RADIANCE

RADIANCE

CARTER SCHOLZ

PICADOR USA   New York

RADIANCE. Copyright © 2002 by Carter Scholz. All rights reserved. Printed in the United States of America. No part of this book may be used or reproduced in any manner whatsoever without written permission except in the case of brief quotations embodied in critical articles or reviews. For information, address Picador USA, 175 Fifth Avenue, New York, N.Y. 10010.

www.picadorusa.com

Picador is a U.S. registered trademark and is used by St. Martin's Press under license from Pan Book Limited.

Portions of the first section of this work were published in *New Legends*, edited by Greg Bear (Tor Books, 1995). Material on pp. 277–280 is adapted from André Gsponer and Jean-Pierre Hurni's technical report *Fourth Generation Nuclear Weapons* (Independent Scientific Research Institute). Used by permission of André Gsponer. The legend of Inanna as told on pp. 320–321 is adapted from *Inanna, Queen of Heavaen and Earth*, by Diane Wolkstein and Samuel Noah Kramer (Harper & Row, 1983). Used by permission of Diane Wolkstein. The voices on pp. 379–380 are quoted from *American Ground Zero:The Secret Nuclear War*, by Carole Gallagher (MIT Press, 1993). Reproduced by permission of Carole Gallagher.

Library of Congress Cataloging-in-Publication Data

Scholz, Carter.
    Radiance / Carter Scholz.—1st Picador USA ed.
    p.cm.
    ISBN 0-312-26893-9
    1. Nuclear weapons industry—Fiction. 2. Physicists—Fiction. I. Title.

PS3569.C52549 R33 2002
813'.6–dc21

2001056018

First edition: February 2002

10 9 8 7 6 5 4 3 2 1

ACKNOWLEDGMENTS

Grateful acknowledgment is made to André Gsponer, Diane Wolkstein and Carole Gallagher for permission to quote from their work. Other quoted material is taken verbatim from public documents issued by the U.S. Department of Defense, the U.S. Department of Energy, and its national laboratories. For additional technical information I am indebted to Andrew Lichterman and Daniel Marcus. Most of all I am grateful to my editor, Bryan Cholfin, for patiently nurturing this book through its long gestation.

I call upon the scientific community in our country, those who gave us nuclear weapons, to turn their great talents now to the cause of mankind and world peace, to give us the means of rendering those nuclear weapons impotent and obsolete.

—President Ronald Reagan, 1983

Out of the crooked timber of humanity no straight thing was ever made.

—Immanuel Kant

1. RADIANCE

ONE

Quine approached the Lab on a road that led nowhere else. The morning light was thick, almost a substance. Past the razorwire of the perimeter fence, cranes and water towers and incinerator stacks rose above the fortress city's sprawl of buildings. Construction vehicles moved on its roads. Beyond, grassland stretched to hillsides sallow from drought and spotted with dark stands of live oak.

Soon he saw the protesters blocking the gate. Cars in both lanes had stopped. The blue lights and red lights of patrol cars flickered on the road's shoulders. Blackclad police formed a line between the protesters and the gate. Over chanting, rhythmic but unintelligible, rang a bullhorn's clipped commands, and the protesters moved off the roadway, the rhythm of their chant stumbling. A few remained kneeling in the road before the gate. Three police holstered their batons and moved respectfully among the kneeling protesters, like acolytes among devouts, helping them one by one to their feet and leading them within the gates to a waiting bus. The sequence of blockade, arrest, and release was by now ritual. The arrested chatted with their captors.

As the cars edged forward, Quine saw once again the darkhaired young woman in the crowd and once again felt the hollowing of his heart. Her resemblance to Kate, any reminder of Kate, still lanced him.

Two cars ahead, Leo Highet's red convertible sounded its horn as Highet leaned out to heckle, —Get a life! The woman flinched and Quine's eyes locked on Highet's head, the bald spot, the wedge of fea-

3

tures visible in the rearview mirror, the broad nose and dark glasses. Once through the gate Highet's car sped into a right turn to the administration building while Quine drove on to the second checkpoint, then through a desert of broken rock, buried mines, and motion sensors erect on metal stalks like unliving plants. Past this dry moat he stopped at a third checkpoint, then parked in the shade of a concrete building with blank walls and embrasured windows, and nervously thumbed the car radio, —affic and weather togeth, while he watched two younger scientists cross the lot and enter the building. Then he stilled the car and went in.

In his office, one horizontal window too high to reach framed an oblong of sky. On the walls, abandoned by the prior occupant and by Quine untouched, hung graphs and pictures, seismographs of bomb tests, the branched coils of particle decay, a geological map, electron micrographs of molecular etchings, a fractal mountainscape, all overlaid by memos, monthly construction maps, field test schedules, Everyone Needs To Know About Classification, cartoons, Curiosity Is Not A Need To Know, a whiteboard thick with equations in four colors so long unwiped that Quine's one pass with a wet rag had left the symbols down one edge ghosted but not erased, and a second desk, loose papers cascaded across its surface, the computer monitor topped by a seamsplit cardboard carton BERINGER GREY RIESLING and buttressed by books manuals folders xeroxes Autoregressive Modeling, Rings Fields and Groups, Leonardo da Vinci Notebooks, Numerical Solution of Differential Equations, Selling Yourself and Your Ideas! and under the desk banker's boxes DESTROY AFTER, and D NULL in black marker. Devon Null, the prior occupant, was "on indefinite leave". But when Quine had moved in, Highet had insisted that he leave Null's half of the office untouched, either against Null's return, or, as Quine was coming to believe, as a monument to disappearance.

Quine checked his computer mail. Most of the messages were notices, chaffing, power plays, trivia.

A memorial service will be held Nov. 1 for Al Hazen who died Oct. 27 following a lengthy illness. He was 51. Hazen worked with the Weapons Test Group at Aguas Secas. Donations in his memory may be made to the

4

American Cancer Society.

One message could not be ignored:

From: Leo Highet <sforza@milano.banl.gov>
Date: Thu, 31 Oct 1991 17:58:36 (-0800)
To: Philip Quine <quine@styx.banl.gov>
Subject: Radiance
Cc: dietz@styx.banl.gov, szabo@styx.banl.gov, kihara@dis.banl.gov, huygens@aries.banl.gov, lb@dioce.banl.gov
Gentlemen:
As you know, the Beltway boys are coming and it is CRUCIAL that they go home awed. I want confidence, energy and style. There are unanswered questions and we will take hits on those. Meeting at noon today to brainstorm our approach, bldg 101, rm E-501.
Highet
===="To apply and direct this vast new potential of destructive energy excited the inventive genius of Leonardo as had few other enterprises."====

More galling than the message was Highet's new computer login *sforza* and his signature quote. This inspirational conceit, that they were all Renaissance maestri under the gentle patronage of Prince Leo the High, had come ironically from Quine, who was reading about da Vinci's eighteen years as military engineer under Ludovico Sforza, Duke of Milan. Leonardo had written, "I hate war, as all rational men hate it, but there seems no escape from its bestial madness." Not while men of genius bend their talents to it, Quine had added. Here was Highet's comeback.

Highet. What a piece of work. Builder and destroyer of his own legend. A fecund theorist but a distracted experimenter, an indifferent administrator but a champion politician. From the start of his career he had traveled to the capital, made himself known to congressmen and their staffs. In reward for such attentions he was at a young age appointed technical representative to a disarmament conference. His conduct was impeccable until one afternoon, goaded by the other side's mendacious presentation and by his own ungovernable need to command the center of every situation, he let slip classified data.

Highet made allies sooner than friends, and enemies sooner than either. After this gaffe his allies were silent while his enemies pounced.

But Highet made the first of the hairsbreadth escapes on which his legend was built. A paper published a year before, cosigned by the President's science advisor, had exposed the same secret. The hearings were dropped and Highet was exiled to an underfunded oubliette of the Lab housed in temporary trailers: J Section.

Anyone else would have languished there. But Highet built by inches a power base, using his charisma to attract the brightest, most driven graduate students he could find, forming in the meantime new political alliances. When Congress at last funded Radiance, all the necessary talent was in J Section, and fiercely loyal to Highet. Soon he was associate director. Two years later, the director retired and Highet filled his place.

J Section. Research And Development In Advanced Nuclear Concepts. Concepts as in weapons. Advanced as in not working yet. Radiance's charter was to develop energy weapons of all types, but Highet's hope and pet was the Superbright: an orbiting battle station of hairthin rods webbed around a nuclear bomb. The bomb's ignition would charge the rods with energy, focused into beams that would flash out to strike down enemy missiles, all in the microsecond before the station consumed itself in nuclear fire.

So far the beams flashed out only in theory. The theory, originated by Null, seemed to Quine sound, but the more he studied his computer model, the less he understood why any of Null's tests had ever produced the ghost of a beam. Yet the farther tests fell behind expectations, the more strident became Highet's public claims. Warren Slater, in charge of testing, had resigned in protest. His letter of resignation was classified and squelched. Bernd Dietz was given interim charge of testing, and to Quine fell the task of finding in disappointing test data any optimism about the promised results.

Meanwhile Highet had grown ever more reckless. He began showing up at high profile conferences and seminars in subjects outside his field: on neural nets, genetic programming, nanotechnology, virtual reality, cold fusion, artificial life, making no discriminations between the cutting edge, the speculative, and the snake oil, as if the force of his character could remake physical law, or at least the local version of it. He spoke in banquet halls at Red Lion Inns, he passed out abstracts,

6

offprints, videotapes, he painted futures brighter and more definite than the present, with himself and his visions at the center of them, inviting the wise and the bold to sit with him in the prosperity and rectitude of that inner circle, outside which was darkness, barbarism, and chaos.

And many have made a trade of delusions and false miracles, deceiving the stupid multitude. Again the voice. In the mind's shadows were countless voices, dead, living, unborn, lost. Since working on Radiance Quine had dreamed them. Now they came into his waking life. This voice he recognized from Leonardo's notebooks.

On his second computer, secure in steel shielding, waited Quine's simulation of the rods. This frail superstructure of hope was raised on a sprawling foundation of faith. Hundreds of man-years of Lab effort and ingenuity had gone into the underlying physics codes. Even so, it was not possible that they could describe the full complexity of a nuclear blast. Simplifications and estimates entered in, acceptable only because their results matched experimental data to some more or less arbitrary tolerance. Radiation transport, magnetic fields, burn products, photon scattering, thermal conduction, ion viscosity, bremsstrahlung, all these imponderables had to be calculated and updated, interacting in every kernel of space, at every nanosecond. If Quine had once puzzled for years over the paradox of a single photon, the complexities here were literally unthinkable. The reward of deep understanding was not part of the package.

None of this cauldron of approximation, this vast rationalization, this ingenious mimickry, was Quine's responsibility. To him it was a black box. His laser simulation ran on top of it all, passing it data, receiving its judgments. Again he ignited his bomb and waited for the nuclear pinball of particles and energies to reach his rods. Color bars and line graphs crept across the screen, the visible satisfactions of programming. The solipsistic machine worlds. It was near to pornography, without nuance. Any halfbright notion could be simulated, the simulation tweaked to an approximation of success, and the success conjured as proof for more funding. Tweak and squeak, as Highet put it. Realization was a "materials" problem. Bend your backs, men, to prove this golden turd of an idea.

The display glitched and broke into the debugger. Lines of codes filled the screen, void qelem, malloc(xarray), atof(nptr). He ceased to see words or even letters, his eyes grasping instead at the pixels, the shards of light within the characters. That radiance within the meanest mote of being.

What is light? Surfaces boil with quantum fire. How comes this dumb swarming to write beauty, alarm, or desolation upon the soul? Eyes are the questing front of the brain, the channel to the heart. The eye may not, as Archytas thought, emit illuminating rays, but our knowledge of its working is no surer than his.

Mind's eye and heart's channel presented him now Kate's russet hair, her full mouth and cheeks, her dimpled chin, her dark eyes framed by wire glasses. Like a key those features fit his heart. They appeared before him like a truth of nature. Mostly he lived in the mundane, scarcely noting what or whom he passed, but at rare moments the world came forward in all its vividness, stunning his heart. Every time he saw Kate, there was that shock of presence.

She was 23, he 37. They'd met in a yoga class. He hadn't pursued at first. He was coupled with Nan, a quiet woman his own age who worked at the Lab. They lived apart but spent half their spare time together. He was content and not content with what they had. But he and Kate talked, and they went out a few times. She seemed interested in him. Her eyes met something in his. Some hope had stirred in him, some need for joy so long put by he'd ceased to miss it. Thus fed his need grew, covert but unchecked. The years separating him from Kate, years he'd squandered in ever more esoteric projects at the Lab, seemed his to reclaim at will. Kate's attention fed in him some myth of starting over. He grew testy with Nan and impatient with himself, seeking not a break between them but between themselves and what he now acutely felt them becoming, burdens and reproofs to each other. Nan waited him out. Her deepening disappointment in him was unspoken but heavy. His desperation grew until he could contain it no longer and he lay it before Kate, blurted it out, a bitter plea. Save me. Who wouldn't flee from that? She regarded him kindly. Oh Philip, the moment's passed. It just didn't happen for us. There's someone else. That the moment could pass. That he had let it. Had not seen it passing.

Such a small thing, that attention, that renewed hope, briefly given and withdrawn, gone now.

The morning too was gone to no end. Every failure now he referred back to that moment, and he saw in his life only patterns of failure and emptiness.

Quine avoided that part of the building where Highet's young theorists worked, X Section, or, as the older men called it, the Playpen. But today his customary exit was blocked by a tour group of weary adults and bored children in facepaint, their guide saying, —tiny robots that actually repair human cells, as he swerved past a sign WARNING TOUR IN PROGRESS NON-CLASSIFIED CONVERSATION ONLY to the swell of the Brahms Requiem in full clash with The Butthole Surfers and a rapid din of simulated combat followed by the admiring exclamation, —Studly! Big win! and laughter fading as he passed an open room in which three refrigerators stood flanked floor to ceiling by case upon case of soda, and veered into a stairwell clattering down metal steps to a metal door held open by a wastebasket and silent despite EMERGENCY EXIT ALARM WILL SOUND and emerged onto a loading dock between brown dumpsters NOT FOR DISPOSAL OF HAZARDOUS WASTE stepping down onto a paved path then jumping back to dodge a white electric cart DAIHATSU jouncing onto a debris of torn asphalt and treadmarked dirt past chainlink CREDNE CONSTRUCTION and three blue PORT-O-LET stalls to vanish behind three glossy cylindrical tanks COMPOSIT PLASTEEL CONTAINMENT DO NOT INSTALL WITHOUT READING PLASTEEL KIT B INSTRUCTIONS, on past temporary trailers holding his mouth and nose against the metallic stench of bright green flux oozing from an open pipe into gray earth, until he regained the main road and passed the checkpoint, showing his badge, to enter Building 101, passing through the lobby where visitors and employees were edified by models of bombs, lasers, satellites, boosters, and photos of the celebrated Nobelists who'd devised them, and on to the conference room where all but Highet had already arrived.

—He was one of these, shall I say, Marxist radical types. His mother cut him out of the family money. Hello, Philip. We're waiting for Leo as usual. So he's in Prague now selling laptops to the Czechs. Ah, the man himself.

—Who's this you're talking about, sounds like he's figured out that free markets are diplomacy by other means. Everyone, this is Jef Thorpe, postdoc from the University of Utah, he's here to look us over. Jef worked with Fish and Himmelhoch on cold fusion, and I just want to say don't believe the conventional wisdom, something is happening there. Jef, this is Dennis Kihara, our new press officer, he takes the heat for my excesses. Bernd Dietz, materials and research. Frank Szabo, systems integration. Phil Quine, our x-ray focusing guru, Philip, Jef's done interesting work in your area, you should sit down with him. Okay, all present? Let's do it.

Highet seated the young man opposite Quine. Jeans, jacket over t-shirt, short black hair, high color, a small gold stud through his left nostril, his presence a breach of protocol and probably security, though the others knew better than to say so.

—You all see the news last night? About the protest? The good news is we won. First they showed the protesters, out on the street, wind noise, bad lighting, and then our rebuttal from our respectable office. We won because we got to go last, and they put us last because we provided closure. That's the model for our presentation: beginning, middle, end. We'll begin by showing footage of successful tests. The middle will be video simulations of the system, where we'll highlight potential problems. By defining the problems we control the questions. And we'll end by addressing the problems and introducing entirely new approaches and spin-off programs. Dennis is running things, but I may break in at any point.

—Leo, can we skip the last part, the science fiction?

—No, Bernd. Past, present, future. Closure. Without this you leave people ready to ask questions.

—We're avoiding questions?

—Not if they're intelligent and informed but we have a few critics and wise guys on this panel and I'd like to keep it simple.

—Leo, I have more respect than you for the intelligence of senators. Congressmen are not always so bright but

—Bernd, it's simple courtesy. We inform them at a level that's neither condescending nor technical, we tell them their money is being well spent, show them how, say thanks so much.

—Salesmanship.

—Grow up, Bernd, a couple times a year I ask you to do this. Is the money well spent? Yes or no.

—Yes, yes.

—I'd ah, feel better if we could discuss the middle part in ah detail, there are just some questions that I'm not comfortable to address without ah, just a little more input. For example the focusing data . . .

—Dennis, only Slater has questioned that data, and he's gone. Discredited. Focus is now Philip's baby.

—So, ah, focus is our main problem?

—Yes, it's one, said Quine. —Focus, brightness . . .

—But we're within an order of magnitude?

—I don't see any quantitative agreement with theory, said Quine. —The tests have shown a few bright spots. That's all I'm willing to commit to.

—That's all you've committed to for what is it ten months now Philip?

—I don't see any fundamentals. I'm beginning to wonder

—Are you pulling a Slater on me, Philip? Because I want to tell you something, all of you. Some people in the lower echelons are making Slater out to be some kind of hero. To me this man was a menace to every one of us because he didn't care about winning. He didn't know what he wanted out of life and wouldn't have been able to get it if he had known. I have no respect for parasites like that.

—Leo, Null had a brilliant notion and we should pursue it, but that's all it is so far, a notion. We

—No one's questioned Null's theory, no one, not even critics.

—Sure but it's a long way from there to even a prototype

—We have supporting test data

—which may or may not mean qualitative agreement may or may not, but never quantitative, we have no understan

—well you're the one with the models Philip lo these many

—and you're the one who said this was a long term project, your words, long term, and now suddenly

—oh sure, and if we all had seven lives

—now that there's a little pressure it's

—what I'm hearing

—it's suddenly urgent

—what I'm hearing from you Philip is that we need more shots. Convey that necessity to our guests when they're here, think you can do that? And put a little urgency into it?

—I won't pretend we have focus when

—You're not going to give me an inch are you?

—Not on the basis of spotty data I can't interpret.

—I tell you what. There's an eighty kiloton shot coming up next Saturday, right, Bernd? Piggyback it, Philip. Get yourself some better data.

—In what, a week? Design and fabricate apparatus in a week?

—Nine days. Jef can help you if he sticks around.

—Now hold on . . .

—Get off the pot. Let's move to Frank's contribution. You've all read it?

—Leo . . .

—We're moving on.

There was a brief silence in which papers rustled.

—Nothing new here, said Dietz.

—That's its strength. We've taken heat on preproduction technologies. This is a simple, viable off-the-shelf option. It's an easy sell. Contractors are lining up.

—It's good show-and-tell, said Szabo. —We can point to a card cage, this is the guidance system a year ago, then hold up a wafer, here it is today. Tangible progress.

Dietz continued to study the paper. —These are Baldur anti-satellite missiles in a smaller package.

—That's right.

—These were shelved over ten years ago as an ABM treaty violation.

—That toilet paper? Let that worry us we might as well give up.

—These are not by any stretch of the imagination directed energy weapons. You want to put, what does it say, five thousand of these in orbit . . .

—We're pursuing many options, Bernd. These would be one layer of a shield. Look, it's a long way to deployment. Oh and we get something else totally for free with Frank's idea. Always think dual use. Put a warhead on these guys they're earth penetrators, aim them downward get a thousand g impact, three k p s terminal velocity, earth-coupled shock waves to destroy hardened shelters. We have a friend in the Pentagon who's hard for that and the Beltway boys know it.

—Wait just wait you mean, this, these ah interceptors are for the presentation? But it's, we need to address the existing problems, that's what they're coming for, we can't feed them something totally new! And with this Slater thing

—Dennis, trust me, it's the best possible thing to do. As far as Slater goes, he's history, a blip, not even an incident. This visit was scheduled long before his snit. Sure we'll get closer scrutiny than we would in the average dog-and-pony but it's an opportunity. Remember NORAD's famous false alarms and screwups? They got a billion-dollar facelift out of those incidents. You up to speed now?

—Well yes, I mean no, not on the interceptors but . . .

—Put Frank's paper in the kit, I'll step in during the presentation. Oh, and make sure everyone gets a souvenir.

—A, I'm sorry?

—A souvenir. What are you giving the kids for family day today?

—Ah, some laser-etched aluminum disks . . .

—Good. Run off half a dozen make it a dozen more etched with the Radiance logo, can you do that? And glossies of the new artist's renderings.

Highet was out the door before anyone else had left their seat. Thorpe, abandoned, stood but did not move quickly enough to follow the older man out. As the seated men studied him incuriously he blushed and exited.

The others then rose. Szabo went out singing under his breath, —It's a long way, to deployment, it's a long way, I know. In the meantime, we have employment, it's the stick that makes us go . . .

At the doorway Dietz said to Quine, —It is outrageous that he should bring a boy into that meeting and criticize you this way. Easy for him to make promises, but when the promises are not so easy to deliver we suffer for them.

—I don't think the boy knew what he was getting into.

—Tell me what you want added to this test as soon as possible. He has put our asses on the line, both of us.

—I'll send you e-mail.

—Souvenirs! He gives senators souvenirs.

Quine had come to the Lab at Réti's invitation, Réti the legend, intimate of Einstein, Heisenberg, Schrödinger, founder of the Lab. Impossible to refuse. Réti had for one semester graced Quine's university with his presence, where he'd sat on Quine's doctoral committee. Quine must have made an impression, for two years later Réti called him. I hear you are working hard on some good ideas. How would you like unlimited resources for this work? Come for the summer, work on what you will.

Quine and Sorokin, a fellow postdoc, had isolated the emission of a single photon from a calcium source in order to determine whether a lone quantum displayed wave-particle complementarity. For two long years they had refined their approach, paring it to essentials, designing an experiment they might hope to realize with the school's meager resources. Elegance born of need. A slow and painful progress. At the Lab, in one month Quine was able to design and build a detector acute enough, and the experiment came off on the first try. Both tunneling and anticoincidence were evident. They had touched the central mystery. Even a single photon is both particle and wave.

Quine stayed. After that it was never a question. Not till much later did he guess that he'd been played. That Réti had his reason for waiting two years before approaching him. That by then his work was ripe for plucking, and the Lab's resources had little to do with its fruition apart from giving them the juice of it.

At the Lab his paper brought him a celebrity near to grace. Unlimited time to think. No assigned duties. And the mysteries ceased to open to him. Idle, he took up one of Highet's endless suggestions, the optics of x-ray mirrors. He welcomed the work, as though it paid some tithe of the mind to the practical. And it was a challenge, but finally it was, as the pioneers had with exact irony called their first bomb, a "gadget". Any solution, even if it laid bare principles, was beside the point if it couldn't kill missiles. So his mirrors never passed a design review. He wrote some computer codes for modeling the mirrors, and those turned out to have some peripheral application in inertial confinement fusion. The weapons work which he knew to be central to the Lab still seemed distant from him. Then Radiance geared up, and his modeling software proved flexible enough to accommodate the next idea: the bombpumped Superbright. Opportunistic as a virus, the Lab took it up. Now he was pressured. Now he was in a competetive atmosphere where the possibility of failure, of weakness, of doubt, could not be voiced even to oneself lest it undermine the resolve needed to get through each day. All the projects here were difficult, at the edge of the possible, and all the scientists worked at their limits and at the limits of their science. You could work on a problem for months only to have your work demolished in minutes in a review by your peers, your competitors, your colleagues. That was what reviews were for: to show up fatal flaws before they became expensively entrenched in a design. So ideas were hammered without mercy. It was and it wasn't personal. If the idea was good, it was yours but somehow beyond you, and if it was bad the attack was on it, not on you. Quine saw men in tears even as they went on arguing and, after it was over, thank their assailants.

Throughout this he kept silent faith with the mysteries. He would return to them when the pressures of the moment were past. Programming took only the surface of his mind; its essence he held in reserve, or so he thought. Quine came at last to understand that he did well at his assigned tasks precisely because he brought them his all. Nothing was left over.

When he left the building the sun was low. The air was thick with heat, and as he started the car the radio blurted —record temp, before he silenced it.

Through the gate traffic slowed. Demonstrators in costume paraded in the road. Quine edged forward through skeletons and spooks with signs and props, TECHNOLOGIES OF DEATH, a longrobed mantisheaded figure towering on stilts above the crowd, tambourines jangling, EL DIA DE LOS MUERTOS, and lab security herding the crowd off the road. As he cleared the crowd a klaxon blared. The mantis swayed, tugging at robes snagged on the perimeter razorwire as the entrance gates slid shut, alarm lights strobing. On the inner perimeter road security vehicles appeared, racing toward the entry kiosk. Then he saw standing by his passenger window the woman who resembled Kate. She wore black spandex bicycle pants and a blue chambray shirt. She was staring at the gate. Quine hesitated, then rolled down the window.

—You want a ride out of here? They're going to start arresting people.

She looked at him, then back at the gate. On the main road Quine saw a flurry of approaching lights. City police.

—I can't wait.

Whoops blasts squeals cut the crowd noise. She saw the vehicles approaching and with something like annoyance got into Quine's car. Quine sped away shutting his window against the shriek of the passsing vehicles.

—I'm Philip Quine.

—Lynn Hamlin. Did you see what happened?

When he looked at her all resemblance to Kate fell away. Same body type, same round features, but hair almost black with a russet tinge, cropped close to the neck. No glasses. Dark penetrating eyes. Tanned calves faintly downed, lithe as a huntress's. No key turned in his heart, just an echo of loss.

—The one on stilts, his costume caught on the fence. It must have set off the alarm.

—Were you there for the demo?

—No. I work there.

His ID was still clipped to his jacket. She'd been looking at it, and now she smiled, as if to confide her little subterfuge.

—What do you work on?

He turned onto a road parallel to the freeway, where earthmovers were parked in torn up lots behind emporia of sporting goods, fast food, auto parts, videotapes, computers, discount carpets. Sun flashed through the struts of a half finished retaining wall.

—Defensive weapons.

—You mean Radiance. Do you believe in it?

And those in the anterooms of Hell demur, saying, I do not approve what goes on inside.

—It's what I do.

—Do you know what Einstein said? That you can't simultaneously prepare for war and prevent it?

—Where can I drop you?

—Corner of Mariposa.

As they passed over the freeway, the sun struck their shadow out toward the golden eastern hills. He sensed her still looking at him, then she faced ahead.

—I like this time of day, she said. —The light.

—I don't, said Quine. —It makes me think of endings.

She said nothing to that. As the car descended into the shadow of the overpass Quine said, —We didn't hear about the protest. The organizers usually let us know.

—Maybe they're tired of playing your game.

—It's not my game. A green sign with white letters Mariposa hung over the intersection. Quine pulled to the curb by a bus stop bench placarded FAST DIVORCE BANKRUPTCY. She turned to him with sudden vehemence.

—These demonstrations won't stop, you know. You don't know how angry people are. . . . Her voice held some doubt, whether for the anger or his belief in it, he couldn't tell.

—Then I'll probably see you again out there, he said.

—Tell me, what's the point, I mean, isn't it obviously a waste now that the cold war

—Look, and hearing the annoyance in his voice he stanched it, —I don't make policy . . .

—Well, that's part of the problem, isn't it. People not taking responsibility for what they do.

Pricked, he turned to her just as a bus pulled to the curb, the squeal of its brakes preempting whatever he might have meant to say. Some hurt might have remained in his eyes. She seemed abashed and held his gaze for a moment longer before reaching to unbuckle her seatbelt.

—Listen . . . would you have lunch with me sometime?

She looked at him in surprise. —Lunch? Why?

—I'd just like to talk more.

—Do we have anything to say to each other?

—We could find out. His pulse thickened in his throat.

—But you're the enemy, she said.

—Me . . . ? He caught, under her serious dark brow, a glimpse of mischief, though she didn't smile.

—Thanks for the ride.

She was out the door before he felt the protest of his heart. So even now he had not relinquished hope.

When he got home Nan's car was in his parking space. Most Tuesday nights she spent with Quine. He went to her place Friday nights and some weekends. But he'd worked late Tuesday, so they'd shifted it to tonight. He'd forgotten.

—Lo, she called, —In the kitchen. I picked up some tortellini at Il Fornaio and a salad, is that okay?

—Fine. As he entered she turned with a wary smile. The sight of her brought him a roil of giddiness, of memory, of guilt, of sadness. Her features were sharp and fine, her skin pale, her straight auburn hair just starting to show gray, her slight body always dressed with a style that in its impeccability read as a brave front.

—Bread's in the oven, can you get that?

He looked for an oven mitt while she talked about her day, some seniority conflict in the personnel department. Quine's patience wore. When, setting the plates down, she bent to kiss his neck, he flinched.

—What's wrong?

—Nothing. It's just Highet's going mad again. A Congressional visit's coming up, it should be routine, but he acts like the whole program's at stake.

—Is it?

—First he drops Null's work in my lap, then today he starts pimping some lunatic idea of Szabo's, and he assigns me a postdoc like, like a chaperone . . . and the protesters.

—What about them?

—They're getting on my nerves.

18

They ate in silence for a few minutes. At last he said, —What would you think if I quit?

—Quit? Your job?

—Yes.

—But Philip, what would you do?

—Well, I don't know. I could take some time off to think about it.

—Time off? I thought that we were trying to save money . . .

—Save . . . ?

—Philip, I'm not trying to pressure you, but I thought we agreed that it makes sense to look for a place together . . .

—I told you, Nan, I can't think about that while this project is on, I can't make big plans like that until this whole thing is, is settled.

—Well, couldn't we start looking just to see what's available, just go to a few open houses . . . ?

—If you want. But I don't see the point if we can't afford it yet.

—The point is to plan for a future, Philip. Haven't you made any progress?

—Progress, I feel like I'm chasing my tail, there's no progress to be made!

—Please don't snap at me.

—I, I can't even discuss it with you, you don't have the clearance.

She stood and carried dishes into the kitchen. He got up to follow. —Nan . . . He came up behind her and embraced her. Her hands rested on his forearms.

—What about Sunday?

—Sunday?

—We're seeing Ginny and Bill, remember? If you came early we could

—Sunday. Look, I have a deadline. I can't. I'm sorry but I just can't.

—You're working? But if you're not getting anywhere . . .

—Well but that's the whole problem isn't it! Meantime there are still short-term goals and meetings.

She sighed and left the kitchen. In the living room the television came on. When after a moment he entered the room he heard her in the bedroom speaking on the telephone. Remote control in hand he viewed a cool panoptic tumble of war famine catastrophe enormity larded with a fantastic plenty of goods caressed by smiling tanned models, to pause on the logotype of Martin Marietta, —a proud supporter for twenty-five years of science programming on public television, his impulse to switch again frozen by the worn, imposing face of Aron Réti, saying thickly, —In science there is a cult of the beautiful theory. But how beautiful is reality? These beautiful theories, these elegant mathematics are not verified by experiment. Experiment shows us a mess of a universe with over a hundred basic particles and three irreconcilable forces. We would like to unify them all, just as we would like to smooth over all the political differences in the world. But experience shows, in physics and in politics, that this is not always possible.

Abruptly the screen glared with the involute radiance of the bomb. Sun's heart. Cosmic ground. Siva and Devi coupling. A thin roar issued from the set and the thick voice rode over it, —The duty of science is to pursue knowledge even if it leads to the unbeautiful. Or to evil. How else learn about evil?

Nan returned to sit beside him. —Isn't that Réti?

The camera returned to the physicist. Emeritus director, Réti was rarely at the Lab; the office he kept there served him solely as a clubroom or a backdrop. Six months ago a film crew had come to the Lab. Quine had heard Réti shouting at them behind the closed door.

—Watch, this is what Highet calls the liberal bias of the media, said Quine as the camera went to the interviewer.

—After the war, many of your colleagues turned away from weapons. Some of them have won Nobel Prizes. Do you feel that your work with weapons has cost you credibility or respect within the scientific community? Has it compromised you as a scientist?

—Never. In fact it has challenged and improved me as a scientist.

—You're closely connected to Radiance. What about recent charges that test results have been faked?

—This is a lie! First, I am not closely connected . . .

—But you've lobbied extensively for Radiance in Wash

—I am no lobbyist! I am a private citizen with some scientific expertise, and when I am asked to testify about technical matters I do so . . .

—But for over forty years you've been an advocate of nuclear weapons. Your authority and influence are well known.

—Now you listen to me. It is an imperfect world, a dangerous world. There is evil in the world. How do you meet it? All ends, even the best, are reached by impure means. Reason is supposed to be the hallmark of science, but I tell you that no one is swayed by reason. A theory, an idea, does not make its own way. It was Einstein who said merit alone is very little good; it must be backed by tact and knowledge of the world. I know of many cases where maybe the data does not quite agree with your theory, no, you think, the carpers will question, your case is far clearer if you discard this set of data, if you report only these results. And who are these frauds? Ptolemy. Galileo. Newton. Bernoulli. Mendel. Millikan. What matters in the long run is not some wishful dream of scruples, but whether you have driven your knowledge home!

Behind the fury in Réti's eyes Quine saw a bright and open wound: more illustrious for his influence than his work, he had failed at everything but success. And Quine's own life, he suddenly saw, was bent around Réti's influence. A man has no wealth nor power but his knowledge, Réti had once said to Quine. But now he said that if power did not lead, knowledge could not follow. Quine stood, ignoring —Philip? what is it? and went to the bathroom. He held the sides of the sink, heart racing. In the cabinet he found the pill bottle.

The spirit is radiant, yet there are two principles of radiance: that of light, and that of fire. Fire comes to the use of those who go not the way of light. And the difference is, that fire must consume its object.

Quine returned to Réti's angry voice, —So I have no Nobel Prize, that accolade of the pure. But Alfred Nobel would understand me well. And history will be my judge, not you.

—What is it, Philip? What's the matter?

Quine turned to Nan, her face in the phosphor light bleak as a rock outcrop. He reached to touch her neck. Unsmiling she leaned her head against his hand. His fingers cupped her nape and he drew her mouth to his.

In the bedroom they undressed on opposite sides of the bed. The television droned on. Between her legs he felt the string of a tampon, and as he touched it she bent double and enclosed him in her mouth. Above the activity of their bodies his spirit hovered sadly regarding the terrain of his life. Lightly his hands cradled her head. He began to pump semen. Deep inside him a talon drove home and brought forth, impaled, his soul, writhing. A minute later he was awash in sleep. Waiting at a counter to pick up xeroxes. Quick tap at his shoulder. Kate. She smiled, her eyes upon him, and he knew it was a dream, and he was happy, and he slept.

TWO

The morning sky, pallid with haze, conveyed yet enough sun to cast
through the high embrasure of his office window a faint rhombus
which crept toward the doorway relentless as a horologe. From his
desk Quine gazed at it half hearing the radio, —ildfires in three coun-
ties, when his phone rang.

—Quine.

—Is this Philip?

—Yes, who's this.

—Lynn. From the demo yesterday?

—Oh. Oh yes. How did you . . . He stood and paced with the phone.
—How did you get my number?

—I called the switchboard. I want to apologize. I behaved badly. Are
you free for coffee?

—Well I . . . not this morning.

—Later this afternoon?

—Well I . . .

—Don't let me pressure you.

—No I, I want to. It's just a surprise.

—I get off work at four. Do you know the Café Desaparecidos? In
the central mall. I work near there.

—Sure I, okay, I'll see you there about four.

As he hung up Jef Thorpe knocked on his open door. Black jacket,
blue shirt, jeans. A faint puck where yesterday the nose stud had been.

—Come in.

—I guess we'll be working together.

—Oh, you're staying.

—If you'll have me. Listen, that meeting yesterday, I didn't belong there, I'm sorry if . . .

—Not your fault. Doctor Highet has his way of doing things.

—Yeah, I see that. Listen, before we started I want to tell you, the single-photon experiment you did with Sorokin was really elegant. I was, you know, sort of surprised to find you here, I thought you'd be somewhere more theoretical.

—I thought everyone had forgotten that experiment by now.

—Oh no. It was very sweet work.

—The detector was critical. We worked on it for two years. We got it only after I came here.

—You didn't follow it up.

—Sorokin thought I was wrong to come here. He said it would be a black hole. He may have been right. Of course things look different from inside.

—Black hole, yeah, I've thought of that. But you know where I come from. That limits my options in the straight academic world.

—You don't have qualms about defense work?

—It's not what I'm here for.

—It's just, you might want to consider your position. I came in neutral about defense work, but before long I was in the thick of it. It's easy to slip into.

—I'm sort of apolitical.

—Well, if that's what you want, turning to the computer which glowed with:

Date: Fri 1 Nov 09:05

From: Leo Highet <sforza@milano.banl.gov>

To: Philip Quine <quine@styx.banl.gov>

Subject: Upcoming J Section Tests

11/4 23:00 PDT, Building 328, Codename "Stelarc", ground-based laser guide star, R. Grosseteste, sup.

11/9 18:00 PDT, Site 600, Codename "Taliesin", 80 kiloton, B. Dietz & P. Quine, sup.

"Mechanics are the Paradise of mathematical science, because here we come to the fruits of mathematics." LdV

—Looks like we're real, said Thorpe.

—You're lucky. It was years before I was associated with a shot.

—Is that luck?

—It's a bit of prestige. A merit badge.

Quine cleared the screen and brought up the Superbright test data.

—You see. Intense brightness here, and here. Very erratic pattern.

—This data is picked up how?

—When the bomb ignites, radiation from the rods bounces off some reflectors to

—X-ray mirrors?

—Yes, something like that. They're beryllium. The data agrees with theory to a point, but when we increase power, we don't get an increase in beam, in fact we get less. We've talked about trying different metals in the rods, we've used gold till now, but mercury . . .

—Yeah, elements seventy-two through ninety-five would be good to try but with the, you know, time constraints, I checked and Fabrication has gold rods ready to go, so maybe those are a good choice and you can, or I mean we can sort of concentrate on sensor configuration . . .

—Sounds reasonable.

Thorpe continued to stare at the screen. —Could this be an annulus? This pattern I mean, could those reflectors be picking up a sort of imperfect focus, you know, the edge of a ring? If we move them in . . .

—I've tried, no luck.

—Can I look at your focusing code?

—Yes, sure, all the files are in this directory.

—That's great. Mind if I work here? pointing to Null's desk.

—Ah, sure. Sure, go ahead. I'm going for lunch and maybe a swim. I'll see you later.

We read of the beaver that when it is pursued, knowing that it is for the medicinal virtue of its testicles and not being able to escape, it stops; and it bites off its testicles with its sharp teeth and leaves them to its enemies.

Gaunt, saturnine, Bran Nolan in a corner of the cafeteria looked up unsmiling from scattered papers to raise a hand in greeting.

—How's our new boyo Kihara?

—Weren't you in line for that position?

—It's my Tourette's syndrome. Terrible liability in a press officer, never know what he might blurt out in public.

—You should have been asked.

—Do you know, I'm happier, if that's the word I want, where I am. Kihara is a little lamb. The last man, Vessell, didn't outlast Slater. And we're not done with all that, no indeed.

—Getting some work done? Quine indicated the papers.

—"The Lab has a longstanding commitment to developing new methods and technologies to protect the environment," the most effective of which to date has been the press release. Do you know we have a toxics mitigation program now? Seems there's a toxic plume seeping into the groundwater under a vineyard off the north boundary. Vines died, soil went gray, the whole field stinks like sepsis. I'm writing an upbeat report about it. And yourself? How's the death ray coming?

—We can maim small insects at a meter. The new concept is interceptors. Small flying rocks.

—Do you know, da Vinci invented shrapnel. He'd have been right at home here with all these advanced minds.

—Yes, that's Highet's conceit.

—Throwing rocks at things. We should be proud, thinking about these old impulses in such an advanced way.

A plump figure came forward shaking a sheaf of papers, from which Nolan recoiled. —Bran, Bran, Bran. What must I do to get you to use a font other than Courier?

—Hello Bob, how's the gout? I don't like this business of tarting up manuscripts. You get enchanted by the beauty of it all. You start to think you're writing the Book of Kells.

—A few attractive fonts, tastefully applied, can spice up a presentation. A little humanitas, you know. Why else, Bran, did we get you that powerful and costly workstation?

—I don't know, Bob, why did you? I was still figuring out the type balls on my Selectric.

The sheaf of papers fell fanning from their clip onto the table.

Shaking his head and chuckling grimly, Bob passed on to another table.

—Humanitas, yes, that's what we need here, isn't it, Highet with his Renaissance, and Aldus Manutius there, need a few more particle men who've read the Tao Te Ching, couple more managers who've studied Sun Tzu, lend these binary views a little tone, dress up the winners and losers, the Elect and the Preterite, the screwers and the screwed. Each man in his station, and keep your distance from the low life, can't have just anyone winning, because if you ever let the rabble ahead, if they can rise, you can surely fall.

Nolan folded back pages, —listen to this bit, "the support of this tight-knit community," support is it now? I'd have said the goading, the ambition, the Schadenfreude, that's what gets the work done. The wife walked out six months ago with the kid, you're eating Campbell's soup cold out of the can, you haven't got a clean shirt, but after a few months of eighteen hour days you've got *data* that everyone wants to see. You *win big.*

—Bran, you work here, too.

—What should I do then, write novels? Or maybe journalism, that's it, *investigative* journalism. Have you met the journalist from Cambridge? Right over there with his tape recorder, name's Armand Steradian. He's researching the belief systems of those who work on weapons of mass destruction, I think that was his phrase. Quite the charmer. He's published one book on scientific fraud, and a paper highly critical of what he calls the defense establishment. You probably don't watch TV but there was a program on PBS last night, Steradian was in it abusing Réti.

—Does Highet know he's here?

—Highet invited him.

Quine headed for the door, passing as he did Armand Steradian, who held a small microphone before a J Section technician, —you're so goldang busy every day you just put off thinking about it, though in Quine's view pressure was a tool well used to put off thinking.

Black cottonwoods around the pool throve despite the drought. Their catkins littered the water. A jet moved on the sky, stitching a contrail across a lace of cloud where a white sun struggled. Quine sat on a towel on the grassy verge and watched a portly swimsuited man enter through the gate, barrel chest glossed with hair, and behind him a woman in a white halter top and shorts, the heads of three men turning to follow. The pool was crowded this Friday afternoon; it was warm, it was the end of the workweek, it was family day; unlike Quine, most worked a five day week, most would depart hence into a forgetfulness. In the shallows of the pool two young girls splashed. One opened her mouth to show her companion a bright penny on her outstretched tongue. A young mother in a black maillot gripped a ladder to raise herself half from the pool and wave at her infant in a nearby stroller, glisten and shadow in the cords of her back, and Quine suffered a pang for a life now beyond his knowing: to be wed, with child, so young. On thermals a black and white winged vulture, *Cathartes aura*, rocked and banked. From the jet thunder fell like muffled blows. The warmth and the sound of water churned by swimmers and the spray tossed up by their passing lulled Quine into a lethargy from which he woke with a start to consult his watch. On the pool's floor danced cusps of light.

The café's walls rose past exposed beams and ducts to the nacre of frosted skylights. Lynn sat in a wirebacked chair at a glass table, face downcast at papers before her. In the moment before she looked up, Kate's face glowed before him. What do you do, Philip?

—Hoy es el día de los muertos, Lynn said in greeting, banishing Kate's image. Angularities all her own moved in her flesh; a small gap showed between her teeth as she smiled.

Quine seated himself and said gravely, —I should tell you I'm involved with someone.

—Gee, I said I wanted to apologize, not start an affair.

—I, sorry I . . .

—And maybe pick your brain about Radiance.

—I'm sorry, I, what did you say before? El día . . .

—Today is the Day of the Dead. All Saints' Day. All of California used to be Mexico, you know, they called it Aztlan. Once my group shuts the Lab down, we're going to reclaim Aztlan for the native peoples. Oh, don't look that way, I'm joking, that's the kind of thing the far right says about us.

—Your group?

—Citizens Against Nuclear Technology. I'm a paralegal with them.

—What's that you're reading?

—Your press releases. She held a sheaf set in unadorned Courier font. —You people have fingers in a lot of pies. When I started my concern was the bombs, but that's just the tip of the iceberg, isn't it. There's also the supercomputers, the lasers, the genetics, the chemicals . . .

—You probably know more about it than I do.

—Your cover stories are so creative. Every one of. Oh, go ahead, order, she's waiting.

—Cappuccino. What you do mean, cover stories?

—Quisiera un espresso por favor. Every one of these quote benign technologies has a pretty easy to imagine military use. Laser x-ray lithography for etching microchips, uh huh, right, and here's one about kinder gentler CBW, "less virulent" tear gas for "crowd control", heavier specific gravity for controlled delivery, if this is the stuff you're public about I can only imagine the rest.

—You're wrong, there's a genuine effort to convert to peacef

—Dual use, I know. Genuine effort to blur the line is what it is, and it goes far beyond the Lab, people in physics and comp sci departments across the country are lining up at the same trough, the grants are there and if they don't take the money someone else will. That's the reasoning. What a waste of talent and resources.

—It's more complicated than that. The people I work with, they're not cynical.

—Yes, I know how people get caught up in their work. I have a friend there, not in Radiance, in another section. He's a Quaker, he calls it "being in the world". At least he's thought about it. How did you get into it?

—Me? I'm, well, a lapsed theorist. But I'm not typical. . . . Was he not? Réti, Highet, Dietz, Thorpe, all had failed in some subtle way that in such a place could be denied. But where was there not failure and denial?

—Do your people pay any attention at all to our demonstrations?

29

—In J Section? Not much.

—We seem to bug your boss, at least.

—Highet?

—In his little red sports car. What about you? What did you think about the big one yesterday?

—It seemed, I don't know, festive, almost a costume party, I didn't realize at first it was Halloween . . .

—But no, that wasn't it. It was a ceremony. An exorcism.

—Oh come on, what, you mean we're possessed . . .

—By arrogance if nothing else.

—That's absurd, you can't convince anyone with some absurd ritual . . .

—It's no different from your rituals, your bomb tests, just as absurd, but really dangerous!

—They're not my tests . . . and he remembered *B. Dietz & P. Quine, sup.* —I'm sorry. I'm no good talking about this.

The set of her features, so poised and eager, softened then and her voice lowered. —I don't mean to attack you. I'm sure you think about it.

—Yes but, but I'm not sure! What to do, I mean. What if it is a waste, what if, if all the money and the decades, all the lives and talent . . . then it's more than just me, it's not just my mistake, but something wrong at the root of it, and what, what can I do about that?

—If it is a mistake, you can face it. You could stop.

—But that wouldn't stop anything. It's almost as if these things we work on . . . they use us to get born. Could use anyone.

—It must be very hard for you. Their eyes met, and the troubled sympathy in hers wrung him. Her face was so concerned for him that he almost cried out with selfpity.

—It's not your fault. I, I need to get back now.

—I really am sorry, can we . . . can we forget about all this and just start over?

—Start over . . . ?

Abruptly he rose and walked away stolid with loathing of his own erratic heart, and of her for stirring it.

•

In the night he woke sweating with a pulse of ninety, reached for the pillbottle next to the small box DREAMLIGHT Unlock Your Inner Potential and its plastic headset. The pills opened a plain of timelessness in which it seemed a lost part of himself dwelled. As he lay in their haze, his fluency returned. Wonderful problems enticed and yielded to his insight, wisdom depended from the sky like fruit. He kept a notebook in case any insight survived his waking. None did.

He attached the headset like a blindfold. At the onset of dreaming a strobe would flicker there and rouse him enough to observe and direct his dream but not to wake. He settled and conjured an image: the battle station shining in the void of space. Slender arms and rods pivoting. The missiles rise in swarms, bright points on the black hollow of a crescent Earth. They blur in a silver mist of chaff. Above the crescent distant battle stations ignite in globes of light, their beams lance out, but swarm follows swarm up from the Earth, far too many to destroy. He pulled off the headset.

The world has changed, the old enemy has collapsed into ruined republics. Yet despite this consummation of all the Lab has strived for, the work goes on, the mood is spiritless, the shots in the desert continue like some ritual of penance, some black and endless propitiation of forces that in losing their fixed abode have grown closer and more menacing.

Stillness. Faint whistle of tinnitus, first sounds of birdcall. Wan dawn light. The enemy is gone. But the work goes on and on.

THREE

For a while Lynn was not among the protesters. Their numbers had diminished to a small contingent by the main gate, holding a drooping sheet painted DIABOLIS EX MACHINA. Quine slowed through the gate and stopped, valves in the engine ticking, for a backhoe lurching across the main road, and closed his window against the dust billowing toward him as he went on past an air hammer breaking a sidewalk to rubble, overtones of its chatter following him across the rock moat and into the building where, too late to retreat, he saw Thorpe seated at Null's computer tapping without letup at Quine's entrance.

—Morning, said Quine.

—Is it? I've been here all night. Something there for you to read.

On top of Quine's stack of journals, a year's unread accumulation, colored slips in their pages flagging articles that at an earlier time would not have waited a day, was a xerox topped with a yellow sticker SEEN THIS? *Physical Review Letters 1954*. A dig at his age?

—I know it's old, said Thorpe. —But I think it applies. See, I started with an EE from a hick school, taught myself quantum mechanics by reading Dirac, so my perspective is sort of, things don't change that much. Lots of good ideas have been left hanging. That's how I found your paper . . . I mean . . . stumbling at having touched as he thought Quine's sensitive point, —not to say, it's just, you know, if you're a student like me, not well connected, not seeing all the latest preprints and hearing all the gossip, you need another way up. So this is my way, sort of looking for old forgotten stuff to build on.

—So tell me about this.

—I came across it working for Fish and Himmelhoch, looking for a sort of nuclear model to explain the cold fusion reaction? Okay I know, the current wisdom is, there's no reaction, it's bogus, or if anything is happening it's electrochemical, okay, fine. But you know, if you model the process in a nuclear way, it looks like a phenomenon called super-radiance. The equations are similar. Highet saw the connection.

—To this? Highet told you about Superbright?

—Very sharp guy.

—That's quite a breach of classification.

—He sort of hinted around it, citing the open literature. Anyway it's moot, I'm cleared now. What do you think?

—I'll read it when I get a chance, dropping it back on the stack of journals.

—But, I mean, we don't have much time. Should I pursue it?

—What have you been doing?

—Well, here, let me show you, I started sort of modifying your code but I had a couple of quest

—You changed my files?

—No no I made copies, changes only on my copies and I

—Okay, but look, just be sure you log all yout changes into the CASE system, okay? You know how that works?

—Yes, sure but I wondered about a few things like where you've got this array of reals here, what's that?

—That's the rod array, angles lengths diameters densities

—Okay I thought so, because see I was thinking if you make that something like ten to the minus ten here

—That's the thickness, we can't make rods that thin it's imposs

—But what if we play what-if with these numbers . . .

—Wait what are you do

—then the beam, oop that's a little extreme but you see what I

—But there's no, I mean sure, you can make the model do any-thing, but it has to correspond to reality!

—Sure, I'm just getting, you know, the feel of the system. But, oh here I wanted to know what this function does, this hyperbol

—Yes that's the response curve of the reflec, look, can this wait?

and without pausing Quine was out of the office as from speakers overhead a pleasant female voice advised, —Attention all personnel. Starting at midnight tiger teams will conduct exercises in this area using blank ammunition . . . and he turned into the restroom where at the end, past a row of sinks and urinals opposite metal stalls, a gym bag hung on a hook and steam billowed as Quine, elbows braced on a basin, looked up from the laving of his hands at a bass voice echoing around the hard tile, —bist du ein Tor und rein, to see in the mirror not his own eternally surprised features but fogged void, and turned from the hiss of his faucet to glimpse through the mist a hard white nude male body emerging to towel itself, still singing, —welch Wissen dir auch mag beschieden sein.

In the cavernous building where Dietz supervised, Quine watched long metal tubes welded one by one to the great monstrance in which the bomb would rest a quarter mile underground. From instruments at the ends of each tube hundreds of cables would run to the surface. Dietz displayed a blueprint of the cylinder.

—We are already welding. I cannot wait to know.

—Can you hold off a day or two? If I had any idea where to put the damn things I'd tell you if I had any idea even how to find what I'm looking for . . .

—We can go ahead with other things for just a little while. For a day. Now the rod configuration . . .

—Unchanged. I'm not touching that.

—Make sure, please, that Highet knows all this. Sometimes he wanders through here and if things are not what he expects he is most unpleasant.

Outside Highet's office Quine, arm raised to knock, from within heard Highet's insistent rasp, —like Kammerer, you know, it's not who makes the mistake it's who takes the blame, and at Thorpe's voice barely audible, —sorry for the poor son of a bitch stuck in his position at his age, barely shows his face, and Highet, —never passed a design review, Quine's ears flared with heat, the door before him turning flat and insubstantial as he lowered his hand and proceeded down the hall unseeing, guided by a familiarity more the prisoner's than the adept's around a corner to a water fountain, stopped before a bulletin board and its overlapping notices O Section, programmer needed to model underground plumes K Section, LASS expert needed Z Section, multimedia guru sought B Section, materials engineer, while two young men passed, one saying, —I have no special loyalty to OOP, and on to a further junction where a convex mirror above him presented an anamorphic view around the corner. There Nan emerged from a cross corridor with a wiry man, white teeth in a tanned face, blackhaired forearms folded. The two spoke briefly. The man put a hand on Nan's neck and bent forward to kiss her mouth. Quine turned back the way he had come, slowing only when he found he had nearly circled the building. He backtracked to Highet's door and entered without knocking.

—Get Thorpe out of my office.

Highet looked up in surprise. —What did he do to you, Philip? You look ready to spit.

—If he's so important give him his own space, I don't want him hanging around me.

—Thought you'd appreciate the company, thought he might be useful to you.

—What's that supposed to mean?

—Thorpe handles himself well, you could learn from him. Show some team spirit. Poor boy's feeling abandoned by you.

—I'll work with him, but I don't have to like him or share office space with him. It's bad enough Null's stuff is still there.

—Thorpe has his own space. You want him out, you can tell him so. By the way, Réti's here for a visit, you might want to pay your respects. Instead of running around down in Fabrication with Dietz.

—Someone has to tend to those details.

—Let me tell you something, Philip, I'm a smart guy but to be brutally honest I'm a second rate physicist. I have the ideas but not the persistence, I've known that about myself for twenty years. But I've learned to position myself and to use other people to get what I want. Win win, you know, we help each other look good. You take my point?

Voices approached in the corridor as Highet went on in a lower tone, —One path in the world is up. There's also a path down. What there isn't is standing still. Now you, friend, have been standing still for quite a little while. I'd say you need to make some career decisions soon, before they're made for you.

Flanked by two Lab factotums, Aron Réti came slowly, stamping his cane, into Highet's office. His eyes, azure behind thick lenses, peered without recognition as Quine greeted him. —Ah, my young friend, how are you?

—You remember Philip Quine, Aron. That beautifully sweet photon detector he built for us.

—Of course, of course.

—So here we are, three generations of first rate physics talent.

—Yes yes, the torch is passed.

—I really must be

—No, stay. Aron, Philip's going to get us the data we need to silence the critics.

—The critics, there is no need to mind them.

—From your eminence perhaps not, but I have to deal with these fools and dupes almost daily. Do you know what a senator, a United States senator, said to me the other day? He called this place a scientific brothel.

—I know the man you mean. Brothels I am sure he knows well, but of science he is ignorant.

—Well unfortunately this ignoramus chairs a committee that oversees our funding, so I have to deal with him.

—Speaking of influence, this left wing journalist, I see him here again, why do you let him in? Six months ago he abused my trust with gutter tactics of the worst sort.

—You mean Steradian? He's a useful idiot. He's so cocksure I let him hear things I want to see in print, look here. . . . Highet lifted from the desktop a folded newspaper, —"Radiance Research Forges Ahead", see, this is solid gold. He's so excited when he hears something that may be classified, his critical sense shuts off. You can see him quiver like a puppy dog.

—Keep him away from me, I want nothing to do with him. What is our testing status?

—We need more. As always. Classifying them has helped deflect criticism but we're still being nickel and dimed.

—What do you need?

—An additional three hundred million over the next year.

—I will talk to the president. This is for Superbright?

—Yes. We can definitely show quantitative agreement with theory. It's only a matter of time and money. Philip will tell you how close we are. He and his new assistant have made tremendous headway, just tremendous.

—So? Tell me about this, my young friend.

—Well, I think it's premature to say so. There's a shot next Saturday. We'll know better then.

—Philip's too modest, that's always been his problem.

—No I just think we need a lot more

—More funding. Basically it's a matter of funding. In the long run we see coherent beams striking out a thousand miles and diverging no more than a meter. We see a single battle station downing every missile any enemy can launch. And Aron, we're also going ahead with your interceptors. As part of the overall system.

—Baldur?

—Smaller, faster, smarter, cheaper. Less than thirty billion to deploy.

—Even twenty years ago I thought that this idea only needed the technology to catch up. It is good we have a history, a tradition, a culture here.

—Like Ulysses, we're never at a loss.

—Really? Never at a

—Philip . . .

—Unless we're trying to produce a thousand mile beam where no test has ever shown

—Philip!

—Well how long do you think we can keep it up! this this

—As long as it takes.

—And you, Doctor Réti?

—My young friend, I am an optimist.

—Philip I want a word with you. Excuse us Aron. One arm clutched Quine in tight embrace and steered them into the hallway, Highet saying in low controlled tones, —One day soon, very soon, I'll stop giving you second chances. Come up empty this time and you're through. Clear?

—Meaning what? You'll what?

—I don't know. I don't know but it will be terrible and final and I promise you'll never forget it. Highet raised his voice to hearty amiability, —Good man! You let me know, and went back into his office.

As night came on the life of the building went to X Section, the Playpen, where the younger men worked on schemes even more speculative than Superbright, and Quine returned for the thousandth time to his simulation with the sinking heart of a man returning to a loveless home. Entrapment. As if fine wire had threaded his drugged veins, and now, as feeling returned, any movement might tear him open. He fidgeted the radio on to, —fades to a reddish color as it enters Earth's shad, and off as he saw again the tilt of Nan's head, the fine whorls of her ear, the man's dark hand cupping her neck. The ridge of her collarbone, the warm pulse of the vein across it.

On Null's whiteboard deltas sigmas omegas integrals infinities in variegated ink still wove like fundamental forces their elegant pattern around a void. From the clutter on the desk he lifted CENTURY 21 LAB QUARTERLY. Changing world betokens larger role for science. Acceptable levels of social risk. Public does not fully understand. World free of threats too much to ask. Revolutionary new technique. Major improvement. Important to a variety of national goals. Unique multidisciplinary expertise. Two young men, one poised to hurl a balloon, caromed past his doorway. He shut the door on guffaws and —teach you some hydrodynamics!

He picked up Black 1954. He looked at the citations, then read from the start. He stopped often to reread, with a doggedness that made shift for his halt sense, once so fine, of the rhythms of scientific thought, the probe and test and parry and clinch that now required his slow and remedial attention to be grasped. As he read, his respect for Thorpe grew even as an emptiness opened within him. When he was finished he stared into space before reaching across the desk to snap off the lights.

The phone chattered. On the second ring he lifted it, holding silence to car for a moment before speaking. In the darkness the computer screen, phosphors charged by the room's vanished light, was a dim fading square.

—Quine.

—Hi, it's Lynn, I'm glad I caught you. I'm hiking up Mount Ohlone with some friends tonight, you want to come?

—Well . . .

—I know it's short notice.

—I should be working.

—Good heavens, all night? We're not starting till nine.

—No but . . . He scrutinized the whiteboard as if this quandary might be expressed there in double integrals. —I mean . . . sure, why not.

—Good! Meet us at the park gate. It's ten miles north on Crow Canyon Road.

In the hallway a length of surgical tubing, knotted at both ends, lay ruptured and limp in a film of water. As he left the building sprinklers came on in a silver mist and rainbows shimmered in the floodlit air. He drove out past parked vehicles and armed men in fatigues.

He arrived early. The sky was starry, the moon full. Some planet was setting in the west, probably Saturn by its color. The V of Taurus pointed back the way he'd come. A car approached, lights snagging in the trees, then came around the last bend lightless and rolled to a stop.

—Mark, Julie, this is Philip.

—Why're we whispering?

—Park's closed. Not supposed to be here.

They went around the closed gate and past a building set back among trees. In a second story window a dim line flickered, a fluorescent tube not on nor off, stuttering between states. Fifty yards further they left the road for a broad path that rose winding under black oak, then bay. An owl called, leaving the harbor of a eucalyptus.

Quine and Lynn walked in silence. Ahead Julie laughed and touched Mark's arm, not a lover's touch, but a gesture of intimacy with the world, the same hand caressing air and underbrush. They talked about people they knew, hes and shes darting in and out of audibility like moths in the dark. Soon they entered a darkness of trees where nothing was visible but shards of the moon fallen like leaves around them. He went more slowly and stumbled. Lynn paused and he heard a rustling. Leaves popped free of a branch and came crushed under Quine's nose, carrying to him a strong waft of mint and resin.

—Sweet bay, she said, —is sacred to Apollo, but this is not European bay, *Laurens,* it's California bay, *Umbellularia.* Her tongue lingered on the liquids.

They kept climbing until they broke from the woods onto an open slope. Moonlight rinsed palely the open range land below them.

—*Artemisia tridentata,* Lynn said, inhaling as she broke from a sagebrush a twig of gray leaves.

It was pungent in her cupped palm. The warmth of her came with it.

—Named for the goddess Artemis. Who loves it. And this is willow. *Salix. Los alamos.* Which is the meaning of Orpheus's name. Who opened doors he couldn't reenter.

—How do you know all this?

—This is where I grew up. This is the smell of my home. This is how I know I belong.

They came up to Mark and Julie at the edge of the grove. The moon hung above them, swollen, no goddess remontant but an airless world already mapped, trodden, and projected for division into satrapies of mining, manufacturing, and defense, occupancy deferred only until these scenarios could enrich their planners at a margin of return greater and more reliable than what current technology assured.

—Let's sit here.

Julie passed around bread, cheese, fruit, a plastic bottle of water. On the grass they sat eating. Somewhere crickets chirred on and off, their presence like a field of energy shifting.

—It's so warm tonight. Almost like summer.

—You from around here, Philip?

—I went to school in the East. I've been working around here for eight years.

—Practically a native. What do you do?

—I write software.

—Friend of mine works for CodeWin, maybe you know him.

—It's a big industry.

—Bigger by the day, said Lynn dryly.

—Where's the Big Dipper? I can't see it, said Julie, standing.

—It's too low to see, said Quine. —That's the handle above the ridgeline. There in the west, that's Vega setting. A summer star. Winter coming in over there . . . pointing to that swarm of fireflies tangled in a silver braid, —The Pleiades. Also called the Seven Sisters. You can count more than seven on a clear night. But not with the moon out. And right behind them Orion, you can see him just coming over the horizon, those three stars in a line. Chasing them. Kind of a bad luck bunch, the Sisters. They were all seduced by one god or another, except for Merope, who married Sisyphus.

—Look! Is that a planet?

Finding the pale green disk where Julie pointed, a handsbreadth from the Sisters, Quine knew it was the beam of a laser ten miles south stabbing to the edge of space where sodium atoms glowed in its heat.

—No, not a planet. . . . Suddenly Lynn's hand was in his. She squeezed it once, and before he could respond released it to run downhill toward a dark grove. He stood for a moment and then he ran too. He ran for no reason he could name, wind in his ears, an excitement rising almost to fear in his heart, hackles alive. Some presence almost, chasing him. Then the darkness of the trees was around him and he tripped and went sprawling. The presence was still there. He feared it though he knew it was benign. It was not death, but it would change his life if he let it.

—Philip? Are you all right?

She stood over him, at the edge of the grove as Mark and Julie approached. He lay there in anxiety, anger almost at how she'd stirred him, at the beauty of her movement, at the way her features held the moonlight.

—Philip . . . ?

—I'm fine. He brushed leaf dirt from his sleeves. The presence was gone. They walked in silence until emerging from the grove and heading downslope. Overhead the green star had vanished.

—So what are you working on now, Philip?

—Oh . . . things in the sky, Quine said. —An aerospace partner wants us to program low orbit balloons a couple of miles across, the apparent size of the moon, sunlit, carrying messages, logos, advertising . . .

—But that's so, Julie began and Mark cut in, —Seems I read about this. The Sierra Club's bringing suit, aren't they?

—I don't know about that, we're just the contractors, I just do my job . . . and Julie glancing at Lynn claimed Mark's arm to move them away and resume in a low voice their conversation of hes and shes while Lynn walked apart, obliging Quine to follow, leaving behind —she sees him as a reclamation project . . . to overtake her on a knoll. She waited with crossed arms. Behind her, the valley was filled with glittering points. At its far verge was te floodlit terrain of the Lab.

—Philip, what are you doing?

—You don't like me as a software mogul?

—Is that your, your cover story? Her face remained still and fixed on him, moonshadow in her eyes' hollows.

—That balloon thing really is a Lab project, they started a small group on it . . .

—You don't want to tell them what you really do.

—No, I . . .

—You think Mark isn't smart enough to see through you? He is. You take his good faith for foolishness.

—Look I, I just didn't know what you told them. I didn't want you to be embarrassed by me. His face heated as he said it.

—Well, that would be my problem, wouldn't it. Now I have a different problem. Because it happens I did tell them. She waited for something he wasn't able to give her, then went on. —When you were talking about the Pleiades you were so, I don't know, at ease. What happened?

—Look, I'm sorry, I just . . . Another breath of warm breeze and he realized he was sweating.

—What happened?

—That green star we saw. It wasn't a star, it was something from the Lab. A laser test.

—A Radiance laser?

—No . . . something else. Unclassified. A guide star for adaptive optics.

She was listening with her arms still crossed. —Why did that change your mood?

—It's just, I'd almost forgotten, about everything except, except for being here. That thing in the sky reminded me. Then Mark asked what I did . . .

—They really have their hooks in you, don't they.

—I know that.

Face still hollowed in moonshadow she stepped toward him. His need to be touched and take comfort welled up, but some stricture unknown yet dreadful held him still. After a moment's wait she turned to face the valley lights. —I'm surprised you haven't quit.

—And do what! Turn from the one place where my, my talents have some use?

—What do you want, Philip?

—Want? I don't know. I can't get it. I want eight years back. Before this I was a scientist.

—They haven't robbed you of that.

—Yes, that's so, I gave myself over, and now I'm on the line for something I don't care about. That's the way, yes, you're going to get screwed regardless, so you should make sure it's for something that matters to you . . .

—What would that be?

—I don't know.

Julie and Mark were calling. They went down the slope and rejoined them. She was still talking to Mark, —so I'm, wait, stop, this is it, these are the boundaries and he's like, what did I do? She turned to Lynn with the pack, —take this? and embraced Mark from behind, arms around his chest, straps of her shortlegged overalls a dark X on her back, bare calves duckwalking the pair down the slope.

In the lot Lynn said to Julie, —Get a ride with you guys?

Quine called out, —Mark, just joking about the balloon.

Mark looked up, fumbling with his keys, smiling. —Oh yeah?

—Thanks, thanks for, for inviting me. He got in the car, opened the glovebox, found a tablet, brushed lint from it, swallowed it dry.

•

In his apartment was a smell like stale smoke and old sweat and rotting food, edged with something fouler, like the metallic stench of the flux from the open pipe. At first he thought it came from outside, where earlier they'd been roofing. But on the deck the air was fresh. He knelt to the carpet and smelled nothing. In the kitchen he bent to the drain and smelled nothing. From a bottle he squeezed a pearl of soap onto a sponge, ran hot water in the sink, scrubbed and rinsed it. He scrubbed the stove top. The ceiling fan was silted over by grease and spiderweb. He fetched a chair and reached to touch it. A black gobbet fell from it to the stove top. He fetched pliers and freed the nuts holding the shield, banging with the handle to break the dried paint around the rim. In both hands he bore the shield like a chalice to the sink.

In its concavities had pooled a glossy tar. He scrubbed it for minutes, smutch washing into the sink. Then he spooled off yards of paper toweling, wet and soaped it, and climbed the chair to wash over and again the sleeve of the fan, the blades, the hub. A viscous brown residue clung to the towels and his fingers. Further into the recess, beyond his reach, was more tar.

Sweat soaked him. He went onto the deck. The moon was dim and reddish, as if the sky held smoke. He stared in wonder and fear until the knowledge that it was an eclipse broke upon him banishing fear and wonder alike.

When he went back in the smell was waiting. He understood that from now on everything would smell like this. For a while he sat at the table with his eyes shut, then opened the newspaper for the memory of CARPETS CLEANED but it parted to 24 HRS OUTCALL DAWNA and LOVE TALK $2/MIN and he stared bleakly at the sullen pout, circleted forehead, hair as wild as if fresh risen from the sea, linen garb pleated in most subtle fashion. His hand found the telephone, and after a distant chirrup a small insinuating voice flicked like a tongue in his ear, and he stepped back from the uncradled receiver, switched off the lights, leaving the voice breathing unheeded into the darkness and the moonlight pooled on the floor.

He showered. In the steam lust swelled in him like nausea. Hot

44

spray lashed him. Incoherent images flashed upon him. Runnels nudged moonwhite globs toward the drain. Depleted he toweled. On the sink were Nan's toothpaste, hairbrush, lipstick, mascara. On the toilet tank an unzipped travel kit of quilted cotton gaped to show diaphragm, jelly, tampons, vitamins, ibuprofen, hairpins, barrette, lens wetter, a glass jar of face cream. A towelend snagged in the zipper as Quine scrubbed dry his hair, dragging the kit. Items hailed on the tile floor. He dropped the towel, then swept his hand across the sink top. He grabbed the kit and hurled it. The jar flew out and smashed against the wall.

FOUR

Dry sycamore leaves scraped over pavement in a hot wind drawn out from distant desert by a stalled offshore low. Over the ridge east of town dust and the smell of manure from the farmlands and a haze of smoke blew fitfully into the valley. As the sun rose through layers of haze Quine, driving to the back gate of the Lab so as to avoid the protesters, passed the dead vineyard by the north boundary. He pulled over, stilling the engine and the radio's —ty thousand acres ablaze.

The gate was closed but unlocked. A bright new sign bore the biohazard trefoil and DANGER TOXICS MITIGATION PILOT SITE ALPHA KEEP OUT. The drone of flies rose and fell like a turbine. Stunted vines clung to irrigation uprights. Bark from one sloughed like ash on his fingers. From deep in the vineyard a warm moist flatus perfused the air. A stink like the chyme of a dying beast. He ran back to the car choking and drooling. At an irrigation faucet he rinsed his mouth, his face, his hair, his hands, yet the foulness, as of corroded metal, lingered. What god loves this?

At Null's desk Thorpe worked.

—Bernd Dietz called. He has to know where to put the reflectors.

—I'm tempted to leave them where they were in the last shot.

—We can't do that, Highet would

—That's why I'm tempted.

—Yeah he's, he can be a real prick can't he.

—Not if you play by his rules. He always has a carrot handy.

—Well I have quite a few ideas but you need to look them over, sort of tell me where they're out of line, you know we're really down to the wire here and

—Okay, let's assume Black's right . . .

—Oh then you've read

—Assume we're looking at quanta as localized particles guided by a physically real field . . .

—Highet, you know he really grilled me on this stuff when he came out to Utah, put me through the wringer, made me prove every assumption, but after an hour I had him convinced, and I thought he really respected . . .

—Typical Highet slap and stroke.

—Now suppose we . . .

—You're good at this. And very fast.

—Commercial software you know, those eighteen hour days tone you right up.

—No don't touch that, we can't change the rod array, I've already told Dietz.

—Can we reorient it?

—Maybe. I'll check.

Under Thorpe's shaping the model gradually began to show correlation. After several hours one run produced an annulus. Then nothing for hours more. They ate dinner in the cafeteria, not speaking, then returned to work. Thorpe coded for a hour, then ran the model. Again the annulus. He rotated the model's rods again and again and at one angle power jumped and the annulus closed to a point. They stared at the screen. Thorpe bit his thumb. —What do you think?

—It looks all right.

—It looks fantastic. It's a hundred times brighter than the last shot. But the model's tweaked to hell and gone.

—I don't see anything wrong.

—No, neither do I. So now if we put the reflectors here . . . see, this is how I work. I'm not a theorist, I don't have your background, I need to, you know, immerse myself in the code, feel the system . . .

—Well, it's a remarkable job. I couldn't have done this. I've tried for months.

—Well, I couldn't have done it if your code weren't so comprehensive. You really worked at this. But it's, you know, at some level it's all just sort of pushing numbers around. I don't know if it's saying anything real.

—We'll know soon enough.

—Do you think something's wrong?

Quine shrugged. —Nothing I can see.

—You're not convinced.

—I don't have to be. It's what Highet wants, isn't it?

—Yeah but, that's not what you think I'm doing, is it?

—No . . .

—Because I would never do that.

—I'm sure you

—Since the Fish and Himmelhoch thing I have to be very careful. They were crucified, just crucified, they're pariahs, their careers are finished. Anything remotely to do with cold fusion is tainted, you may as well say you're working on perpetual motion. And I was on that team, I was in that lab. So I have to be very careful.

—Perpetual motion, you could probably sell that to Highet. At least as a talking point.

—It's not funny to me. I had nothing to do with that debacle, just so we're clear on that.

—Sure. I understand.

—Sorry I'm touchy. Just, you know, tired. You've been generous, letting me work with your code and all, I really thought you'd stick me with the scut work but you've done it haven't you, all the test details, and let me do the interesting part. This could take me a long way and I'm grateful.

—Why don't you go home, get some sleep?

—Yeah, okay, I'm whipped.

—Take tomorrow off. I'll tell Highet.

—No no, I'll be in. We have to write up a work order.

—I'll do it, don't worry about it.

—Are you staying?

—God no, what is it, midnight?

—It's, oh Jesus, it's two a.m.

—No, I'm leaving in five minutes. I'll write the work order tomorrow.

—Oh I meant to, here's something else for you to read . . . and, hesitating a moment, Thorpe placed a stapled xerox on Quine's stack, held his gaze for a moment, and departed.

It was a new paper by Sorokin. At CERN now. Quine skimmed it as if reading news from a distant galaxy or a remote epoch. It solidified and extended the work they'd done together, the experiment that had separated them. It was clear that it was a field now and that Sorokin owned it. He stanched an upwelling of envy and selfpity.

But instead of going home Quine broke apart Thorpe's code and studied the changes. He gave the model a new set of energies: points clustered around the focus. Again, with different energies, the same focus emerged. Something was wrong, he could smell it; his instinct was not yet dead.

Near dawn he found it. Along with the sensor positions, Thorpe had tweaked the sensor response function. Playing the system, as he said, to get results. But now the function emphasized certain wavelengths. As might the sensors themselves when struck by the bomb's radiation. The brightness data from the earlier tests might be nothing but reflection, instrument error. When you put that error into the focusing code, the code naturally confirmed the data. Glue in a house of cards. And down in a corner of Null's whiteboard, half erased, was it? yes, the same function, the same tweak. There in the corner of his eye for months. Wasted months. Wrong from the start. Error or fraud? No way to know. Maybe started as one, became the other. But wait now. If you removed the tweak, if you stopped trying for a beam, chaff fell from the problem and the expressions said something else entirely.

A presence entered the room. Air gravid and light adance. There appeared to his mind's eye the battle station lost and insignificant in a tide of radiance, all the universe's light at wavelengths and colors beyond mere vision, streaming in intricate brocade, weaving and mediating between matter and energy, wave and particle, the phenomenal and the noumenal. Here was the mystery, at last, open for his knowing as he hovered between fatigue and ecstasy, and he knew he was unready to pass through the gate of revelation into this realm of light. He drew back. And the presence like a roebuck in forest startled and was gone. The tide of light receded. He was left with only the particulars of rods and reflectors. But he had found their flaw. Mystery might elude, but the information was sure. Thus angels must feel, radiant with the certainty that flows from their single devotion to right.

—Bernd, I need some reflectors.

—For Taliesin.

—Yes.

—I know, I have a work order already, this morning, from Thorpe.

—No, I need more.

—We do not have time to add

—I have to have reflectors made of something other than beryllium.

Dietz was silent. He began leafing through a logbook. —Do you know, try as we might we cannot keep traces of oxygen out of the beryllium. I have told Highet this. Long ago.

—Really.

—I have proposed hydrogen in the past.

—Why haven't we tried it?

—"Don't mess with success."

—I see. I'd like to try it.

—Does Highet approve?

—I'll take responsibility.

—Without his approval I can do nothing.

—Bernd. This is what Slater thought, isn't it. That the beryllium reflectors were giving false brightness. And Null knew it too, didn't he.

—I did not see Slater's report. Dietz did not look up from the book.

—Make some hydrogen reflectors for me. Cable them separately from the beryllium.

Dietz shut the book. —Send me a work order. I will have to send a copy to Highet.

Kihara came through the doors with a following of suited men. —Won't be a minute gentlemen, don't let us disturb you, you can see here the precision engineering we're capable of, bang-up job of inventiveness, maximum return on investment, the answer to reversing the balance of trade deficit, innovative federally generated technology transfer to industry, improves the nation's economic competitiveness as we work deliberately and consciously to build partnerships, a new class of information with commercial value, very creative cooperative efforts, freedom to negotiate intellectual property rights, fees and royalties, cover the technological waterfront, take for instance these fine-grained superplastic steels, not to mention x-ray lithography . . . and Quine returned to his office rummaging through CENTURY 21, Rings Fields and Groups, Computer Addict Wholesale Microcenter, TeX Technical Reference, to come upon WORK ORDER Form 4439A Authorized Use Only, and sat for a minute holding a pen above it suddenly frozen at the sound of Thorpe's approaching voice, —you have to invoke the world control option from the command line, relaxing as the voice receded, pen moving to spell SECONDARY SENSOR ARRAY.

From Highet's open door he heard, —You want less pressure, try the Institute for Advanced Salaries, it's a fucking retirement village for the reality-impaired! and a lower voice unintelligible in response, then —I don't care, I want results! the lower voice growing sharper, —is cheap. My people have to make it happen, as the door opened and Dietz, pale and shaking, came out past Quine glancing at him without a word and stormed down the hall, Highet following to the door, calling out, —A beard without a mustache, does that make you an honest man? and to Quine, —You. I don't want to talk to you now. Send me e-mail.
　—I think you'll want to hear this. We can show quantitative agreement.
　Highet looked at him with loathing. —You want to change the reflectors. The day before the shot.
　—I want to try hydrogen.
　—That's an incredibly bad idea, that's totally braindead, to introduce a new measurement technique at this stage. You have to calibrate, you have to
　—If Slater's right, if the beryllium shows false brightness, it's only a matter of time until we know it. It might as well be now. Or do you want to spend fifty million on another shot?
　—I'd love to. Who told you Slater said that?
　—It's common knowledge. We'll have to address the issue eventually.

—Common knowledge my ass.

—Then it might be wise to preempt questions about it. The shot's so close to the presentation, we can't be expected to have data that quickly. But we could say we're investigating. If we have to.

—You're sure about the quantitative agreement?

—The simulation's excellent. I won't take credit for it. Jef Thorpe did the work.

—Did he now. Well, we're a team. Good results show good management.

—I'd like Jef to give the presentation.

Highet's eyes fixed in calculation on Quine as the phone rang and Quine waited for the dismissive wave with which Highet ended audiences, but instead he spoke a moment, then covered the mouthpiece and said, —Want to make some money Philip, Devon Null's taking on investors, and uncovering the mouthpiece, —Yes, application's outside the envelope no problem there, keep me briefed, and in another moment hung up, leaning back and clasping his hands over his thinning crown, gazing at the ceiling.

—Well that's fine, that's very fine. Wonder if we could work up a little something. I could invite some key people to the ranch for the shot, some unnamed sources, goose the process a little, can we get Thorpe in on this?

—He's probably in my office.

—You may work out yet Philip, Highet grudged as one thick finger stabbed the phone. —Jef? Leo. Get over here, rising to pace past framed and signed photos of three Presidents, another of Réti and himself with the current President, artist's renderings of the Superbright and of a fusion driven spaceship, cartoon of a mushroom cloud WHEN YOU CARE ENOUGH TO SEND THE VERY BEST, certificates from professional societies, a length of cable, a circuit board. He stopped at the window, gaze caught by something, and parted the vertical slats of the blind with his fingers, speaking softly, almost to himself.

—Do you know the darkness that's out there? Do you realize how tenuous this all is? Twenty thousand years of civilization, and only in the last few hundred has rationality begun to displace superstition. I tell you I would sup with the devil, I would risk armageddon, not to lose that. When I think of those fucking tree huggers out there . . . and turning back to Quine, voice low and insistent, —Think the ills are in a system, think it's that simple, Réti and his anticommunism, your new girlfriend and her peacenik buddies, wonder why's she drawn to you?

—Now wait just a

—Darkness and malady is in the human heart, Philip, don't you know that? The enemy is the heart. You can't hide from that darkness . . . as Thorpe entered in black linen jacket, red t-shirt, nose stud, eyes eager, and Highet's demeanor switched to the cheerful, —Jef, my man. I want to wow the rubes when we go to the desert. We have a ranch out there with T3 data lines from the test site. What can you do that's portable and fantastic? I want flash that makes you reach for your checkbook.

—I've got an interface toolkit from my CodeWin days, I can throw something together. Just tell me what kind of data I have to work with.

—I'll e-mail you the details. Shot's tomorrow evening, not too much for you, is it?

—Demo or die, I know the drill, said Thorpe, grinning.

The evening wind whipped dust across the highway, vibrating the cars stopped in three lanes behind flashing lights at Codornic s EXIT NLY as Quine punched —illion in property loss, over to —noninjury accident being cleared at the Codornices Road exit not blocking lanes for you, drowned in a siren blaring up the shoulder OHLONE VALLEY RESCUE ƎƆИA⅃UᙠMA as Quine edged against horns and unheard curses into the exit lane and cut back onto a commercial strip behind the central mall, the reverse of which colonnaded and pedimented facade, its raw concrete stained by rains, caught with a sort of wounded dignity the sun's last rays as they likewise gilded Estancia Estates An Adult Community where Quine parked and for a moment held in his gaze a prospect of identical bungalows arrayed on lawns billiard-green out to the surveyed boundaries of chainlink and dry pasture beyond.

—Oh! Philip. Come in. I wasn't expecting you, your deadline . . .

—Well it's Friday night, I thought

—I'm glad you, but, if you'd called I would have made dinner . . .

—I wasn't sure I was coming.

—Your work is done?

—There's a test. I fly out tomorrow afternoon. And there's a presentation Monday.

—Can you stay tonight? We can go out for . . . is something wrong?

—I need to ask you something.

—Yes? What is it?

—Who's the guy with the curly black hair and the good tan?

—The, what?

—I happened to see you the other day. In a hallway. He was acting kind of proprietary.

—Proprie, her face flushed and she turned to look across the room, one hand resting on a table. Quine waited.

—How long has this been going on?

—His name's Ben and he's a good friend, and it's been, we've been friends for years. Since before I knew you.

—You still see him?

The flush darkened, and as she turned back to him her mild features contorted into a stiff anger he'd never seen in her. —Do you mean, do I sleep with him? Yes. I have. Once or twice since you and I have been together.

—Once or twice. You've lost count.

—Oh, Philip! Why are you, this is hateful!

—It hurts me, Nan.

Her face was a mask of plain misery. —We never

—Never what, laid down rules? I didn't think we had to, I thought some things went without saying.

—Without saying what! That I'm yours alone when you don't give me anything, for God's sake Philip I didn't turn to Ben for sex, just for, for kindness, for friendship, just to feel that I mattered! To someone! Five years of my life Philip, I'm no longer a young woman, do you want to know when it was I saw Ben, when I went to him after you and I were together?

The coldness, the absolute coldness of the moment.

—You don't, you don't even care do you. It hurts you, but I can see in your eyes, you won't listen to me. How can I possibly explain when you won't even give me credit for, for loving you, Philip? When you and I met, at that picnic, and I was so charmed by you, by your intelligence, your modesty, your reserve. Do you remember, the thunderstorm? I hadn't seen one since moving West. And afterwards you took me home, we were drenched, and I loaned you clothes. Oh Philip, it was long over between Ben and me, he was like a brother, I just wanted to say goodbye, to tell someone close to me how happy I was. How happy I thought I'd be.

—And the second time?

—Yes, that's all you want to hear. Two years later, when you didn't come to dinner, didn't call, and I waited and waited, so it was only an anniversary just a date on the calendar that's all, but I called Ben and he came over to be with me, and he didn't, didn't even want . . . cut off by her sobs.

—But I, you knew I was working, you could have

—When you come here and, and sulk for hours, barely acknowledge my existence, don't call for days on end, then expect, how do you think that makes me feel . . . I would have told you about Ben if you'd asked if you'd ever shown any interest at all. If you even know who I am!

Within him a stone fell and fell, soundlessly turning.

—Philip, talk to me! Don't turn away like this!

—I have nothing to say, and he was out the door, where streetlights had come on, knowing that his leaving now was worse than anything gone before, a withdrawal he could never make right. Don't tell me, don't tell me we don't feed the emptiness in each other.

F I V E

In the Great Basin of Nevada thousands of acres of waste and infecund desert had been reclaimed for science as the Aguas Secas Weapons Test Site, and one hundred miles further west was the Advanced Research Institute of the Eastern Sierra, a ranch at the edge of the Owens Valley, a black facility whose funding appeared in no budget. Leased to the government by a conservative businessman, it served as a layover site for Lab personnel on their way to the desert. It nestled in the broad base of a canyon near a creek's loud runoff through lateral moraine. To the west the ground rose in the space of a few miles from six thousand feet to a twelve thousand foot crest of granite crags. Below, a few miles to the east, the north-south highway lay like a dropped ribbon across the wrinkled valley floor, and a hundred miles further across desert dotted with sage under a flotilla of thunderheads was the chalk white sink of Aguas Secas.

Even before joining the Lab Quine had seen ARIES. On his first trip west, while switching planes at Phoenix, he'd been paged and diverted to a single engine craft bound for a Kern County airstrip, where a sheriff's four by four awaited him. The first Radiance shot had just gone off and at the ranch they were celebrating. Quine met Highet there. Highet was beating a twelve year old at chess, telling the boy, I'll trade a bishop for a knight anytime, I love knights, they leap barriers, they face eight ways at once.

A month later Quine was at Aguas. Rank smell of sage hovered in the predawn cool, immensities of desert air quivered to the horizon.

They drove with the sun rising behind them, the young initiates joking, group leaders and guards and observers in DoD hardhats silent and grim. Roadways of cables led from instrument trailers over desert pocked with the collapse craters of previous tests to the distant borehole. Above it a red crane pointed straight up. The count reached zero. And the earth rippled. A wave rushed toward them and the ground shook as if a train were passing and passing and passing. When it stopped the air was a clear plasma of exaltation. To know that the binding forces of matter were yours to break, the wealth of nations yours to squander in such sublime force, this was a deep and secret sweetness known only to the few.

At the ranch now Thorpe was joking with some grad students from X Section. Others were there from J Section, and some stern faces he didn't know, military or intelligence, and Steradian alert as a corrupt deputy. Highet arrived in blue jeans and tooled leather boots, carrying cases of soda, chanting in a false twang, —Twaace the sugar, twaace the caffeine . . . followed by a Western senator cadaverous and grinning in white Stetson, and his young aide plump and groomed to a sheen, with the zealous black eyes of a pullet.

—Look at em, young, brilliant, confident, said the senator. —That's how I felt at their age. They own the world.

—The world? retorted Highet. —They own their genitals. The rest of them's mine, raising his voice to introduce, —Gentlemen, the right honorable Howard Bangerter of Utah . . .

The aide asked if physics had yet succeeded in finding in the traces of Creation the fingerprints of God, and Highet nodded, a slow smile spreading and his tonguetip darting as his hands rose to conjure, —Not God exactly . . . as Quine walked onto the deck where three barbecue grills sizzled, and a keg of COORS LITE sat amid greasy paper plates bearing the ruins of meals, and the sun had long since chased the waning moon, itself pursuing Venus, behind the mountain wall. Although the sky retained day's blue a chill came down from the remote and snowless peaks.

—This young man, Highet's voice carried out from within, won last year's Heinrich Hertz Fellowship in Physics, a prestigious award I happen to administer . . . and Quine stepped down from the deck, crossing dry grass to the creek's rockstrewn willowed bank where it trickled through small pools and clumps of rotting leaves. Quine followed it upward, breath laboring. He stopped at a large boulder long ago tumbled from a higher place, and sat. Little residue of the day's warmth remained in the shadowed stone. The western ridge above him was a great dark wave. In the east a glamour of rosetint clouds swept up from the horizon. The ranch was small below him. A cold wind came down the great wall of rock. Into this wilderness he might ascend and be lost.

But he returned. Thorpe's voice came up as he slid open the glass doors, —background, you know, trucks on the highway, that sort of thing. Other side of the spool you can see some small temblors we had this afternoon. When the shot goes off we'll see more than a wiggle. But the real action's on this screen here. At the site they're recording everything for later analysis but data's also piped to this workstation where this autocorrelation software gives us an immediate window on what's happening. Red is intense energy, blue is, you know, less intense. We're looking for sort of a red ringlike structure.

Quine watched the stylus quiver as about him others conversed. Without warning the stylus jerked. The screen of the workstation came to life, numbers flowing down its right edge. Colors coalesced on screen. The senator and his aide leaned in enrapt. A minute passed. Blue and green surrounded a corona of yellow and a jagged red core flecked with white.

—We have brightness, Thorpe said. —A hundred times the last test. More. Could be a thousand times.

—Three orders of magnitude improvement, declared Highet. —At this rate we'll have every enemy missile on Earth neutralized in a few years, and raising his tone with his glass, —To Team Superbright! Leonardos of the age. You people are the best in the world.

Grunts and howls of triumph went off like rockets. The senator's aide leaned smiling to whisper in the senator's ear.

A second wave of guests arrived, a dozen men in suits adorned with MAMMOTH CONVENTION CENTER NAME COMPANY and a few women packaged as brightly as new software, and Quine moved off through the manic younger men hopped up by caffeine and sugar and the shot.

—Need now's another little war where we can demo this stuff. Feed some tinhorn tyrant some antiquated missiles and provoke him to use them.

—PDP eleven downstairs running spacewar

—thought Malibu was bad but Acapulco's about three inch waves

—guy at the Cloudrise Seminar, he blasts wheat into stubble in a shock tube at mach ten, calls that science, eighty k a year

—maybe the moon's changed its orbit or

—thou shalt not piss on a colleague's funding

—translate the project into terms attractive to DARPA

—well Mazatlán then or Valparaiso

—think I'll propose rye

—dup rot swap drop

—corn smut

—know better than to say that in public with troops on the border

—shell game

—call it Virtual Wilderness

—I hear Sara squeezed it out

—boy or girl?

—people make money on it they're more likely to go along

—girl I think that's what Moe said

—why leave home to get away

—he didn't go deep enough

—photo and topo database with fractal interpolation software to smooth the animation

—a quagmire like Viet

—substantive working relationship with at least six major US companies

—get USGS or Interior onboard

—hell why not go worldwide

—translate the project into terms attractive to DOE

—not this time, this is Southwest Asia

—get on your NordicTrack put on the goggles you're up in the Cordillera

—and somebody from the insurance company's selling records of who owns what where to thieves

59

—take out the infrastructure of the whole frigging country if we have to

—get up close to extinct animals

—everybody makes out, homeowner's paid off, insurance company raises rates, thieves fence the stuff, fence makes a profit

—ought to get the Basil Zaharoff memorial award

—as defined in paragraph R of section 11 of the Atomic Energy Act of nineteen fifty four

—in Caracas this guy went by on a bicycle sliced the damn finger right off for the wedding ring

—knowingly and with intent

—living things probably get wiped out in a pretty thorough fashion every few million years

—better than real

—so cool cause like the program's working but you don't know what it's doing so there's these emergent properties

—sophisticated encryption algorithms deserving of patent protection

—control the flow of information, do it by classification do it by misdirection principle's the same

—incorporating certain aspects of prior art such as multiplication

—translate the project into terms attractive to Disney

—object oriented

—get this straight, if I say nine times six is seventy two I'm infringing?

—yes but when your story comes back it has your fingerprints on it then you know where it's been

—I have no special loyalty to DNA

—must have misjudged my audience

—but if you codify your knowledge that nine times six is sev, ah, fifty-four in any machine executable form

—sometimes the envelope pushes back

—women at that high energy conference in Tsukuba

—held research positions at four universities published thirty papers before anybody realized

—won't impact the users of the algorithm, or affect the multiplication market, only the vendors of such algorithms

—kinbakubi kenkyu kai?

—lineal descendant of ibn-Musa al-Qarizmi that being the first publication

—no PhD not even a BA all his papers copied from obscure journals

—seme-e?

—Go for it, Bruno, do the meat thing.

Quine edged into a hallway and down a narrow flight of stairs as behind him music began pounding, catching as he turned a last glimpse of Thorpe, cheeks flushed, smiling at a circle of admirers the impartial smile of triumph.

Nature is more ready in her creating than Time in his destroying, and so she has ordained that many animals shall be food for others.

He continued downstairs toward a light. In the cellar seven or eight young men from X Section were gathered around an old rackmounted minicomputer and a pool table.

—so he goes, learn to hassle people and lie with a straight face.

—Excuse me, I need to get back. Does anyone know the arrangements?

—Excellent advice, dude.

—Excuse

One glanced up. —There's pool cars outside somewhere.

Full dark. A dozen cars. E108637. DEPARTMENT OF ENERGY OFFICIAL USE ONLY. Key in the column. The seat harness slid up and drew in over his chest and waist as a chime sounded and dash lights blinked red then glowed teal. The car swayed and bounced for a mile down the dirt road. There the highway stretched north and south into void, under stars like chips of ice. He could go anywhere. But time was a field that moved with him, inescapable, close as the blue light in the cabin. He drove for hours without stopping, radio for company, wash of noise, hollowness in his being. Mountains that a century ago killed emigrants with their rigors fell to his vehicle. Descending to the flats he saw brushfires crawling on far ridges like luminous cells writing some teratogenic message across the land, and the farm cities on the ancient seabed added their sulfurous light at the meetings of capillary highways glowing with the heat of a summer long past its term, and booming through the car's windows when he opened them was the smell of dust, manure, smoke, exhaust, chemicals, and he crossed the last ridge into his valley of a million souls, of all the places he might go, for all the freedom he had, here again.

In the dark apartment he stripped, dropping rank clothes behind him on the way to the bathroom. The mirror's sudden light showed, before selfhood interposed its protective assurance, the face of a stranger, aging and vulnerable. Lowering his eyes from the brightness he stood voiding for long seconds. A ribbon of urine twisted along the axis of its arc as it splashed into the bowl. Standing thus he blinked, faded, woke. The gates of sleep stood open and he was through them, uncleansed, as soon as he lay down.

S I X

Gathered before dawn the crowd set out for the main gate, to be met by police as later arrivals swelled it further, until Lab workers began to show up in their vehicles and county and city police were called to divert traffic to the north gate against the columns of people still coming, and the south road was closed to vehicles and state police summoned, and still the spectacle slowed traffic to walking speed, so that Quine was late to Highet's office. Highet stared out his window at the south road.

—Those people out there will never understand. It could be so much worse. On the other side, entire cities, entire regions have no civilian industry at all, it's all military. Here we cut our deals as needed but we still do real science. We bring in people like you. We roll back the darkness.

—There's a problem.

Highet turned. —What.

—The beryllium and hydrogen reflectors were cabled separately. Thorpe's analysis at the ranch used only the beryllium. I looked at the hydrogen data yesterday. Nothing. No brightness. No beam.

Highet turned again to the window. —I see. The hydrogen reflectors which I asked you not to use. You know, I almost stopped that work order, came that close. But I wanted to see what you had in mind.

—As supervisor it was my decision.

—Yes it was. So where's your quantitative agreement now?

—You saw at the ranch. The beryllium shows it. Spectrum peaks here, as predicted. But that's not an x—ray, that's oxygen in the beryllium glowing at just the right wavelength. It looks exactly like the new model's predictions for focus.

—And where did this new model come from?

—Thorpe has been modifying my code. I found a routine of his where just this set of frequencies is amplified.

Highet came from the window, pacing past the photos of Presidents and artists' renderings, touching the length of cable.

—So it's all Thorpe's fault! That's yout story?

—The CASE system shows all his modifications.

—I see. Well, it's bad for him, then. Especially after Fish and Himmelhoch. He has a history.

—I wouldn't call it intentional. The ideas he brought were good. I worked with him, I didn't see this, it could have happened to anyone.

—It doesn't matter. He has a history, voice sharpening, —quackery or carelessness, you think it matters? You think you can ever walk away from your history?

Quine said nothing.

—Now those hydrogen reflectors, let's talk about these, you piggybacked your own little test onto the piggyback, that was very cute. Did Thorpe know about that?

—You saw the work orders.

—He knew he was getting feed from the beryllium only?

—It was his demo.

—Yes, you saw to that. All right. We'll keep him on for a while. Then you'll write him a letter of recommendation. Down the road we'll issue a report on the false brightness. You'll be group leader on that.

—You want me to . . .

Highet's voice was tight with controlled fury. —I want you to take some responsibility. Show you're serious about this. It's about time you moved up or got out.

—Okay.

—You begin to interest me, Philip. I thought I knew what to expect from you.

—At least we caught this now.

—Okay. I listened to your story. Now you listen to me. We haven't caught a thing yet. What we need now is another test.

—I don't want to sound naive, but you're not going to mention this at the presentation?

—Today? I think not. I think I will not at this moment give the enemies of reason grounds sufficient to bury our project, our knowledge, our aspirations. Highet lifted from his desk a small device etched with a craft undreamed of even a decade before, raising it before him like a talisman, weighing it in his hand. —I believe not.

Nolan came through the door bearing a red folder, acknowledging Quine with a minute change of expression, as the phone rang and Highet lifted it, —No I can't see anyone right now.

—Very clean data from your shot, Philip, Nolan said.

—no damn it I can't Chase is coming in an hour

—Oh, you've seen it?

—what, what do you mean he's here now

—We prepared the overheads. A match with theory unparalleled since Mendel's peas. Kid's a barn burner is he?

—well damn it keep him down there

—He'd like to be.

—fucking hero of the people can just wait

—You're taking him under your wing.

—don't care! Do whatever it takes! Have to do everyone's job, what's this Bran?

—Overheads of the Taliesin data.

—Fine, leave them. Bernd there you are find the rest of the team will you get them up here we have a little problem god damn senator arrived just a little ahead of schedule he's downsta, Dennis where the hell have you b . . . Nolan — !

—Oh! I just, sorry, didn't see your foot

—Sorry Dennis let me help you up . . .

—Nolan will you get the hell

—my slides! here don't step on

—Nolan!

—just put these back in order, with the ah integrated 24-bit color TGIF animations and music in standard MIDI files

—Dennis

—little problem with the synthesizer all the instruments stuck on the cowbell patch so when we played the Apocalypse Now music, I mean the Wagner Valk, rather intriguing actually but hardly

—Dennis will you

—then our Silicon Graphics machine couldn't read the TGIFs so we had to convert them to Video Postscript but somehow they came out black and white one inch square so

—Dennis will you please

—go low tech instead, keep it simple, four synchronized slide projectors overheads eight track digital tape

—Dennis, get up! Leave the, will you leave the slides on the floor. Go to the lobby. Keep Senator Chase busy down there.

—But I

—Go! and pacing to the window, parting the blind, —Fuck's this going to play like, must be hundreds of them in the road.

—The news said a thousand, said Dietz.

—Bullshit. Supposed to keep these assholes away from the main gate put them up in the north corner, I want to know how word of this got out! glaring at Quine, —I want to know who's been talking to these people, who let them know Chase was coming today. Who do we have out there? Federal protective, local police, I want county I want the Chippies, bring out the goddamn transit cops if we have to!

—Leo, it's symbolic. Today's Armistice Day, you know?

—Shit on that, it's to embarrass us. All for Chase. Man keeps calling me up about twenty kilos of plutonium gone missing, I keep telling him we don't stockpile plutonium here.

—But we do, Leo.

—Well, Bernd, Chase doesn't have the clearance to know that, and picking up the phone midring, —Yes? Damn it Dennis just, look, take him to the downstairs conference room think you can do that? . . . no will you forget the fucking slides, thumbing the phone's button, — Where's Szabo? You all go down, I'm right behind you.

—Senator, glad you could make it. This all? Expected to see more of your colleagues . . .

—Doctor Highet. These two gentlemen are from the General Accounting Office. You'll be seeing more of them.

—Why don't you all take a seat and we'll begin.

—I have just one question, Doctor Highet. Is the Superbright going to work?

—I believe our presentation will address any

—I don't want a presentation, I want a yes or no. At the present moment, judging from everything you have to date, is it a viable system, within the budget and timeframe we have?

—Beyond question. In fact we have new results that show

—A new Superbright test? When?

—I can't discuss that in open session.

—Then maybe you can discuss claims of exaggeration and fraud from Warren Slater.

—Those are lies. Slater sabotaged my teams repeatedly. He had reasons of his own to derail this program.

—Such as?

—I can't discuss that in open session.

—Slater's not the only critic. Some of your own people

—Those are not my people. Those are people who've made up their minds that certain technical problems are too hard to solve. They're wrong. They could be making a contribution, but instead they find fault.

—So why are you behind schedule?

—We're not.

—According to your own timetable

—Senator, we have brilliant, creative people together here doing important work. Leave them alone and they accomplish miracles. But if you put limits on them . . .

—You're not answering me. I didn't ask about miracles.

—I am answering you if you'll let me. You cannot nickel and dime a program like this in the research phase, not if you exp

—Research? I thought you were engineering phase.

—Very nearly.

—You sent the president a letter claiming engineering phase.

—I do not acknowledge that. If such a letter were to exist it would be top secret, and you lack the clearance to see it or the competence to evaluate it.

—Doctor Highet I'm tired of this, you have put in motion a program that all told has squandered thirty billio

—Senator

—you have stonewalled, you have defied

—Senator

—gress, you have hidden behind classifica

—Senator, you're an asshole. You might even be a traitor.

—I will not take that from you, sir!

—You don't have a clue what's at stake here, one look at those hippies out front you're ready to cave, sell out this nation's security its technological edge its, breaking off for the figure in the doorway who bowed his head in apology.

—Gentlemen, we have a bomb threat. We need to clear the building.

—Good God.

—Your peacenik constituents, Chase. Good work.

—I'm not through with you, Highet.

—Fine, I'm willing to sit right here play Russian roulette.

—Gentlemen please, security is coming through, you'll have to move to Building 101.

Clipped static blurted in the hallway. Gallop of many feet approached.

—Clear this area!

Outside in the sunlight a security squad came running in a wedge, helmeted and visored, black gloves holding batons at port arms. Leather creaking, heels clattering, radios jabbering, they broke through the exiting crowd and Quine was swept the wrong way, out past an unmanned checkpoint before he cleared the surge of people onto a lawn where men in jumpsuits trailed strips of CAUTION tape on two then three sides of him and he dashed through the open space as behind him shouts were raised. Between windowless walls he took a stairway down to where two workmen rounding a corner dealt him a blow with the plank they carried, —Jesus watch it! hurling him to his knees against a chainlink fence trembling at the lip of a great pit. In this excavation five, seven, ten vehicles labored grinding and roaring in desperate intensity, beeping hollowly as they reversed or clanking furiously forward over a terrain of pale mud. Vast as the pit was it would not bury a millionth of the dead the bombs could kill. Quine

pulled free of the fence with a tearing of fabric and went over a walk-
way of plywood sheets, pausing before a trailer CREDNE CON-
STRUCTION in which doorway two t-shirted men eating lunch
regarded him with dispassion as with a handkerchief he rubbed dirt
and blood from his palms and the knee visible through ripped pants,
then went down another stair of raw wood stained with mud, glancing
back at concentric terraces gouged from the hillside. *The city is built
on two levels, lords and palaces above, common workers below.* He
rounded a corner to where a stream of people hurried past guards at a
checkpoint.

—Look I need to

—Move on, there's been a bomb threat.

—Yes but I'm in an important meeting I need to get back to

—You can't come this way, this is a secure area.

—I'm cleared dammit! clapping his breast where no photo ID, but a
torn flap of pocket, depended, —oh Christ, look my name's Philip
Quine can't you call

—Move away! The guard shoved him back into a stream of people
advancing slowly toward the main gate. He made his way through and
broke into a jog on a path that led to the perimeter road, where he doubled back to the entry kiosk from its far side passing and passing close
on his left the unending mass of protesters just beyond the fence. He
stopped short of the entrance gate where cars were blocked by the leading edge of the crowd coursing out and around them like a stream
around rocks, while bullhorns blared —personnel, do not exit by this
gate repeat do not, and outside the gate protesters swirled in place like
debris at a confluence of cataracts, held back by a skirmish line of county police vainly trying to keep them separate from Lab personnel. Quine
stood sweating and panting until four cars slewed to a stop on the
perimeter road and discharged Lab security, one of whom leveled his
club at Quine, not clearly part of either crowd, and cried, —You!

Quine ran for the kiosk. More Lab police had arrived there, forming
a wedge to divert Lab personnel from the gate. Quine was suddenly
before two of them who linked arms to bar his passage. Their visors,
opaque and bronze, mirrored twin Quines, elongated and dismayed.
He pointed past them.

—I belong inside.

Then he was seized and pushed through the gate into the street. A helicopter swept overhead. His crouched under its roar, hands against his ears.

Let us now speak the truth as we know it. Say that the sun is round, and bright, and hot. Say that it fires its acolytes, darkens their skins, elevates their wormridden souls. It rises in our birth and it sets in our death. Its prints upon our flesh the spots that adorn its face. It is in us whether we labor under it, or hide away from it. It strikes through our souls, it ignites the light of our being, it limns the shadow of our denial.

In the crowd he saw Lynn, her dark head appearing and vanishing among others, nape and shoulders bare and tanned below the cropped marge of hair, sun blazing on the straps and back of a white top.

Light is a wave and we are carried upon it. Light is a particle to pierce us with revelation. Light is the sun or the moon, a heat that tempers or a gentleness that silvers with love.

He pushed toward her. At the end of its circuit the helicopter turned and came again.

Say what you know, that love is lost. That light is extingushed. But see, loveless our souls still blaze. Our sun has not gone out, for fire comes to those who go not the way of light. See, we blaze and are not consumed.

He called her name and the call was lost in noise. The crowd shoved them together and she turned to him, eyes surprised. It was not Lynn. Pressed by the crowd they unwillingly embraced. He clung to her until another surge felled him. The cut on his knee opened and he bent to stanch it. When he rose he was among figures wearing skulls of papier-mâché and skeletons painted on black tights. Tambourines jangled, clattered. Around him people tied kerchiefs over their faces. The helicopter roared. Its belly glistened like a spider's, then it rocked and moved off leaving a silver mist that fell gently onto the crowd like a spring rain. Tears leapt to Quine's face and he dropped to his knees gasping and blinded, clinging to the nearest figure, saying over and over, —I belong inside.

11. DUAL USE

Past the toll plaza the bridge stretched into morning fog and low clouds that obscured bay and sky alike until the center span climbed out of this gray limbo into a brilliant haze through which sun smote the driver's window and curdled the horizons to brown smutch, while a jet poised like a raptor overhead and thundered in falling glissandi as Highet pressed A/C MAX and turned up the radio to, —first day of spring in the Bay Area record highs expect, punching over to the orotund tones of, —Great American Broadcasting network, your host Tuck Eubanks ladies and gentlemen, the conservative voice of truth, prosperity, and fun, back in a moment, and hurtled down the span's far side through Redwood City where the only trees to be seen were blue gum eucalyptus and sycamore, past Your Company Name Here 415-282-0110 and SINATRA 4th Show Added Mar 31, tapping the brake as taillights reddened in all lanes ahead, swerving from behind SQUANDR to thread between 386SX and FOOBAR, punching the radio to —clones lowest prices guaranteed at Computer Addict Sunnyvale, downshifting to third then second as Versant, Data General, Hexcel, Informix, and Failure Analysis Associates went by, cutting in front of ELUESIS to brake sharply under a small black billboard in white Futura italic SAVE US FROM WHAT WE WANT as the radio continued, —Caltrans hazmat team on the scene 101 southbound at Moffett three lanes closed, and stabbing the selector again, as if a more congenial reality awaited on another channel, —my friends, I am expounding and commenting on a cultural decay happening in this

73

culture, his hand traveling on to pick up the cellular phone, —Dan Root, please, this is Leo Highet, as traffic locked to a dead stop.

—Dan, it's Leo. I'm stuck in traffic, 101's a parking lot. I'll meet you at the restaurant soon as I can, pulling as he hung up onto the shoulder, accelerating past the stopped cars, punching brakes and horn together and sliding his window down to shout —Asshole! at another driver also edging into the shoulder, and to swerve up the offramp where again he jammed brakes to join two lanes merging under a stand of blooming acacias, as the radio warned, —Friends it's alarming but people do judge you by the words you use. Semantech Dynamic Language Cassettes give you the essential power words you need to dominate any, itch rising in his gorge to trigger a violent sneeze contorting his face and leaving it a mask of suspicion until he spied the high cascades of yellow blooms tossed in the caress of a warm breeze, —Ah shit! and jammed the window button to slide the glass unhurriedly shut, other hand reaching for the glove box, eyes streaming as he reached for his inhaler and again punched A/C MAX, removing sunglasses to dab at his tearing left eye, glimpsing in the mirror angry red skin under a pale brow as horns blared behind him and the radio asked, —Have you ever wondered if hair transplants are for you? and eased the clutch to inch forward from the offramp onto a six lane divided thoroughfare where he chose his opportunities to advance through gaps and openings among cars streaming in a semblance of purpose complex to the edge of chaos past two miles of low featureless office parks and condominiums shrouded by olive and eucalyptus until SOON YET loomed and, cutting across two lanes, he glimpsed his left eye swollen, his nosé reddened and enlarged. —Great, just great.

Near the restaurant door DISABLED PARKING ONLY. Highet parked, the car alarm yelping as he pressed keychain to arm it, and paused in the foyer to ask of an impassive Chinese, —Dan Root? and followed the pointing hand to a bellow of laughter rising over the clatter and din of plates flatware talk and the plume of smoke curled there above the massive figure in white Stetson and black shirt with red and white embroidery across the yoke, and he edged down a narrow corridor past a potted ficus and a woman laughing into a pay phone and entered the men's room where a mirror set upon mauve and avocado

74

tile showed him a face divided, right half normal, left half angry with welts and distended into a despairing expression of forsakenness and misery, the eye a furtive and evil bead in swollen flesh, the lip lifted to expose teeth, as though presenting a threat while the rest of his face apologized for it. He cranked a chrome lever to reel yards of paper toweling into a basin under a faucet that every few seconds pinched off its flow like a prostatitic urethra until he banged the springloaded tap to restart it. The last of the toweling tailed into the sink and he lifted the soaked paper to his face and held it there covering the welts, regarding stolidly the unafflicted yet still unlovely right side until he recoiled —Damn! from moisture seeping at his shoulder, collar, and hair, and flung the toweling onto the floor, turning in vain for another towel dispenser, shaking his wet hands in the air in a desperate mudra of fury, running them through his thinning and awry black hair before reentering the dining room where the massive figure at table six craned his broad neck around and exhaled smoke in greeting.

—Why, you look like sumpin the cat's all done with.

—And a good morning to you too, Dan. You're in form.

—Oh, I am. Dim sum, a double corona, and technology transfer. It's all a man really needs to be happy. Leo, you know Orrin Gate. Orr's chairman of Gate Cellular. He was out to the ranch after your last shot. I think you met there.

—Yes, good to, pardon my, no towels in the men's, cut off by an obstreperous fit of coughing at the table behind him, —enjoying the cell phone you sent, very clear signal, never a problem even in the car.

—I'm glad. We are very good at what we do.

—Pull up a pew, boy, here on my right, said Root, handing him as he sat a napkin to dry his face.

—These allergies will kill me yet.

—He'll have two of these and two of those, Root said, taking from a passing cart four small plates.

—What's this?

—Duck feet, and these are jellied

—Excuse me, came a sharp voice, as Highet turned his bad eye wincing into Root's exhalation of cigar smoke, —This is the non-smoking section.

Root shifted his bulk and thrust his shoulders back in thunder-struck disbelief. —What did you say, sonny?

—Your smoke is ruining other people's enjoyment of their meals.

Root's pale blue eyes narrowed in the fat ruddy face framed by lank gray hair and beard. The tooled ivory clasp on his red string tie rose gently and gently fell on the placket of his black shirt, and a slight smile widened his mouth.

—I'm Dan Root. And you are? extending a hand which the other man took reflexively.

—It doesn't mat, annoyance turning to concern as he flinched in Root's grip.

—Ruin, is it. I guess you don't know what ruination is.

Root touched the coal of his cigar against the base of the thumb gripped in his hand.

—Jesus . . . ! as for a fraction of a second the hand writhed in Root's grip beneath the coal, then was snatched back and cradled like a wounded pet.

—You best put some ice on that.

—You're crazy! The man backed to his table staring at Root, face lit as with the fire of revelation. Root turned back to the table and set the cigar in an ashtray.

—I sheerly love to take the righteous down a peg. It's almost worth a spoiled ash.

—Someday one of your victims will call a cop, Highet said.

—That man won't call a cop. Why, until now, he thought he was Wyatt Earp.

At his table the man upended a water glass and wrapped ice in a napkin. His companions bent forward in earnest discussion while the man stubbornly shook his head.

—Try the parchment wrapped chicken, Orr. No no, unwrap it first. Now, Leo, what's all this crap I'm hearing about Superbright problems?

Highet looked distastefully from Root to Gate and back. —Dan, I know what an omniscient view you have from your ranch in the mountains, but some of us down in the trenches

—I just want to know if we got trouble.

—This is a classified program, Dan, I'm not going to start talking technical details to the unsanctified.

—Unsanctified? asked Gate.

—Security, Orr, he's worried about security.

—That's right, Dan. We're not all freelancers like you.

—Simmer down son.

Gate cleared his throat. —Perhaps I can start. I'll express our interest in general terms, so that any inadvertent classification breaches won't jeopardize you gentlemen. As I understand it, the Superbright component of the Radiance project is not coming online as quickly as anticipated. Consequently, a secondline component of Radiance may be frontburnered. This second program has aspects of interest to us outside its purposive antimissile envelope. Fair enough?

—Go on.

—Gate Cellular is eager to enter the growing digital information market. To play in this market requires vast amounts of cable. That or satellites. The larger players have a formidable lead in the cable markets, but there are parts of the globe where, for political or geographic reasons, cable can't be laid. Some companies propose to serve these areas with a small number of geosynchronous satellites in high orbit. We think there's a better way: a few hundred small, cheap, moveable satellites in low orbit. Research and development costs are high, so we're looking for strategic partners.

Root pulled from a shirt pocket some papers and unfolded them. — Long as we're bein so circumspect. . . . This is from Aviation Leak. "The Slingshot orbiting interceptors kill incoming enemy missiles by impact. Simple and small enough to be deployed by the thousands, they are little more than a camcorder, a guidance computer, and hydrazine thrusters." Put a high speed switching network onboard, what've you got.

—Slingshot? asked Gate.

—That's what we're calling them now, said Highet. —A David and Goliath thing. Little pebble of a missile knocking out an ICBM by kinetic force.

—Or any other target, said Root.

—Dan . . . , Highet warned.

—As I understand it, Doctor Highet, the Lab wishes to move into more commercial applications.

—Wish has nothing to do with it, it's a Department of Energy mandate.

—In any case, they're encouraging Cooperative Research And Development Agreements with industry, correct?

—Yes, said Highet. —But Slingshot isn't a candidate for a CRADA. It has classified components.

—Orr's application is outside the defense envelope, said Root, folding the papers. —I say it's dual use.

—Looked at the right way almost anything's dual use. But DOE won't open a CRADA on this, I guarantee you.

—CRADA, who wants a CRADA, I'd sooner have cancer. You're getting prissy in your old age, Leo. You didn't talk this way back in the days of Transfinite Polygonics.

—Didn't have a senator on Appropriations out to hang me then.

—Shit, Leo, you remember when you and Réti and me came up with these orbiters, called em Baldurs then.

—Dan . . .

—Remember? That weekend at the ranch? Hell, I got patents that overlap all this stuff. You saying I don't have a right?

—Look, last thing we need right now's even the appearance of improp

—What's your damn trouble, Leo? Those Superbright tests?

—Dan, will you shut up before you

—Gentlemen, permit me. The press has suggested, with whatever truth, that delays with Superbright may jeopardize the entire Radiance project, including the Slingshot interceptors. Now it seems to me, if the defensive value of Slingshot is seriously questioned, a parallel commercial mission could save it. It would seem wise to have that commercial mission in place before such questions arise.

—Listen to Orr, Leo. He knows his stuff. Orr went to school with Undersecretary Rip Whipple.

Highet dipped a corner of his napkin into his water glass and held it to his swollen face. —Can we get some more tea?

—Doctor Highet, the men's room is, where? Past that ficus? Thank you. Pardon me.

Root watched Gate's departure, then turned on Highet.

—What the hell's wrong with you? Why the hissy fit?

—Whipple's about to resign, Dan.

—What? How come?

—His Radiance Liaison Office at the Pentagon handed out half a billion in contracts last year, all approved and overseen by the same four people. Turned out all four used to work for him.

—Shitfire. What's he gone do?

—Back to private industry where he can make five times what he made at Defense.

—And they wonder why they can't keep good men. But so what, that's not your problem. What is?

—Got all those patents, Dan, you don't need me.

—We need Sand Hill Road, that's Orr, and we need the Beltway, that's you.

—I'm not exactly Beltway Bob these days.

—Did those test results get leaked? That shot with the sensor problems?

—Jesus Dan let's, a little louder, let's call CNN why don't we. You haven't seen it in the papers, have you?

—That's it, isn't it, that's why you're sweating.

—Those results are classified.

— Is there a trail back to Null? You have to tell me that.

—There's no trail. We're writing a report to make our own trail.

—Who's doing the report?

—Quine.

—Who?

—He wrote the x-ray focusing code. And he supervised the shot, along with Dietz. That kid we fired, Thorpe, the scapegoat, he was working under Quine.

—What's Quine like?

—He's a fuckup.

—So why you letting him write this report?

—He and Dietz supervised the test. You know Dietz. So I tapped Quine. I bumped him up to deputy associate director.

—You crazy? Deputy associate of what?

—Of enough rope.

—Slater's old post.

—I think people will get the message.

—How about what's his name, Szabo?

—I don't trust Szabo, he'd use this to get a leg up on me.

—Thought you had that degree thing on him.

—Why waste it? Anyway Quine pulled a fast one on that test, he set up that kid, Thorpe. Very down and dirty. I want to see how he writes it up. His head may yet end up on a stick.

—Better his than mine or yours.

—What do you want with Slingshot, Dan? You know how to do comm sats.

—We want those thrusters of yours, boy. Mine couldn't keep a bird in low orbit for a year. You're claiming ten years? Is that for real? With those dinky little fuel tanks?

—Classified.

—Fuck you too. What's our lead time?

—First tests in August. Next round of CRADAs in November.

—These birds really gonna work?

—Jesus Chr, you sound like Senator Samuel Fitzfuck Chase, are they going to work, they're *tests*, Dan, that's why we do them, because we don't fucking know. If we knew it'd save us all a lot of time wouldn't it now.

—Boy, you're on edge. You need a vacation. Whyn't you come up the ranch? Take us a couple horses up to Steelhead Lake, catch some trout. Not much snow this year, gonna be an early summer. What do you say?

—Coming up Sunday for those Hertz recruits, aren't I.

—I mean a real vacation.

—I'm fine.

—Why's Chase worryin you? Our bud Howie Bangerter chairs that committee.

—Howie and his Mormon butt boys.

—Don't say that to Orr, he's LDS.

—You're kidding.

—I mean it. He's a deacon or something.

Highet turned to see the blacksuited figure returning past the ficus in the hall.

—Gate know what he's doing?

—Five years from now he should own this market. We're talkin billions, boy.

—If the crick don't rise.

—There you go. That's my Leo. Don't you worry now.

—Gentlemen.

—You know, you're not the only interested party, Dan. I heard from Stone last week . . .

—Stone! You're not serious. Any man who'll play for nickels can't be trusted.

—Mister Gate, question for you, why do you want a low Earth orbit for comm sats?

—Please, call me Orr. A big reason to go LEO is signal delay. Geosynchronous sats have a perigee of twenty thousand miles. By the time you've bounced your signal off them there's a perceptible delay. That's not acceptable for time critical uses.

—Isn't Motorola on this turf?

—Yes, they are. But they plan to orbit fewer satellites quite a bit higher.

—This seems, I'm just freewheeling here, a system this size seems like a risky commitment for an unproved market and a small company.

—That's why we're looking for allies. But the market's there. If not for cellular, for something else. As I was saying to the vice president, and Root shot Highet a glance while Highet looked bored, —we think of the satellites as delivery systems. We're still looking for content providers.

—There's a question in my mind what we get out of this.

—We bring to the table high speed high capacity packet switching and routing technologies. Linking the Slingshots in a networked system could make them viable for a wide range of applications. Weather monitoring, pollution tracking, global positioning . . .

—Okay, I think I can package that.

—Now let me ask you this. I understand that a Cooperative Research And Development Agreement grants an exemption from the

Freedom of Information Act.

—Our working model gives a five year FOIA exemption.

—Good.

—But getting DOE to sign off won't be easy. Slingshot is a defense program, they're sticky about that.

—Shit, Leo . . .

—Surely, pardon me Dan, surely the Department of Energy can be made to see the benefit. Their CRADA program is, from what I hear, unsuccessful so far. This venture could be a showpiece for them, wouldn't you say? And I understand that Slingshot itself has a shall we say clouded future.

—Can't speak for DOE, they have trouble seeing the sun on a clear day, but I'll do what I can. We'll draft a letter of agreement, see where we go from there.

—Excellent. I'll fax you our latest business plan.

Root raised his hand in a scribbling gesture and across the room the manager left the man clutching his wrapped hand and darted over to slide the check under Root's hand freeing from a gold clip three hundred-dollar bills. Root winked at the manager. —Somethin for the help.

The three men rose and walked leisurely to the door. Gate said to Root, —I'm sorry Mister Kim couldn't make it.

—Mister Kim? said Highet.

—Oh, another potential investor, said Root. —He's kind of a recluse.

—Mister Kim. That Sand Hill Road, Dan? Or Seoul?

—Pyongyang. He he, see his face, Orr? See it? Had him going.

In the vestibule they threaded through a crowd coming and going, past the phone booth where a wrapped hand rose gesticulating above the partition and snatches of talk emerged from the background din like complexities at the surface of chaotic systems, —got to get back I'm about to slit a cat stem to sternum, and —soon's I quit I get two offers not even looking, and —Christ it's hot for March, and two small boys darting either side of them, one shouting, —I win! I'm king of the world! as the three men emerged into sunlight and Root pushed up the brim of his Stetson and dropped the stub of his cigar to the pavement where he ground it to smoldering pulp beneath his boot-sole.

—Got you a love note there, Leo.

Highet followed Root's deliberative gaze from the curve of a horse-tail cloud slipping across the sky's pale dome between a stately pair of eucalyptus, leaves shimmering like unheeded semaphores, flanking a squat white savings and loan 11:30 82F 28C and finally down to SFORZA and the black vinyl bib stretched across the snout of the red hood into which was tucked a parking ticket.

—Well gents, as the great Karl Friedrich Gauss said, Go you forward and faith will come to you.

—Thank you for your time, Doctor Highet.

—Mister Gate, we'll be in touch. Dan, always a pleasure.

The car yelped as Highet disarmed it, Gate flinching from the sound as Root cast an arm around him, saying, —Leo'll eat anything that don't eat him.

On the bridge, hurtling down the far span, the ticket fluttered like a trapped bird till it tore free as the car boomed past a mobile home named for that tribe whose tale of Little Brother, so similar to that of Phaethon and Helios, did not punish but rewarded its hero with wisdom and respect for his snaring of the sun, and raced mere feet above the bay, accelerating past NO TOLL THIS DIRECTION and the leaching pools and the industrial parks, one hand scanning past —it's your constutional right! to an orotund voice that had —nothing to be ashamed for! as the freeway broadened to eight lanes sprawled like a flattened snake up green hillsides turning gold so early in the year after —seventh year of drought for Cali, while elsewhere, —flood waters so severe, seemed to demonstrate the chaotic extrema of a global climate under assault by the effluvia of —traffic and weather togeth, until, satisfied for the moment that no news, of himself at least, was good news, Highet silenced the radio and slipped a silver disk into the slot of the CD player to let the doomed guitar of Robert Johnson carry him back to Codornic s EXIT NLY and past the city's central mall, cutting across a chorus of horns and around Estancia Estates, where CREDNE CONSTRUCTION earthmovers pushed back still further the chaparral behind the open frames of identical unfinished houses, and banners flapped in the hot wind STARTING AT $150,000.

Coming then to the main gate of the Lab, fortress city of ten thousand souls behind razorwire, slowing past the demonstrators in their motley, with their handmade signs FRAUD DECEPTION STOP NOW, the darkhaired woman absent today, the woman he'd first singled out for heckling because of her beauty, Highet swerved to flatten a rolling paper cup under his wheel, stopping at the kiosk to show ID, —Morning, Jake, and continuing through the doubly fenced desert of broken rock and motion sensors, into Building 101's parking lot, RESERVED DIRECTOR, noting with distaste Philip Quine's battered white Subaru parked at the far end near a yellow backhoe <<ULTRA-DIG>> beyond which rose the terraced adumbration of a building, its southern facade cloaked in mauve and avocado tile while the northern half, an unfinished cliff of raw concrete spattered with pale mud, fell away to a terrain of rutted earth and pools of bright green flux, all enclosed by chainlink and plywood sheets stenciled ADOBE LUMBER and CREDNE, the halfmade bulwark oddly deserted by its builders although the workday was at its height.

—Morning, Dolores, as he entered the outer office, frowning at the radio declaiming in carefully modulated outrage, —typical liburrul modis operendy. He calls my logic cheap and my facts hazy and my reasoning fellatious, until Dolores reached the knob to silence it, and Highet plucked the Ohlone Valley Herald from a box of mail in which a smaller carton held two and a half doughnuts, —Think we can keep the jelly off the correspondence? rounding the desk to come —Ow! hard against heavy boxes sealed with a gray cover sheet Final Environmental Impact Statement and Report For Continued Operation of Laboratories.

—Geez, you look just awful. Take a doughnut if you want.

—Thanks so much Dolores. Might as well, there's most of one on the newspaper already. What's all this junk?

—That's the EIS back from the printers, you wanted three copies.

—Three? Looks like a flat of phone books, prodding one box with a foot.

—It's seven volumes, six thousand pages. You have calls

—How many of these things did we print?

—Two thousand sets. You have

—I love it, we're clearcutting the Pacific Northwest to print environmental impact statements. Is Conor here?

—He was. Your new computer arrived. You have

—At least something went right while I was gone.

—You have calls from EPA, DOE, DoD, the university regents' office, Philip Quine, Bernd Dietz, Doctor Réti, Senator Chase, the vice president

—Of what?

—Of the United States.

—God, I love to hear those words. You put all this on the mojo?

—No the network is down, that's why I'm telling you. Also William Venham, your sister Thea, and Cedars-Sin

—Why's the network down? Conor! Get him in here.

—and you have a one o'clock

—Don't remind me, as he pushed open the inner office door and the voice rose up again behind him, —my friends, it's demonstrative that, and the door swinging wide banged a tower of cartons, —Fuck! toppling them in a spill of bubblewrap, styrofoam, spiralbound manuals, warranty cards, and cables bagged in plastic across the floor to where a black box aXon with matching monitor, keyboard, and printer sat on his desk. Highet put down the newspaper and the doughnut and his blunt fingers touched its matte surface, which took briefly their sweaty imprint then swallowed it like mist, as Conor entered yawning, slim to frailty in a black t-shirt SEROTONIN $C_{10}H_{12}N_2O$, fine black hair in a ponytail, trim mustache and beard, a reliably complaisant witness to Highet's pleasure or displeasure.

—Sorry about the mess, boss, I'll clean it up. I didn't know if you wanted to keep the boxes. What's wrong with your face?

—My face? Not a thing. Feel good about yourself, Conor, the world will love you. Is this thing sexy or what?

—It rocks. Conor stooped to gather cables, deftly mating socket to plug, snugging keyboard and mouse. The machine gave out a suave chord and the screen lit with chiseled icons bright along its border.

—The operating system was written for aXon by grad students at Cambridge. They got chump change, and the aXon execs are all driving Ferraris. What is it about you students, you're supposed to be so smart.

—We are Zen mind.

—Is that why you took the network down so I have to collect my messages by sneakernet?

—Mu, o master. We had a little incident. Somebody put some pornographic GIF files up on an open server. We had to take it offline. Unfortunately it was also a mail server.

Highet grimaced. —Christ, don't people have anything better to do with themselves? How long were the files there?

—The creation dates vary. Days, months, don't know.

—This was on an open server? Save the files, I want to know what's going on there. Now what about my mail?

—Behold the little mailbox. Every time you boot, he knows to check for spooled mail on the server, and there, leaning in to smartly tap the black teardrop mouse, —you are.

—Are those my messages from Dolores? Okay, you can keep your job. But get rid of these empty boxes.

—Do you want to store them?

—You kidding? Shitcan them.

—And the manuals?

—We don't need no stinkin manuals, pivoting with one hand to tap in his password ••••• and burst open the iconic mailbox as Conor hovered nosily.

—Chaos on the edge of complexity?

—Just the usual noise. Now clear out of here and let me start taking out the trash. Come by at four and we'll talk about your Rayleigh-Taylor project.

—Cool.

As the door closed Highet slumped back in his chair. His breath came harshly and with suspensions. In his bowels dim sum moved restlessly. Opening his eyes he stared blankly at a slick card aXon Warranty Tell Us About Yourself, picked it up, and flipped it spinning to ricochet from the lip of the trash can to the carpet.

He took the Ohlone Valley Herald and cellular phone into his private bathroom, resting the newspaper on the sinktop while he unfolded the phone, loosened his belt, lowered his pants, settled sighing onto the seat, and then punched SEND. —Dolores? Get me an hour in the gym at four. Yes I know, don't remind me, punching END, raising the newspaper to Grand Jury Indicts 4 LA Cops, Estancia Expansion Given Green Light, turning to the editorial page where, —Son of a! welts on his face reddened as he took the phone, selected a number from its display, punched SEND and waited. —Doctor Réti please. It's Leo Highet, and scanned the text, post-Cold War era, needless expense, environmental hazards, peace dividend. —Aron, have you seen today's Herald? What? Oh, that went fine, I think Gate's on board. But the Herald, listen to this, lead editorial, Stop Nuclear Testing Now. What is this crap? We employ ten thousand people, we *made* this fucking cow town, where does he get off? No, don't placate me! I don't care about the editorial, paper's a joke and everybody but Greer knows it, I just want to know why he's getting feisty. And it's not just him, I've got calls in from Chase, DoD, DOE, the vice president I mean what's going on? Who's talking to who? Yes I'll be here the rest of, wait, got a meeting at one but I'll have Dolores put you through. Find out what you can, pressing END, and the phone instantly trilled in his hand and he shifted his nates, sighing. —Highet. What is it, Dolores. Tell her, no, never mind, I'll take it. Hello Thea, how's mother. Uh huh. Yes I did. Well, they've done what they can. If it's chronic, there's nothing . . . no, I, look, Thea, she's seventy-eight years old, she's had a full life. No. No I can't poss. Well, you do what you like but I. Thea, are you listening? I just said I can't. I run a billion dollar laboratory here, I can't just take a week off and come to Lancaster, it's out of the. Look, don't start. Call Mark and hassle him why don't you. Uh huh. Thea, lis, Thea, listen to me. I'm hanging up. I don't have time for this. I'll call you when you've got mother home. Goodbye, Thea, pressing END, —Jesus suffering Christ, and dialing again to wait through, —Thank you for calling the Ohlone Valley Herald, if you know the extension of, and punched 4 3 1, refolding the newspaper and spooling off a length of toilet paper while waiting through — J Frank Greer is not in his office right now. If you would like to leave a message, please wait for the tone.

—J Frank, it's Leo Highet. You know, out at the Lab, where your son works. I'm in a small room with funny furniture. Your editorial is in front of me. Highet rustled toilet paper at the mouthpiece. —Now it's behind me. He snapped shut the phone.

He rose then, wiped, and flushed, gazing like a haruspex at the spiral arms of the swirl as the auguries were swept away. Red pepper, sausage, pasta. Fragments rose in the ebb unflushed and he flushed again. In the miasma was a faint scent of asparagus. He washed his hands. At the doorway, hitching his belt, he thumbed on a fan and shut the door behind him as both desk phone and cellular phone trilled together.

—Already? Thank you Dolores. He glanced at his watch, and took a folder from the desk drawer, opening it to confirm its contents and stepped over the threshold where the toe of his loafer came down on aXon Warranty Tell Us skidding him past Dolores startled from YOUR IMAGE YOUR SUCCESS How To Polish Your Management Style to turn down —friends, I am the epitome of, as he caught his balance to stride out and down the hall, pausing outside the conference room just long enough to hear, —therfucker can't imagine anyone doing anything for decent reasons, he thinks everybody has an agend, silenced by his entrance into air stifling as a bunker under high sealed windows like embrasures.

—Morning Leo.

Dietz, Szabo, Karp, Quine, sitting there, sweltering, jackets over their chairs, shirts spotted with sweat. Looking at his swollen face. No one saying what they thought. Highet laid down his papers, put on halfglasses, and remained standing.

—Like an inferno in here, what's the problem?

—I called physical plant. They say the air conditioner's screwed up.

—That's really great, we need physical plant to tell us that?

—They say they're working on it.

—What about the other conference room?

—They're painting it.

—I thought we painted it last year. Oh, I remember, one of those idiotic use it or lose it budget items. Speaking of which, where's Kihara? I asked him to be here.

—He, ah, said he had a brush fire to put out.

—He say what it was?

—Something about an EIS.

—Frank, did you take that meeting with Jeremy Rector this morning?

—Yes, sir. Him and two other federal-looking gentlemen from the General Accounting Office.

—And?

—They'll be back.

—Okay, let's start without Kihara. Yes, what is it, Bernd?

Dietz rose and held out a white envelope, its end trembling. —I must tell you. I cannot continue here. For a long time I have known this. I hear rumblings, it is like a great building with a bad foundation, a few cracks appear, the collapse begins, no, I cannot stay on, this is my resignation.

—Bernd, sit down . . .

—Last night someone from CNN calls my home, to ask about charges of fraud.

—Did this someone identify himself?

—Armand Steradian.

—Wasn't he that PBS guy used to hang around here, Leo?

—Ex-PBS. After that backstabbing special of his I made some calls. He'll never work for them again. What did you tell him, Bernd?

—Nothing! But I can read the writing.

—Bernd, you're overreacting. This is nothing more than our friend Chase leaking rumors. If he had anything real, he wouldn't be phoning in anonymous tips to Chicken Noodle News. Show some nerve. He's just waiting for someone to bolt.

—But I tell you I cannot

—Bernd. Do me a favor. Put that envelope back in your pocket. Keep it there over the weekend. If you still feel this way on Monday, we'll talk.

Highet looked around at the rest of them. Not saying what they thought. Sweat ran down his ribs.

—I'm glad Bernd brought this up. It's stressful but it's nothing new. The Radiance program has some unresolved issues, we know this. We also know that we can resolve them. But in the meantime our critics are getting vocal. Is there anyone here who can't take the heat?

Dietz glanced at Quine. The others held their poker faces.

—Okay. Let's move on to business. You all know how DOE is talking up dual use technologies. We hear this so often, the old plowshare polka.

—Dual use technologies, said Szabo. —I've got one of those in my pants.

—Thanks Frank, I'm sure we all

—Looked so nice out this morning I thought I'd

—appreciate your wit. Here's my point. This is an opportunity. We can start moving Radiance technologies under the dual use envelope.

—What about the GAO investigation? asked Karp.

—I'm not worried. The report isn't due for a few months. You've all given your interviews, right?

Quine was readying to speak. That habitual wounded look. Always about to flinch. As Quine's mouth opened, Highet spoke.

—Philip, you were reviewing the recent Superbright tests. Where are you on that?

—I'm finished, pulling several spiralbound xeroxes from a black nylon carryall.

Highet stared in disbelief. —I thought your timeframe was longer.

—I'm done.

—Well, hold those. It's not appropriate to discuss them now. Not till we've all seen them.

The wounded reproach in Quine's eyes did not flinch but hardened. —I thought I'd distribute them now.

—I said hold them.

Something like rage there now. But no followup. Highet held his gaze for a second longer as Quine fingered the bindings.

—So, future directions. We've got CRADAs in x-ray lithography. Fusion research can cover a lot of programs. Frank, talk with P Section and see what all we can get under their umbrella. We're looking at reduced underground testing, very possibly a full ban. Bitter as that is, it's an opportunity for computer science, simulation codes, and for hydrodynamic and hydronuclear testing. What else, people? What else can we package?

—There's the toolmaking code we gave GM a few years back.

—A lot of astronomy stuff could fall out of our adaptive optics work.

—Astrophysics is always good cover.

—We have fabrication techniques that could prove adaptable to commercial manufacturing.

—Very good, thank you, Bernd.

—All this is more like a garage sale than technology transfer, said Szabo. —What about the Slingshot orbiters? Plenty of potential there.

Highet looked thoughtful as sweat slicked his inner thighs. —Really. What kind of potential?

—Well, lots of things. They're just orbital platforms. Off the top of my head, astronomy, weather monitoring, comm sats . . .

—What about the classified elements?

—Most of the Slingshot tech is off-the-shelf. It's a matter of what you put on them. Different hardware, different software, that's all.

—Can you write a white paper on this, Frank? Identifying areas outside the security envelope?

—Kind of busy right now. But yeah, I could.

—Do it. The rest of you, I want something in writing about programs in your areas.

—Ah, before we, can I just bridge in here? What's our advantage going after this stuff? Karp leaned crossly forward, bare forearms resting on the conference table's oak veneer.

—Why, Henry, said Highet, —we get the satisfaction of enhancing America's global competitiveness.

—So we go from national security to appliances? I'm not very excited about that. I remember the last time we did this crap, designing wind turbines in the seventies. About as sexy as bell bottoms.

—I was there, Henry. Labels change, the work goes on. You all know I've got the entire Lab to consider, but you also know this is where my heart and history is. Nuclear design, directed energy weapons, missile defense, this is our work, the work of the age. I won't let anyone cut the heart out of our mission.

—I hate this shuffle, complained Karp. —We'll have crackpot realists coming down off the woodwork to get on the gravy train.

—If we don't get it the pickpockets will.

—That's right, Frank, said Highet. —I know it's a pain in the neck. It's meaningless and it distracts. But rise to the challenge, people. Think of it as diversifying our portfolio. Anything else? Then let's get out of this fucking sauna. Philip, in my office.

And like Virgil quitting the underworld, damp thighs chafing, he led Quine to his office pausing to hold the inner door for the younger man to pass in first, then following him in with a slam. Quine flinched.

—Don't you ever try that again. Make an end run around me.

—End run? You assigned me this report, you

—Don't tell me what I did!

Quine dropped the bound xeroxes on Highet's desk, An Analysis of False Brightness Readings in "Taliesin" Test of Radiance "Superbright" X-Ray Laser Component.

—This is my draft report, submitted for comments exactly according to protocol, exac

—Protocol! Don't give me protoc, breaking off to grab from the desk an inhaler, glaring over its barrel as he pumped it, then, after inhaling noisily, —Where, just where do you get off, returning this favor I did you, the great favor of letting you head this group, of promoting you to director level, you repay me with this bullshit? I'm speechless. It is understood that you run this kind of report by me privately, first as a courtesy and just incidentally so you don't make an ass of yourself.

—I'll risk that.

—No you won't, you'll sit down this minute and we'll go over it line by line. Dolores will clear your afternoon, reaching for the phone which trilled stopping his hand momentarily before he lifted it. — Highet. Yes, Aron, what have you got? EIS? What's that got to do with. No, it's just back from the printers I haven't even opened, it's six enormous vol. Oh Christ, not those jerks again. All right, don't worry, I'll. Yes I'll deal with them. Don't excite yourself. Never mind the EIS, I need, never mind it, I need to know about the Taliesin test. The last Superbright shot. Whether those results were leaked. You haven't said anything to anyone? Okay, I think someone here is selling us out, glaring at Quine. —No one's called you? Okay. Well, you say no comment, of course. Call me if you hear anything at all.

—I'm not going to do this, said Quine.

—Excuse me?

—I'm not going over this document with you. I'll put it through channels.

—What do you think you're playing at, Philip?

—You, you think this is some kind of game, winners and losers, the screwers and the screwed, think you can change reality by, by wishing, by lying by

—People like you, Philip, you suffer reality. I make it happen. That's no game. It's serious *because* you win or you lose. It's you fucking amateurs who screw things up.

The phone trilled again. —Dolores, hold my calls. What? Tell him, no, send him in.

Dennis Kihara entered bearing six hefty gray volumes cradled in his arms then skidded —Look out! across the carpet, stumbling to a stop at Highet's desk where he deposited his burden and bent to pick up, —What's this, Tell Us About Yourself, looks like a warranty c

—I'll take it, what's your problem Dennis?

—The EIS, have you seen? well of course you have, here, page IV-C-238 let me, oh sorr

—Dennis, just

—because we wait, let me, Map of Planned Construction, see, right next to Building 101

—Yes, that's us right where we're always been.

—Well it's, gosh, I reviewed this map myself, and I don't know how it happened but we have to issue an erraticum.

—What's the problem?

—Well look!

—It's a map, it

—No, there, out the window! following the point of Kihara's trembling finger past the slatted blinds to a bleached sky half obscured by a mauve and avocado facade.

—Don't like that tile, looks like a men's room, but what are you

—It's not there!

—Dennis what are you

—The building, the new building's not on the map!

—That's ridic, scanning the foldout graphic and the text across from it dotted with gray overprinting designating changes from the Draft document, —look, List of Construction Sites, it's right here

—Yes but the map!

—Well . . . , finally seeing the unmarked void in the pregnant swell of the main road where the new construction was underway, —well that's unfortunate but hardly a major, we'll just issue an erratic, I mean an erratum.

—We need to send it asap, I have a list, I tried to e-mail you but the network is down.

—List of what.

—Of people and places I contacted.

—You what?

—I just, I, I called some places to advise them that there were problems with the EIS, didn't go into detai

—Called what places.

—Well I started with our FedEx list. Congressional offices and citizens' groups mostly.

—Really. Ink's not dry and you're on the horn telling CalPIRG CANT Greenpeace and Senator Chase that we have some reality problems, that's just great, just incredibly efficient Dennis.

—Well thanks I just, you know, it's my job

—Take the rest of the day off, let me handle this.

—Oh no, I couldn't, it's my mistake.

—Yes it is, but you've done so much already.

Kihara glanced from Highet to Quine uneasily. —Well, I

—I'll come back later, said Quine.

—No you won't. You stay right there, transfixing Quine with all the fury he kept from Kihara. —Dennis, what I need from you right now is a list of everyone you called, pushing a blank sheet of paper across the desk.

—Okay, I can email you

—I said now.

—Well, I think I can remember most of. . . . Fumbling, he unclipped from his shirt pocket a blackbarreled pen, nesting barrel in cap as

Highet calmly waited and watched Quine.

—You know, Dennis, nobody notices an oversight like this in a document this size unless you point it out to them. What you do is you wait a few months, and then you file an appendix buried in a bunch of other documents. Like a cat you hide your shit in the sand, you follow me?

—Um, yes, okay, I'll, yes I think so. The pen hesitated and continued.

—But you don't ever, ever tell the people who want to shut us down that we fucked up. These people are the enemy.

—Sorry, I, here . . . pushing the sheet to Highet with one hand as the other returned pen to pocket, clipping it in place.

—Don't apologize, it makes you look weak. Just never do it again. If there's ever a question in your mind, ask me. You're sure that's everyone?

—I, yes I think

—What about CalPIRG?

—Oh yes that's right

—Never mind, I'll add it. You get any callbacks?

—Yes, Lynn Hamlin, and Highet saw Quine tense, so he did know her, —from Citizens Against Nuclear Technology, she wants me to speak at a meeting tonight.

—No chance. Forget it. What time is this meeting?

—Six p m at the, ah, First Unitarian Church of Kentwood, open forum on, let me see, the role of the Lab in a post Cold War

—Yes, well, they can open it without you.

—They've invited a speaker, Tony Luz.

—Luz? That prick. We went to Caltech together. Makes him think he knows science.

—Well, he's fairly well known, I thought another point of view

—Adman turned enviro. Don't loan him credibility. Got a little problem there, Dennis.

A round black stain had spread across Kihara's shirt pocket where the pen was clipped.

—I, what?

—Your pen is leaking.

—Oh? looking down in confusion to pluck it out with a snap, staring in chagrin at the silver clip on the cap topping the black barrel narrowing to an exposed gold point. He dropped it —Damn! on the desk, touching the stain futilely with fingertips that came away darkened, as Highet pulled two tissues from a box. —Damn, damn . . . holding the tissues as he gathered the volumes to his chest. Highet followed to push the door shut almost on his heels.

Highet capped the pen and clipped it in his own pocket. He looked at Quine in silence for a moment. —I'm too good natured. I like to give people a chance. Guide them along. Like you, Philip. I promoted you, I gave you this opportunity, handpicked you to manage this report, told everyone to cooperate with you. You let months go by, you don't talk to me, and now you drop this, this sack of shit on me.

—The, the whole point of an independent

—Independent? The hell you think you're doing! You want to go it alone? Like Slater? You want to see firsthand what happened to him?

—Slater, yes, and Dietz

—Dietz, defecting in the middle of the fucking meeting, did you put him up to that?

—He's been trying to see you all week, you don't even answer his e-mail, and, and Slater, they knew, didn't they, that the computer model was rigged from the start, all the way back to Null.

—Now it's Null's fault? Thought you were blaming young Thorpe. Keep your scapegoats straight. The fact is it's your model, Philip, your computer code, and if anyone goes down for this

—but you put me on it, didn't you, gave me Null's code and the bad data from earlier tests, let me waste over a year on something you knew couldn't work until Thorpe tweaked it to give those bogus results

—behind Thorpe's back, that stunt you pulled with the backup reflectors, I should never have let you

—because otherwise no one would have known, that was the heart of it, wasn't it, those beryllium reflectors, they glowed exactly as the model predicted, but they weren't measuring anything but their own radiance, the backup reflectors showed just a spike in the background noi

—Listen to yourself, you're saying that even your backups showed brightness

—six orders of magnitude below what you claimed, six orders! a million times less! and twelve orders from what you promised, you overstated the power by a billion times! and you knew it all along, how did you think you could get away with it, fake something like that at the heart of this program?

—Watch what you say about what I did and didn't know, and be very careful about using that f-word, because it's your problem, you're the one who couldn't do your job! So don't tell me what I know, I know it can be made to work, but you couldn't do it!

—You think you can do science by PR, by

—Do you think this, pacing to the wall and tapping the framed facsimile of an ancient letter in a small precise hand, —wasn't PR? "Item, I have a model of very strong but light bridges, Item, I also have models of mortars, Item, in case of need I will make large bombards, mortars, and firethrowing engines of beautiful and practical design, in short, whatever the situation, I can invent an infinite variety of machines for both attack and defense," sure, think this wasn't blowing smoke, think Leonardo had ever built any of these, think he had off the shelf hardware ready to go, no, but he got the job and he did it all, gave Il Moro satisfaction for nineteen years didn't he

—bring up Leonardo you might talk about the string of projects he left unfinished

—and Slater, don't give me Slater, a fuckup and a substance abuser, little lesson for you there

—and just who is this Devon Null? Nobody in J Section has ever seen him, one day I'm sharing his office space, the next all his books papers folders xeroxes are gone, cleared out, personnel won't even give me his employee records

—Ask your girlfriend. I mean the one in personnel, not the one in the antinuke group. Although with the information sieve around here the other one might have them too.

—What business of yours

—My business is to keep this place going, you want to walk around here on Valium making wild accusations remember that.

—Now wait just a

—You consider this report finished, is that right?

—Yes.

—Fine. I'm accepting it. You're done. Your group's dissolved. You're on leave. Now get out.

—Now wait a

—Did you hear me? Out, now!

For a moment Quine stood, then zipped shut his empty carryall and went out past a slender young man carrying a calfskin case who looked up from Dolores and in at Highet.

—Oh, Doctor Highet, I just dropped by to set up a meeting.

—Why don't you come in for a minute, Jeremy, holding the door as his eyes followed Quine into the corridor.

—I don't want to barge in . . .

—No, I'm glad to see you. Just one minute, as he went around the desk to lift the phone with one hand and with the other casually pulled open a drawer and swept An Analysis of False Brightness into it. —Dolores? I want drug tests immediately for all employees in J Section. Yes, I mean this afternoon.

—I'm glad that's not my investigation, the young man said, smiling.

—So, Jeremy. How was the meeting this morning? I'm sorry I missed it, you know how it is, complexity on the edge of chaos. Frank Szabo take care of you?

—It went well. There are one or two points I think we'll take up in a future meeting.

—What points?

—Written statements from Doctor Réti to the president and the secretary of defense. They seem to overstate the Superbright's power by a substantial amount.

—Doctor Réti is emeritus here. He's not involved in daily operations, so he may not be completely up to speed on Superbright details. But he can still express his opinions as a private citizen.

—Well, yes, but on Lab letterhead?

—He keeps an office here, it's natural he'd use the stationery. I wouldn't make too much of it.

—Don't you, ah, review his official letters?

—No. Why should I?

—Well, you are the director.

—Jeremy, put yourself in my place. Réti's the founder. He's a living legend. I can't vet his correspondence.

—Yes, but, even compared to your own test results, his estimates of the beam's power are high by a factor of um, a billion? He says that the last test, Taliesin was it called? indicates a major breakthrough?

—We saw substantially increased brightness. A billion times? No reason the beam couldn't be made that bright.

—Doctor Réti used the words "engineering phase".

—Our bottleneck isn't the science, it's the funding.

—Well, concerns have been raised

—Jeremy, concerns are always being raised, you don't mean the GAO's investigation hinges on a couple of letters, do you?

—Well, but even your own numbers from previous tests have been questioned by some of your own people

—Not Slater again, is it, totally unreliable

—Szabo said this last test, Taliesin, is under internal review by uh, who is it, Philip Quine?

—That's purely a technical review. We tried out a new detector arrangement. But the old detectors worked fine, they gave us all the data we needed. Actually, Quine's been dragging his feet on that report. I'll have him finish it and get a copy to you, but frankly any problems there are technical and not substantive.

—One last thing. What do you know about uh, Transfinite Polygonics?

—That some kind of non-Euclidean geometry? Nuclear chemistry's my field.

—It's a holding company, or possibly a consulting firm. Doctor Réti seems to own quite a lot of their stock.

—And?

—Certain technologies licensed through Transfinite originated in the Lab. There might be a conflict of interest.

—We often waive commercial rights.

—Well, if he's advising the government on matters in which he has a financial stake

—Oh look, Réti's no sharpshooter. Some of our people go into private industry, it was probably some former student he wanted to help out, I'll bet he's forgotten all about this stock. Is there anything else?

—No, that covers it. But the issue of the tests and the alleged overselling. I wouldn't take those too lightly.

—Thanks for coming by, Jeremy.

Highet flipped open his phone, arrowed down until its display showed ROOT DAN, and pressed SEND to hear, —The Gate Cellular customer you have called is unavailable or has traveled outside the coverage area. Please try your call again later.

The gray face of his watch blinked 3:55. From under the desk he took a black gym bag blazoned aXon, unzipping it for the hand that opened the drawer to transfer An Analysis of False Brightness, as the desk phone trilled and, —Highet. Yes, Bernd. No, that's all right . . . fingers drumming, he checked his watch for 3:56, and tapped the phone's cradle, —Hold on, Bernd, that's my other line, at once hanging up and passing into the outer office —I'm gone, Dolores, waving off her —But the Vice Pres, as rounding a corner behind him a black t-shirt SEROTONIN stopped to watch his back vanish into the warmth of the afternoon sun and pass briskly into the shadow of the unfinished facade, still oddly deserted, past plywood and chainlink where yellow CAUTION CUIDADO tape now stretched taut between stakes around a terrain of ruts and pools of bright green flux.

On a machine of matte black steel and padded vinyl, Highet pumped and pedaled, pale pudgy thighs kissing and releasing the damp seat, and inhaled the stink of his wet clinging shirt. All around him, the creak, clank, huff of exertion, the smell of work, the tithe that flesh exacts from mind. Three times a week, since a spell of tachycardia had scared him to an emergency room, he forced himself through this hour of pain, seething at every pump of calf, every stab of outraged quad. At thirty minutes he quit and went through the locker room, pausing at a fountain to gulp from the weak quavering arc of water brought forth by his thumb on its chrome button, then peeled off sodden t-shirt and shorts for swim briefs, and headed past PLEASE SHOWER BEFORE ENTERING POOL into air cool on his moist flesh and sunlight glinting on black cottonwoods, burnishing a golden haunch clad in bright spandex, tinging with russet black hair that vanished into a white cap. He freed from his gym bag dropped on a redwood bench a pair of smoked plastic goggles, and sat at pooledge, legs immersed, and rinsed spit from the goggles before fixing them in his orbits, waiting for the white cap to flipturn at the wall by his feet before plunging to breaststroke a few lengths behind the scissor of golden legs, the wink of bright spandex.

After ten laps he pushed up out of the water, toweled, brushed fallen cottonwood catkins from the bench, and sat. Nearby a pair of gardeners glanced at him then returned their attention to the trees. —¿Porqué los álamos no sueltan semillas? —Hace dos años rebajamos las hembras. El jefe tiene las alérgias. —¡Ay! Entonces los hombres álamos ya no difrutan mas. He opened An Analysis Of to *beryllium excited by the trigger glowed at precisely the wavelength of the predicted laser light,* blinking away from the bright page for his sunglasses, seeing across the pool a thin pale man in blue trunks, suede hat, and hiking boots watch a trim woman passing, his eyes sliding in a lean humorless face. The woman entered the pool and a moment later the thin man removed his boots and hat and lowered into the same lane to swim breaststroke a few lengths behind the woman. Highet called to the lifeguard.

—Why don't you tell him to move to a slower lane?

—Who?

—The blue suit. He's in the way.

—Looks fine to me.

—Don't tell me! I've been sitting here watching him for ten minutes, you haven't even been looking.

After a hesitation the guard went to pooledge and thrust a blue kickboard in front of the man as he came to his turn. Highet flipped pages to *defective reflectors duplicated and therefore confirmed the brightness predicted by the computer model.* Like a child probing a scab he skimmed to *throwing all previous test results into question,* whispering —Fucker, and plunging a hand into the gym bag feeling for the spiral edges, did I get all his copies? Of course not, he'll have a backup, glancing up to see Quine's girl, the one in personnel, talking warmly with a wiry man darkly tanned. What was her name, he'd looked it up just last week. Should have seen this a few hours ago, before dealing with Quine. Drive the knife deeper. A white cap appeared at pooledge and golden arms straightened and a golden leg came up to vault glistening spandex from the lane and russet hair tumbled free from the white cap, cool blue eyes meeting Highet's shielded gaze as he shook free of revery, zipped his gym bag and strode back into the dimness of the locker room, sunglasses fogging as he passed the steaming showers, detouring to a row of urinals where he dropped the bag and spraddled tugging aside the crotch of his briefs, staring ahead at tile, as on his cooling back dampness dried and his stream rang in the bowl, misting faintly the hand holding his stub of flesh. On the porcelain shelf was a small uncapped vial. While right thumb and index shook and tucked his flesh into his briefs, he turned the empty vial between index and left thumb, —Son of a, to display URINE LUCK • Tersolene • Directions: Add contents of the vial to eight ounces (8 oz.) of urine. Mix slightly.

Near chainlink now wrapped with CAUTION CUIDADO, in the shadow of the facade, Bran Nolan, saturnine and gaunt, stood wearing the look of his namesake, son of Febal, upon his return from the magic year of sojourn that spanned mundane centuries, to learn that the shore of home had become fatal to him.

—Evening, Bran.

—I hear Kihara screwed up the EIS.

—That's the truth.

—Do you know what's going on here? Nobody's working.

—It's five-thirty, Bran.

—Nobody's been here all afternoon. The caution tape, who put that up?

—I don't know. Bran, have a minute? Step inside, would you?

Highet led inside and down the hall, through the empty outer office, kicking aside in passing aXon Tell Us About, gesturing Nolan to a chair near the black matte computer.

—You put your guests in the death seat, I see.

—What?

—The back end of your monitor's pointed at me. That's where the ELF emissions are highest.

—ELF, elf is right, that crap's about as real as leprechauns. While you're here, your draft response to this GAO thing, I have a language question, skimming through pages to where a yellow highlight stopped him.

—Which GAO thing? We're got five pending.

—The property management one. You say here, "signals an accounting discrepancy". Isn't that a bit strong?

Nolan put on glasses and studied the page, lips pursed. —Our December statement said, "excellent security management of sensitive materials." The same month an internal audit reported ten kilograms of plutonium missing. That signals, you might even say highlights, a discrepancy.

—Suggests.

—What?

—Suggests a discrepancy.

—Oh no, not at all. An off-record comment in the cafeteria suggests. A heavily edited and reviewed document signals. Or denotes. Or even highlights.

—Something softer.

—This is soft.

—Softer.

Nolan crooked a finger. —Indicates. It indicates a discrepancy.

—That's acceptable. Highet moved a pencil across the page. —Thank you. What's the story on the building?

—I heard that Kihara tripped some alarms. I thought I'd see if they'd unearthed any bodies out there.

—Bodies? What bodies?

—I don't know if you remember, but in the planning stage we had two consulting firms prepare environmental reports on that site for us. Chivian-Harris found soil toxicity well above EPA action level

—I remember.

—which they blamed on leaky retention tanks and a faulty sewage system. So we called in a second firm, Boole & Clay

—Eric's company.

—correct, who suggested cleanup procedures and gave us a more forgiving report on the tanks. So we cited Boole in the EIS. Their findings suggested that the soil could be treated as low-level waste. Then the soil engineer reported.

—Soil engineer?

—Before the contractor can pour concrete the engineer has to certify that the soil is dense enough to hold a foundation. They use a nuclear density testing machine, it's a small radioactive source and a counter, like a smoke detector. The design originated here in the Lab. You put soil in the tester and it blocks radiation from the source, and from the absorption you can infer the soil density. Well, the tester went off the scale. Credne, the contractor, came down on the engineer, said his machine was out of alignment, they got him to give a visual approval. Then Credne trucked the soil away, and Chivian tested again and this time we came up clean. So we cited the clean report in the EIS.

—So what's the problem?

—Why do you think the tester went off the scale? The soil wasn't absorbing, it was emitting radiation.

—How hot was it?

—Not low level.

—Where did that soil go?

—We don't know.

—We don't know?

—Probably to another Credne site. They have some complicated leaseback scheme with a trucking subsidiary. Their records aren't so good.

—That's Credne's responsibility, isn't it?

—I'm not a lawyer, I can't answer that. Point is, both Boole and Chivian are cited in the EIS. The two reports are on file, anyone can look them up, and if they do, they'll see the soil engineer's readings.

—How likely is that?

—Some group like CANT might wonder why Kihara's so frantic about his mistake with the map. They might get curious about the paperwork.

—What's the worst case scenario?

—Well, this isn't Site Alpha. We can't just fence it off and call it a toxics mitigation program. It's in the middle of our plant. Oh, and about Site Alpha. The winemaker's been talking to CANT. He's suing.

—Christ, we bought his land, what more does he want?

—Damages. Loss of livelihood.

—Shit, thought that was all wrapped up.

—Funny thing about PR, it bumps into reality once in a while.

—Keep telling you, reality's what you can get away with. Write him a check, see how fast his reality changes.

—Where does the money come from?

—We have a special access fund, use it.

—You know . . . the plume keeps spreading.

—What does that mean?

—The toxic plume. Under Site Alpha. It's not contained. We can't keep buying up land around it.

For a moment the plume was apparent to Highet, clear as a computer simulation, a subterranean cloud of false colors, arms extended, breaching the boundaries of the Lab, which expanded to follow and enclose it.

—You say CANT is behind this suit?

—That's what I hear.

—I never cease to be amazed, Bran, at how much you hear.

—It's my job.

—You go above and beyond it sometimes. You know, Bran, I tried to get the search committee to promote you instead of that young idiot Kihara.

—Thanks for looking out for me. But I'm sure you're better served by Kihara. Journalists can't be trusted, everyone knows that.

Highet looked at him. —You're a real hard case, Bran. You won't give me an inch.

—Is there anything else?

—Take down that caution tape out there.

Outside as the light slanted toward dusk he slowed near the handful of demonstrators just beyond the gate, alert to a camera crew interviewing a woman, her full face radiant in sun, intense black eyes beneath black hair tinged with russet, her beauty a thorn in his heart, lifting his sunglasses as he passed to blink twice at her dazzling flesh, as if to capture not an image but an essence through which desire might be gratified, intimacy possessed, and redemption grasped. As her eyes tracked his passage the head of the reporter turned, and

Highet accelerated away onto the main road seeing in the hollow afterimage of his blink not an essence but its negative. Traffic thickened into town, and under a white on green sign Mariposa he turned too sharply into the wake of a bus pulling away from the curb to trap him behind its tailpipe and rear placard admonishing Police Recommended Don't Park Your Car Without as the traffic light above him changed and oncoming vehicles edged honking around his rear until he gunned around the bus before cutting back in and slamming brakes short of a truck backing slowly into his path, beeping in disconcerted hocket with Highet's horn as he jammed the gearshift to R only to see the bus's headlight fill his rearview mirror as the truck's step How Am I Driving? 1-800-328-7448 scraped loudly across the red hood.

—Stop! You son of a bitch stop! It lurched a yard short of his windshield as a head leaned down from the driver's cab.

—Where'd you come from?

—Just, just, move it, you imbecile! Pull it forward!

In a blast of smoke it pulled away, as he reversed the car, arrested by a blare of bus horn where its glassy eye loomed in his rear window. Shifting to 1, Highet went in a squeal of tires around the truck, left arm held high out the window in profane salute, wind booming through the open window street after street until at last he slowed at First Unitarian Church of Kentwood turning into a parking lot half full, noting with less surprise than disdain the battered white Subaru with Lab sticker on its rear bumper.

Paper signs taped to walls CANT MEETING -> led to a side room FELLOWSHIP HALL depressing as all childhood memories of church, where the after-service klatches in the basement, folding tables laden with cakes and pastries too cloying, smell of burned coffee in chrome urns, fading sun aslant through blinkered windows to fall in exhausted lines on a scuffed linoleum floor, the empty chatter, the waste of time, had never failed to fill him with a metaphysical nausea. Fifty or more people sat now in folding chairs, listening to —the easy availability of dual-use technologies makes it almost impossible to constrain nuclear programs in other countries and raises serious questions, as just inside the door, Quine started back from Highet's, —You.

What are you doing here?

—I have a right

—If I find out you've been dealing with these people

—What will you do, put me on leave?

Highet stared at him for a moment, then went on around the edge of the room, where, near the platform, a russet tone in nightblack hair snared his eye and sped his heart. The serpent of invention entered him and he stepped up next to her, as if better to hear the speaker, —Next question, yes, and turned to gaze at her strong profile, seeing her awareness of his gaze in the faint throb in her neck. He murmured, —Are you afraid of me? Is it fear makes your heart beat? Or excitement? while beyond her stony profile Quine glared with concern or was it panic as Highet went on in a mild undertone, —Are you afraid of getting what you want? I've seen you out by the gate, hating us. Her eyes narrowed but remained locked ahead while Luz said, —other countries with or near nuclear capabilities look skeptically at our own commitment to nonproliferation, and across the room Quine paced and glared, his distress a goad to Highet's invention. He leaned still closer to her, saying, —It's not fear you feel. It's wildness. The wildness of wanting. What is it you want? When you know, taking it is easy.

—Is it, she said, fierce black eyes locking on him.

—Yes. Yes it is.

—I want to talk to you sometime.

Now his heart was wild. —Name the time.

—Now? Arms folded under her breasts.

—Right now?

—If you're serious. There's a café in the central mall, Café Desaparecidos. I can meet you there when I'm done here. Seven-thirty?

—That's a deal.

Scattered applause died and people milled around. Tony Luz came forward. —Well, the Prince of Darkness himself. Last place I expected to see you, Leo. What's wrong with your face?

—Nice line of talk, Tony. Won any Clios lately?

—Same old Leo. Smiling, Luz raised a fist and lightly pressed it to Highet's shoulder. —People, this is Leo Highet, director of the Lab. I feel like I owe him equal time. How about a little informal Q and A, Leo?

—Matter of fact I've got a plane to catch.

—Five minutes. Five minutes, Leo? You don't want to run from us, do you?

—Yeah, I do. Most pointless thing in world, arguing with you guys.

—Five minutes.

Her hard black eyes studied him. He raised his wristwatch and touched buttons. —Five minutes.

—Why do you classify hazardous waste by the building it's stored in? Why not by the program that generates it?

Slogan t-shirt buzzcut three day beard. Cheap shill pumped full of citizengroup coredump data. Answer in kind. —Accounting for materials and wastes is done by building to provide information for emergency response services and to assure that the buildings meet safety requirements.

—Doesn't that just make it easier to hide the fact that the weapons programs generate most of the hazardous waste?

Cocky amateur. Give him what he thinks he wants. —Good point. Maybe we should track that information, but we can't. Our procedures are dictated by federal regulations. Talk to the feds about it.

He stopped paying attention, these were just the old neverland arguments he could handle on autopilot, the uninhabitable utopias of good will to be brought about by some wishful convergence of niceness, the very word *nice, ne scient,* not knowing, ignorant, he stressed it like a secret insult, —Yes, I agree, it would be *nice,* very nice, if the world could be saved by recycling, and so on, she was at the door now, talking to Quine while Luz asked another question, and Highet parried it with his own, —Tony, why are you so down on dual use? Isn't that what you want, get us out of weapons?

Luz shifted his weight slightly back, disengaging, as Highet watched Quine and Lynn go out the door together. —Don't see that happening, Leo. Dual use policies have weakened export controls on rocket technology, we're selling missiles overseas, last year the US accounted for fifty-seven percent of world weapons sales. Some of these systems are being turned back on us.

—Good thing we know their vulnerabilities.

—Leo, as long as we keep designing and selling these weapons

—You've got that lunatic in Baghdad, you've got twenty thousand warheads floating loose in the so-called republics, you think now's the time to cut antimissile programs?

—It's welfare for the defense industry.

—Free market, what have you got against capitalism, Tony, capitalism's been good to you. Drumming the fingers of one hand against the back of the other, trapped by his ego, center of the situation while she moved off without him. He tapped a button on his watch. The watch beeped and he held it high for all to see, touching it to silence, —That's five minutes. Now I have a question for you. Anyone here read H G Wells? The Time Machine? No? You're Eloi. Look it up.

In the lot, Quine's white Subaru was gone. He passed SFIST as acceleration spilled warm evening air through the car, cutting back across two lanes to Codornic s EXIT NLY, turning smoothly without slowing past STOP onto a commercial strip that looped behind the central mall, where stains of rain and rust on a colonnaded and pedimented facade stood stark as melanomas under sodium light. He parked under the red and white glare of SMART & FINAL, and his car alarm yelped as he strode under a portico through smoked glass doors into the oasis of an atrium ringed with Target Clothestime Kinko's Tower, fixing on Café, where, visible through the broad entrance, black hair with russet tones was bent forward over some papers, the skin of her neck taut against vertebrae, and pale where it touched the fringe of her hair.

Highet sat down, saying, —Thought you might have stood me up, leaving that way. With him.

—He offered me a ride. She swept up the papers and tucked them away.

—What does that mean, indicating the sign, —desaparecidos? The café of desperation? Abandon all hope?

—The disappeared. Those taken by death squads.

—Oh, of course. In El Salvador. Or is it Guatemala? Part of the profits from every latté. Have you eaten? Thai place around the corner makes great mee krob.

—I ate before the meeting.

—I haven't eaten since this morning, I'm starved.

—She's waiting.

—What? Oh, give me a mint tea. And a, what have you got, a blueberry muffin.

—Quisiera un espresso por favór.

—Saw a woman outside the gate this evening, looked like you, talking to CNN.

—That was me. I saw you drive by.

He played to her amused tone, examined her critically. —That was you? Did you cut your hair? How'd you beat me to the church?

—I got a ride. I saw you turn right at Mariposa. That's the long way around. You've been watching me?

—Know your enemies. Legal observer at CANT demonstrations, Stanford grad, good grades, *nice* family. You want to close down my Lab. That's what I know about you. What do you know about me?

—I know that you sold the president an unworkable and ruinously expensive antimissile program

—But, he raised a finger, —ruinously expensive for whom?

—Do you know that the Cold War has cost five trillion dol

—You know what? The Russians wish they had our deficit. They wish they could run up a debt. You follow me?

—Is that what you're, gracias, what you're telling the GAO?

—The GAO, right. Talk about your waste of money, as he leaned forward to bite into the muffin.

—But, is that really your line? That you knew all along it wouldn't work, but you made the Soviets think it would?

—That would be a policy decision. DOE sets policy. I'm a simple scientist. Not even that, really. I administrate. The science is done by people like your friend Philip. Where did you meet him?

—He gave me a ride once.

—You don't own a car. For ecological reasons.

—The more you drive the less intelligent you are.

—Repo Man. I love that movie.

—I wouldn't call Philip a friend.

—You like him.

—I don't dislike him.

—He tell you he's a bomb geek?

—A what?

—That's what they call us, the, how should I say, *pure* scientists who work at the Lab and take our money but want to show that they, you know, disapprove of bombs. They call us bomb geeks. Did Quine tell you he's one or did he pretend to be pure?

—He told me that he works on weapons. He's torn about it.

—Torn. That's good. It's good to have scruples. Without them we're no better than the beasts.

—His work is all he has, and he said to me, you don't know what's happening there, what I'm up against right now . . .

—Did he. That's very interesting. He go into details? Sitting back and smiling, eyes on hers, Highet unzipped his case to take from an upper pocket a sheaf of pages, slyly tipping the pages toward her to reveal in unadorned Courier font "TALIESIN" RESULTS PRELIMI-NARY SECRET. —Give you this, maybe? Or this? and like a conjuror fanned to An Analysis of False Brightness, as her full cheeks reddened and a pulse twitched where vein crossed collarbone under downcast eyes, thick lashes, and the fine black hair of her brows.

—No.

—No. But you have seen them before, he said in a tone almost caressing.

—What if I have? Dark eyes locked on his.

—Oh, well, breaking the gaze, sitting back, still smiling, replacing the sheaf in his case. —It's nothing to me. Old news. Your people talk to Senator Chase's office?

—Of course we do.

—Ever convey documents?

—What does that mean?

—You know Bran Nolan. One of our press officers. He's dealt with your group before.

—I know the name.

—He passed these to you. No? Then who? Philip himself?

—You've got some imagination. Dry voice, but a tremor in it.

Leaning forward, hands clasped around his teacup, sincere gaze. —All

I want to know is, how long you've had it. And if Chase has it too.

—I don't know anything about that.

Hardness biting through her tremor. Standing up to him. His heart sped. —You know, it's not as though your side doesn't have enough arguments without resorting to this. It doesn't serve your purpose. You shouldn't antagonize us, because no wait, now listen to me, because we're on the same side, yes we are, and I'll tell you why. You want the bomb work to stop, and I don't agree, but you know what? I can live with that, really I can, so long as we stay cutting edge on other fronts.

—It's weapons work that gives you your lock on federal money.

—That's changing. We're moving away from that.

—Oh, that's right. Dual use will change everything.

—Isn't that what you want?

—You're good at this, I'm almost believing you.

—Have some muffin.

—No thanks.

—I can be persuasive. If you let me. Why don't you come around? Let me give you a tour.

She lowered her eyes to sip her espresso. —Where do you know Tony from?

—Luz? We were classmates at Caltech.

—I didn't know he went to Caltech.

—Lousy scientist, but he always could work a crowd. You know he was in advertising?

—You're still friends?

—Sure, why not. We're useful to each other.

—But, is that what you call friendship? Use?

—Friendship. Is that when we all sit around, like, holding hands? I'd rather have allies. Friends, you know, *sympathize* with you. Allies help you get things done. I'd like to be your ally.

—That sounds too lonely for me.

—Oh, I could be friendlier. But let me ask. Quine, your Philip, you think he hasn't used you? To get things done? Think he hasn't maneuvered as much as anyone? I could tell you about that shifty little shit. Luz and I, you may wonder at that, but we know what the other is. Quine, though, you never know what he's doing.

She studied him for a moment. —In some ways you're very like him.

—Like who?

—Philip.

Which warmed him until he saw the pointed coldness of her eyes. He laughed. —I don't think so.

In the atrium, a metal gate thundered down beneath Clothestime. Highet regarded her. —You'd be quite attractive if you'd use a little makeup, fix your hair, shave your legs.

She looked away, across the café, smiling and shaking her head. —What you're doing now, it's so . . .

—I know, he said, getting to his feet. —You've got me all figured out and it doesn't help a bit.

She rose, face darkening. —I do day care. I see this in children, they want to own every situation. I don't need this in my adult life.

His heart seethed. —Adult life? You're so young. Those kids at your protests, that rebellion doesn't age well. You'll see.

—Some of those protesters are your age. Or older. There's a seventy year old Episcopalian bishop. There's a single mother with three children who works forty hours a week then another twenty doing this. They're the finest people I know. She opened her purse.

He dropped a bill on the table. —This is my treat. I insist. Call me if you want that tour.

And went with ballooning heart into the lot, free as the paper bag KFC skipping across asphalt in the warm night wind flattened by his front wheel as the vacant moonless sky trembled unseen past the glare of light poles, a glare that brightened and dimmed, dimmed and brightened as he drove, arousing a frustration that would not be calmed, an urge that could not be channeled, a lust to abase himself before her and thus abase her, until, cued by the car's approach, lights snapped on over the garage and the door rolled open. He stilled, shut, and locked the car, red light blinking on the dash under teal 8:45, garage door rumbling shut as he entered through the kitchen silencing the alarm's squeal with 3 1 4 1 6 # as the light went from red ARMED to green SAFE, passing and ignoring the blinking MESSAGES on his answering machine, as kitchen lights came on for him to lean against the open refrigerator door, drumming fingers, stooping to come up with a greasy box PapaGeno Pizza, punching the microwave START and plucking from between Fines Herbes and Italian Seasoning a small bottle LactAid, shaking out two pills and swallowing them with Peach Iced Tea from a cold and glistening can while thumbing the small television where CNN drew a baleful glare for —ongoing probe of Radiance missile defense program, and the oven chimed and the phone trilled. He turned off the phone and zeroed the answering machine's volume, touching the CD player for —got a kindhearted woman do anything in the world for me, and crossed back for his pizza, steaming and succulent, pausing to jab his thumb against ant after ant streaming across the counter in braided lines, then carried plate to table and as he ate skimmed the newspaper, Exxon To Pay Fine, US Steps Up Iraq Air Patrols, State Budget Shortfall, Why Gate Cellular Is Forging Alliances, A's Shine In Training, the edges of the newsprint soaking up a smear of grease from his fingers as the pizza diminished, his eyes at last drifting to 24 HRS OUTCALL above a sullen pout and forehead circleted with dark hair wild as if fresh risen from the sea, and he unfolded the phone, clearing his throat, for —Lombard Escorts, while Robert Johnson sang on forlorn in the empty living room against the rush of a shower, interrupted by the chime and the quick stride of muscled calves beneath a belted robe opening to, —Hi, I'm Dawna, running a hand through hair not dark or wild but bright as a carrot under the porch light, beyond which a sky as empty of stars as of folly, error, sin, and avarice turned through empty hours carrying a sliver of waning moon, thin as a nail paring, in pursuit of Venus through a brightening sky in flight from the sun rising to flood the bedroom deck with morning light on slim white legs stretched from red satin briefs barely covered by the fall of a translucent shift.

—Do you mind? Highet called out. —I have neighbors.

—Don't we all, honey, as she came in sliding the door shut behind her, taking from between his outstretched fingers three tightly folded bills. She sat on the bed and pulled on hose. He stepped into the bathroom to dress. When he emerged she was picking hairs from her brush and dropping them into a waste can. The brush went into her bag with a snap and she smiled brightly at Highet as she turned and went out.

As he shut the front door behind her, he saw the light on the answering machine. He pressed PLAY for, —Leo, it's Dan, some son of a bitch hacked my cell phone, and walked to the sink where he jammed the lever to blast hot water across a tide of ants twined from the pizza crust lodged in the sink drain across counter and linoleum to a garbage pail, returning to, —ran up eight thou in calls to Bogotà, new number's 326-7668, give me a, pausing the machine to punch the seven digits.

—Dan, it's me. Yeah, doesn't say much for Gate's security, does it. What? Chase? That son of a bitch, what's he trying to. My performance review committee? as steam billowed from the sink. —Okay, give me the rundown. Dullard Quack and Logjam, they're on our side . . . what? Well that's Quick's own fault, if he hadn't been a year late and ten million over with the last mainframe we ordered he'd still have the contract, now what's Logue's problem? Well again, that's his, if he hadn't talked to the press, I told him you cannot win playing with the press, you're always going to lose. Okay. Okay, Dan, cut to the, what do you mean probably? You mean Dillard's our only sure vote? How can that be? What, tomorrow? They're meeting on a Sunday? Christ, as if I didn't have enough . . . Why. Why should I. No I don't see what being there in the flesh does for me. It's only a recommendation, what do the regents care, the university gets their money no matter who's director. What do you mean cuts both, of course it does, but we have enough friends on the regents to override, don't we? A new regent, what do you mean, who? A noname, oh that's great, little bit of Monte Carlo in the mix. What else, Dan? shutting off the hot water and walking to the window.

—Christ Dan that was years ago, I was still out in the trailers. And if you want to know whose bright idea it was to rig a homing beacon on the missile's target, ask Warren Slater, that prick. Anyway, you know what? The only test of four that worked was the one they didn't rig.

Outside a city truck moved slowly past as two men in its bed deposited TOW-AWAY NO PARKING placards at the curb.

—What else. Who . . . oh come on, Steradian couldn't find his dick if you held it for him. Yes he called me, he called Dietz too, forget it, he's fishing.

He flipped yellow pages for Exterminators stopping at a display ad, Nekrotek 24 Hour Pest Control.

—Dan, Bill Venham is a troglodyte. Yes I know, rich and powerful, so's the vice president, I don't return his calls either. What? Oh he calls because his son went into some telecom venture after that savings and loan thing, maybe he's trying to weasel in on our Gate deal. But Venham, there's no way I'm going to his fucking fundraiser. I know Réti's going, ask me it's pathetic the way he hangs around these rightwing creeps. Oh yeah, you know how long I've been just showing up at these things. Uh huh. Uh huh. All right, Dan. I said all right, I'll do it! That, and the review committee on Sunday, quite the itinerary you've got lined up for me. What about the Hertz kids, does that have to be Sunday night? Oh, the shot, of course, I forgot. Yes I'll make it. One of the few things I still enjoy. I'll be exhausted but I'll be there.

Reading and punching digits for, —Nekrotek, he gave his name and address, jabbing his thumb against ant after ant braiding onward across the counter, —Ants, yes. Well look, I'm leaving town can you fax me the paperwork? I'll sign it and leave it with a key in the mailbox, okay? Yes you'll take a credit card . . . ? and hung up, turning to the answering machine MESSAGES and touching >> for a beep and —tor Highet, this is Armand Steradian of CNN. I'd like to talk to you as soon as possible. I'm finishing a story on allegations of rigged tests in the Radiance program, my number is —Fuck you, and touching >> for the beep and —Frank Greer returning your, —can't believe this twerp calls me at home, and touching >> for the beep and —York Times, if you'd care to comment, then leaning in to read the display, —fifteen messages! punching >> for —alleged violations, and >>, —questions about your environmental impact statem, and >> —call at your earliest, and finally STOP for a peremptory knock at the door sounding with the chime. For a moment he stood frozen, then walked lightly to the bedroom. From its window he saw in the street a van bearing a dish antenna. The bell and knock sounded again. After a third try, two men, one shouldering a video camera, returned to the van.

From the closet he took a garment bag and checked its contents: his impression-management suit, a tie, two clean shirts, socks, a pair of Rockports, a personal kit. Again he lifted the phone. His left eyelid began to twitch. Phone in hand he pressed a finger against it. With the other hand he punched 276-7384. Behind him his fax machine purred.

—Aron, it's Leo. I need your help. Please call me. It's urgent. I hope to see you tonight in Burbank at the Venham dinner. I'll be on the road till then, you can reach me by cell phone at 544-4438.

Outside, the van had gone. Pages had fallen on the floor behind him. He picked them up and scribbled his signature. He zipped his laptop computer into its nylon carry. From the dresser he took a spare house key and five hundred dollar bills. At the front door he checked the fisheye lens for an empty street before swinging it wide and dropping the spare key and the faxes into the mailbox. On the way back through the kitchen to the garage he unplugged the answering machine and again picked up the phone.

—Thea, it's me, looks like I can shake some time loose after all. When is mother getting home? Uh huh. No, if I leave right away I can be there in. No, not a problem. I can take care of some other business at the same. I'll be glad to see her too. Okay, look, don't go to any trouble. See you about three.

The garment bag fell on the passenger seat as the garage door rumbled open, and he was on his way.

The dead seabed, the broad valley, sundered the state top to bottom. Speed Enforced By Aircraft. Power lines fell and rose in catenaries to cross the road's dead places as a crescendo buzz rose to bury —wouldn't stand a prayer, and fell away behind, —here we are in the quick of it, as the radio scanned to —another anointed message from the Reveal Christ To The World Ministries, to —with significant tax deferral benefits, to —this, also from the Washington Times, to —Inland Empire checks in accident free, to —Jesus was never impressed with size, the size of your organ, as the sun reached zenith and declined glinting on the lake at Elev 4819 where he turned off the freeway to descend into tender green hills and an orange dust of poppies blooming, and silver violet sage trembling palely in the relentless wind, leading the eye out over an immensity to distant mountains naked and wrinkled as ancient skin. From above fell a hollow roar. Two blunt black triangles banked against blue emptiness.

Tumbling from the edge of his vision something dim and gray crossed the road and splintering tinder sheared from the windshield as the tail of the car shimmied and stabilized with one branch of the tumbleweed lodged in the hood trembling in the slipstream. His heart slowed and his attention came back to the road where the works of man now came more thickly, Joshua Estates blazoned over a brick drive flanked by banners snapping and New Townhouses From $59,999 We're Leasing Come See Why, Spacious Skies Senior Living Small Pets OK, then City Limit Elev 2376 and a grid of vacant dirt roads, W 280 Ave W 270 Ave W 260 Ave, then mini malls and LANCASTER FACTORY STORES, identical red tile roofs and beige walls and empty parking lots reproving the immensity in which they lay.

The house, once at desert's edge, was now deep in a tract of others like it. Locust trees shaded the street, their roots heaving the sidewalk. Forty years ago the saplings were slender and staked, no taller than himself. His eyes and mind, inapt tenants of time, still expected to find them thus, continued to seek in a place, a face, what first they had found there.

Sun glared on the concrete walk. He was sweating before he reached the house. No answer to the bell. Neighborhood Watch Armed Response. Key under the rock as it had been for years. The unlocked door stuck until he thrust his weight against it.

Stale air of home. Anxiety of passing time. This place he had always wanted to escape. On the bare dining room table lay a note. He read it, then lifted the phone and dialed. Through the handset came unanswered chirrs. As he counted them, Thea's car pulled into the driveway. Her key turned in the lock. The door stuck, then flew wide.

—Oh, you're here.

In one hand Highet held out the chirring handset, in the other her note. —Your answering machine's turned off. I don't believe this Thea, you couldn't have called me? When did you find out?

—They want to do just one more series of tests before they release her.

—Great. Just great. I'm going home.

—Oh, Leo . . . that's absurd.

—I'm not waiting around in this house.

—Why don't you go into town for a while? You know, your high school reunion's tonight.

—My what? Is this one of your airball agendas, Thea? If I need that level of excitement I'll sit in a Motel Six and watch the Weather Channel.

—Fine, do what you want, you always do.

—You've got that right.

—I have to be sure everything's ready. I still need an IV stand, to hang a drip from. I'm sure we can rig something up, it just has to be tall.

—Rig something. Sure, I know, let's use the coat rack. Dress it up with some Christmas lights, a little tinsel, there you are.

—Leo, don't be sarcastic.

—I'll buy the damn thing, okay? Where's the store, give me something to do.

—The hospital gave me some addresses. There's one in Pasadena.

—Perfect, I'll stop in at Caltech on my way to the high school, make a clean sweep.

—Oh, is there a Caltech reunion?

—Joking, Thea, just a little joke, checking his watch, —How late is this place open?

—Leo, it's all the way in Pasadena!

—I'll leave now. Make sure the hospital gets their kickback from the referral. Got to go down that way anyway for

—You've just driven seven hours. You

—Five hours.

—must be exhausted, Mark and I will stop on the way back from the hospital with Mother.

—Stop on the, yeah good, let Mother sit in the back seat staring at the crutches and bedpans in the window while you shop around. Come on Thea, there's got to be someplace nearby, where's the phone book.

—Leo, will you just, just stop it!

—Thea, you're the one wants everything ready, only you want to do it on the cheap at the last minute, like always, you've had, what, six weeks to get this stuff, you knew you'd need it

—Do you think you can come down here for a few days while I've been dealing with this for months, and you think

—Who said anything about a few days.

—What?

—I never said a few days.

—How long are you going to stay?

—Told you, expected Mother to be here already, thought I'd stay overnight, hit the road in the morning.

—Oh, I see. I get it. You want to buy your way out of spending any time with her.

—Buy my way, Jesus, Thea, who's paying the hospital bills?

—Mother's Medica

—I mean the rest of it, after the deductibles and everything Doctor Said won't accept assignment for, you know how much that comes to? Buy my way, Christ that's good, not with a lousy IV stand, if she had to rely on you for money she'd be dead already.

—Oh that's rotten Leo, I don't care about the money, she needs to see you, did you think of her feelings, it may be the last time, did you think of that!

—Well you're the expert on feelings, I can't compete there.

She looked at him dully, then rummaged in a gray woven carryall blazoned with a crossstitched mandala. —I don't know why I thought this time would be any different.

He looked away, around the room. —How's business? Sell any houses recently?

She stared into space for some seconds before reaching, as it seemed, less an acceptance of his question than a resignation to it. —The market's flat. I got into it at the wrong time, at the end of the last boomlet.

—Upholding the Highet real estate tradition. Ever sell that land of Dad's?

—No.

—What's the house worth now?

She looked around, appraising it. —I could ask one fifty, I might get one thirty.

—You going to sell?

120

—You mean after Mother? I suppose so. I haven't really thought about it. Oh, I wanted to ask you. The market's better in your area. How would you feel about me moving up there?

—Up to you. Where are you looking?

—Ohlone Valley. There's a development called Estancia Estates, units starting at one fifty . . .

—Estancia . . . ? I wouldn't live there.

—Why not?

—You can do better.

—For two hundred I could, but I don't have it.

—Any time you want a loan, Thea.

—It would be a business move for me. I have no reason to stay here once Mother's gone. Without Bob. Mark has his family, I don't see much of him. Leo, whatever happened to that girl you were seeing last year, Jan? I liked her, I thought she was good for you.

—That's over.

—Are you seeing anyone now?

—Yes, as a matter of fact.

—Well, what's her name?

—Dawn. Her name's Dawn.

She looked at him skeptically. —Are you thinking of settling down?

—Married to my job, you know that. How's Mark?

—You'll see him tonight. I thought we'd all have dinner at my place.

—Little problem there, I've got something this evening.

She stopped in her rummaging, looked at him bitterly. —Can't you, can't you ever

—Look, I'd rather not go to this thing, it's

—ever just

—one of those things

—do anything for someone else

—It's to honor Réti, told you I'm obligated

—Leo, this is your mother!

—I'm here, all right? When I said I'd be! Don't lay this on me Thea, it's not my fault you got your signals crossed.

Abruptly she rose. —All right. I don't want to discuss it. Here's the key.

—When are you leaving for the hospital?

—Now. We should be back by eight.

—Christ, how did she end up at a hospital two hours down below?

—Leo, you know how she trusts Doctor Said. He recommended a man at Cedars.

—Don't want to be, you know, unfeeling here, but it's terminal isn't it, how good does he have to be.

—Leo, I'm going. There are towels in the guest room.

—I'll be back tonight. Will Mother be here?

—I expect so. I'll see you in the morning.

The front door shut, grunting. He flipped through the phone book. Antelope Valley Medical Supply. Medi-Mart. Mid-Valley Surgical. Free delivery. Typical Thea, didn't even look. He picked one, wandering into the kitchen as he talked, —Expires six ninety three. Can you hold delivery till nine p m?

The clock on the stove was broken, hands frozen at 2:10, though a stub of a second hand ground and scraped on. Outside the kitchen window the old fig tree nodded in the wind. On the table was a newspaper. He unfolded it to AF Base Has Clouds With Its Silver Lining and its sidebar Cold War Relics, then put it aside. From the living room he carried garment bag and laptop to the guest room, past the sampler hanging in the hall, Bless This House O Lord We Pray, pulling back the drapes to see the long view of his childhood, the distant ancient mountains, now enchased by hedges, fences, light poles, power lines, returning to the living room where he snapped on the television in passing to his mother's room. A new chrome walker stood by the bed. Back in the living room he punched channels to —Headline News, and stood watching, the fingers of one hand drumming against a thigh, one foot tapping. After several minutes he switched it off.

At the end of the hall he went down six steps to the basement study, where a dispiriting smell of mildew hung. He sat at the small desk with its brass lamp and blotter, the framed photos of his mother and father, Thea, Mark, himself, Dad in uniform, Dad between two high school players in his sweatshirt LANCASTER COACH BOMBERS. Shelves of teak veneer sagging on metal wall brackets held what passed for a library yellow with ten years' worth of National Geographic propped against Patent It Yourself, Encyclopedia of Estate Planning, The Book of Business Knowledge, Secrets of Super Selling, Everyday Health Tips 2000 Practical Tips, and How To Avoid Probate! abutting the fifteen brown volumes of Compton's Pictured Encyclopedia, their gilt bands touching The Merck Manual and Bartlett's Familiar Quotations and The World Set Free slanted against The Martian Chronicles and the sober dun bookcloth of The Rise and Fall of the Third Reich and Lancaster High School 1960 1961 1962, the sequence ending as abruptly as Gerald Hunter Highet's career there. He took down 1962, blowing soot from its top edge. A strip of paper marked a page. On the strip, his mother's looping hand: *sometimes I wonder why I spend the lonely night.*

Tenor voice on the phonograph. Mom and Dad dancing. Leo darling, your father and I have been married ten years. Dad smiling. Not a smiling man, but a collector of jokes. Son, you know what a ball bearing mousetrap is? Leo tried to picture the mechanism. It's a cat, son. The lined face, graying crewcut, bleak eyes, tight mouth, jowls under the square jaw. Jerry to some friends, Hunt to others, Captain (ret.) to the rest, depending on how they'd met. Petty hustlers, most of them, from his Army days, his years at Lockheed, his bootless dabbling in real estate. Then the high school for three years, chemistry and coaching. Until the scandal. Nothing proved. What do you think I am? I never touched a one of them. It's political, the superintendant has it in for me. Left under a shadow, as they said. Then failure after failure. The real estate. The orchards. The telemarketing. His run for selectman drew a visit from the local Republican officials: best for all concerned that you withdraw. But he wouldn't. Leo had been proud then of his father's stubbornness. Later he saw it was desperation. A debacle: thirty votes out of three thousand cast. Then the cancer.

From the marked page Leo's photo at age sixteen looked warily out over Math Club, Science Club, Chess Club, Honor Society. Young gawky prig thinks he's on his way to a Nobel Prize.

On the opposite page was Chazz Hollis, his best friend. Curly blond hair, open smile. Orchestra, Band, Swim Team, Track, Language Club,

Key Club. Summer days in Chazz's cool basement. Leo used his father's keys to swipe chemicals from the high school lab. Potassium nitrate, aluminum, sulfur. Outside the sun bleached, the hot wind scoured the world. They bicycled to the edge of town to set off bombs, out where tank tracks remained from Patton's army training to fight Rommel. Or they drove out to Edwards to watch pilots rack up flight time with touch-and-go landings. Once in a while something secret would be tested. If somebody's father were involved in the project, you might hear about it. One night he and Chazz drove on dirt roads to the eroded hills behind the rocket lab. They lay on their bellies overlooking tarmac where a rocket engine on its side thundered and spewed flame, a hard white fountain that filled the night with noise, light, power.

Spring hike through Death Valley with a dozen other boys. His father's idea. Toughen you up. Chazz is going, you like Chazz. Unspoken was the expense, nothing to Chazz's family, to theirs a sacrifice. So he went. Hating every minute and hiding it. Bone tired every night, always the last one into camp. Weak boy, can't hike, can't climb. Nights dark as the void, desert sky lustrous with stars, meteors, and the occasional wanderer, Sputnik could it be? Even Chazz mocked him, best friend Chazz, golden Chazz, whose father was a state senator, Chazz who never worked for anything, who always had a new bike, new microscope, new drum set, new radio, new girlfriend. That day on the cliff, twelve of them shouting and climbing, Leo last, fifty feet from the ground, ten feet from the top, suddenly empty and weak, rock biting his palms. Chazz leaning over the edge, tongue out, dribbling spit on him. Being beaten, being second, being mocked. Never again. He clapped shut the book and reshelved it.

In the shower he prodded with blunt fingers the roll of fat at his hips. Soaping under his arms he probed lymph glands. Wiping mist from the mirror he leaned to examine his broad nose, the creases around his eyes, the stubble sprouting more white than black, the nascent dewlap, the thinning hair. His swollen cheek had subsided, leaving only a slight puffiness. He shaved. In the guest room he unzipped the garment bag, thinking ahead to his drive, the 14 to the 5, low sun in his eyes, an hour if traffic didn't thicken through the valley. Waste of time, this whole weekend. Never mind. Just show up. In the hall mirror, behind sunglasses, was no trace of the young gawky prig but a sober harried face in late middle age, its sourness fixed by habits of mistrust and anger and just showing up.

The sun was setting. A/C MIN, he lowered windows for the spill of cool air as the car crested the pass above the lights of San Fernando, a splendor as intricate and baffling as the brain's net of cells, as brighter stars rose to break free of the net and bank in the air above HOLLY-WOOD-BURBANK AIRPORT where he turned at Convention Center into a knot of cars waiting for Valet Parking behind a familiar white Mercedes NKB3 just pulling away as under the awning an elderly figure, limping, was escorted inside where Highet, a few minutes later, followed, past MULTIMEDIA EXPO to a smaller ballroom ARETE FOUNDATION Tonight Guest Speakers Tuck Eubanks Dr Aron Réti and a concentrated display of wealth sapient of little but itself, object of its own desire and scion of its own begetting, demurely awaiting some intelligence to possess and shape it, to cherish and obey it, and finding no lack of supplicants: media consultants between jobs, econ postdocs, freelance historians, sociologists, engineers, futurists, grant writers, lobbyists, intellectual property lawyers, direct mail wizards, PAC men, Ponzi schemers, and free market ideologues who, like the pious of an earlier age, would have been horrified equally at having their faith doubted or at seeing it practiced, producers and providers and panders of one content or another, aspirants to this bridal altar, charged with an excitement sexual but not carnal in the face of such dumb bounty, eager to court and preen and fawn and possess and find themselves, in turn, possessed, until in this happy consummation it could not be told who was using whom or even that use could be separate from being.

In tailored pinstripe, at the center of a captivated group, an obese and blustering figure held forth in orotund tones with an animation that danced between belligerence and deference, choler and comity, feinting aggressively then falling back in submissive attention to the flattered figures of the vice president, eyes dull as his lusterless blue suit, William Venham in black mohair, and, a little apart from them, Aron Réti, wizened and rumpled as exiled aristocracy, wearing on his ravaged features a thin forbearing smile that might have masked a displeasure not with hierarchy itself but with its current occupants.

—My friends, I understand the President, I truly do. I had an encounter with him that was really profound on me. He's a good guy but he just doesn't *get* it about taxes that it's *your money* . . .

With his ear for public affect, Highet judged Eubank's voice so near to excellent that its lapses, at least those that were not calculated, offended. Vulgarity and laziness mixed in its upper reaches, where an ugly hard resentment was slurred with venality and easy contempt. Groomed ferret on a leash. Sucking up to the vice president.

—What we truly need in this coming election is a truly conservative candidate, a man like yourself, sir . . .

Highet approached Réti, only to be caught by an arm in black mohair. —We-hell! The man himself!

—Listen Bill, give me a minute with Aron would you, I need t

—Bad time, Leo, our guest of honor's pretty busy.

—This is important.

—Man's pleading your case to the vice president and the assembled masses, what could be more important?

—My, pleading my what? turning quickly as from behind him came Réti's voice, rumbling and deliberate. Off balance, he bumped the man behind him, who put hands out to steady him. It was Orrin Gate. Gate's mild face showed only mild concern, unless that faint smile hid more than recognition. But Gate had come from a blind spot off his radar. Here in the very lap of power and influence, where he needed to be alive to every current, he was missing cues. He glared malevolently at Eubanks, still at the center of the group but silent at last, small eyes glittering in the piggish face, while Réti in his oracular mode stood leaning on his cane. The vice president listened, mouth slightly agape.

—So I ask you. We deploy Patriot missiles to defend Tel Aviv. Should we not so protect our own borders?

—Well, I can't, ah, speak for the president, but I would think, that we, that is, it does look like something, ah, we would want to look at . . .

—I am certain that the president understands the importance of missile defense. But he must *express* that support! With conviction!

While, frustrated at the attention withdrawn from him, the obese figure again struck its orotund tones, so familiar to so many whose pursuit of truth stopped at the nearest radio. —He's right! Folks, the reason conservatives are winning is that moderates don't have conviction. If you ask people what's wrong with the president they'll say he isn't convicted!

Highet turned to Venham, who was, he saw now, observing him.

—Your case, is it? Venham's eyes glittered.

—You said that, Bill, not me.

—I meant that Aron's arguing the Lab's case.

—because I think the President discredited himself when he raised taxes after he promised

—Bill, I need to talk to you about this regents' meeting coming up.

—Not now, Leo, too much happening.

—Hello, it's Doctor Hite, isn't it?

—Leo, you know Stan Flack? Stan, Leo Highet.

—Sure, we've met, hello Doct

Venham leaned in, lowering his voice to confide, —You worried about regents, Leo, Stan's the man to talk to.

—Oh? But, you must be the new reg, turning, off balance again, to take the extended hand, which vigorously pumped his, —sorry, missed your name

—Aron! Let's

—Flack, Stan Flack. Won't you join me at my table, Doctor Hite?

—Yes, sure, just let me, freeing his hand, —Aron! as the elder scientist's ice blue eyes fixed on him briefly then returned to Eubanks.

—Catch us later Leo, said Venham as the vice president and Réti joined in Eubanks's professional laughter. —Got to get things rolling here.

A snub? He'd never. Like a son to him. Get a few minutes with him later. Meanwhile the regent went forward through a press of people, Highet a few steps behind, dodging past, —destroy America without firing a shot, and —no injustice, their external circumstances fit their level of development, and —like actually paying them to have children, and —sell them all to private operators, while a nasal voice cut through, —steal a man's style, about the lowest, and Highet turned to face the back of a scuffed brown leather jacket lined with a red silk scarf nestled under curly blond hair past which a stunning woman in a white silk blouse said, —Chazz, I think he considers it homage, —Homage? Maybe he'd like to come rob my house, call that homage too, the nasal voice lost under, —just love Tuck's show, all his, his down home spun-nisms, and —Here we are Doctor Hite, won't you sit here? ushered by the eager voice to a table at the far edge of things, where a querulous old man in a wheelchair was soothed and settled at table by an atten-dant to the glares of a chubby young man whose lapels bore one a gold cross and the other an enamel pin of Old Glory, as —dees n jelmen, burst from a podium hung with a banner azure partitioned by the chevron of mountain peak over the legend αρετε encircled by the motto SCIENCE LIBERTY COMMERCE. A klaxon of feedback swelled and warbled before it damped back to, —tention please

—so glad I ran into you Doctor Hite, we need to talk

—Yes we do, about this upcoming regents' meeting

—because my people are ready to move on this multiplication thing

—pleased to have with us tonight

— . . . multiplication . . . ?

—one of those black intellectual conservatives when there weren't too many and now more have come out of the woodpile

—follow up on our discussion out at

—Wait a minute. Aren't you the new UC regent?

—No no, we met

—You're not a regent?

—out at Bill's ranch a while back, drowned by applause rising to meet the obese figure ascending to the podium as Highet muttered, —That lying sack of

—Thank *yew!* You know my friends, this is a thrill for me, because my whole life I've always tried to meet people who are the best at what they do

—may remember, Doctor Hite, that we had established a priority claim for the operation of multiplication

—ah, you're the, yes, I remember you now

—people whose energy and entrepreneurism and inspiration define

America, with the ideas that are inspirational on American life

—know this guy, came the querulous voice, used to insult people on the radio in Sacramento

—inspiring people to be more than they can be

—hey do you mind, I'm trying to listen to Tuck

—in the free marketplace of ideas, my friends, where the truth always wills out

—hard to believe a mind that small has a mouth that big

—ideas like family, excellence, competition, and self-reliance

—if you don't like it go party with Jane Fonda and her elite liberal media husb

—people we need in this battle for ideas, people with a lot of passion for their ideas, because by gosh passion is key

—Spanish Inquisition had a lot of passion too, didn't it

—will you, just

—cking moderate

—way things *ought* to be, because people are at their best when they look out for themselves

—bring you up to speed on our patent application

—look

—folks, I was just talking with our brilliant guest of honor Doctor Réti, the father of the

—prior art consisting of al-Qarizmi's book

—but this is simple, you don't need to be a genius. Let's put the dots together. Missile defense is not rocket scientology

—where's the food

—it's not E M C equals, it's not time travel

—expressing the multiplication operation as

—look whatever your name is there's been a misunderstanding, I really don't

—hostile world, and just because the Soviet Union's gone dunt mean we're home scot free

—ask a man to dinner, feed him malapropisms

—just good sense that we need to be competitive in this arena

A young waiter, goateed and smug, came round Highet's right holding a tray. —Do you want the chicken peccata or the salmon rushdie?

—I'll have the chicken.

—Good, we're out of the salmon.

—soul of brevity my friends and as Shakespeare said, brevity is the soul of wit. That means, the least amount of words you take to say something, equals the more power that it will have. So without further

—don't know what's happening to the Grand Old Party, these rude young upstarts, religious fanatics

—and finally thank you for inciting I mean inviting me to host a pogrom with so many prestidigious names. Our first speaker

—so now we're preparing a summary of every existing computer algorithm for multiplication so we know who to go after for infringem

—a man the elite liberal media love to hate

—man who can't spell his own name

—the most unique individual I have ever met

—say young fellow, how much salt is in this chicken?

—Vice Present of the *Yew*nited

—nk you Tuc, and the microphone cut out as the deer eyes flickered between podium and audience, —k you all. Like you, I am here tonight to founder, er, honor the foundation of the Arete, ah, all right, Foundation, named after, uh, the Latin, ah, Greek word for ah virtue. Coined by that great Greek, uh, soph, sophisticate, Pro, Proto, goras who said, ah, Man is the measurer, and I think that is clear, and clearly the lesson of that is, uh, that man is the, the one who measures, just as we, ah, as men, or women of course, owe it to our fellow man to make sure that he, or she, ah, measures up, as I am sure all the members in this room would like to be measured . . .

—Dear God, someone put him out of his

—so what we need from you Doctor Hite is a list of computer multiplication algorithms that might be infringing on our

—What I need is a chance to eat my chicken peccata, you mind?

—honor for me to introduce a man we all ah, honor, I mean, a man to whom this great and beautiful count, the microphone again skipping, —deeep debt of ah, skipping again, —Réti, applause rising as the old man limped to the podium, scanning the audience with ice blue eyes as he pushed the microphone back an inch.

—Today the Arete Foundation, indeed the nation, has a special challenge before it. For we stand on the threshold of a new era, a turning point in history. Today, nuclear weapons are obsolete.

—not trying to claim exclusive rights, just a modest licensing fee

—If I promise to look at it, will you leave me alone?

—thank my young colleagues at the Lab, for developing the Superbright laser, cornerstone of the Radiance antimissile defense. For security reasons we cannot reveal the actual intensities we have achieved with this remarkable device. But I assure you that the skeptics will be confounded.

—just a small fraction of a cent per operation

—yes fine here, here's my card, call me, just

—But our work does not stop here. Tonight I will tell you of a remarkable new development. A system of fast, small interceptors that hurl themselves like stones against missiles. Thousands of these devices in low orbit will constantly monitor the globe for threats. If a missile is launched, an interceptor will spot it and knock it down. Today, thanks to startling advances in miniaturization, this system is practical and even cheap.

A sudden crash of dishware from the back of the hall brought the ice blue eyes up and glaring.

—Critics now ask, who is our enemy? The Soviets are gone, should we not divert this money to peaceful uses? I will not answer this dangerously naive criticism. Except to say that the prospect of ballistic missiles, in the hands of twenty different governments, makes an effective defense *mandatory*.

Réti's voice, slow and heavy with a Transylvanian accent unrelinquished after sixty years in America, was the aristocrat to Eubanks's plebe. A sales talk all the same, and so what? From Plato to Planck, science was persuasion. Galileo's dialog of Simplicio, Sagredo, and Salviati was written to persuade, not to prove.

—But this is not all. The Slingshot orbiters perfectly fit the new mandate for dual use. In addition to defending against manmade threats, they can protect us from natural calamities.

—not just a floor wax, it's a dessert topping

—will you shut

—extinction of the dinosaurs caused by an enormous meteor impact. Such an impact, if it occurred today, would cost business over eight quadrillion dollars. And these impacts do occur, about once every hundred thousand years. Thus, simple division shows that killer asteroids cost us eighty billion per year, against which our proposed research budget of two billion per year is if anything too modest.

—never thought of it that way, amortize the apocalypse

—Arete's parent organization, the respected think tank NOUS, the Nexus for Optimal Use of Science, has endorsed Slingshot. They have provided Congress and the president with the scientific analysis they need to make informed policy decisions. But science, though necessary, is not sufficient. The Arete Foundation will provide the political will to make the correct choices. For as Einstein once said to me, "All the wisdom on this earth remains without success if force does not enter into its service." May that be the watchword of the Arete Foundation as well.

—Coffee?

—No, pushing away from the table as applause rose to bury —Wait, Doctor Hite . . . !, as Réti limped from the podium and was lost from sight. Highet skirted tables as people stood, blocking his way, coming against —Did himself in with that *read my lips*, wait and see, and edging past —billion acres of so-called wilderness ought to be in private hands, as chairs were backed into his path, past —impossible to get reliable help, as the crowd thickened and he pressed through —what with the deficit, we can't afford not to sell off some assets, sighting Venham near an exit with the vice president and Eubanks and Réti smiling and shaking hands with a burly man in blue serge, as the nasal voice nearby again nagged, —drive six hundred miles a week, get home I have a right to some peace, while Réti turned laughing to Venham, and black mohair fell across the stooped shoulders, —want to build a transmitter in the middle of Alaska, one point seven gigawatts beamed straight into the ionosphere, where he lost sight of them, —told Vicente to pull out the olive trees, the fruit was staining the pavement, replace them with oleander, as black mohair hove briefly into sight again under EXIT, —turns out the proposal came from an Arco scientist, they just happen to have thirty trillion cubic feet of Alaskan natural gas they'd like to sell on site instead of having to pipe it, breaking through to reaching the exit just as two Secret Service agents pulled the door shut and moved to block him.

—Sorry, sir, no exit here.

In fury he turned and was blocked again by the back of a curly blond head, red scarf, scuffed leather jacket, the nasal voice nagging, —gone all week long, but when I get back Friday at six there he is with uprooted stumps and dirt all over the drive, it looked like a clearcut, with his Salvadoran friends backing a pickup through my rhododendrons, as Highet was jostled forward and the blond curls turned to face him, annoyance on the snub features turning to surprise and sly pleasure.

—Leo Highet! Is it you? My God, what are you doing here?

—Chazz? Chazz Hollis?

—Barbara, this is my best friend from high school.

—Hello. Her warm hand in his. Beautiful smile. Sheer silk sheath. Her eyes quickly shifting from his. —Chazz, I'm going to talk to Renata.

—All right. We'll leave soon.

—Last place I expected to see you, Chazz.

—I'm so embarrassed. I had no idea this would be so political. Do you know Bill Venham? He invited me. He's been a real friend to the Philharmonic.

—We've met. A little conservatism won't hurt you, Chazz.

—What did you think of Eubanks?

—Not much.

—His radio show is enormously popular.

—Is it really.

—Some people say he could run for president.

—Any idiot can run for president.

—How long has it been, Leo? Twentieth Lancaster High reunion, wasn't it?

Ten years ago. Out in the trailers licking my wounds. Mercedes liberal looking down his nose at me. Still building bombs? he'd said.

—That's right. You'd just put out a new age album under the name Proteus.

—Oh my gosh, that's right. You know, I did that as a lark, but they turned out to be my cash cow, those Proteus albums. You're where now?

—I'm director of the Lab now.

—So you've done pretty well for yourself there.

—And you?

—Oh, I'm juggling about four careers. There's a new computer music research center at the university, they've created a chair for me, endowed by a recently deceased film composer. Quite a good composer really. All his life in addition to his film work he wrote symphonies, chamber works, an amazing output, but they were never performed. I'm conducting an evening of his quote serious music at the Hollywood Bowl this summer.

—Didn't know you conducted, Chazz.

—Oh, yes. Another cash cow. And I have a Proteus album due out in November, though I'm moving away from that. Oh, and Leo, you'll be interested in this. At the research center we're designing some AI software.

—All that and AI software, too, you're a versatile guy, Chazz. How'd you get to be so smart?

—Oh, my assistant, he's here somewhere, he's quite brilliant, he works at the Navy's Complexity Institute. It's ironic to be adapting his work to music, but I think it makes a statement, converting military technologies to cultural uses. Of course, I use a Macintosh for my own composing, but the research at the Center is much more advanced. We're working on a program that can be trained to write in any musical style. It's a challenge. One knows very well how Mozart differs from Haydn, but to get from that rather intuitive knowledge to a working program is quite difficult. The university has an intellectual property interest in it. They want to patent algorithms that embody compositional styles. They've trademarked a dozen major names, Mozart, Bach, Beeth

—Trademarked?

—For marketing new works in the style. Of course we have no idea if this will pan out, but it doesn't hurt to stake a claim.

—Speaking of technology transfer, we might be able to help you. We've done a lot of AI research in house. This algorithm works how, exactly?

—Oh, I can't tell you exactly, some sort of chaos theory, chaos on the edge of complexity, you should talk to, there he is, Jef! Jef Thorpe, this is Leo Hi

—You.

—Oh you, you know each . . . ?

—Jef used to work for us at the Lab.

—Oh is that where . . . ? What a coincidence.

—Small world.

—Ah, you two, ah, must have some catching up to do, I'll, head swiveling as it tracked the crowd past Highet, dispensing a smile here, a nod there, hand groping in an inner pocket for —my card, Leo, the home phone's changing next week, I'm moving to Palos Verdes, actually that's why I'm, ah ha, I see my realtor over there, glad I ran into you, Leo, we'll talk again. Jef, see you Monday . . .

Thorpe, blackjacketed arms crossed over red t-shirt, said, —Someone told me, the fish rots from the head.

—Let me explain something to you, Jef . . .

—No need, I understand.

—Do you really? Do you understand how Quine screwed you? With those secondary reflectors?

—Yeah. I also know the primaries were giving bad data all along. That's what got me jigging the code in the first place. Because I trusted the data and I saw how to make the simulation correspond.

—You think I wanted to blame you? Quine was group leader, you were his assistant. Your fingerprints were on the code. And you had a history.

—What does that mean, a hist

—Fish and Himmelhoch.

—That's totally unfair! I had nothing to do with

—What's fair got to do with it? Quine was my man, I protected him. Even though I despise him. He's gone now, if it makes you feel better.

—Well, so am I, gone.

—Learn from this, Jef. Protect yourself. Be ruthless.

—Man . . . shaking his head, —I'm not sorry I'm gone.

—Enjoy your honeymoon at Complexity. But stay in touch. That Richtmyer-Meshkov work you were doing is hot, we can use that.

—This, what, this is unbelievable. Why should I share anything with you?

—Because in the long run we're on the same side. I won't forget that and I'm betting you won't.

—Man, there it is. The Highet Effect. That reality distortion field. It's amazing. You'll say anything, won't you.

—You heard Réti's speech. Knowledge and force.

—I heard it. Einstein my ass.

And turned from Thorpe, going into the corridor towards MEN, where a hotel employee blocked him with a mop held like a quarterstaff, —Closed, there's another down the hall, and on past Space Reality Space Fantasy Art Expo where orbiters and battle stations and shuttles and starships were clustered in promiscuous congress against airbrushed starscapes no telescope had ever viewed, past a booth where a woman in hot pink jogging bra and satin shorts, wool socks, heavy boots, and backpack walked a treadmill, face hidden in a helmet stenciled VIRTUAL WILDERNESS above a smile fixed in Cheshire Cat detachment at the mountain landscape projected on screens for the spectators' benefit behind her pumping legs, and went on past CodeWin, where the pressure of his bladder led him into a dim alcove lit by a screen with the image of hair not dark or wild but bright as a carrot, lips pouting and slim, white legs raised for —Missile defense! as a cacophony burst from another booth where one boy urged another facing a barrage of incoming graphics, —Fire! Fire! Fire! and on past AMNESTY INTERACTIVE where high resolution graphics and digital audio lent the prison cell and repetitive screams a gritty chic, finally attaining the relative peace of MEN where two figures at urinals, one in black mohair, one in blue serge, backs stiff and legs spraddled to produce in porcelain tones an intermittent tenor aria and a profounder chiming continuo, over which serge was saying, —*agenturnaya razvedka*, information coming through network of undercover case officers. Codename Star wished that his information may not be traceable to anyone on Manhattan Project staff, and Bill Venham turning slightly saw Highet, the tenor flow stuttering and ceasing, —Leo!

Pull up a pew. Say hi to my new friend Vassili.

—Can't get away from you, can I, Bill. Thanks for setting me up with old Stan there.

—Stan?

—Stan, Stan Flack, remember? Of course, not being a regent, he didn't know a hell of a lot about my situation.

—Oh hell, that's all over, Leo, you should be looking for new possibilities, that's why I hooked you up with Stan there.

—What do you mean, that's all over?

Venham shook, tucked, and came to the sink, while serge continued his relentless basso under the soprano and alto of two faucets.

—Regents, DOE, that's the old order, Leo. Give us a couple years and we'll close down DOE, move it all into the private sector. We've got a position paper on this, I'll send you a copy.

The chiming in the Russian's bowl tapered off, then began again.

—Who's he?

—Vassili's in from Moscow. With some very hot info about a certain Manhattan Project scientist who passed atomic secrets to the NKVD during the war.

—Not Aron, I hope.

—Ha ha! Oh, Vassili's a gold mine of information on the Stalin era, I'm offering him a position at NOUS. Say, that reminds me, did you get my letter?

—Been a little busy, I'll ask my girl.

—We're keeping a pew warm. There's a place for you anytime you want it.

The basso continuo at last diminished, retarded, and ceased with a heartfelt sigh. —Bozhe moi.

—Got to be going, Bill, stopped by a hand plucking his lapel, tucking a light green vellum envelope into his inner jacket pocket, then smoothing the fabric.

—Give it some thought, Leo.

—Where can I find Aron?

—Aron? He's long gone. Listen Leo, about this cold fusion thing . . . but Highet likewise was gone, out past MULTIMEDIA and the airbrushed infinities, past abandoned mop and bucket by Out Of Order, pausing only in the lobby for MEN and the relief he had not earlier taken.

Didn't even get to talk to him. Call him tomorrow. Might be too late. Driving up from the bowels of the garage, surfacing to wait for the flash and shriek of ƎƆИA⅃UꓭMA passing and in its wake traffic streaming then thinning as the city fell away behind him. Stars above thin cloud. In the valley a misty rain began and his wipers switched themselves on. The syncopated rhythm lulled him over the pass. Wasted trip. Down to a bright grid flat against void, and off at J Street.

Thea looked up from reading as the door stuck then flew open to strike the IV stand that fell clattering.

—How was your dinner?

—Didn't expect to find you still here.

—I wasn't sure you were coming back. I didn't want to leave Mother alone.

—I see the stand arrived. Place right here in town Thea, they even deliver, if you'd look in the yellow pages.

—Well now we have two.

—Oh for Christ's sake.

—Well, you didn't tell me you were going to buy one.

—Okay, so return it. How is she?

—She went to bed a little while ago. She was waiting up for you, but she tires easily. Her light's still on. You might say good night.

—Listen, about dinner. I told you I had things to do while I was here.

—I know, Leo. I know nobody's going to change. Mark is coming tomorrow morning for breakfast. Is that all right? Do you have something else? Just so I know.

—I need to be in Westwood by noon. Breakfast is fine.

—I'll be here about eight. Will you say good night to Mother?

—Of course. See you tomorrow.

Light under the closed door. He stood by it for a moment, then went in.

—Leo, dear. It's so good to see you.

—Hello Mother. He stood by the IV, not looking at her. Hanging plastic sack, D5 Half-Normal Saline Dextrose 5% 1000 mL OSMOLARITY

273 mOsmol/L (CALC) STERILE NONPYROGENIC SINGLE DOSE
CONTAINER. Blue plastic gauze pads on the bedside table. Brown
plastic pill bottles. Chlorambucil. Small milky plastic cup holding a
tablespoon of clear liquid. Spot of dried blood on the pillowcase.

—Leo, I'm so glad you came. Her thin gray hand reaching for him.

—How are you?

—Oh, Leo. I'm so tired.

—Mother, can I ask you something about Dad?

She looked away, then turned back brightly. —Do you remember,
when your father taught you to shoot? You'd go after jackrabbits, you
two, and come home hungry as hunters, and I'd have dinner waiting
and I'd say, Home are the hunters. Do you remember, Leo? Oh, you
loved that. Because it was your middle name, Hunter, yours and your
father's. After your grandpa. But you wouldn't eat the rabbits.

—Yes, I remember. Mother, listen, when Dad lost the election

Her eyes pleading. —Leo. All I ever wanted from your father was a
body to hug and a soul to cherish. He was such a distant man.

He patted the thin gray hand.

—I need to take my medicine. Hand me that little cup, dear.

—Here. What is it?

—Morphine. She swallowed. —And then he put himself beyond
me forever.

—I'll be down the hall if you need anything.

In the hall ghost voices chattered and nagged. Her radio, constant
irritant of his childhood, her distraction and defense, all day and all
night, one in every room. To drown that memory now he shut his
door and switched on the radio on the night table, whence sprung a
voice rich with the false resonance of digital signal processing, —space
music, reflecting the, natural cycle, of birth, life, and death. For the
next hour, space travelers, Earth Journey . . . the voice fading to a mix
of bells, flute, rattles, talking drums, bass guitar, and the nasal whine of
synthesizer. He unpacked laptop and cell phone and plugged them into
their chargers. Groping behind the night table for the outlet he saw a
corner of faded blue in the dust and cobwebs. A small cotton sack filled
with catnip. Lancelot. Orange and white tom butting his head against
your leg, loud growling purr. Thirty, forty years ago. Toy can't have

been back there that long. No, of course, Mother had that skinny Siamese died last year. Pellet of paper back there in the dust. Smoothing it open to her looping hand: *you are not my keeper.*

—Jesus, he muttered, kicking off his shoes. Nobody's going to change. He turned off the light and reclined on the coverlet staring at the ceiling, holding the cat toy. Lancelot would climb onto his chest to sleep. Purring hum at his breast. He missed it now.

—space music, celebrating the, natural cycle, by the, Los Angeles based composer, Proteus. For a playlist, ask for program, three thirty nine, Earth Journ, and snapped it off.

The natural cycle: homage to cruelty and waste. What use heaven makes of its beings. Sets them to strive and build under incommutable sentence of death. If he were younger he might pit all his force and resolve against this enemy, this faceless minion of heaven, if not to beat death at least to put it off. Why shouldn't people live for centuries? What could they not accomplish?

All I really wanted was to do physics. The structure of the universe. The nature of matter. Members of the Academy, ladies and gentlemen. And what have I accomplished? Chemist of people, catalyst, holding the place together so others can do the real work. Like young Quine, that paper he coauthored with Sorokin years ago, that was the real thing. Still know it when I see it. Well, he'll never get back to it now. Bitter satisfaction there. Reduced to living on others' failures.

It's coming apart. Dietz's building, falling. Hanging on to the cliff, looking for the next handhold. Rock biting his palms. No one tells you what you need to live.

Leo had to pee. In the hall he saw light under the basement door. Leo opened the door and went down the stairs holding the rail tight. Come here boy. Light glowed amber in the shotglass. Papers and maps overflowed the desk. These are streets, see. Placentia, Palm, Pioneer. We live here. The new streets will be here. Vacant parcels in A-17. Land's cheap now, but it'll be valuable. The sharp smell as Dad sipped from the shotglass.

Dad yelling at mother because Gramp wouldn't loan him the money to buy property. Worthless patch of desert. Shortsighted old fool, it'll double in three years! Finally he forged the old fool's name on a check.

What a stink over that.

Vast echoing dimness. Endless rows of lockers and benches. Blurred voices, the smell of sweat and mildew. Leo comes to an arena of light and steam. All the showers are running. There his father stands naked with a sullen young man. Father pulls at the player's swelling penis and looks up unsmiling at Leo.

Abruptly awake. A sigh almost a moan escaped him. Best for all concerned that you.

Fuck them. Fuck them all. Let them try it. They can't do this to me, they don't have the votes. He rose and crossed the hall. He stood voiding. The floodlight outside dimly lit the bowl. In its light noiseless rain drifted down a fathomless sky. On the distant highway, trucks whined, wheels hissed on wet road. As he returned to his room and lay down, he felt a wave of weakness, almost the body's disgust with itself. I have nothing left for this fight.

Leo at the back door snapped on the floodlight. In its glare, half hidden by a creosote bush, stood a long slim canine with the slinking frame of a scavenger and a bushy tail upright. Its eyes were golden coals and in its narrow jaws it held the neck of an orange and white cat with head and paws dangling, tail curled under. Lancelot turned his head into the light and his pink mouth opened in a silent mewl. The coyote bolted into darkness with the cat.

Get up. Get dressed. Are you angry with that coyote? We'll get him. In the dawn halflight his father stood. Dumb with sorrow and sleep Leo dressed. He took the rifle his father thrust at him. The sky grew light and they hiked into the sandy hills behind the house. Nothing moved for miles in that pale ungiving light. Leo wanted to ask if Lancelot might have gotten away, if they might still find him, but the question died in his throat.

Eyes wide, he listened to the hollow ceaseless hiss of the universe. He reached for the inhaler, cylinder cold in his hand's warmth, an exaltation like freefall as the spray struck his sinuses.

Dad. Tell me what I need to live. Read to me like you did.

Once there was a man, a rocket man, in his coalblack uniform coated with stardust, a man alone in the night of space. A proud man, and brave. On his shoulders lay the fate of the world. His rocket ship left the Earth on a pillar of fire. It climbed up and out of the gravity well. Spewing a hard white fountain of flame. Behind it the Earth dwindled, and all he had ever known dwindled with it: his family, his friends, his past. The Earth dwindled to the size of a basketball, a grapefruit, a blood orange, a lemon. A ball bearing. Lancelot . . . ! And deep in the void waited a sickness and a disease, and it came upon the man, and it was called the Loneliness. Deep, lustrous desert sky, still as death, and in its darkness waits the hidden enemy, Sputnik could it be? A strong man took the leadership in war, one who had once blinked at the sun and dreamt that perhaps he might snare it, and was roused to convey to his brothers that indeed he had done so, and had thus led them out of the caves and finally into space itself. There! And there! Points of light. The enemy. Deep in space, cruciform in a ship no larger than a bodysuit he fingered controls in his gloves, he darted and fired at his opponents. Fire. Fire. Fire.

And the sky gathered color as a sun still unrisen scattered rays across a serene paleness cut by a blunt black triangle outracing its own hollow roar, as though to assert that the day alone did not suffice, its beauty a goad and a challenge to the discontent spirit. A key scratched in the front door which gave its grunt of resistance and paper bags rustled to the kitchen and water ran in the master bathroom through pipes singing beneath the house, the dirges of childhood, as he stared at the same ceiling he had forty years ago. Highet thrust himself out of bed.

At the dining room table sat Thea, reading a newspaper. —Good morning.

—Thea, what are these? fetching from a pocket and flattening *sometimes I wonder why I spend the lonely night,* and *you are not my keeper.*

She sighed. —Oh, the fortune cookies.

—Fortune cookies?

—It's what Mark and I call them. She's been leaving them around the house for years. I find them under sofa cushions.

—These were downstairs and in the guest room.

—We think they're her way of dealing with Father's death.

—That's twenty-five years ago, Thea.

—Well, she hasn't ever wanted to admit . . . you know.

—Twenty-five years and she still thinks he just dozed off with the motor running in the gar

—Leo, hush. Please. I hear her coming. The pipes stopped singing. Then, rising, her voice brisk, —I'll start breakfast. Mark will be here soon. You see if Mother needs help.

—Not the kind I can give her, sweeping the paper strips into his pocket. —You're up on this pop psych stuff, you know the word denial? Dad with the booze, Mark with the sports, Mom with the radio, you

—You with the science, Leo. Would you please

—Fine, all right. Mother! Do you need help?

She was in a housecoat and slippers leaning against the chrome walker at the bedside.

—Do you need help with that, Mother?

—I hate this horrid thing. If I could lean on you, darling.

—Here. He extended a crooked elbow.

—I'm sorry to be a bother, dear.

—It's no bother.

—You look so handsome in your suit. Like your father when he ran for office.

—Hope I do a little better here than he did.

—He would have won, dear, but the local machine was against him. A little slower, darling. Her fingers dug into his forearm.

—You're a tough old bird, Mother, you'll outlive us all.

—Sit there, Mother, I'll bring you some juice. Mark will be here soon.

—Thank you, Thea. Leo, darling, would you turn on the radio?

—Oh Christ.

—Tuck Eubanks is on.

—How can you listen to that crap?

—Now, I don't agree with everything he says, but he makes some very good points.

—Leo? Can I see you in the kitchen?

He turned from the skull so visible under the thin white hair, as the orotund voice sprung from the radio, —this attempt to tug people's heartstrings has wrung dry, and strode into the kitchen where his sister waited, arms folded.

—What, Thea. You mean I should just shut up and let her listen to that poisonous buffoon?

In a tense whisper, —Yes, that's exactly what I mean. And keep your voice down. You're acting like a spoiled child.

His voice fell likewise. —She does that to me, she always has, you know that. This is a mistake, me being here.

—You're making it one. You're making it one so that you can avoid dealing with it, as usual. You are so ungiving.

—Right, got about fifty urgent things need doing, went out of my way to clear some time drove three hundred miles but that's not enough, you know what it is Thea, nothing's enough, you turn everything into some kind of drama and if people don't play their part they're ungiving. If you want to know, that's why Bob finally left you, your constant dramatizing, and he tried to go along with it all, playing a dozen different parts, kept giving till there was nothing left to give.

—Leave Bob out of this.

—There you go, Bob's not in your script any more, so leave him out.

—You're the last one to talk about relationships.

—Oh, no doubt, but I'm talking about you, Thea, how you've got zero tolerance for anything not in your movie.

—You always have to win, Leo. I know that so well, but it always surprises me. Everything's a conflict to you. No wonder you're good at your job.

—Just look around sometime Thea if you don't think everything's a conflict, just look around you for one goddamn min

—Thea, dear? I think Mark is here.

—Thank you, Mother. All right, Leo, could we have peace for, for just one hour? Just through breakfast?

He went out the kitchen door into the back yard. The fig tree, barren of bloom, burdened with the weight of its own branches, swayed stiffly in a warm and steady wind. A heavy dry scent from some unseen flower itched his nose, heavy with mucus, and he blew to clear it. The doorbell turned him back inside.

—You're looking more and more like Dad, Mark.

—New car, Leo? Very sporty. Pity about the scratch on the hood.

—How's life in the trades?

—Locally, it sucks. But we've got enough work out Newhall way.

—How are Mary and the children, dear?

—Good good, they're good, Mom. Gary just started Little League, he's real excited about that. How's with you, Leo?

—Complexity on the edge of chaos. Had to run off last night to a dinner.

—I heard.

—How do you all want your eggs? Mother, I know you want poached. Leo? Mark?

—Scrambled, Thea, thanks.

—Just coffee.

—You don't want anything, Leo?

—No, got something else at noon down below.

—Sit, sit down, all of you.

—Say, Mark, got a construction question for you. When you truck fill away from a site

—Away? Usually you truck it in.

—Well say you've got too much of it. What would you do with it?

—Well, if it's good fill, nonexpansive, you'd take it to another site that needs it.

—One of your own sites?

—If you've got one that needs it.

—You ever hear of Credne Construction?

—The statewide low bid kings. They've cost me work. Why?

—Just curious. They're doing some work at the Lab. I pass their trucks every day.

—They do industrial work and tract homes. Those new developments out by Adelanto? That kind of thing. I don't know about their industrial, but their tract workers get paid by the piece, not hourly. That's incentive to cut corners.

—Thea, you hear this? Credne's the contractor out at Estancia. Tell her she doesn't want to live there, Mark.

—What the hell do you care where she lives, Leo?

—Just want to keep her out of my neighborhood.

—Well, don't ask my help.

—Mark, please . . .

—I'm POed, Thea. He's been doing this since I came in, how's life in the trades, I look like Dad . . . I don't need this from a guy we see once every five years.

—Okay, don't let it get to you, Mark, I'm leaving.

—Oh Leo. Mark why did you have to

—Me? He's blowing us off, and it's my fault?

—Nobody's fault, sit down Thea, just got to run, some things I have to

—Leo, please sit down. Finish your coffee . . .

—Thea, I don't need this any more than he does.

—Please, dear . . .

—He's great at this, always has been. Toss a stink bomb, get every-one fighting, and he's out the door.

—Please, let's not fight.

—Mark. Mother's right.

Mark looked at Thea, then at Mother. His nostrils flared, his mouth tight. Like their father. Then it passed. Mark rose and held out his hand.
—Sorry, Leo. If you have to go, you have to go. Stay in touch, will you?

—It was good of you to come, dear. We are all so proud of you. Thin arms reaching for him. Smell of medicine. He accepted her hug.

—Take care of yourself, mother. I'll call.

Thea came to hug him. —Goodbye. I'll call you about Estancia.

—Yes, all right I, hesitating at the front door as it stuck, —seems, . . . seems like I'm forgetting something. Turning back to the three pairs of eyes fixed on him as he raised sunglasses in a halfhearted token of farewell, donning them against the glare that broke in shards on the concrete walk and asphalt and again on the distant glitter of tall build-ings and again on the pebbled glass under his parked wheels by the yel-low tape CAUTION CUIDADO knotted like some superstring of dis-tress and disruption through the world, reaching it seemed from the Lab to Westwood, as he followed the shards past boarded windows as two rollerbladers zipped by in t-shirts NO FEAR trailing a sound newly in the world, a sly hiss from their carbide wheels, another spinoff of a Lab project in composite materials, its ingenuity knotted throughout the world, his mark, putting resolution into his step as he went under a granite architrave FIAT LUX and down an echoing hall to pause at an oak door, hand stilled on knob by the patrician voice from within, —strategic deception, that's what Whipple called it. He claimed that the entire point of the program was to force the Soviets to spend

Cool light through slatted shades, dark conference table lustrous as old coin. He recognized some of the faces.

—Sir, this meeting is closed . . . Doctor Highet?

—I believe you're discussing my contract.

—This, this is, your presence here is most inappropriate.

—Inappropriate? And him? pointing to the figure who upon his entrance had gone silent as a pallbearer, —He's just giving a little impartial advice?

—Senator Chase is here at our invitation.

—The senator wants my head. I know this. You know this. I'd like to defend myself.

—Doctor Highet, you know how performance reviews work. When we've gathered enough data

—Enough rope, you mean.

—We really cannot have

—This is just the sort of antic he's

—Hell, Charles, let the man sit in, what harm can it do? Senator?

—Fine with me.

—Well it's irregular and I want it noted that I don't approve.

—So noted.

He seated himself at the far end of the table, facing Chase, two chairs away from any regent.

—Doctor Highet, one of our concerns is your evident lack of support for the post-Cold War mission DOE has defined for the Lab, specifically technology transfer. The perception is that you are heavily invested in the Radiance antimissile program.

—I've long been an advocate of technology transfer. I've spearheaded many collaborations with industry. We've just made an agreement with Gate Cellular that will double the net worth of our dual use technologies.

—Some evaluations of your performance . . . well, here, underestimates difficulties and time frames, more concerned with public perceptions than realities, combative style, profane and tactless, abrasive sometimes abusive, serious problems accepting criticism, ten bad ideas for every good one . . .

—Who wrote that?

—and recent articles in the press about Radiance tend to support a view of, well, here, numerous inaccuracies, misleading statements, unresolved issues, out of control, emerging picture of mismanagement and impropriety, does the competent and honest scientists at the Lab a disservice . . .

—I should get the name of your clipping service. Don't tell me you take that seriously?

—The university takes these accusations very seriously. They reflect on our oversight.

—Press gets hold of a few rumors, plays right into the popular mistrust of science and government, pretty soon you've got a feeding frenzy.

—Well, you've got five ongoing GAO investigations, two DOE, six congressional

—Well Doctor Beckman half of those aren't us, they're you, it's the university's oversight being questioned.

—Without laying blame, Doctor Highet, it does seem that the Radiance program and all its ah unresolved issues are associated rightly or wrongly with your personality.

—Maybe you don't want a scientist at the helm. Maybe you want a salesman.

—It seems to me we have that already, said Chase. —Thirty billion dollars wasted on a fraud, a deception

—Senator, you got your money's worth. Radiance spent the Soviet Union into oblivion. Nothing fraudulent about that.

—Do you deny that you deceived, misled

—War is deception.

—Do you hear that? That's exactly what Whipple said to me. Are you admitting that this program is a deception?

—Not at all.

—Please, Doctor Highet, Senator Chase, we're not going to resolve the larger issues, I really think

—Yes, let's cut the, to the, bottom line, what happens to me? Got that figured out yet?

—I don't think it's approp

—Come on, I'm here, let's have it.

Hum of overhead lights. Sun slanting through dust. Jet scraping past far overhead.

—We think it best for all concerned that you resign.

—My contract has over a year to run.

—Absent a resignation, we will recommend that the regents terminate your contract.

—Resignation to be effective when.

—In one month.

—Then you have a replacement in mind.

—For the short term we will appoint an interim director.

—It's, you know, *appropriate* to consult with an outgoing director about his successor.

—It's premature at this time.

—Come on, who's on your short list, Ware? Szabo? Karp?

Glances exchanged. Chase sat back, his face blank, until after a pause Beckman spoke up, —We're impressed by Doctor Philip Quine.

—Quine!

—Doctor Quine addressed the problems of the Radiance program with candor and resolve.

—Quine!

—Doctor Highet, we

—You know that he's been put on leave?

—Yes, for writing a report critical of Superbright, I gather, said Chase.

—If you'd read that report, you'd learn that he had a major role in what you're calling this deception.

—That's what I mean by candor, said Chase.

—The candor was mine. I ordered that report.

—I ah, for one, I think that is wholly to Doctor Highet's credit.

—Ordered it and then suppressed it, said Chase.

—You can't jump a man from deputy associate to director.

—Can't, Doctor Highet?

—There are ten associate directors with more seniority, there are scores of group leaders with twenty and thirty years experience, you can't just pass them over, especially for

—Doctor Highet, I can't say I appreciate you telling us what we can or can't do.

—Listen to me. Philip Quine is the classic bad hire. For eight years he did nothing. I finally found something I thought he could handle and he screwed it up and tried to assign blame.

Pages turned. —You hired him, didn't you? Kept him on? Promoted him?

—Yes I did. That was poor judgment on my part.

Highet caught Chase's faint smile at that. —I'm warning you not to make the same mistake. Quine has no experience, no stature, no leadership. He's incapable of making public statements.

—That's a plus, said Chase, still with his calm tortoise smile.

—He's erratic and unreliable, and he has a drug problem.

That interested Logue. —Really? We have no evidence of

—I can supply it.

At last Chase was annoyed. —Oh come on, he's doing it again, don't get drawn into

—Know something Senator? You're gone. Next election. Wait and see.

—Why, are your rightwing friends going to target me?

—Please, Senator, Doct

—Think you can use this nation's security as a political football you'll find otherwise pretty damn quic

—Security is exactly what worries me, Highet. I want you and your mouth gone before the entire Lab is tainted by your commitment to this disastrous program.

—And if I won't resign?

—Do I have to spell it out? Lying to Congress, misappropriation of funds, conflict of interest . . .

—Conflic

—If you think I don't know what you've been up to with your shell companies and your job shops, selling knowledge and technologies developed with public funds

—Come off it, there's nothing illegal about spinoffs, and besides

—Do you want to go through a hearing? I think you remember what that's like.

He had a picture of himself then. Twenty years ago in Geneva. The Soviet delegate looking at him in disbelief as he said what everyone there knew: that the Soviet antimissile system being offered as a bargaining chip was made worthless by the new American MIRVs. And then the awful silence in which he knew that he had ruined himself. In that silence he had learned how disliked he was. No one stood up for him, no one attempted to cover for him. That silence followed him as he walked afterward by the lake, with the swans gliding by, followed him through his years of penance and obscurity in the Lab's temporary trailers as he slowly reconstructed his career, working on deadwood projects no one wanted, through years of swallowed pride and cagey maneuvering, the silence that could be covered only by doing and more doing, and it was here now, as they all looked at him, saying nothing. He was as alone and unprotected as he had ever been, like his father when the hammer had fallen on him. And in that silence he heard that temptation of a stillness in which doing might cease.

—Please, gentlemen, no one wants . . . this.

—Think you're God's gift to the republic, don't you Chase, scourge of the military industrial complex

—That's not what this is about.

—What, then? Why do you have it in for me, Chase?

Chase squared his papers in an oblong of sun. He took off his glasses. —Last autumn, when I visited the Lab, you called me a traitor. I don't take that from anyone.

—You hear? said Highet hoarsely. —It's personal. He has it in for me.

—Your judgment is the issue, said Chase. —That showed extremely poor judgment.

Dillard cleared his throat. —Do you have anything more to say, Doctor Highet?

—No. But this is not over.

And went out under FIAT LUX into sun hazed by high cloud ridged and swirled, light congealed there in strange and lovely tumult, as if some angel of chaos had passed through the air. Not until he was on the freeway did he open his phone and arrow to Réti's number. Six times it trilled in his ear. When the answering machine picked up, Highet held for a moment, then pressed END. He must succor himself. Settling sunglasses he was soon through the suburbs and out of the valley, climbing past FAR-GO Mini Mart and IN-N-OUT BURGER, and on past Elevation 2000 Ft to Agua Dulce Airport, then descending past the sandstonered rooftops of new developments, Willow Creek Village from $59,900 to Antelope Valley Urgent Care, Best Buy, Target, K Mart, Grace Christian Superstore, on past Assembly of God, NO MAN COME IN THE FATHER BUT BY ME NOT BY MIGHT NOT BY POWER BUT BY MY SPIRIT, while he thumbed the radio for —the Lord commended the unjust steward, for the children of this world are wiser than the children of light, and silenced it at a flashing in the hills out beyond Mojave, synchronized points of light, hidden as the road wound up among slabs ribbed vertically by erosion, tilted layers and stony hummocks of sienna, brick, and chalkgreen, and on this sandy paleness dark clumps of sage, juniper, joshua, rising to a plateau stitched by power lines, where colonies of windmills flashed in the dull sunlight on both sides of the road.

At the crest he stopped. He stilled the engine and stepped out. Wind whipped at his hair and clothes, and he felt a strange peace. He watched the windmills flash, the two and three vaned propellers, the eggbeaters. After Geneva, in the temporary trailers, he had worked on all these designs. Though disgraced, he realized, he had been happy then. He had nothing to do but rise.

He pulled on a cotton jacket and began walking. A dirt road led up the nearest hill. Cloud moved in the wind and its mottled shadow hurried across the valley below. Even in the lee of the hill the wind was strong. Above him blades flashed and sang. He hiked following a chainlink fence, his soles slipping on the long dry grass, until the fence gave way to barbed wire, where, hand on a weathered post for balance, wire shaking under his shoe, he vaulted over.

He stopped near a twovaned rotor. The Lab had waived commercial rights. His first Devon Null spinoff. On a twenty meter pole sat a white nacelle, surface mottled with rust, blades blurred in the wind. Up there a hawk beat against a crosswind, stalled in a cloudbreak of sun blazoning its broad rufous tail. Its shrill whistle fell, and a gust hurried it on toward the tower, wings taut and swerving, but the wind swept it into the blades, and their song trembled as the hawk struck and traveled on, rising and falling away in a long arc like a tossed stone.

He found it fallen in some sage. Big dun body striped with black bands. Head lolling from the broken neck's ruff, eye half open, a drop of blood at the beak. Strong horny claws grasping nothing. Already an ant moved across the feathers. Bitter smell of broken sage. In the sun rotors flashed like pitiless clockwork. Against the wind he walked back to the car.

They'll do it. They'll take Quine because he's a good gray drone, never done anything worth doing, but he looks clean to them. They'll give him a year or so, let the place run on autopilot till the stink of scandal clears, and there's a new secretary of energy, and he'll be out. But I'll be long gone.

Under a sky gone flat gray the car shuddered in a gust past Land of Many Uses and THIS IS A HOME RULE COUNTY handlettered and flanked by two crudely painted American flags, and the mournful voice of Robert Johnson —stones in my passway and my road seems dark at n, n, n, the disk skipping with a cold digital chatter, a sound newly in the world, —nemies have betrayed me, have overtaken poor Bob at last, and with a finger he stilled the player which extruded its disk like a silver tongue, as a small town passed in a blur of FRYING RABBITS & BABY BUNNIES, Very LA Cellular & Pager, PICK & PULL SELF SERVE AUTO PARTS above two fenced lots beneath high tension lines stretching on past sagebrush and joshua trees, Federal Prison Camp, Living Ghost Town, Litter Removed Next 2 Miles The John Birch Society, featureless acres of Mitsubishi Cement rolling by while the catenaries of power lines rose and fell between towers, rhythmic as the hand that absently began to press the firmness in his lap rising less from desire than from boredom, from the body's inscrutable tyrannies, even as the detector on the dash chirped and flashed the presence of K band radar bringing both hands back to the wheel and the speedometer needle dropping below 80, 70, to hover at 65 for the oncoming black and white cruiser's U turn across the divider to follow at a distance, as his eyes traveled from mirror to road to dashboard to mirror until the cruiser's abrupt turn back across the divider to recede, lights flashing, in pursuit of a less attentive speeder heading south, and the needle rose again past 70, 80, 90, wheels consuming the stripe of road that led north to a horizon jagged as some graph, while to the west the nearer peaks vanished into a turbulent mist, and wind whipped across a dry lake bed to lift alkali in twisting columns white as chalk in sudden sunlight moving like smoke across the dappled plain toward the arid eastern range wrinkled and dark under dense lenticular clouds flowing from the western crest across the valley and trailing dark streamers.

The highway climbed into that darkness, past Elev 6000, until he reached his turnoff and snow flurred in the bitter evening halflight. Flakes had begun to collect in the ruts of the dirt road PRIVATE Posted No Trespassing at the end of which was parked a van Department of Energy Official Use Only with three inches of snow on its roof. Lights shone in the windows of the ranch.

In the entranceway, duffels carryalls and laptops were piled. Highet removed his coat, and from a wallpeg lifted and jauntily donned a billed cap $e=hf$, hanging his cotton jacket on the freed peg. Within sat Dan Root on the large sofa with five young men on hassocks and chairs, reaching to the low circular table for bowls of chips, salsa, popcorn, sodas, beers. They wore jeans and t-shirts NO FEAR, $\aleph_0$, And God Said $e_0 \int E \cdot \delta A = \Sigma q$, Highet knew them only by their transcripts and their e-mail names: miko, n8, baryon, thomxen, jre.

—Gentlemen, welcome to the Advanced Research Institute of the Eastern Sierra.

—Leo, you made it! Pull up a pew. We just microwaved some tamales.

He sat glowing and glorified in the light of his admirers, young knights-errant hungry for the award money, for an internship, for a career, for a world they couldn't yet imagine.

—Give me some of that healthy hacker food. I haven't eaten since the rubber chicken last night.

—Leo was out hobnobbin with the vice president.

—I saw him almost complete a sentence. It was scary. Looks like you hit some snow, Dan.

—Had to put the chains on. The boys did, I mean. I just sat inside keepin warm. You get any comin north?

—The last few miles.

—Doctor Highet . . .

—Leo. Call me Leo, and he's Dan. We're all colleagues here.

—What is this place? D, Dan wouldn't say. He called it the Castle of, what was it?

—Don't know your Wagner? Monsalvat, that's the Grail castle. Can't tell you what it really is, yall don't have your clearances yet.

—That's right, you should have blindfolded them.

—It's a cool place. I've gone rock climbing near here.

—Tom, you want to toss another log on the . . .

—We bring you guys out here so you don't think it's all work and no play. You'll work hard. But trust me, you're going to love it. The resources are incredible. So I want you to think big. If you could work on anything, anything at all, what would it be? Let's hear your wildest dreams.

Sitting back on the sofa, arms crossed, eyes narrowed and shaded under the cap brim, the rhythm of travel still in his body was distracting him. He listened not for what they said but their saying of it. The dreams themselves were always puerile variations on the same themes: escape, power, revenge for injustice. He listened for how their voices handled, and how their minds harnessed these raw energies.

—I want to build a starship. Get off the planet before we destroy it.

—Barry?

—I guess I'm with Mike about the planet. But getting off it seems like, well, like it's okay to use up this planet because we'll just get another.

—Use it up how?

—Overpopulation, pollution, resource depletion . . .

—But Barry, overpopulation isn't a problem. When you increase the population you get more scientists, hence more solutions.

—Yeah Barry, going into space is all about environments, life support, terraforming. I mean, it's going to happen, so let's get good at it.

—anyway the carrying capacity of the planet

—Planet's here to be used, isn't it?

—anyway we won't be able to get everyone off the planet, we can't afford it. So who decides

—Most people are just excess baggage, that's what Hume thought.

—anyway why do we have to transport bodies? The important thing about humans is their intelligence, not their meat packages. You can move that software to a more durable chassis. See that's what I want, backups, copies of myself, lots of instantiations, dozens of little Nate-daemons surfing the Net and doing science.

—Hey, if my instantiation can't go climbing I don't want it.

—Yeah but see your daemon could be doing physics while you're climbing, and if you had an accident it could keep on doing physics

—Hey Barry could be the first posthumous Nobel Prize winner. Or hey Barry, network your daemon to one of those Virtual Wilderness systems, let it solo the Eiger while you're

—don't want to knock human beings too much, but should we restrict ourselves to human intelligence? I have no special loyalty to DNA.

—If a person is the pattern of their thought, you can record and store that pattern. You could raise the dead. Resurrect Newton from the thoughts recorded in his works.

—A composer friend of mine is doing exactly that. Creating new works by dead European white males. Beethoven's Tenth and so forth.

—Wow, I'd like to talk to him.

—I can make that happen.

—But who decides who's to be resurrected? You think we have an overpopulation problem now

—Bigger hard disks! Memory's cheaper every day.

—Well, the ones who haven't contributed, who've left no trace, there's nothing to resurrect . . .

Logs burned to embers, confirming time's arrow even as Tom was saying, —Time machines are easy, you just spin ultradense matter until the continuum uncurves

—no but the matter you spin has to be infinitely long

—anyway once you have a working time machine you could

—Leo, it's gettin time.

—Okay, Dan, I'll wrap it up. Why did I want to hear this stuff? I wanted to hear it because we deal in futures. If we're smart enough and our ideas are good enough and we convince enough people to invest their time, their money, their talents, above all their belief, we can bring some of these futures into being. Nothing we've said is really impossible, just difficult and expensive. I look at things from the point of view of some infinitely advanced civilization limited only by the laws of physics, not by lack of time or talent or funding. Only if you think that way do you have a chance of having the ideas that can truly advance civilization. Give you just one instance, Mike, you can use this for your starship. We're close, very close, to breakeven from intertial confinement fusion. We need more funding, better facilities, but it's going to happen. And then there are no limits. Then mankind has all the cheap clean power it wants. And then we go to the stars, Mike. That's what I think.

A lozenge of light flashed across the ceiling, as Root's thick fingers dropped a silver disk in a player for elegiac violins suspended over the hushed growl of cellos and an oboe melody. —Little soundtrack. Could be the last time we get to see that needle jump.

—Last time . . . ?

—A hundred miles east of here in the desert we sometimes engage in highly classified events that cannot be discussed with the unsanctified. But whether or not those events are or aren't happening, you can watch the seismograph, where you might see some effects, which are unclassified.

Grinning, Barry said, —But can we trust the effects? Any sufficiently advanced technology is indistinguishable from a rigged demo.

Highet gave him a sharp look. —Barry, we don't even joke about that.

The needle traced a trembling path of ink on the turning drum. A baritone voice leapt and feinted to stretch the syllables of —Kar . . . frei . . . tags . . . zaub . . . er. Then the needle leapt.

Yes. Spirit is loosed from rock, freed of matter's tyranny. We open a crack through which light blazes, waking the life in every mote. Once more Ahura Mazda, the wise Lord, defeats Ahriman. A world without this radiance at the heart of things would be nulliparous, without man or mind. Yet no life awakes save through human mind and will. In the wakened world, agents of will move and collide, cooperate or battle. The great work of consciousness is to form and direct alliances among the agents in oneself and in others, and so to perfect the world. To protect and nurture this spark in the sea of night.

—This is what it's about, gentlemen. Bringing light into the world. Signing your name on a tongue of fire.

—Man, that's . . .

—What is it, Barry?

—It's, maybe this is a bad time but I feel weird about this. I have kind of a problem with weapons work.

—Oh man . . .

—Come on Barry, give the man a break.

—No, it's okay. Barry, nobody's going to make you work on weapons.

—But to be in a place where

—Listen, for nineteen years Leonardo worked for the Duke of Milan. He was hired to design armaments. He also painted and sculpted. You think he fretted over that? Think the soul can split itself? Think you can have the Last Supper without the Greek fire? The human spirit is fire. No light without heat.

Highet paced to the fireplace and drew back the steel curtain.

—What if you wish away uranium. Set the initial conditions of the big bang so the particle soup's less dense, you don't get fast neutron capture, nothing heavier than bismuth forms. Nothing fissionable. Do you get life in that universe? Do you get intelligence? I don't think so. I think you get cold rocks spinning in a waste.

He picked up a log from the bin and tossed it on the low blaze.

—Reason has to be built, fought for, spread. You think knowledge always advances? For every Leonardo there's a Paracelsus. For every Mendel a Lysenko. Darkness follows our every step.

The log caught flame as air pulled past it and up the flue. He drew shut the curtain. —You have to understand that it's win or die out there. And if your ideas are good, you have a responsibility to put them into the world.

—Barry, said Mike. —I don't like the weapons stuff either. But I want to get to the stars. I don't care whose back I do it on. They can have their bombs if I get a fusion drive out of it.

What he owed these kids. To grind them in the mortar of necessity so that their talent, in the grinding, could emit its radiance.

—Listen to me. We're just vessels. Science is a godly force that works through us. Honor the god wherever it appears, in yourselves, in others. Make friends and be loyal to them. Always stand up and speak your mind. Take up space, because timidity gets no respect, the meek inherit nothing. Make enemies by choice, not by accident. That's my advice to you.

A bitter exaltation entered him, near enough to love for their bright faces admiring not him but what was in him, his joy embittered by the knowledge that he would not be there to see them through. Yet they would come to him, some of them, regardless.

—Yall scat now. Leo and I got to talk. Downstairs there's a game room, a billiard table, some workstations, and the ARIES collection of old tech. If you ever wanted to play Spacewar on a PDP-10 now's your chance.

—Cool! as Root went with them to the stairway. The music had changed to a moody essay in winds and strings. Highet switched it off. When Root returned he carried a green bottle Laphroaig and two glasses. —Bit over the top, weren't you? That honor the god stuff.

—Don't believe in God, Dan?

—You want to be careful feeding that hunger.

—You don't say.

—You're so concerned about rationality. About the light. Upset by Howie Bangerter and his know nothing creationists. But do you know how many of your heroes were washed in the blood of the lamb? The great Joseph Priestley wrote commentary on Revelations. Michael Faraday was a fundamentalist. James Clerk Maxwell wrote out daily prayers.

—You left out Babbage and Newton. Different times, Dan. Protective coloring.

—Thing about God is, he ain't around much, and it's got to be someone looking out for the chickens.

—Don't pour me any of that.

Root poured a glass for himself. —Coyote baptizes the chickens, you know that story?

—Wish you'd lay off the, the down home spunnisms.

—Seems one day Coyote went calling on a hen. He says to her, these chicks of yours, they're fine chicks, but why don't you baptize them? Baptize, she says, what's that? Says Coyote, Baptizing makes them big and strong, you leave it to me, and he takes one chick away. Next day he's back, says, your chick's doing real well, but he's lonely. So Coyote takes another chick and

—eats them all, so what's your point.

Root grinned. —You do lead em on.

—Without a little religion they'll end up jarwipes in D Section. That a Havana?

—It surely is. You want one?

—God no. Just wondered if you're still supporting the corrupt regime.

—Long as they keep rollin these on the thighs of virgins.

—You're a piece of work.

—And how noble in reason. Root turned the cigar slowly in the flame of a match, watching Highet as smoke rose. —How'd it go in LA? How's your mother?

—Dying.

—I'm sorry to hear that.

—What's that supposed to mean?

—Christ, Leo, bite my head off why don't you. Just tryin to be a decent human being.

—Don't strain yourself.

Root studied him. —What happened?

—I'm out, Dan. Out on my ass.

—What?

—If I don't resign, Chase says he'll prosecute.

—Prosecute!

—He won't do it. But they let him say it. They let him say it.

—Who they gone replace you with?

—Quine.

—Quine! The deputy associate. I warned you, Leo.

—They'll regret it. He's a pure fool.

—God looks out for them, I hear.

—I'm glad God's got work.

—Well, what the fuck, they can't do that. They can't raise him up like that. There's a pecking order.

— I gave him the Taliesin report to write, so he's whistleblower of the hour. Every other candidate has deep roots in weapons, in Radiance. Quine looks clean to them, but not too clean since he's been mucking in J Section. Maybe they think he knows where the bodies are buried. From their point of view it's an easy sell, the new broom.

—Chase must have some regents by the balls. Well shit, the governor has to approve it, he's still a Republican. You can fight this, Leo. It ain't right.

—You're the one who said the regents are deserting us, Dan, think the governor's going to second guess them on this?

—Somethin stinks here.

—Chase is putting pressure, I don't know how.

—What about that GAO report? Isn't that auditor fellow Rector a friend? That could change some minds.

—Months, that's months away.

—You can hang tough that long. Did you talk to Bill Venham?

—I asked Venham for help with the regents and he seated me with some schmuck who wants to patent multiplication.

Root smiled. —Stan Flack. What's Bill got to do with him?

—Oh, Bill's got lots of interesting friends. Last I saw he was holding some Russian's dick for him. Some ex-apparatchik trying to sell the line that Uncle Julius was a Sov spy.

—Oppenheimer? He was, he was. Who was this Russian?

—Vassili something. So, what, they suck up to some KGB thug just for a payback? Christ Dan, they reminded me of Stalin and Lysenko.

—Lysenko wasn't so dumb. Got himself a sinecure.

Highet held out a folded page of light green vellum watermarked Cranes Crest Old Money, with ϑoϑσ debossed over small widespaced type Nexus for Optimal Use of Science.

—There's your sinecure.

Root took the letter and read it. —That's a nice offer. You gone take it?

—Sit with a bunch of burnouts writing white papers? How does

Réti stand them, those god damned consultants with their valet thinking?

—NOUS is respectable.

—Used to be, before Venham stocked it with his used scientists his distressed intellectuals his right-thinking gigolos. Man has more money than God, but that's not enough, is it, has to buy a think tank buy a broadcaster that stalkinghorse Eubanks on the radio, you ever listen to him? Ratfucker ought to be selling used cars or slinging insult comedy in a Tahoe lounge, but there he is chatting with good old Bill and the vice president.

—Cut it out, Leo, we owe Bill. Where'd this ranch come from? Think we'd have sold Radiance to the president without him?

—You remember when Venham wanted me to start a section at the Lab for creation science?

Root chuckled. —You coulda spun it to DOE as alternate paradigm research.

Highet's mouth twisted. —Christ, you're shameless. You'll say anything.

—Think your man Leonardo didn't have to hold his gorge every day?

—We're not talking Sforza here. Half these nonecks think the dinosaurs died in the Flood because they couldn't fit on the Ark.

—These are our allies, boy.

—They're thugs, Dan. They're enemies of reason.

—Common cause, Leo. You don't have to share a pew with them.

—Common cause? What cause?

—Power, money, influence. Commonest causes there are. Who gives a shit what they believe?

—You remember when Schott won his Nobel? A year later he was pushing master race eugenics.

—What are you gettin at, Leo?

—Just because you're smart don't think you can't be stupid. Give them an inch and see what they take. Venham and his buds want to shut down DOE now.

—He's just makin a point.

—A *point*? What point, he and his cronies aren't happy with the cost-plus contracting deals they get now?

—The entire DOE budget's what, seven billion? Chump change. Why suck a dry tit? Move the weapons to DoD where they belong, hand over the rest to the private sector. That's their thinkin.

—And you think DoD is that stupid? Don't you remember that the joint chiefs wanted no part of Radiance? Said it would never work, recommended against it?

—But they took the money now didn't they?

—The whole defense industry's ready to implode Dan, you know that.

—Soviet Union imploded. Nice opportunity for some business-men.

—You talking about Vassili? What is he really, KGB or some Mafiya goon?

—I don't ask less I need to know.

—You know, you can keep your business opportunities, Dan, because if all the nuclear programs go to DoD that's the end of the Lab.

—Come on, Leo. The players change, the game goes on. Anyway, since when you got any use for DOE? As I recall they put you into windmill design.

—They did. And I learned how to play them. Learned how to get my people what they need. I'm not going to stand by while these thugs steal that.

—See, this is why we set up Transfinite and Nullpoint, boy. Get ourselves paid even if the feds give it away.

—I owe something to those kids downstairs.

Root snorted, then stood looking into the fire. The hand holding his cigar rested on the mantelpiece. —You want my advice, Leo, you take Réti's cue. Nothin wrong with consulting.

—Think I want to end up like Réti?

—One of the most powerful scientists in the world? I think you do.

—If it's about science, Dan, Réti hasn't done any since the War.

—Well, it hasn't been about science since the War, now has it.

—Then what is it about? What do you get out of it, Dan?

—Me? A good time. Son, there's people out there write fat checks just to scratch an itch. Way you or me want a beer, they want a summer house, a yacht, a nonprofit foundation. A fellow can live pretty good off the fallout. I don't need to own a ranch myself when I got the run of this place.

—Some people call that leeching.

—"Make to yourselves friends of the mammon of unrighteousness; that, when ye fail, they may receive you into everlasting habitations." If it's good enough for Our Lord . . .

—Turning devout, Dan?

—Dammit Leo, it's our moral duty to skin these piggies. Capital's like blood, it's gotta flow. Like Leonardo, we can divert rivers, rivers of gold . . . You remember that German rocket company in Zaire? The launch site on the Luvua River? Didn't you visit me there when you was a postdoc?

—You've told me all about it.

—It was like havin your own damn country. Big as the state of Virginia. Mobutu let us push out ten thousand Bushmen. Up on that plateau, I felt like another King Leopold. I might still be there if that consortium hadn't gone broke. Still, we put a few items into orbit, yes we did.

—That's it, then? Smoke a good cigar, put a few items into orbit . . .

—You think any of us gone win a Nobel Prize? Got something better, we do. Those thugs of yours, to them we're wizards. Nuclear weapons, missile defense, cold fusion . . . just say the magic words, and the vaults open. Oh, the world's a wicked place, Leo, and freedom ain't free. If you want freedom, somebody's got to fuck a rat. So let the thugs do it. While we run free.

—And science? Knowledge?

—You think people want knowledge? Last thing they want. They don't want to know. They want to be saved. And the only salvation . . . is to forget. Without forgetting, there's nothing but loss and regret.

A log fell and fire leapt in the grate. Ash swirled in the updraft. Root gazed as at the apparition of a thing long past hope, then shrugged and drew on his cigar.

—Anyway, what else you gone do? Teach physics at South Bunghole State?

—Maybe I'll disappear. Like the reclusive Devon Null.

Root looked sharply up. —I don't want to hear that. Somebody has to take the heat. That's why you're director, so there's a scapegoat.

A gust swept moaning down the flue, and the fireplace spat sparks against the hanging metal curtain.

—I was bringing in a billion dollars a year, Dan. I thought I was invulnerable. I let my guard down.

—Crap, Leo, you're the most guarded man I know.

—What else could I have done? I went as far as I could without killing Radiance outright. Call it dual use, counterproliferation, stockpile stewardship, just get it off the weapons menu. I'm tired of this shell game.

—Come on, son. Radiance isn't dead. This stuff never dies, cause good soldiers like you and me keep the faith alive during these long winters. Don't give up now. The players change, but the work goes on.

—Does it? I mean shit Dan, what's next, privatized missile defense . . . ?

In the dying firelight Root's face was stone. Woe, like wind in the flue, the merest tongue of a gale, stirred in Highet.

—What does Gate want with those orbiters, Dan?

—Like the man said, he's still lookin for a content provider.

—Shit, that's it, isn't it? Gate doesn't want comm sats. Why, you son of a bitch. Seoul or Pyongyang, which is it?

Root studied his cigar. —Afraid you're out of the loop on that.

—The players change.

—Yes, they do.

—Saw this coming, did you Dan? Made to yourself some friends?

—Take that job at NOUS. We'll do business again.

—But for now you'll work with Quine.

—If he becomes director I got to, don't I.

—I warn you, Dan. Don't do it.

Root looked up from his cigar, incredulity on his features. —You *warn* me?

A pale face appeared in the stairway. —Doctor Highet? Doctor Root? There's something on CNN you should see.

Downstairs the other students watched a missile chased to destruction while the nagging voice of Armand Steradian rode over, —test managers installed a homing beacon on the target to guide the interceptor. Undersecretary Whipple defended the rigged tests on grounds that the deception was part of a so-called special access program devoted to disinformation.

Whipple's haggard face appeared. —At that time there was no obligation to inform Congress. Of course Congress is now being informed of all special access progr

Film of the missile looped again. Into the room's stricken silence Highet said, —Ancient history. DoD ran those tests years ago. He's trying to make this sound like it's our doing.

—series of scandals. The program's centerpiece, the Superbright laser, is under criticism from without and within. An internal review is said to dispute the extravagant claims made by director Leo Hi

—That prick! I should never have talked to him.

—Meanwhile, Laboratory founder and antimissile proponent Aron Réti is in stable condition following a stroke

—Oh my God. Dan—!

—It's news to me.

—perhaps the most controversial physicist of the twentieth

—Come on, dimbulb, tell us the hospital.

—Likely Stanford. Root unfolded a phone.

—financial interest in Transfinite Polygonics, a firm that has profited from technologies developed at the Lab, according to the General Accounting Off

—Did Aron know about that GAO probe, Leo?

—He knew all right, knew it was without merit, but this publicity would have been a blow.

—for CNN this is Armand Steradian

—Fucking vulture, I'll tear his heart out. Change the channel, who else has it, skipping past, —Rottweilers terrorize churchgoers at eleven, to a man holding a microphone before a gate where motley figures wavedsigns FRAUD WASTE STOP NOW as a red sports car SFORZA sped out of frame, —audit found widespread evidence of financial malfeasance and gross incompetence and concluded that the Laboratory can no longer be trusted to police itself, cutting to a full face radiant in sun, dark eyes intense beneath black hair tinged with russet, —Our concern is

—Turn it off. Did you get the hospital?

Root closed his phone. —He's there. Stable. No calls. Visitors two to six tomorrow.

—I'll go see him then.

Root's heavy steps followed Highet upstairs.

—Well, it don't rain but it shitstorms.

—It was bound to break. Almost a relief it has.

—What's this about an internal review?

—Told you, Quine's report. Chase was waving a copy around this morning.

—Where'd he get it? From Quine?

—Quine hasn't got the balls to leak

—Had the balls to write it, didn't he?

The plume still spreading, like the bitter miasma of Root's breath now close on him, the glitter of his eyes.

—You said Quine was under control.

—Who am I, Dan, Rasputin?

—What's wrong with you, boy? Ain't you learned yet? Root's hands squeezed his shoulders. Highet shook them off.

—What, Dan? Learned what? How to stay ahead of every last asshole who wants a piece of me and sell out the ones who don't?

—How to manage your people!

—Who the fuck are *my people*, Dan? Quine? Dietz? Szabo? Venham and Eubanks? Mister Kim? You? I'd really like to know who the fuck *my people* are!

—Take it easy.

—Screw you. I'm going.

—What? Where?

—Tracy.

—What, you mean Transfinite? You crazy? Six hour drive in the snow, you got chains?

—I'll manage.

Root stood. His body moved between Highet and the door, the stub of his cigar held aloft. —What are you up to, Leo?

—Afraid you're *out of the loop* on that Dan, turning for his jacket draped on the wallpeg.

—Hold on, now hold on here.

—Got to get my resumé together, don't I? Chase gets his way Radiance is dead, Gate and Venham get their way everything's for sale to the first bidder, Luz and that woman get their way we're all out on the street with clappers and bells. So I'd better make to myself some friends. Better become a, what did Gate say, a content provider.

—I got private papers there in Tracy.

Highet pulled his jacket on, adjusted the brim of *e=hf*. —I mean, fuck a rat, Dan, I need something to sell like everybody else, need to come out of this with a little *content*. Don't want to end up hosting multimedia conventions or infomercials, don't want to be left behind on Mike's dying planet, do I.

Root's big hands came up. Highet flinched from them, then held his ground. They closed around his head, the thick fingers cradled his skull, thumbs pressed painfully on the hinges of his jaw. Between two fingers the cigar stub smoldered. Smoke and heat brought tears to Highet's eyes.

—Don't trust me Dan?

—Don't you sell me out.

—Is that even possible?

Root's grip tightened. He crooned, —Don't you know that I love you like a son? Like you love those kids?

—Let go of me, Dan. You're an asshole.

Slowly Root smiled. His breath stank. His teeth were yellowed and stained with tobacco. His gums were white and puffy. In the depths of his mouth gold gleamed. —That's right. I'm the asshole that shits on the world. Do you see the god in me? Do you honor it?

—I see it.

—What? What do you see?

—What's in you . . . is in me.

The grip relaxed. Highet stepped back. Root whispered, —Go you forward.

Past Carson City and CHAINS REQUIRED he climbed into cloud, as a voice battled drifts of static, —Lord I knew that thou art a hard man, and flakes fell faster and thicker in the cones of light the car projected as it gained Elev 7120, where the voice returned, —and cast ye the unprofitable servant into outer dark, the road now white in his headlights as he downshifted and skidded sideways, static on the radio like a held breath as he straightened and snow clumped to be swept away by groaning wipers down past Elev 6000 at last to plowed and glistening black streets reflecting the neon glare of casinos and motels, the voice rising urgently out of static, —in mankind's darkest days my friends? God's Word tells us that one generation of believers will never know death, but they will be lifted from the earth in a rapture before the great tribulation, before the end time, before that ghastly epoch of pestilence and famine and the fire and the blood. When the fire falls, where will you be my friends? Will you be lifted from the Earth to meet your Lord and Master Jesus Christ in eternal life, or will you drown in the blood and burn in the flood of the nucular fire and starve with the sinners and the unbelievers in the great tribul, and he punched to a familiar nasal voice —well Terry, I think it makes a statement, converting military technologies for cultural uses. In my Concerto for Horn and Electrified Conductor the artificial intelligence actually composes an accompaniment as the conductor beats off, silencing it as the road dropped into chaparral, and further down the slope cities on the ancient seabed sent their light up to a heaven stained with thinning cloud no longer dampening the highway or the potholed access road to DA-NITE SELF-STOR 24 HRS, behind razorwire and lights stark as low suns on some lunar horizon. He rolled to a stop at a stanchion and punched the keypad 3 1 4 1 6 # for the gate rolling open on an alley between corrugated tin walls dull in the lunar light, until, stilling the car near a scuffed door, he stepped out into the humid stench of chemicals from a nearby slough and the freeway's whine just over a concrete soundwall, above which the sky was a dark void where an unseen jet passed screaming between landfalls.

Upstairs was a warren of corridors. At each turn was a black plastic wedge POISON on the floor, gray pellets in its recesses. At 211 he hefted the padlock in its hasp and inserted a cylindrical key. He threw a switch and a bare bulb in a wire cage came on overhead to light a narrow walkspace between cartons stacked to the ceiling, AR-KIV, STOR-ALL, DESTROY AFTER, BERINGER GREY RIESLING, and hasty scribbles in black marker, ~~Transfinite~~ Nullpoint, ~~Baldur~~ Slingshot, LHH Personal, LHH Papers, DR, HR, boxes seamsplit and overflowing with xeroxes, printouts, books and manuals stuffed into the gaps between them, Rings Fields and Groups, Numerical Methods In Ratfor, How To Sell Your Ideas, Notebooks of Leonardo, on across the floor to a spill of procurement documents, patent applications, source code printouts, spools of data tape, boxes of floppy disks, notebooks, conference proceedings, advisory reports, expired radiation badges, cassettes of Réti's speeches, fundraiser menus (veal marsala, purée of winter roots, braised Belgian endive, 1975 Robert Mondavi Cabernet Sauvignon), minutes of L5 Society meetings, drawings of space stations and railguns, a plan for using subways as civil defense shelters, a plan for using nuclear bombs to dig canals and harbors, a plan for spaceships propelled by fusion bombs, for machines the size of molecules (with and without sex organs), for machines that travel faster than light and machines that travel through time, for psychokinesis and communication with the dead, plans for the endless mortgaging of an untenable present to finance an impossible future, all to answer the night's secret hope, untempered by experience, that morning will bring renewal, though morning has never renewed anything but yesterday's conflict and chaos where it left off.

Light glinted in a recess from the green of Laphroaig, which he grasped, brushing off cobwebs to unscrew the cap, tipping it to his mouth, then resting it among the detritus on the floor as he pulled down boxes one after another to look for a salvation not in forgetting the painful conviction of what one might have been or had meant to be, but in the hard coin of what one has become.

LHH Personal. Record of every accomplishment and debacle. Here was the transcript of the hearing after Geneva. Here was the official reprimand and reassignment, and the letter from Réti that had saved him from dismissal. Here were dossiers on each of his Hertz recruits, and documents from J Section as it grew. Stubs of paychecks at each new salary level. Clippings announcing his directorship. The President's speech of commitment to Radiance. And here, out of order, was the dossier he'd assembled on Quine for the Hertz board during the first days of J Section. Here was the paper that first brought Quine to his attention. A wave/particle experiment with original insights and meticulous design. What Réti had said: —This is first rate. This shows real imagination.

—Oh, you can pick them all right, Highet muttered, pushing aside the opened box to make room for ~~Transfinite~~ Nullpoint. Salvage part of it at least. Throw a bone to the GAO and get Chase off the trail. That hint about shell companies. How much does he know? Come out of it with a clean bill for Transfinite and Nullpoint. All the rest, all the Lab business, the EIS, Credne, the plume, the investigations, can go hang. Leave some surprises for Quine. See how he likes it.

He sat on the floor among the boxes. He found a clean folder and plucking a pen from his pocket wrote on its tongue Transfinite Systems: Technology Transfers. He began to sort pages, the damaging from the damning. Root and his schemes. Supposed to make us all rich. Help our employees. Doing well by doing good. Never should have listened to him. Into the folder went a waiver of commercial rights to a wind turbine design. Never saw a dime from it, the wind power market just died. Back into the chaos of unsorted papers went a transfer of laser technology to a retiring employee represented by Transfinite. That blue-green laser the Navy wanted, we moved it outside the Lab into a spinoff and all we got out of it was an investigation. Réti bought their stock, the Times got wind of it, he didn't speak to me for months. Into the folder went 3D modeling software given to a motor company. Back into outer dark went a computer architecture, developed at the Lab and released to Transfinite, that had made a Hertz kid rich when it was sold back to the Lab by Quick Data Systems, the kid's new employer. Try to help people this is what you get, investigated. No good deed. So it went until the folder was a sheaf, and the level of Laphroaig had dropped by half, and he replaced the pen in his shirt pocket.

First rate. Shows real imagination. Who'd ever said the same of him? He pulled down LHH Papers, the record of his own life in science, the alembic in which all baseness was to be redeemed, all impurity to drop out like precipitate, leaving knowledge pure. Yet it seemed now, as he turned those pages, tipping Laphroaig to his mouth, hemmed in by AR-KIV STOR-ALL DESTROY BY, that these papers, whether they proposed weapons or defenses, fantasies or fixes, no matter how technically sweet their arguments, were all made for trade rather than for truth, were made for the trade in truth.

The rising bile of pity and loathing for the life and work so baldly laid out there before him was arrested by Laser Compression Of Matter For Thermonuclear Fusion. 1974. Réti, Highet, Szabo, Snell. When he was the Lab's newest wunderkind. The old man would drop an idea, a hint, and he'd work all night on it. The whole thing took months. Here it was, boiled down to three pages in Physical Review Letters. He read it through. A certain amount of handwaving, of course. The full paper was twenty pages, but it couldn't be published, too much of the material was classified. What was here was a fan dance for a presumed audience of nonclassified fusion scientists, Soviets, and US funding sources. The full paper was more exigent, and at this remove he could barely follow the reasoning through its pages, but he turned to the crux it had taken him a month to work out. Yes. Light pressure and momentum flux got you just so far. Much higher pressures could be generated by shaped laser pulses, by imploding the fuel sphere and ablating the outer layers like rocket exhaust. Szabo and he had written computer codes to simulate the process. Those cranky old mainframes. The all-night runs of data. The shortcuts and hacks. Tweak and squeak. But they got there. They showed you could start a breakeven thermonuclear burn with only a thousand joules of energy. In theory. It was brilliant. Better than Quine. Not just the science, but the implications. Fusion power. Pure fusion weapons without fission triggers. Best of all, they could build it. The vaults would open to them.

They did. They built it, the world's most powerful laser. But the fusion experiment failed. They rewrote the simulation codes, raised their estimate of the power needed, raised it again, got more funding. The laser program took on its own life, as more and more powerful and expensive machines passed in succession, but by then Highet had moved on, become a group leader, a section chief, was more and more abstracted from the work that had started it all for him.

—Still, some damn clever stuff here, paging faster through the rest of the box, —yes, we put a few items into orbit, rising unsteadily to deal a vicious kick to the lowest box in a stack —fuck! that crumpled it, —a! and brought down the boxes above it, —rat! bursting like a leafstorm across the floor, and knocked him to one bruised knee scooping papers wildly with both arms. —But isn't this what they want? Isn't it? Bridges very strong but light, mortars and bombards and firethrowing engines, cheap lighting, unlimited energy, cure us of certain disagreeable things, of cancer, consumption, and death, but don't inflict vision upon us, give us salvation but not knowledge, magic but not imagination, papers flying around him now like a vortex of bad ideas, of wishful thinking, of aquavitae and aether, of perpetual motion and phlogiston, of N-rays, polywater, and cold fusion, wishes that would not die but returned again and again like Nemesis, reclothed in the style and rhetoric of the day, those palaces of time, space, and power bedizened by cinnabar, jasper, electrum, antimony, radium, uranium, plutonium, cavorite, or carolinium, as for instance Zero Point Quantum Dynamic Energy, The Prospects of Immortality, A Many-Worlds Approach to Physical Law, How To Prevent Proton Decay, Steganography: A Novel Approach To Data Hiding, and fallen across them a dozen musty paperbacks unopened since high school, brittle tea-colored pages broken from their bindings like spilled cards, lurid covers flaking at their edges, The World Set Free, From the Earth to the Moon, The Shape of Things To Come, he bent to read "hitherto Power had come to men by chance, but now there were those Seekers, seeking, seeking among rare and curious and perplexing objects, sometimes finding some odd utilizable thing, sometimes deceiving themselves with fancied discovery, sometimes pretending to find," and again, violently, he scooped through more papers, seeking as if for a last chance to turn back history and take another track, nothing impossible about that, physical law is CPT invariant, no idea how this will pan out, but it doesn't hurt to stake a claim does it, as an itch rose in his throat and nose, —Ah ah *ah*, and a violent sneeze spattered mucus across the cover of Artificial Life, —Shit! fumbling for the inhaler as his eyes filled and streamed, chest heaving with coughs, gradually subsiding until he tipped Laphroaig for the last drops of its aquavitae, its promise of timestop and forgetting, then lurched to vomit the reflux over Inflatable Kevlar Space Station and Perpetual Motion of the Third Kind, and Dark Matter As Projectile Weapon.

He dabbed at the moisture at his chest. On his shirtfront —Damn! a black stain had spread, and he plucked out the pen, flipped it away, its gold point glinting as it spun upwards end over end toward the globe of the light, the tip slipping through the wire cage to penetrate the bulb which with a last flash went dark. He subsided then onto the papers, curling up where enough light yet sifted through a mesh transom to guide his hand to buttons on his watch, sifted and fell across the progress of digits and the beep on his wrist chasing off dream images of the beep from defensive consoles tracking the beep of enemies approaching the beep silenced by his finger on watch, showing 7:00 in segments swallowed inexorably by 7:01 as he sat up coughing in the miasma of dust and ammonia.

—Pull yourself together, he told himself. Mucus and vomit had dried on his swollen face. He wiped at the crust. He set empty Laphroaig into a recess and crumpled to a wad Inflatable, Perpetual, Dark. He opened the neat folder Transfinite and in the cubicle's halflight doublechecked its pages, finding much that tantalized but nothing that damned. At last he closed it and went limping into the gathering predawn, under high harsh lights raking a truck where two men rolled a cart loaded with canisters Dichlorodifluoromethane CFC-12 Freon and looked up in furtive alarm at the yelp from the red sports car SFORZA soon joining the dawn traffic already thickening past sumps and leaching pools and industrial waste ponds, one car among thousands streaming in lines twined like the involute treachery of the heart across flat empty land as infecund as it was interminable, this procession climbing more slowly to where wind whipped past turbines and tore apart the morning fog at Anabase Pass Elev 1835, and far off in the valley below, at the edge of town, diminished by distance, the fortress city of the Lab stood as ever, adumbrating some new frontier.

Descending toward it, Highet opened his phone and arrowed to RECTOR J. —Jeremy? Leo Highet. Hope I'm not calling too early. I have some papers to help you clear up this Transfinite Polygonics business. You free for brunch? Good. Dim sum place in Mountain

View, I'll give you the address.

Sun warm on his face, he lifted sunglasses from the dash, put them on, punched another number, waited, and said, —I'd like to speak to Mister Venham. This is Leo Highet. Yes, he has my number. Yes, he'll know what it's regarding.

Coyote, First Angry, enemy of all law, wanderer, desert mind, outlaw, spoiler, loser, clown, glutton, lecher, thief, cheat, pragmatist, survivor, bricoleur, silver-tongued Taliesin, latterday Leonardo, usurper Sforza, adulterer Lancelot, tell, wily one, by any means, of the man with two hearts, of knowledge and desire safely hidden from each other. Did not Paracelsus command us to falsify and dissimulate so that ignorant men might not look upon our mysteries? Did not the noble da Vinci hide the meaning of his thought by the manner of his script? What man has not two masters, two minds, two hearts? Tell of the man so wounded in himself that he tore his second heart from him and cast it out, naming it the world, and swore to wound it as it had wounded him.

In the valley he turned at Codornic s EXIT NLY, the stale smell of his sweat heavy in the car despite A/C MAX, a chafing under his arms and at his groin, socks stiff on his feet, as he turned past TOW-AWAY NO PARKING to an abrupt stop at ROAD CLOSED UNEVEN ROAD SURFACE where the roadbed dropped six inches to dirt and broken asphalt as further down the road an airhammer chattered in the shadow of an immense shroud NEKROTEK secured by thick ropes around his house, and fumbling for the phone, unfolding it, — Hello! You people were supposed to come and kill some ants for me on Saturday, here it's Monday and my house is tented, what? Highet, H I G, no I can't hold! hello? as the airhammer renewed its assault at a more penetrating pitch and then fell silent, —Yes I'm here, what's. No, not Hite, it's H I G, G as in George . . . no! that's not my first name, it's . . . what? No! It's *ants*, not termites! What do you mean tox . . . A week? I've got to get into my house right now! hello? hel, as workers gathered around the silenced airhammer removing hardhats to peer into the damaged earth, —I'll give you environmental impact you f, the phone splintering in two against the radio which leapt to strident life with, —throw them off the bridge and let them sink or swim! How far longer is this subhuman uncivilized conduct to be tolerated? this cocaphony of, slamming the gearshift into R, then 1, 2, 3, weaving onto the freeway, 4, 5, to —relentless pursuit of the truth which always wills out, stabbing again and again in search of a more congenial reality, which the radio, now locked by its trauma onto one station, declined to provide, as the center span carried him high above the bay and the orotund voice ripened, —Folks, I had a great time. I met the vice president, and on past Data General, Versant, Failure Analysis Associates, tapping brakes at a small black billboard in white Futura italic DISTRACT US FROM WHAT WE KNOW as the voice rolled on, —heh, not running for President, you people can just forget about that, although you know, if I *did* run, I *would* win, Highet muttering, —don't agree with everything he says but he makes some god damned good points, swerving up the offramp where he jammed brakes to join two lanes merging beneath a stand of acacias, rolling the window shut despite his own stink against the yellow blooms tossed in a warm and fragrant breeze, again punching A/C MAX, as the radio informed him, —Something exciting is going on in America's bathrooms, and he unzipped the garment bag with one hand for the electric razor humming against his jaw as he joined the six lane thoroughfare and cut across two lanes of complexity to SOON YET where a black Infiniti pulled past him into the last free parking space, DISABLED PARKING ONLY, its driver setting a blue and white plaque on the dashboard before slamming the door and walking smartly away.

He found an unmarked space near the garbage dumpsters, checked his watch against the savings and loan 10:32 84F 29C, and walked in the richness of his own stink to Open Visa Mastercard Push, pausing in the crowded foyer to flag down an impassive Chinese and press into his hand a folded bill, —Table for two in about ten minutes, going on down a narrow hall past a potted ficus into the men's room where a mirror set upon mauve and avocado tile showed him a face stunned and swollen. Pushing open a stall he lowered the toilet lid and placed his folder and clean shirt on it, removed his jacket and slung it over the open door, noting a deep black stain on the lining, and, turning back to the mirror, seeing its duplicate on his shirt pocket. He stripped off the shirt and the t-shirt with its own copy of the stain, the reek of his unwashed flesh rising, and stuffed both shirts into the trash bin below the empty paper towel dispenser, grabbing from the stall a roll of thin gray toilet paper, banging the tap to release a flow of water that every few seconds pinched off until he banged again, wetting gray wads of paper in the sporadic flow to scrub futilely at the stained flesh over his heart as he pumped the spigot of the soap dispenser yielding nothing, then rubbed his wet hands over its scummed chrome surface as if petitioning a miracle, and with the thin lather thus coaxed laved his face, chest, underarms, holding the tap with one elbow while rinsing with both hands. Toilet paper pilled in his body hair as he scrubbed and patted dry his arms, sides, and torso, its shreds floating in a basin of cloudy gray water. He shook open the folded shirt and pulled it on. The jacket smelled not too bad. He straightened its lapels and ran a wet hand through his thinning and awry hair, turning away from the pools of water on the floor, the wads clogging the basin, the scraps on the mirror, to reenter the dining room where a young man in blue pinstripe stood, scanning the room.

—Jeremy! There you are, offering a wet hand, —Pardon my, some slob messed up the men's room, no towels left. Here's our table, following the impassive Chinese to a corner where at once a cart rolled up.

—Pull up a pew, Jeremy. He'll have two of these and two of these.

—Ah, what's

—These are duck's feet, and this is parchment wrapped chicken.

—Uh . . .

—You'll love them. Now, I brought all the documents I could find relating to Transfinite Polygonics. You're right that Réti holds an interest, but it doesn't amount to much, a few patents about to expire, nothing that ever came to market. Company's been inactive for many years.

—Ah, may I? reaching for the folder. Highet's hand remained on it.

—You know that Doctor Réti's in the hospital?

—I heard something about it.

—I'm on my way to see him. Jeremy, I'm convinced that the publicity of this thing brought on his stroke. He's a gentleman of the old school, he can't stand publicity. Anything you can do to keep this out of the press . . .

—I assure you that I don't talk to reporters, Rector said coolly.

—I'm sure you don't. Ever have duck's feet?

—No, I . . . and while Rector's attention was on the plates, Highet slid the folder across and removed his hand.

—You'll see a couple of items in here that might be poor judgment, but nothing illegal, I think. It's an interesting field, intellectual property. Did you know that in '34 Szilard tried to patent the nuclear chain reaction?

—I'll look at this later, tucking it under the Ohlone Valley Herald open on the table, where Highet read as Rector watched him read, Lab Consultants Charged With Fraud, Audit Reveals Contract Abuses, —You do have your share of troubles. I saw on the news last night

—You know, there's lies, damn lies, and CNN. With these witch hunts going on, I can barely do my job. I'm thinking of resigning. Réti's stroke made me realize, life is too short. We never know. At any moment, and Highet snapped his fingers.

—Yes, well, I understand. Of course these new charges don't bear on my investigation.

—I'm impressed by your thoroughness, Jeremy. By the time this business is over you'll know more about the Lab than I know myself. Have you ever thought about leaving civil service?

—Well, you know, the benefits, the security . . .

—May I ask how much you make?

—Well . . .

—You should look at our job descriptions for management analysts. Salary starts at fifty k. Maybe more for somebody with your experience. We're always looking. We could expedite it, get it done within the month.

—Really? Of course the timing, the appearance of improp

A momentary hush fell on the room, and then a short sharp shock rattled crockery, rippled water in glasses, and set overhead lights swaying. In its wake was a second of silence, and then, outside, car alarms ignited in periodic blasts of horn, sirens ramping up and sweeping down, a buzzing and warbling complexity on the edge of chaos, as conversation tentatively resumed and phones were unfolded and some patrons rose and went out into the lot as Jeremy Rector closely examined a duck's foot, saying, —I'll give your offer some thought.

—Try the parchment wrapped chicken, no, unwrap it first . . .

The work goes on. The great work goes on.

III. STEWARDSHIP

ONE

Beneath the jet, as it dropped like a raptor in a thunder of falling glissandi through low clouds, the line of the bridge divided baywater scuffed by chop and the wakes of sailboats near the far shore, where salt leaching ponds fit one into the next like puzzle pieces of greenstone and jade and cinnabar slipping from sight as the jet closed on whitecaps spraying a verge of crushed rock. Then the sudden blur of runway. The jet touched, bounced, settled, reversed engines with a roar. Quine reached under the seat for his case. When he came up the window framed a view of identical houses on the flanks of brown hills, dissolving the charm of distance into the rude immediacy of the mundane. The jet halted. Eyes shut, Quine waited for the aisle to clear, then stood and reached his suitcase from the overhead. Stale air dispersed as California winter, only slightly cooler and mixed with exhaust, made its tentative way in past Starbucks and Simply Books and NewsPort into the open cavern of a men's room, where Quine surprised in the mirror a pale and distressful face hard to call his own yet undeniably familiar from some other place and time. He set both cases between his feet, held his hands under a tap, splashed his face, turned to an empty towel dispenser.

—Paging American passenger? J? Powers? Please report to the information desk, where a sliding conveyor doubled his walking speed to Ground Transportation -> and through sliding glass doors to the roundabout where BayPorter was cutting off Avis Shuttle before ramming the back of Mount Extreme Vacation Bible School. A white sedan E108637 came forward with Conor leaning across the passenger seat to open the door DEPARTMENT OF ENERGY OFFICIAL USE ONLY.

—Perfect timing, said Conor.

—Sorry to spoil your morning. Quine handed in his larger case and Conor wrestled it over the seat into the back as Quine sat and fumbled for the belt.

—No problemo, jefe. I exist to serve.

A whitegloved policeman waved them around BayPorter and Mount Extreme where a short dark man in a turban and beard gestured and argued with a stolid white man in a black suit and tie.

—You look tired.

—Got up at four to catch the flight.

—Sleep on the plane?

—Not really.

—So how'd it go? Are we still open?

—For a while. The secretary's setting up a task force.

—What do you think that means?

—I really can't say.

Conor's hand moved to the radio for —when there is a clamor across the land, who turns a tin ear? My friends, libberuls may ask for equal time, but I, Tuck Eubanks, *am* equal time

—Conor, do we have to listen to this, this idiot?

—Sorry, jefe. Just trying to get the traffic.

Quine half closed his eyes. Leaving the airport they drove through a maze of construction. Ramps ended in air. Cranes and gantries surrounded concrete pylons crowned with rebar. Through his drowsiness the world came and went harmlessly. Failure Analysis Associates, Informix, Hexcel, Data General, Versant. RAGS2AU. They sped up the approach to the bridge, named after that gospeller who recounted the parable of the talents. A faint smell of burning, remote and dry, as if something beneath the surface of the world smoldered.

Inertia woke him as the car turned. Past Codornic s EXIT NLY, the hills were green at last with the first winter rains, fresh growth vivid almost to tenderness over the blackened memory of last summer's burns, cut by a sudden lattice of steel beams and open floors, the shell of an office building gone up since last he'd looked, extending the hegemony of the former outliers AmeriSuites Efficiency Studios Opening Soon and R G L C N M S M X. Then the Lab lay ahead of them like a city on the plain, some new Atlantis fenced by TRESPASSING LOITERING Forbidden By Law California Penal Code 602. They drove more slowly past the half mile of chainlink and razorwire to the west gate. Conor slowed for the security check, slowed again for the inner checkpoint, and parked at Building 101, dull under sunlight now hazed by high cloud and a wind out of nowhere that cut through Quine's jacket as he opened the car door.

—By the way, your car's in your space.

—Oh, you picked it up, thank you. Did they fix the CD player?

—No, they said you'd have to take it to the installer.

—But the last owner . . . oh, never mind. Thanks for the ride. Listen, can you . . . and a muffled boom from somewhere beyond a chainlink fence CREDNE CONSTRUCTION jolted him, —can you stop by later and take a look at my computer? It's crashing a lot.

—Sure thing, jefe. Around six?

—I'm going to try to leave early. Call me around three.

As he went through the door he caught a glimpse of a figure moving deep in glass, carrying a case, his stride fast yet unbalanced, as if he might at any moment veer in a new direction. Not a calm cell in that body. That baffled fury in his stride. He went through the entranceway in exaggerated haste and preoccupation, past a couple of faces he knew and several he didn't. A poor photo of him appeared each month over the Director's News column in Century 21, but few of the Lab's employees, he hoped, paid enough attention to spot him in the hallways. Still his guard was up until he reached the fifth floor and entered the outer office where an orotund voice declaimed, —these people are nothing but a bunch of plebiscites! and was cut off a moment ahead of his —Dolores would you pl

—Calls from Paul Zalman of aXon Computer, Senator Chase's office, Lynn Hamlin of CANT, and Frank Szabo. Orrin Gate will be a half hour late for his two o'clock. Jeremy Rector wants an appointment. Armand Steradian from PBS wants you to call him. And Doctor Réti wants to see you in his office.

—What, is he here today? I thought he was in, in

—He's back early.

—Well, I don't have time today, Dolores. Tell him, is he here tomorrow?

—No, tomorrow and the next day he's at NOUS. Then next week he's in Washington.

—It'll have to be after that. I'll see Szabo at the meeting. Chase, that was his office?

—That's right.

—Okay thanks, and get me Rector's personnel file, will you? I'll . . . leaving unspoken just what he intended as he passed to the inner office, dropping his suitcase on a bare expanse of carpet between bare walls keeping their distance from a nearly bare desk where he paused to open his case and draw from it a sheaf of papers and a yellow legal pad, pages turned back. The suave startup chord of the computer ushered him into the bathroom where he stood for several seconds with eyes shut, hands on sink, breathing deeply. He turned a tap and let it run, raising his eyes to a face not wholly unfamiliar, but still suspicious and fearful of what it might find there. Opening the mirror, he reached for St. John's Wort Extract, shook out two capsules, filled a cup, swallowed, did the same with Ginkgo Biloba, then shut off the tap. Water stood in the basin inches deep and the drain gurgled once.

At his desk he tapped a computer key, then opened his case, frowning at the papers there. From outside came a din of construction, a tattoo of warning beeps, a wail like lamentation. Quine turned to stare through polarized glass down on earthmovers, any one of which deployed the power of a pharoah and all his slaves, roaring and lurching with a purpose hard to discern over pale rutted terrain, in the middle of which the cab of a crane pivoted slowly, its derrick level with him, a chain reaching from its apex almost to the ground where a thick metal plate swung and rotated as the chain wailed. Workers waved the plate over an excavation in which lay cylindrical tanks stenciled COMPOSIT PLASTEEL CONTAINMENT DO NOT. One side of the plate came to rest against the ground and the wailing ceased. The workers stepped back and the plate dropped to earth with a boom Quine felt in his feet. He yanked a cord and blinds fell rattling, cutting off his view of the pit, the crane, and the mauve and avocado facade of the new building opposite, completed but not yet occupied.

He lifted the phone, punched 0 0 0 1 #, then 1 2 3 4 #, for —You have, twelve, new messages. He listened through them without expression, occasionally making a note on his pad, until reaching the cool contralto of —Philip. It's me. Welcome back. Will I see you tonight? Call me.

Turning to the computer he scanned his e-mail, the trace of a smile on his face giving ground to trepidation at

Date: Wed, 6 Jan 1994 14:51 -0800
To: quine@lucinda.banl.gov
From: sforza@nous.com
Subject: Orrin Gate's CRADA
Delay Gate's CRADA. Orbiters purposed for something other than telecom. Foreign partners. Export control violation.
Highet

Still standing, he paged through his address book, slowing raising the handset to his ear only to hear voices already in converse, —so he says, trust but verify, —oh, his wife's having an affair, tapping the hook for another line and —llo? Who's, tapping once more for —Dolores? Are we having phone problems again? Can you get me an outside line?

—not sure of himself

—won't last long you can be sure

Slamming down the phone, face reddened by something he could barely name, he drew from his case another sheaf of papers, looked at them briefly, pushed them aside and lifted the phone again. He dialed and waited through two rings for —Nexus for Optimal Use of Science. How may I direct your call?

—Leo Highet please.

—May I say who's calling?

—Philip Quine.

—One moment.

He looked at his watch. The wall clock. The papers before him. Staff meeting at noon. Make sure you know everyone's name.

—Doctor Highet is not in his office. Would you like his voicemail?

—No, and he tapped the hook for a new dial tone and touched

MEM 1, turning to face the window, his expression gradually soften-
ing as he waited through four rings.

—This is Lynn Hamlin. I'm not at home right now, but if you'll

He tapped MEM 2 and waited. —You've reached the offices of Citizens Against Nuclear Technology. If you know your party's, punching 303 for —Lynn Hamlin. Is not in her office. Please

He replaced the handset and sat down, scanning the pages before
him. Core competencies of the Laboratory. Our mission in a post-Cold
War. Execute in accordance with best business practices. Matrix management. Successful integration of spirit, marketplace, and politics. He
paused now and then to mark something with a highlighter, staring
past the inscrutable words, as if meaning resided literally between the
lines. He glanced at the computer, and reached to swing the mouse,
causing the speaker to chime as the sailing cursor froze despite his jig-
gling hand.

—Oh for, lifting the phone and pressing 2666 for

— lo?

—Conor? Is that you? This is Philip from my office. Can you hear
me?

—

—Conor I can't hear you, there's something wrong

— 're ving a litt roubl ith th pho

—Can you come up here?

— ca

—Conor? Can you

—

He dropped the phone into its cradle, glanced at his watch, and
swept papers into his case, rushing out past —something called capitalism which has as its divine right something called supply and
demand, his stride down the hall fast yet unbalanced, slowing at a corridor to veer in a new direction up to E-501 WET PAINT where the
door was shut and the knob with all the equanimity of the inanimate
frustrated all his trials, until he saw taped to the wall Staff Meeting In
E-533 and went more quickly down the hall glancing at his watch,
turning left at E-525 full tilt to a corner where he slowed in confusion
at a silver sign E-530 -> which he followed to another turning, slowed

at E-550, turned again, and burst finally into E-533 where a waspish voice, —thought I'd leave it out, fell abruptly silent.

Ten of them at the long table. Deputy and associate directors, group leaders, every one with more seniority than he had. Taking it for granted that he would last a year at most. As he sat he gripped the table. On the underside wood veneer gave way to some rough composite of sawdust and plastic. Frank Szabo sat beside him with a yellow legal pad and a styrofoam box.

—Sorry I'm, didn't know the other room was. How's everyone?

—Morning Phil, came Szabo's waspish voice. —Good flight?

—Frank, would you mind very much calling me Philip . . . what's that?

—This? Szechuan eggplant. Want some?

—No, I just, yes ah David?

—It's awfully cold in here. Is there some reason the air conditioning's on in the middle of winter?

—Frank? Any idea?

Szabo shrugged. —I could call physical plant.

—Would you please?

Again Szabo shrugged, took out a phone and unfolded it.

—Okay. I know you're all curious so I'll get right to it. I met with the secretary. I met with unders and deputies and assistants. You remember Reese Turbot, he was here through ninety-one, he's now under for DP, defense programs, so we have an advocate there. We talked about our mission in a post-cold wa

—Plant says they're having a little trouble.

—Did they say whe

—No ETA.

—Thank you Frank. So I presented all your concerns. I think I put across our ah core competencies. I acknowledged that in light of some ah past problems we need a better management model. I said we're committed to, to executing in accordance with best business practices to serve DOE's customers who are of course the President and the Department of Defense.

—A corporate management model? You really think that works for us?

—Arn, the secretary is setting up a commission. They have a year to write a report on the future of all the government labs. There are corporate people on the commission. The secretary comes from that world. We have to act as if we're listening.

—Are we?

—Yes we are, Bill. Because the alternative could be disastrous. So our immediate mission is, let me just . . . shifting papers on the table before him and trying to focus not on the words or their evaded implications but on the yellow highlighter marks, —"to assure the safety and reliability of the nuclear weapons stockpile in the absence of underground testing".

—Absence of testing?

—The upcoming series of fifteen tests is canceled.

—Canceled? And you went along with this, Phil?

—It wasn't up for discussion, Frank.

—But Phil, you're supposed to look out for our interests. You're supposed to make it a discussion.

—She'd already talked to the joint chiefs. They agreed the series was unnecessary. The administration wants a comprehensive test ban treaty. Talks start in Geneva this month, and testing would jeopardize that.

—We employ three thousand people out at Aguas Secas.

—Nobody wants to close the site. Subcritical tests are still on the menu, pending the treaty.

—Give up testing, I do not believe this.

—Frank, we're already not testing.

—When Leo was here

—Leo's not here.

—No, he sure isn't.

—You don't understand the situation. You should see the bills being introduced in Congress. Cut our workforce by one third. Close us down entirely. Eliminate the Department of Energy.

—All of that is such pardon me Phil bullshit. Do the rest of you remember the video DOE sent when that ditz was appointed? What she said? "The most important challenge facing the Lab in the coming decade is diversity." Ten thousand nukes loose in the former Soviet

Union, proliferation in rogue states around the globe, decaying warheads in our stockpile, but first things first: hire more Hispanics.

—Well what do you expect she used to be a utility exec

—Okay, now look

—take anything she says seriou

—ever get a real scientist in that office

—canceled that test series just before Leo left, you know her reason
then? "I can't explain this to my grandmother."

—Okay, look everyone, can we get back on tra

—guess now we're in the elder care business

—All right! Let's cut the, cut to the, I mean we've got a lot to do
here.

—My point, Phil, is that our destiny is in our own hands, and these
proposals from these out of touch jerkoffs don't mean squat.

—I'm telling you what we have to work with. They understand the
difficulty of doing this without testing.

—Do they understand the difficulty of ceritfying new designs
without testing?

—There are to be no new designs.

—Well, blow me.

—That's the official ah position, no new designs unless, let me see,
supreme national interest

—Oh, okay, you had me worried for a minute.

—What do you mean?

—Supreme national interest means this statement is operative
until it's not.

—So Frank, you're saying that DOE is holding open an option to
design new weapons, and any assertion to the contrary is just public
information.

—I thought you talked to Reese.

—He told me no new weapons.

—Not the same thing as no new designs. Okay, so we can't test.
What can we do?

—Anything short of a chain reaction. Subcritcal burns. Hydronuclear tests. Henry?

—There's some debate whether those will be allowed under the

proposed treaty. Some countries are insisting on a zero-yield defini-
tion. They say anything using nuclear materials is a nuclear test.

—Well, that's just foolish. No way we're giving up hydronuclear.

—Frank, please . . . I think that's a matter for the treaty negotiators.

—The hell it is.

—Just what does that mean, "safety and reliability"?

Again his eyes sought highlighter marks as he paged forward to,
—"assurance that the primary will achieve ninety percent of its
design yield, and ah predict with high certainty the behavior of full
weapons systems in complex accident scenarios."

—And how are we supposed to assure and predict if we can't blow
things up?

—That's our job, Arn. Find a way. What's on the table is something
called science-based stockpile stewardship.

—As opposed to what, theology-based stewardship?

—Frank . . .

—Phil, do these morons even know what the fuck they're talking
about? When Leo was here

—All right, Frank, that's really enough, we can do without the, the
Leonid meteor shower.

—Just trying to help us out here, Phil. Somebody should.

—The other approach as you all probably know is engineering
based. Meaning, turned by a loud squeak from the styrofoam box as
Szabo sawed at its contents with a white plastic fork and knife.

—Low blood sugar. Go on, I'm listening.

—I wish you'd

—Do I have to file an environmental impact statement to eat
lunch?

—Just do it quietly. Meaning we just remanufacture decaying warheads. So that's an option. Dave?

—Well, we already do that. But we can't keep doing it indefinitely.
Too much of this stuff is only in people's heads. What we've got now
is highly skilled physicists working as librarians, just documenting
what they did years ago.

—This wasn't documented at the time? Bombs were built without
plans?

—No no, of course there are plans, but, but, you never worked directly in weapons, did you, Doctor Quine?

—J Section.

—Yes well, let me ah try to explain. You can dismantle two devices of the exact same mark and rev but with different serial numbers, and the insides differ. I don't mean the physics package, although sometimes you have differences there too, but just, you know, the glue, the hardware, there are thousands of parts and when a part becomes unavailable you substitute, so even if we had complete plans, some subcontractors are gone, some parts or processes are unavailable. The only way to do it, really, is to have people around who know how to do it, not just technicians who can follow plans. I mean, pardon me Bernd, I have the greatest respect for technicians, but the design and construction of these things is really very intricate indeed. And we do periodically upgrade a design, make a new rev, and that requires a good deal more than, than remanufacturing skills.

—And anyway, as Dave says, we do that already, remanufacturing gets us nothing new.

—Yes okay so to maintain core competencies . . .

—Well, we have to keep people interested. Attract new people. In other words, base it in science, not engineering.

—Henry?

—I agree, but our first priority should be archiving and knowledge capture activities.

—You mean talk to the old guys.

—Well yes Frank, exactly, our knowledge base is aging, we have to archive and capture before all our designers retire.

—Talk about your elder care . . .

—But for the long term, on an ongoing basis, we need to attract a new generation of ah stewards if we're to ah maintain core competency.

—Dave, in your opinion does "core competency" include the ability to design new weapons?

—Well, of course if you've truly got the ability to ah steward in the full sense that would include that ability, yes.

—How does that square with the department's public information?

—Well, having the ability doesn't necessarily mean using it. I personally separate the act of designing a new weapon from physically building it. I advocate maintaining the capability to design by exercising it, not by cutting new metal.

—Yes Frank?

—How the hell do we attract good people if all we have is maintenance and cleanup? Wanted, nuclear janitors, I don't think so.

—Well, that's where Avalon comes in, said Ware, spreading his hands.

—Avalon will attract new talent?

—The most powerful laser in the world? Oh, I think so. That's a draw.

Szabo's plastic knife squeaked against the styrofoam. Held aloft on his fork was a limp spear of eggplant. —So this is the deal? We give up testing and we get Avalon?

—Not in so many words, but that seems to be what's on the table, said Quine.

—But they're committed to Avalon anyway, aren't they? I mean key decision zero went through . . .

Quine looked again for highlighting. —"Approval of Mission Need", yes, but key decision one is the important step. That approves the baseline budget and the site.

—You know, this thing is going to get built one way or another. Since the SSC was canceled, DOE needs a long term big ticket project to keep their budget up and we deserve to have it.

—The SS, I'm sorry, Bill, I'm not up on

—The superconducting supercollider? The scientists thought they could find the Higgs, the managers thought they could write off Texas style parties. They got defunded after digging a two billion dollar ditch outside Austin.

—Doctor Quine, I agree with Bill. You may not realize it, but we've pushed for Avalon for years now. The participating ICF labs signed on last year.

—ICF, that's inertial confinement fusion, Phil.

—Thanks very much, Frank, I know what it is.

—Bill, you laser guys have wanted Avalon for years, but why should I care? What does the weapons side get out of this?

—You get to go on living, Frank.

—Oh, that's cold, Bill.

—Come on Frank, remember what Leo used to say, always think dual use. You get high energy densities, radiation flow, hydrodynamics, equation of state, opacity, and even something that should interest you Doctor Quine, x-ray las

—Listen you know, I'd like to stop using that phrase, dual use. How about benefit? Can we start saying dual benefit?

—Jesus, Phil, if it's such a problem for you, we can call it dueling banjos.

—Anyway my point is, Frank, this machine is great for weapons science.

—Except that if we sign on, testing's gone for good.

—Frank, have you been listening? Testing's gone anyway.

—It's a huge mistake to accept that. We can outlast this administration. We should hold our ground.

—We heard you Frank, said Quine.

Szabo turned his attention to Szechuan eggplant, white plastic knife squeaking.

—All right then. The secretary wants a full conceptual design report. If you'll look at these sheets, as the room's stasis was broken by the creak of chairs, rustle of papers being passed, of bodies leaning forward.

—Jesus.

—All this by May?

—That's the time frame. Let's look at, at what else do we need for this program. Marshall?

—Computer simulations. A sort of numerical test site.

—Simulations never capture all the details you need. This is how we got into so much trouble with Superbright, if you'll recall.

—Not the same thing, you were trying to model something that didn't exist yet, but we've got data from actual shots to test our models against. Over a thousand tests, going back forty years. If we can't shoot off new stuff we can look at the old tests again. Archive and reinterpret.

—Are we calling this science? Sifting through our archives?

—Frank . . .

—Also faster computers. I mean much faster. I mean teraflops. If not petaflops. The great dome of Marshall Mosfet's bald head inclined to a pad. —We're talking at least a three times ten to the seventh problem with some portions running for more than ten to the fifth cycles. Even with optimization, simulations will require say hundred teraflop computing speeds and tens of terabytes of memory. We're looking at arbitrary Lagrangian-Eulerian and adaptive refinement meshes. We're looking at end-to-end first-principles simulation capabilities based on high resolution adaptive numerical methods. We're looking at massively parallel architectures. Full-system full-physics 3-D simulations validated using AGEX facilities and past underground test data. We're talking scalability. Figure we'll need to increase everything by a factor of ten by the time we're done. The bald head came up and the gleam in Mosfet's eye seemed to follow teraflops and petaflops up into some cybernetic empyrean. —We've been talking to aXon about prototyping. They already supply workstations to the physics groups.

—Still with us, Phil?

—Sure I, just a little jet lagged. So is this all possible?

—Just give us the funding . . . the funding which, as the politician once remarked about a few billion here and a few billion there, started to look, with the addition of each new ballpark figure on the whiteboard, like real money, a reality it generously extended on credit to the still-prospective program names alongside the figures: Avalon Laser Facility $1.1B, DARHT Dual Axis Radiographic Hydrodynamic Test Facility $120M, ADAPT Advanced Production and Design Technology Program, ASCI Advanced Strategic Computing Initiative $122M, APPF Atlas Pulsed Power Facility $43M, AHF Advanced Hydrotest Facility $422M, MESA Microsystems Engineering and Sciences Application $400M, HEAF High-Explosives Applications Facility $45M, FXR Flash X-Ray linear induction accelerator $85M, CFF Contained Firing Facility $48M, ARS Advanced Radiation Source $240M, ECF Explosive Components Facility $28M, BEEF Big Explosives Experimental Facility, all with —goals and milestones, start drawing them up, stifling a yawn. —Okay? Anything else? Are we done? Yes Arn?

—We're rushing to get the sensors ready for the Persephone shot.

—Shot? There are no tests . . .

—Moon shot, Phil. A joint NASA-DoD project. We're supplying the instrumentation and guidance.

—Oh, that. I just hadn't heard the, the name.

—It's on the cover of this month's Century 21, Phil. Somebody wrote a Director's News column about it under your name.

—Yes all right, I know the project, I just don't have time to, to keep up with all the cute names.

—Your ah column has it entering lunar orbit in early February. It'll actually be March.

—Four weeks from launch to lunar orbit? Why so long?

—It'll be in earth orbit for a while.

—Doing what?

—I ah, I don't think everyone here needs to know that. Also, there's an added leg after the moon, a rendezvous with a near-earth asteroid . . .

—And?

—Just want you to be clear on the entire mission.

—Okay, now are we . . . ? when a sudden dampness on his thigh drew his eyes down to a dark stain spreading from a drip off the edge of the table where black tamari had pooled under Szabo's styrofoam.

—Frank . . .

Szabo followed Quine's gaze, and the practiced annoyance on his features flickered into genuine chagrin for a moment before he pushed the box aside and stabbed at the pool with a napkin. —God, I'm sorry Philip. I must have cut through the, I'm terribly sorry, I'll pay for the cleaning . . .

—It's okay, Frank. Look, why don't we call it a, yes Glenn?

—We do have one little problem I'd like to bring up. This ah crackpot group, CANT, they're suing us. They claim we didn't list new construction on an EIS and that we're hiding waste disposal information related to the site.

Quine looked guardedly around the room, where only blank masks looked back.

—Yes Glenn, I think I know what that's about. Counsel's already on it. Bring what you have to my office. Oh, ah, while I've got you all, is anyone else having trouble with their phones?

—Phone fax ethernet you name it, they're pulling new cable, supposed to give us T3 lines in every office but meanwhile it's a mess, I'm getting other people's voicemail and I don't know what.

—Frank?

Szabo looked up from folding the soiled napkin to say, —Afraid there's no helping it, we're upgrading all the lines because of the network integration, secure wide bandwidth fiber optics, bound to be some growing pains.

—Okay, are we, are we done? See you all la . . . while at the back of the room behind the rising figures a door opened as Quine glanced up to see —Dennis, is that you? I thought you were on leave.

—Entrepreneurial leave of absence, yes, but see I'm working on something, and I wanted to show y

—Dennis, this meeting is for section heads onl

—I know, that's why I thought you should all have a look at this, see I was visiting CERN in Geneva where this guy Tim Berners-Lee came up with some really neat stu

—Look Dennis, we're fin

—sort of hypertext plus pictures, calls it the World Wide W

—Aren't they doing this at SLAC? Converting their high-energy physics database. Weenies.

—Well see I thought we might want to get involved at some level, I brought my laptop so I could show anyone who

—I'll have a look, Dennis, said Szabo. —Let these other machers get on with their day, as some drifted out into the hall, muttering, —going to get criticism that Avalon has weapons applications, —well of course it has weapons applications, who are we, General Foods? —good thing it's a construction project, always good for the local economy, probably get the support of the Herald, —geez, we always get the Herald, editor's son works here for Chr, —except when he's been talking to that CANT group and he forgets which side his

—Is that a supertwist display?

—Okay you all, I'm

—Just so we don't waste a lot of time here, Dennis, believe it or not we've heard of the World Wide Web.

—Oh, good, so you see the commercial potential.

—Commercial . . . ?

—This is called a brows

—That's Mosaic.

—Oh you know about it.

—NCSA.

—Right, National Center for Supercomputing, this guy there Marc Andreesen showed it to me, see you can, as HTML ERROR 404 FILE NOT FOUND appeared, —oops, let me just, as the screen filled very slowly, top to bottom, one line at a time, with a profile of carrot red hair, a young woman's arched brow and sultry eye.

—See they're letting Andreesen take the code and turn it into a commercial product, he's looking for investo

—How many megs RAM you got?

—Why the hell would anybody want to sit around waiting for pictures over some crappy twenty-four hundred baud modem

—Depends on the pictures doesn't it, as the young woman's snub nose fell fetchingly to a suggestion of rosy pursed lips just beginning to appear.

—Ninety-six hundred is here, fourteen four is just around the corner and eventually

—eventually we'll all

—commercial? I don't think

—But see if you could browse a catalog and just click on items you want to buy

—And this would be for who, people who find mail order too challenging?

—What's she sucking on?

—Ah, these are some graphics files from a Lab machine, the sparta node

—Jesus Christ, that's gotta be nine inches long.

Kihara's face flushed as he stabbed at ESC, —Um, let me just, system's a little slow responding, let's go to another

—thought we purged those files months ago

—Got to hand it to you Dennis, you give good demo.

—Okay, everyone, I'm go

—What's this now?

—Wow, right between the

—This one from our digital mammography program?

—Sorry sorry, I don't know where these came from but anyway you get the ide

—Hey Dennis can I try? In a moment the screen blanked to collective groans while below the windowbar ANDREW'S OFFICE a vacant room slowly accreted, fluorescent lights, file cabinet, wall posters, computer, chair. —This is live from my friend's office at CERN, he's got a slowscan camera hooked up to his computer, updates the image every two minutes. Is this cool or what?

—Okay every

—Wait, slowscan . . . Kihara poked at a device in his palm with a stylus the size of a golf pencil. —What's his URL?

—everyone, I'm going. See you . . . as no head turned to follow Quine out the door and into the hallway where the machers had dispersed leaving the way to his office clear except for —Bran! Have you got a minute? Walk with me, and Nolan, haggard, fell in step. Past the open doorways where countless managers sat bemused by their computers and past a conference room where a point made too emphatically sent a dry marker skating out across the hallway.

—Philip. Check your e-mail today? Our sister lab in New Mexico is offering five hundred dollars each for the internal organs of workers like ourselves. After one's demise, of course. The tissue analysis group studies them for radiation effects. They have quite a collection. Some of Karen Silkwood's bones, relics worthy of pilgrimage. No premium for management organs, I'm afraid. Have you heard the one about the dean's brain?

—Bran, is it common knowledge that you're ghosting the Director's News column for me?

—If anyone thinks about it at all I think it's naturally assumed that you have more important things to do.

—Szabo needled me about it.

—Szabo needles everyone. How was the meeting?

—Well, apart from Szabo interrup

—No, I mean Washington.

—Washington? Oh. We met in the SCIF, you know what that is?

—Sensitive Compartmented Information Facility, we've got one. Basement room with no windows, EM shielding in the walls. And what did you come up with down in the bunker? If I may ask?

—Science-based stockpile stewardship.

—Difficile est non satirum scribere.

—What . . . ?

—Who came up with that lovely word stewardship?

—The secretary. I think she got it from some management consult-ant.

—What happened to your pants leg?

—What? Oh, it's just a, a spill, I should . . . but his intent went unstated as they came into range of an orotund voice raised in raptur-ous self-appraisal, —President Eubanks, it just has a nice alliteration to it doesn't it? and —Dolores? Please . . . as the voice faded complete-ly behind the closing door.

—Guy's running for Congress, did you know that?

—What guy?

—On the radio.

Quine came out of the bathroom dabbing at his pants with a hand towel discolored by tamari. —Glenn Boniface brought up something we need to look at, lawsuit from CANT, something about an EIS?

—How much do you know about that?

—Nothing, really. We should go over it but I don't have time now. Tomorrow?

—I'll check with Dolores.

—Thanks Bran, as the phone rang, —Yes? Already? Okay, just a min, covering the mouthpiece, —See you tomorrow, to Nolan's nod and exit, passed on his way out by a cleancut younger man on his way in, suited coiffed and dentifriced to a standard somewhat higher than the lab mean as Quine came around the desk towel still in his hand.

—Orrin Gate.

—Right, pleased to, excuse me, my hand's wet, let me

—I'm very glad to meet you, Doctor Quine.

—just get some things together, opening then shutting his case, opening then shutting one drawer and another, —here, sorry about this, just back from Washington, a little disorganized . . .

—Take your time. Did you get the phone I sent? The account is activated, just go ahead and use it.

—Yes well, it's not something I really need.

—You'll come to rely on it. I promise you, five years from now everyone will have one. Moms, dads, kids, one in every car.

—You're interested in our orbiters, said Quine.

—Our satellites need a low earth orbit for minimum latency time. We're thinking of a constellation of a few hundred, though that may change.

—The problem here is that this CRADA basically asks for access to subsystems of our Slingshot antimissile interceptors, which is a classified project.

—Doctor Highet assured me that it fell under dual use. You can put in place any firewalls you need to.

—We're calling it dual benefit now. The Slingshot thrusters, why are those of interest?

—Low earth orbits tend to decay quickly. My understanding is that these thrusters permit stable orbits for a longer time frame.

—Can I ask what this means, in ah Appendix A, the Statement of Work, "to establish the optimal topologies of a reconfigurable constellation of low earth orbit satellites under a variety of conditions"

—Because of latency and bandwidth issues we may need to fine tune the constellation once it's in place. You see

—You want to put satellites in orbit and then move them around? I've never heard of that.

—It gives us flexibility our competitors lack.

—And these are civilian comm sats.

—Civilian, military, possibly both.

—You don't know?

—At this point in time, we're not sure what our content will look like. A constellation of satellites might have to be reconfigured quickly to take advantage of rapidly changing markets. We need to maintain fluence and modularity. We need to handle multiple channel rates, protocols, and service priorities and to support a wide range of applications including the Internet, intranets, multimedia communication,

LAN interconnect, colocation, wireless backhaul, et cetera. Many of the applications and protocols we'll serve in the future haven't been conceived yet.

—Well in that case how can you, I mean, that's not the business plan I read.

—Well, no, what you have must be half a year old. And I must say, this slowness is discouraging and costly.

—Yes well, I have to run this by the book.

—At other labs, I understand, NASA labs for instance, directors can approve CRADAs directly.

—Yes, that's true of the GOGO labs but we're a GOCO

—Contractor operated, yes, but NASA labs are GOGO. Now this Slingshot technology is being used on an upcoming joint NASA-DoD mission, lunar mapping, is that right?

—Where did you get that information?

—Aviation Week. I was hoping to gain access to the thruster performance data from that mission. And the sensor performance data.

—The sensors? Why?

—As I say, our content is still fluent. Weather, environmental tracking, surveillance, all are possible missions for these platforms.

—Look, this is extremely broad. We can't share classified DoD data.

—Well, of course the data would be reviewed by DOE and DoD before we shared it with our strategic partners.

—Partners. What partners.

—If the CRADA were in effect and you were properly nondisclosed I'd be more willing to share that information.

—Are your partners defense contractors?

—No, at least not for the US.

—Not for the US? They're foreign partners?

—One is.

—Then we can't possibly share this data. It raises all sorts of, of export control issues. Anyway, you see here, where is it, here, Article 22, "US Competitiveness, products embodying intellectual property developed under this CRADA shall be substantially manufactured in the United States."

—I think I see the problem. This is about Mister Kim, isn't it? Doctor Highet was suspicious of him. Mister Kim is head of the aerospace division at Hyundai. If all goes well they'll be assembling the sats for us. I tell you this in strict confidence.

—These platforms were designed to be kinetic kill vehicles. You're not interested in that part of their mission?

Gate stared at him for a moment, then laughed. —Well that's . . . Was that Doctor Highet's idea? But then, he's known for his flamboyant imagination. No, we just want maneuverable, low orbit platforms.

—What you want them for seems ah fluent.

—Doctor Quine, I'm a visionary. In my industry you have to be. That doesn't mean I have a single vision, I have many visions, constantly adjusting to the market. I thrive on chaos. When other people run in fear, I see an opportunity.

Quine touched a throb in his temple and shut his eyes while outside some engine unseen went on with its building, then he refocused on the pages before him.

—How do you plan to launch these?

—We're inviting bids from international launch providers including the US, Russia, China, and Korea. Candidate rockets include the Atlas, the Proton, the Long March, the No Dong . . .

—No Dong? Isn't that a North Korean missile?

—I've talked to Senator Chase about this, and he's eager to move things along. I really need to expedite this before the Persephone launch.

—That's in two weeks.

—That's why I'm here. Can we go forward?

Quine stood and extended his hand. —I'll be in touch.

—Seriously, Doctor Quine.

—I'll review this material with the Slingshot team and let you know.

—Let me know when?

—When we're done.

Gate leaned slightly forward and clasped Quine's hand briefly. —Thanks for your time.

In the vacant office Quine glanced at his watch, then the wall clock, then lifted the phone to hear a waspish voice, —terrible administrator, lost control of the meeting, and replaced the handset, face burning, the heat diffusing into a kind of despair as he stuffed papers into his case and snapped it shut.

—Dolores? He stepped into the outer office where, —no no no, heh heh heh, a bully pulpit is not a pulpit used by a, as Dolores stilled the radio and looked up. —Is this, is this guy ever off the air?

—Sacramento reruns the show three hours later.

—Okay look, I'm leaving early. I had almost no sleep and, and, what?

—Your appointment with Jeremy Rector?

—Oh Jesus. Can you, oh never mind, let's get it over with, and he retreated to the inner office, where the noise of jackhammers rode over the din of some compressor as he went into the bathroom for Naproxen 220 mg and saw as he turned the tap an inch of water still standing in the sink. He swallowed the tablets, then jiggled the drain lever repeatedly until a few small bubbles emerged and the water slurped away. He sat at the desk and opened a folder Jeremy Rector Principal Management Analyst, and frowned at the vitae inside for a minute before slapping it shut. The jackhammers fell silent.

Rector entered, clothed in a brown wool suit, swinging a calfskin case.

—Jeremy, sit down.

—Thank you Doctor Quine, as the calfskin case clicked open with a snap and a stack of folders came out onto the desk.

—Can we, before we start, I've been looking at your vitae . . .

—Oh, is there a problem?

—No but, I mean, you came here straight from the General Accounting Office, is that right?

—Yes, I was looking for a change.

—Highet hired you?

—No, it was after he left.

—But you talked to him at some point?

—We, ah, had a discussion, yes, brief, informal. Why?

—Because it seems, I mean, Highet is implicated in some of these investigations, it could appear improper that you were hired at a time when . . .

—I went over this with Lab counsel. You know, IRS agents sometimes go into private practice, you can hire them to represent you if you're audited. To me this is similar, an audit just goes easier if you have someone who knows the ropes, who can clarify issues for the auditors. I think Doctor Highet understood that, he certainly never said I was supposed to, well, cover anything up.

—No no I'm not suggesting, just want to, to clarify . . .

—What?

—Well, my position. That I'm not condoning anything but full cooperation in any ongoing investigations.

—Of course.

—Then if we can, I want to look at this buffer zone business.

Rector opened a folder. —Right. Well, it seems that the toxics mitigation pilot program, Site Alpha, you know, the vineyard over the toxic plume, needs to be expanded.

—Expanded? Why?

—Well, the plume is spreading offsite. The expansion brings it onsite again. Anyway, some people in E Section got wind of this, recommended it actually, and they bought land in the expansion zone.

—They thought they could make a profit selling the land back to the Lab? But that's, what's wrong with these people, don't we pay them enough, that they have to pull this crap?

—I think we can convince GAO to drop the investigation if the people involved make restitution.

—Is that enough?

—If you want to reprimand them in some way, that's your choice. But in the interests of the Lab's ongoing situation, I'd say settle it and move on. Now we have the missing property and the unassigned overhead costs . . . as Rector shifted the first folder to the bottom of his stack revealing the next, one inch thick.

—Look, Jeremy, I'm sorry, but is this urgent? I mean twenty-four hour urgent?

—Well, no, I mean we have months to respond, but there's a lot to get through and I thought

—I know, I just, I'm just kind of jet lagged and I can't really concentrate, so if you don't mind . . .

—Fine, and the calfskin case clicked together with the chirm of the phone.

—Hello?

—Enjoy your weekend, Doctor Quine.

— jefe?

—Conor? Is that you?

— old me to cal

—Conor, I can't, the phones are still, can you hear me?

— ay?

—Look I, if you can hear me, I, I, let's not meet today, I'm going to leave early. Okay? Okay?

— k

He dropped the handset on the cradle, muttered and swept papers into his case, latched it, and strode into the outer office where —a grass roots bottoms up effort, was suppressed as he entered.

—Okay Dolores, I'm

—Doctor Réti is on his way up.

—Christ! Didn't I tell you, as a knock sounded. His eyes darted around the room for an escape he knew wasn't there from the inevitable he'd been putting off for months by cautious scheduling.

Morose, limping, Réti entered. He bore a gnarled staff taller than himself, and the expression of a man who'd spent too much time with fools.

—Doctor Réti, it's, it's good to see you. Come, come in . . . and Quine led the way into the inner office as Réti glanced dispassionately around the room.

—So. How is our young director getting on?

—Not so young. Forty.

—Before I was forty, we had dropped atomic bombs on Hiroshima and Nagasaki. Just a few years later, I argued to build a laboratory, this one, to learn everything we could learn about nuclear weapons. So you are right. Forty is not so young. And now, almost half a century after the first bombs, we go on learning.

Quine said nothing. Réti stared past him at the drawn blinds, beyond which a jackhammer opened fire.

—May I sit? Réti gestured at a chair.

—Forgive me, of course, please.

Réti limped slowly to the chair and lowered himself into it. The staff leaned against it like a limb of Yggdrasil. —But that history is not important now. What is important now is to keep the Radiance program alive.

—Doctor Réti, the administration and the Department of Energy have decided that our work on Radiance is over.

Réti pointed at him. —This important knowledge, for which you and so many others fought so hard, must not be lost.

—The knowledge gained was not, in my view, primarily scientific.

—You do not yet understand, there are ways to keep programs alive, to reorganize their component parts. I will tell you how.

—Yes, but

The pointing finger raised. —One moment. Many years ago, when I was for one semester a visiting professor at your university, and on your doctoral committee, I read your dissertation and I thought, here is a young man who understands physics. And when your paper on quanta was published with Sorokin, I knew that it was so. I lobbied strongly that you should have a Heinrich Hertz fellowship to come here. And you did excellent work. Now you are director, a rise of meteoric speed, and I wish to put at your disposal some of my experience.

—You flatter me. My understanding of physics is not that deep. And the work I did on Radiance was deeply flawed. It led to a scandal.

—The work is not flawed. The scandal is in the political necessities.

—Doctor Réti, perhaps you forget. I worked on the Superbright x-ray laser for years. It didn't work and we pretended it did. And we suffered the consequences.

—May I remind you that despite your own highly critical, one might almost say self-lacerating report, our entire team was exonerated by the General Accounting Office. The idea is still a good one. And that is why we must proceed with it on different terms. Now listen to me. I will tell you what we must do.

—Sir, with all due respect. I am director, and I am responsible to the Department of Energy. It is my decision.

Réti's brows came together. He breathed heavily. —You are not like Highet.

—No, sir, I am not. I believe that's why I was appointed.

Réti sat forward in his chair. His hands met between his knees.

—Look. My friend Leo Highet is an enthusiast for new ideas. Like me, he is an optimist. There is nothing wrong with that.

—In this case optimism became fraud.

—I spoke well of you to the regents. I supported your candidacy. Despite that Leo Highet was my friend, and in my opinion ousted unfairly, I did so for the good of the Lab.

—I appreciate that, sir.

—I remember too that you visited me in the hospital. I should like to think of you as a friend.

—You do me too much honor.

—My friend Leo Highet has his weaknesses, I do not deny it. But whatever else, he has passion. And he understands the political necessities of funding.

Leaning forward, Réti grasped the staff and stamped it upon the floor. —Funding comes from the threat. Now, this administration does not think that Russia is a threat. I say they are wrong. But even so, there is no shortage of threats. There is another great threat, and I do not mean the threat from north Africa to southern Europe. There is a threat of being hit by a comet, or asteroid. The last time it happened was in Tunguska, Siberia.

—In nineteen hundred and eight, said Quine. He had heard this before. It was part of Réti's road show. Following Tunguska he brought up Chicxulub (Mayan, some said, for devil's asshole) where, during the Cretaceous Period, a meteor had hurled enough debris aloft to darken the earth, change its climate, and cause planetwide extinctions.

—Yes, in nineteen hundred and eight. I was then five months old. It was an aboveground explosion of ten million tons equivalent. Had it happened near a populated region, it would have been the biggest disaster, and we have excellent reason to believe that this disaster with appropriate notification can be averted. Here is a threat that is less probable than most other threats, but when it happens, it can become so big that, you know, it wiped out sixty-five million years ago the dinosaurs. That I think is a very interesting threat.

—According to the secretary of energy, said Quine, —the Lab's mission is now stockpile stewardship and management.

Réti fixed his eys on Quine. —I understand you held a meeting. I would have liked to attend.

—I'm sorry, I thought you were out of town. It was urgent that we move forward.

—I have no official duties. It is your prerogative to include me or not. But I will say that other directors have profited from my experience. I will say that I have always been notified of meetings.

—I'll see that you get complete minutes. It was a discussion of the stewardship program. We

Again the staff struck the floor. —Stewardship. Do you know what that word means? It means you are warder of the sty. A keeper of pigs. Is that what you wish?

—The stewardship program has interesting elements. For example, the Avalon laser.

—Yes, Avalon, do you think I don't know? Avalon is ours by right. We have planned it for years. Since the very beginning of this Lab we have pursued inertial confinement fusion. I wrote the first papers on it. Now, this new administration wants a test ban treaty, which is impossible because Russia will cheat. And they think to buy our compliance with Avalon. I say we should have Avalon plus Radiance!

—That's impossible. All missile defense work is now run by the Pentagon.

—The Pentagon will not continue the x-ray laser.

—Perhaps not.

—On which you worked so hard, gave so much.

—You could look on Avalon as a way of continuing and vindicating Radiance's x-ray laser work.

—What will happen to J Section?

—I can't say at this time. There will be cuts.

—Listen to me. You must make a project to investigate the possible results of an asteroid impact. And the possibilities of protecting us from such an impact. And then you will find that much of Radiance, including Superbright and Slingshot, is also good for asteroid defense. Lasers, orbiting interceptors, nuclear weapons, all this can be repurposed. There is time to get all this into the budget request. There is support in Congress. We must have this!

—Frankly, sir, I'm not sorry to see this missile defense work gone.

Many feel it's a violation of the antiballistic missile treaty.

—That treaty is no longer valid because the Soviet Union no longer exists. In any case, this work will never stop, because it has many powerful allies.

—What do you mean?

—You will see what I mean. And you will be sorry you let it slip away from you.

—Doctor Réti, our budget may be down this year but

—It is not just the money! They cannot be allowed to tell us what to do. And in our work there must always be a nuclear component. Do you know why? Because they fear the nucleus. They respect it. And we are its masters. But now they would reduce us to simulations. This must not be. This would be our end.

—We have no choice.

—Do you understand something, when Radiance started, I could go directly to the president and ask for funds. On one occasion I secured a hundred million dollars, just by asking. On another, sixty million. Just like that, and gnarled fingers rose and met but did not snap, —From black budgets. Now we have a new president. I cannot do that with this new president. So you must.

—I can't.

—You must! Why do you resist this?

—Sir. Radiance cost us credibility, we lost good people over it, we lost the trust of our owners. We'll have nothing further to do with it, in name or in fact. That's final.

Réti looked up sharply. Pale piercing eyes sunk in sagging flesh. He thrust himself forward, trying to stand. The head of his staff swiped the air. —You must not! Must not! Permit such an end to our experiment. We must find the next enemy.

—Please! Quine stood at the moment Réti sank back into his chair, eyes cast to the floor, mouth open, lower lip pendulous. —Don't excite yourself.

At last Réti looked up at Quine, eyelids trembling. —I am stupid, I am emotional, I am old. I had such hopes for you. Why do you not ask me? Months you have been here. You do not come to me, you do not ask me for advice, for counsel, for anything. This is not right.

—I apologize. I, I've been busy, and you're often not here.

—Or perhaps you believe, as outsiders do, that I am some kind of monster? But you know better. In the old man's eyes was an entreaty, in his voice a belligerence. —Do you know that I argued for a demonstration? To drop one atomic bomb over Tokyo Bay, or on an uninhabited island. There was not time enough, they said. It would be too difficult and expensive, they said, to build another bomb. That was the last time I attempted to influence policy. It is not a scientist's place. But! I am not afraid to express my opinion as a private citizen! And for a moment Réti was silent, reflecting no doubt on the many times he had expressed, sometimes on Lab letterhead, his opinion as a private citizen, but the memories were perhaps not uniformly happy, for his eyes narrowed and when he went on his tone was confidential, as if he were unfolding some elaborate mystery.

—Now I will tell you something. During the War, we all worked together, we all knew that the Bomb was important science and it was important to the world. We all felt that. When the War was over it changed. We were no longer together. There were two camps: make more, better bombs, or stop there. You would think that men so smart, so excellent in their field, could agree. It was obvious the Russians would build one. But no. And the strange thing was this. We were all excellent, all first rate, but even so, some were a bit above the rest, yes? And the very best, these were the men who did not want to go on making bombs. So when this Lab started, I became director, because I had no competition. I was the best of those who remained. The best of not the very best, do you see? I had won by a forfeit. My friends were no longer my friends. Now I talked with generals and senators, to whom physics was a magic trick. To whom I was a magus. That was my compensation. Nobel prizes for Bohr, Wigner, Einstein, Lawrence, Fermi, Urey, Rabi, Bethe, Bloch. For me, the ear of generals and Presidents. Now you know something I never told even my good friend Leo Highet. Something I am maybe a little ashamed of. So that you will understand what this place is to me.

He extended the staff. —But I will tell you further. I am right and they are wrong. The age of the heroic individual scientist is over. The bomb changed everything forever. From then on we work always in teams, always funded by government. And government is not interested in *physis*, in *scientia*, they want *techne*. I saw this sooner and more clearly than any. So we give them what they want! And in return they permit us to go on with our work. And we are *not*, and Quine shrank from the fury and loathing he saw in Réti's eyes, —we are not *owned*.

Leaning on his staff, Réti got to his feet, shaking off Quine's hand. When he had left, Quine sat trembling. He cleared his throat as if he would speak but said nothing. He rose and went to the bathroom where he ran water into a glass and reached for Valerian 500 mg when the shrill of the phone turned him. He glanced at the mirror to find something vicious in the face there, something that hid itself as quickly as it had appeared.

—Yes Dolores? All right, tell Conor I can't see him this evening. I'm leaving now.

By the time he reached the road an anticipation of night stood in the east where the sun's last rays raked tender green hills, an island of serenity beneath the ridge's stubble of windmills, relics of a time before his time at the Lab when, however briefly, its mission has encompassed the passive generation of energy as well as its explosive deployment. The enemy? Where now is the enemy? His distracted gaze moved over the stopped traffic and the unfinished pylons of a freeway overpass separating on the one side a lighted plinth of signs Circuit City, Toys "Я" Us, Barnes & Noble, Office Depot, Bed Bath & Beyond, from its counterpart on the other side proclaiming CompUSA, Zany Brainy, Borders, Staples, Linen 'N Things, and past those to the redtiled roofs of Estancia Estates which recalled an era so bygone it had never existed, a dream of California begun when Cortez's men landed on the Baja peninsula which they mistook for the setting of the romance *Las Sergas de Esplanadian*, whose author Garcia Ordonez de Montalvo averred that somewhere hereabouts was an enchanted isle of gold and pearls and griffins where Queen Califia's black amazons dwelled and welcomed men once a year for purposes of procreation, and Cortez's men in their hope (two girls for every boy!) or disappointment, or irony, gave the peninsula that empire's name, whence the name traveled north to the Alta mainland and into a further dream of gracious caballeros and señoritas kept ever fresh to meliorate the zeal of the friars Gaspar de Portolà and Junipero Serra, who in their exigent grace converted nearly as many natives as they enslaved, leaving the land vacant for the newest dream of Gracious Living in The Valley Starting in the $150,000 The Vineyard Starting in the $250,000 and The Glen Starting in the $350,000, where the only visible gold and pearl were the headlights and taillights of innumerable cars crawling past that green island of serenity dotted with the frames of new homes rising in the sun's last rays like a tide of wrack up the hillsides. His eyes darted like animals in the cage of his anxious face, leapt from the darkening ground of nature to the lighted figures of man's improvements upon it and back as if somewhere in this vast scribble and sprawl were signs to unlock the meaning of his slow unsteady progress, but the sign before him said EXIT NLY, and led only to more of the same.

As he entered the house he called out, —Lynn? coming into the kitchen and glancing to the refrigerator where the calendar JANUARY was marked 6 PHILIP BACK and a red line crossed 24 through 31 LYNN IN GENEVA CTBT CONF and under 25 VANDENBURG LAUNCH, and then to the sink, where apron strings were drawn tight across the trim back and flat shoulder blades up to closecropped black hair touched with russet. His shoes squeaked crossing the blue and white vinyl. She turned to him shaking water from her hands, smiling, wiping them on the apron. —Welcome home.

—I'm glad to see you. God I'm tired. What a day.

—I knew you wouldn't call me back. So I just showed up.

—I did call, I called you at home and at work.

—But no message.

—I don't like talking to machines.

—And you don't want to be overheard talking to me.

—Oh, come on, I

—Everyone knows about us anyway.

—Do you think so?

—You don't sound very happy about it. She put her wiry arms around his neck.

—I'm very happy.

—Thank you, so am I.

—It's not a problem at work? Nobody's mad?

—No, they think I'm going to convert you. And I will, too. Except Tony Luz is mad at me.

—He wants you for himself.

—Too bad for him.

As he leaned in to kiss her a weight in him shifted but didn't settle. Her lips smiled under his.

—Now let me cook. Here. She handed him a glass of wine, golden and heavy.

—Thanks. What's this about a lawsuit? I hear you're suing us?

She bent to the oven, its door protesting as it opened. —Who, me? You must mean that peacenik outfit I work for.

—They're the ones.

—It seems you've been careless with your EISes.

—You don't mean that oversight in the building plans, do you? We issued an errata.

—Need to know? She looked up, black eyes glinting.

—Okay, sorry. I won't ask. What are we having?

—Grilled portobello mushrooms, risotto alla milanese, salad. Into the oven she slid a baking sheet bearing two mushroom caps big as hamburgers.

—You spoil me.

—I do indeed. Will you set the table?

On its surface was a vase of alstroemeria shedding striped petals into a bowl holding two Bosc pears and two green apples, and onto a strew of newspaper clippings, US Forms Radiation Task Force, Inexcusable Experiments, 33 Hospitals Were Involved In Cold War Radiation Experiments, Human Radiation Tests Were Widespread, Prisoner Irradiation Probed.

—What's all this?

She turned to him, a shallot in one hand, a paring knife in the other. —You haven't seen?

—I've been busy.

—Philip, this is a huge story. Doctors injected cancer patients with plutonium, they irradiated prisoners' testicles, they fed pregnant

215

women radioactive iron, all without their knowledge or consent. It really has the Auschwitz touch. And it's not just them. It's the downwinders, the

—Down what?

—The people who live downwind from the test site. All through the fifties when the bombs were going off, and they had no warning, no precautions, no compensation, the cancer rates are unbelievable, if you could hear these people talk, Philip. It's heartbreaking. Can you hand me the salad bowl?

—Well, but, with testing stopped . . .

—That's not the point. This is the department's history. You can't bury history.

—I thought you were preparing for the treaty talks.

—I am. I'm following this because Janine, the reporter, has worked with us. You couldn't have a better example of why people don't trust DOE. They stonewalled Janine at every turn. Some of the documents were almost fifty years old and they still won't come clean.

—The new secretary wants to change things.

—She did the stonewalling.

—But, she extended the ban on testing, she's declassifying, and she did admit to these experiments, you saw her openness press conf

—She had no choice after the articles appeared. Anyway, she's only admitted to eighteen victims, there are probably thousands. Now they'll form a task force and in a year or two they'll still be arguing over compensation.

Outside, beyond the black glass of the kitchen window, the yard went suddenly bright in the wind bending a tree tripping a motion sensor. He looked out at the tossing of the hedge some ten feet away, a wild motion constrained, chaos on the edge of complexity, until the floodlight snapped off. Then he returned to the clippings, Aguas Secas Desert Witness No More Bombs No More Tests.

—Did you go to this? Were you at the test site?

—Oh, that. No, I stayed home this year. You show up, you listen to the usual homilies about peace, you get arrested and released. You spend three days validating each others' righteousness and at the end of it all nothing has changed. I always come home tired and grouchy.

Anyway I had too much to do getting ready for the CTBT. Are you changing the subject?

—No, I just . . .

—Philip? Our agreement?

—You don't need to know anything about it. Really.

She scrutinized him. —All right. I trust you. Sit. Eat. You look exhausted. Holding a baking sheet in an oven mitt she raised a mushroom on a spatula and placed it before him.

—What a day. First the flight. Then a terrible, long meeting. Then Réti came to see me.

—Réti?

—I'd been dreading it. He went on and on about this asteroid defense stuff, still trying to keep Radiance alive through it. He won't give it up.

—But surely after all the scandals . . .

—He thinks we've been exonerated. He thinks it's a great success that we spent the Soviets into oblivion. Maybe he thinks we can out-spend the asteroid belt too.

—He can't keep that program alive, can he?

—I don't know. Not as it was anyway.

—You're under a lot of pressure.

—You won't believe what Highet did. Our new principal management analyst is one of the guys who wrote the GAO report on Radiance.

—Are you really telling me this?

—What do you mean? Of course. It's so Highet, I thought you'd appreciate it.

—So are you going to fire this guy?

—Why? He's been vetted, and anyway he may be able to tell me something about Highet.

—You've really got it in for Highet, don't you?

—You don't?

—Could we, I just want to not talk about it.

—I always wondered where you got that report on Superbright. You had a copy even before I turned it in.

—Philip, you know I can't tell you that.

—Was it Bran? Bran Nolan?

—Please, I can't tell you. Have some salad . . . Arugula, watercress, sliced pears, hazelnuts, walnut oil, raspberry vinegar, rinsing it with the last of the Chardonnay, and then, —I have to look at some papers, here let me . . . He rose to clear the table as, across the last of her wine, turning the glass by the stem, she watched him cross to the sink with dishes and return to the clippings bunched under the alstroemeria, pausing at Aguas Secas Desert Witness finally to say, —Is it necessary to call us Doctor Strangeloves in your literature?

—That's not ours, Philip. That's another group.

—Well . . .

—It is strange that I love you, don't you think? In her eyes something worried, then fled. She stood up and pressed her mouth to his. Her breath to his. After a moment she broke it off. —But I do love you, Philip.

—Yes, I . . . I know. But . . .

—Do you remember the first time we made love? I came over and told you to take my clothes off.

—I remember.

—I didn't want to be carried away by the moment, I wanted to decide it. For so long I thought that getting involved with you was a terrible idea.

—But you kept calling. I wondered if you wanted to use me.

—There was a little of that. But you, you wanted to be used.

—Yes, I did. By you.

—You look, sometimes, you look so frustrated and disappointed, but under it there's something else. Like you're still looking for something. You haven't given up. You didn't just walk away from it all.

—Are you sorry now that you have me?

She looked almost smiling up at him. —No.

They passed through the living room where the dead eye of television reflected the entrance to a side room. —I don't want to keep you from working, she said, a hand poised at her blouse, soon held in his, moving to caress and hold, as breaths quickened, hands moved and plucked more urgently where limbs stirred and came down in darkness on the bed as her heat enclosed him hungrily, her legs drawn back for the swell of his entrance, her arms raised in a kind of supplication, the pale light from the street sketching her smoothness and firmness no longer an instigation but a reproach to his haggard flesh as he rolled onto his side and she came nestling after to embrace him and press the fronts of her warm thighs aginst the backs of his.

—You poor. You're so tired. Just sleep.

—I'm sorry. I . . .

—It doesn't matter. Just sleep.

As his eyes closed his face slackened to a repose almost like its childhood, some mocking semblance of an innocence he'd inadvertently held through the passing of time and buffeting of experience that had turned it into this lined and sunken parody.

Somewhere within this stricken countenance he wandered in hallways that turned one into another, past WET PAINT and curious figures turning to watch, the corridor narrowing to a closed door where the knob turned and turned unavailing and a waspish voice said, —a terrible administrator, lost control of the meeting, thinks you can bury the past, and —Philip!

—Huh, what!

—You were having a bad dream. It's all right.

He shivered as she held him. In the streetlight the line of her lip was archaic, without sympathy or flaw, more unforgiving than her youth. He thought of Nan and his heart quailed.

TWO

Rainless January gave way to winter storms that blew in one after another with no break, stacked like waiting furies over the Pacific, driven to landfall by a jetstream which, satellite photos showed, thrashed like an unmanaged firehose yet somehow kept its business end trained on the Bay Area, so that as the new year wore on what had been the driest winter on record threatened to become the wettest, said the newspaper Quine shook free of its yellow sheath, water falling on the seat beside him, and turned braking for orange cones around a truck EBMUD at a broken hydrant laving the flooded street as booted workmen in orange slickers waved him to DETOUR the wrong way down Codornices, onto a curving road at the edge of town heading into a rain that obscured any landmarks. He fidgeted the radio on to —widely expanded alcohol and drug testi, stilling it for the slap of wipers barely clearing the sheets of water that rippled over vagueness until the Lab gates loomed and he parked under RESERVED DIREC- TOR. He dashed through the outer door and in the hallway still rush- ing overtook two men talking who didn't glance up from, —Thou shalt not piss on a colleague's funding . . . as he turned a corner into —Bran!

—Morning Philip. Slow down you'll live longer.

—Listen I need to talk to y

—I'm on my way to a diversification seminar, can it wait?

—Well sure but

—Too bad, I'd like to miss this thing.

—Well come by my office later, will you . . . ? as he jabbed an unyielding 5 for the blessed but temporary solitude of brushed stainless steel, pulling Ohlone Val from its plastic sheath and unfolding it to Lab Hiring Criticized By Antinuke Group, for a stunned moment —Damn her! and a trail of water tracking him to his office where the radio was —worried he was going to do danger to himself, until he closed the inner door and stopped short of his desk where —Conor? sat.

—Think I found your problem. Disk is all messed up, you should have a lot more free space than it says here. Looks like a partition was removed but not erased, I'm trying to recover it . . . come on now, give me a break here, as Quine came around to peer at the screen.

—What's this, thirty eight directories thirteen thousand files three point one gigab

—Looks like he never threw anything away.

—Highet?

—I'd've thought he'd encrypt everything, look at these directories, docs, contacts, 4thgen, xxx, what's xxx? Thousands of files here, as the screen filled with a face framed in carrot red hair and lips pouted to kiss, —What, Conor, what is this?

—Well it's not a Polish sausage is it. Looks like one of those GIF files they found on the sparta node back when. Want me to delete them?

—Thought we did that, yes Dolores what . . . ? turning to follow her stare back to the screen beyond them. —Some old files of Highet's, we were just

—You're due in the conference room at ten.

—Right, just one, as the door swung shut. —Why that woman doesn't knock . . . Conor, can we get back to this later?

—Yeah sure, just let me, uh huh, here we go, I thought so, as down the screen spilled

Type Bits/KeyID Date   User ID
pub 2048/0276B74D 1993/05/10 Leo Highet <highet@styx.banl.gov>
—--BEGIN PGP PUBLIC KEY BLOCK—--
Version: 2.6.3
mQEPAzlqPx0AAAEIALEPWTHRLZ6x0n75VZkUwjpOFl3coOOVmB35xXcw

Gym+Du8biuNgKrK+KwkHvJxdaywtkixRZkl/IEKEktWviruj520c1tuy5DNV+
MR0pZUDKZbbjlI2PsCuTS9D4qFRXQ/hNKbTtFjQD9RavfBr2kTHEFqzqn-
mJY9KOlm2bK312Wz054RiHPPlYyzDMLahtCCHHxx2IqlyeFx
aqVgTR9BVGYBdTnsQG26Yfq9HyEByrQ+KrlOaElxOjmQ96WGvfW441hPjuj
7QXJYfOFMmSVhxgBBEu1RRiEi/CdXjycyvUfiGQh1dWGYVulMpjy9gmgvM0
IWIOQ03HBetyTgJ2t00AEQEAAbQcTGVvlEhpZ2hldCA8aGlnaGV0QG5vdX-
MuY29tPokBFQMFEDlqPx4F63JOAna3TQEBwWsH/jxevyVRovVKhr1FYN-
MbWyZ6VfcTg7WdDcsJXW2ZBm6ZnnBKwuXV6t7vOzlex+gvJ2f+zbhk49y
3cUlsPLbrCONA31/UC45OQcBzLbTmmvekpsdWAUM5dxkFraoc4vKDFtaFv
y9HM2yeuYt7KPNnxHE/KGdVU9cJxLN5xAEW4pCXFYtTNuMlk2vnLr7QbK
1WCAqHRQ5okVlJKOBPnOtPN3rvwQEChut0cw/ggwPrqAbZqF+ZNJZXCljF-
FlXCgWbC5JypguLQzcMH/EdOw4A87IkheC0FnfENZBzUng9bLwxraqCyi-
ADgz5AzcXZyDAKS1KzBQcVEto6MLqblDsyEQ2wl═JWor
————END PGP PUBLIC KEY BLOCK————

—That's Highet's public key. You know, Pretty Good Privacy, Phil Zimmermann's encryption software? The feds call strong encryption a munition, they're prosectuing Zimmermann for exporting munitions.

—I thought, I mean, isn't DES the federal encryption standard?

—Guess he didn't trust it enough to use it on his personal files.

—Can this PGP be cracked?

—In theory, anything can be cracked. In reality, this is a two thousand forty-eight bit key. DES, that's only fifty-six bits. Give me a week on our fastest computer and maybe I could crack DES for you, but this, forget about it. Unless you can guess his password.

—Did you ever see him use it?

—PGP? Nope. But his mail password had six characters, all lowercase letters.

—How do you know that?

—I watched him log in often enough.

The door opened again for —Dolores, would you very much mind knocking, my open door policy doesn't mean I want people just walking in every, yes I know I'm late, Conor could you

—Oh listen, the P Section codes problem. Apparently it's a hardware error.

—A hardware error? In the new aXons?

—Something's wrong with the math chip. Every one of them gives the exact same error, for just one pair of operands. Weird huh?

—Well tell them we want a fix.

—They won't talk to me, they want you. We put out an advisory on the Internet. About a million users want that fix now.

—I don't have time to handle every little thing like this, this should be a, a warranty repair.

—Believe me, I tried.

—All right, I'll call. Now I really have to . . . but as soon as Conor was out the door he paused at Lab Hiring Criticized, frowning as if it were some vermin that unchecked would spread.

—J Frank Greer, please. Philip Quine, tell him it's urgent . . . Waiting with the phone to his ear he tapped a computer key.

From: lhamlin@igc.apc.org
To: quine@lucinda.lab.gov
Subject: CTBT
Date: 4 Feb 1994, 10:30 (-0000)
I love you, I miss you. Geneva is incredible. I think this treaty has a real chance. Wonderful news in the paper that the US testing moratorium is continued. You didn't tell me! You're so bad. See you soon.
xoxo
Lynn

For a moment a smile flickered there under the set brow and his hand on the mouse fidgeted up a window Reply only to Cancel a moment later at a voice in his ear, dropping his eyes to Lab Hiring Criticized.

—Frank, it's Philip Quine. I just saw your page one article about our auditor I mean analyst. Would you mind, in the future, would you mind very much running this kind of thing by me or my press officer? What? Yes of course he spoke to me. No. No I don't have a problem with the. My point is I didn't think it would run. Off the rec, no I didn't say that because. Because it. Yes all right but. No I'm not saying that. I think we need to stay on good terms. But sometimes there's no good reason to, to stir up shit, you know? No I'm not asking for, just a friendly call, okay? Just so I know when an article's going to. Yes. Yes I will.

He dropped the handset and strode through Dolores's office, ley Herald folded under his arm, harassed by an orotund voice, —both of them running on the mantle of reform, into the corridor where he turned left full tilt past E-530 -> to burst into E-533, —Sorry I'm la ... vacant but for the long table. —Oh for ... and back around three bends to E-501 and the smell of fresh paint.

—Christ ... ! he exhorted the empty table and chairs. He headed back to his office, waylaid by a placard Diversification and Strategic Management of Laboratory R&D Portfolio, stepping uncertainly into a dim conference room where a small group sat facing a viewgraph harried by the red dot of a laser pointer.

—'ve got your stars, your cows, your dogs, your question marks, you want to optimize the cycle so that your question marks become your stars and your stars become your cash cows that can be milked to nurture new question marks before they become useless dogs that have to be put to slee

—Excuse me. Is Bran Nolan here? Bran, can I see you?

Nolan came to the door as the consultant resumed, —Now we turn our attention to optimizing our diversification. The model that we use consists of two functions. The first is the total return, and Quine had a glimpse of

$$R = N_b p_{sb} R_b + N_s p_s p_{su} R_b + N_s (p_{ss} - p_s) R_s$$
$$I = N_v C_b + N_s p_s (1+r)^N C_b + N_s C_s$$

before Bran guided him into the hall and the door swung to behind them.

—Thanks for the rescue, thought I was getting the fifty-drachma course.

—Bran is this the, the what?

—Prodicus, a Sophist, sells his skills with language. I thought this ace was going to start using Navier-Stokes equations to figure market share. Our share of the nuclear weapons market is pretty nearly a hundred percent isn't it?

—Bran, should I be in there?

—I don't think anyone should be in there.

—No I mean, I'm supposed to be in some meeting somewhere, but the two main conference rooms are empty.

—I wouldn't worry about it.

—I'm going back to ask Dolores. Did you see this? Quine unfolded

Lab Hiring Criticized for Nolan's outstretched hand. He read it impassively.

—In future why don't you refer calls like that to me? Anytime you say something to a reporter you can expect to see an unreasonable facsimile in print next day.

—But I thought, you know, a few months ago they did that flattering profile of the new director, I thought we had a rapport . . .

—Greer's run that paper since we were the biggest employer in the area. Every so often he just has to kick the company store. It'll blow over.

—Well, I've spoken to him, I made it clear that we want to be notified of something like this.

—Why don't you leave him to me? Highet tried to micromanage press relations. Did more harm tha

—Doctor Quine!

—Dennis, are you still, I mean, how can we miss you if you won't go away?

—Hi Bran, I'm glad I ran into you both, have you got a minute?

—Not really.

—Dennis, I'm late, can we

—No you're not, we're just starting.

—What, is this the . . . ?

—Yes, come on in . . . to where half a dozen men, two or three of them managers whose names escaped him, sat at a table facing a pale lined projection of a computer screen littered with icons.

—This is Jerry Seller CFO, Jerry this is Philip Quine director . . .

—Pleasure sir. So how you know Dennis?

—Dennis was ah our media guru here. He's on leave, but we still seem to see a lot of him.

—Yes I'm moonlighting I guess you could say. Now before we get started I hope you don't mind I need you all to sign this, purely a formality, this form just a standard

—nondisclosure agreement, whereas 3Vid possesses certain business, product, technical, marketing and strategic infor

—so if you could, yes there, and on the next page, and the rider, and initial here. . .

—What's so hush-hush Dennis, a personal missile defense?

—Sorry I just, my clients need to protect their intellectual property, yes thank you, ah, and, is this everyone? Everyone has signed? as
he turned to the laptop and the arrow cursor danced nervously across
the projection. —Now if you'd all just put on these . . . as he handed
around cardboard eyeglasses with red and green cellophane lenses. —
Eventually we'll market this as a standalone flat panel display you can
hang on any wall, but we coded it as a screensaver as a sort of proof of
concept . . .

—We going to watch The Creature From the Black Budget, Dennis?

—No let me just, I have to switch modes here, as the screen display
fractured into a tangle of green and red images.

—Where's Waldo?

—Okay now everyone if you'll put these on . . . until they resembled a crew of dissolute arctic explorers, —stand about here, ah, you
may have to squint a little . . .

—What's that, Hieronymous Bosch?

—Um, here, if you option-click on the upper left, oops, I mean the
upper right you get

—A copyright notice? You copyrighted Bosch?

—We licensed the entire National Gallery, they own the individual
copyrights, but our collection of them is um proprietary, yes and here,
the upper left, you get the title, um, Garden of Earthy Deligh

—It changed.

—Right, see that's the whole thing, it keeps changing so you don't
get bored, and you can set the cycle time or randomize . . .

—Sure, don't want to be stuck looking at the same painting for
more than a minute, what's this?

—little glitch there, sometimes the screen doesn't clear completely,
ah, we seem to have part of Saint Sebastian mixed with, ah

—Magritte? I like the bowler hat.

—press control F1 for a refresh, oop, oh see, this is another feature,
password protection, just let me ah

—That an Annunciation?

—but what's that in her um

—Another of those GIF files, not exactly an immaculate conception is it

—Seems to come right out of the screen at you.

—don't know how this got into our database, some kind of mistake, as he jabbed desperately at control F1.

—What's that annoying music?

—Oh, that's Mozart.

—Mozart? Sounds like Salieri on the zither, that relentless deedle deedle . . .

—Um well here, you can alt-shift-click on this uh squiggle, this little icon here . . . ?

—That's a treble clef.

—and see, here's the help file, MicroMuse version 1.4, trademark, Smart Markov Autonomous Recombinant Melody generator, patents pend

—What's the matter, couldn't license the real thing from the Köchel people?

—The, the who . . . ?

—Never mind.

—See, here in this popup here you can pick any style or composer, Franz Lisp, CPU Bach, Mostly Mozart . . .

—Think you're infringing there on a Lincoln Center trademark there.

—Oh really? Kihara made a note on his tablet. —And here, instrument selection, choose your orchestra, some of the General MIDI instruments are a little rough but when we get better samples, as the deedle deedle changed to the tuneless clangor of —cowbells that's not right, let me just, eventually we'll have world class samples, we're trying to license Yo-Yo Ma's violin . . .

—He's a cellist. But maybe he moonlights.

—Dennis, I'm, why are you showing us this?

—I thought we might want to get involved at some lev

—Dennis, I've got to, walk with me will you . . . as he guided the eager young man down the hallway for —This is a government laboratory, not a multimedia startup.

—Well yes, Mister Seller is the startup but I just thought because flat panel displays are in our portfolio we could

—Denn

—get involved at some level in a partnershi

—Dennis!

—. . . what?

—Look, I appreciate your ah enthusiasm, but we're not, I mean, could you concentrate on, on something a little more relevant to our mission here?

—Well but see I thought this could be packaged as a security enhancement, you know how X Section leaves their computers on all the time, even when they're away from their desks and this could be a secure screensaver also a kind of battlespace display for the strategic modeling that X Sec

—Look Dennis, why don't you get back to your demo, we'll talk about this later.

—But Doctor Quine . . . flinching from a raised hand that came away holding green and red lenses no longer confounding the eye but upsetting afresh the mind that had adapted to them, until it came through a familiar doorway to —Dolores, get ah, what's his name, Steve Task of aXon Computing for me. I'm returning his ah, what is it Conor?

—Here's that directory tree.

—Okay, thanks, and close the door would you. He sat down as the phone blurted. —Hello. No Dolores I won't hold, get him on the line then call me back, his eyes going blank for a moment in which it seemed he might almost relax before they tensed again to fall on the sheet Conor had left as the phone chirped.

—Yes this is Philip Quine. Yes I know about the problem, I don't know why you want to talk to me, this should be a simpl, what? Stan who? Flack? Lawsuit? Patent pending on multiplic, wait, what are you talking about? What do you do mean he got us on board? CRADA? With who? Systems Concepts And Methods? No, look, this is the first I've heard of. Anyway what does this have to do with the errors, I called because our physics group is getting multiplic, okay now wait will you. Will you please just. What do you mean not an error. There's one pair of operands that returns the same error every time you multiply them, the same error every time, so, so . . . what? On purpose? You built a math error into the chip on purpose? But what do you mean a different algorithm, a mistake's a mistake. Infringe on what. Look this is, I really don't know how this whole mess I don't even know this Stan Flack, but we're committed here to building a massively parallel supercomputer with these chips and this is just unaccep. Internet? Users screaming for a fix, well of course they are, what did you expe, what do you mean they'd never have noticed if we hadn't, we, we put the word out? How? Well sure, someone here might have posted to a newsgroup it's still your mistake! Software fix, yes, we'd like that as soon as poss, I, I really don't care how much it's going to cost you, no I don't care about your first quarter earnings we have our, our own prob. We are not to blame for the whole thing! All right. All right then fine. Fine then. See you in court, tapping the cradle for a dial tone but getting instead a waspish voice, —Who, Mister Dial Tone up there? Just wonder how long he's going to last.

He dropped the phone and touched a vein beginning to throb in his temple, Quine brought frontmost a window he'd opened that morning:

cd /highet/contacts

ls

grep -Fi 'null' address_book

>Nullpoint Systems, PO Box 314, Tracy, CA, 95378.

as the phone rang again and —Send him in, and through the door came Jeremy Rector, smoothly swinging a calfskin case.

—Good afternoon Doctor Quine. We missed you at the meeting this morning.

—Yes, there was some, some confusion . . .

Rector sat and his case came open with a snap. —You've seen this? passing him a report in blue covers, Adopting New Missions And Managing Effectively Pose Significant Challenges GAO/T-RCED-94-113. Quine opened to the executive summary where *Experts and agency officials agree that the laboratory's new missions need to be clarified if their resources are to be used most effectively* before he closed it.

—Yes I, I testified that, that the lab's new missions have to be clarifi

—That's one down. Now about this missing property . . .

—Jeremy, you've seen this? pushing Ohlone Valley Herald into

Rector's gaze. —When we talked about your hiring you didn't tell me you'd worked on the GAO Superbright report.

—I assumed you knew. My name's on it.

—Of course I read it, but that was before I knew your name. Is there some reason your report failed to mention my report . . . ? Quine opened a drawer and drew out An Analysis of False Brightness in the "Taliesin" Test of Radiance "Superbright" X-Ray Laser Component. Rector examined it.

—I never saw this.

—Highet didn't give you a copy?

—No. There were various classified materials which were summarized for me, but I didn't have access to them.

—Because I have to agree with the Herald here, given my own involvement, that GAO report on Superbright read to me like a whitewash.

—As I knew the facts it was an accurate representation of what was provided.

—It came out shortly after you hired on here, didn't it?

—Let me think. October? After Doctor Highet had left at any rate.

—It exonerated Highet.

—Too late to save his job.

—Weren't there some other matters under investigation? Something about a shell company.

—As I recall there wasn't enough to investigate.

—Was the company called Nullpoint?

—I don't recall. Look, Doctor Quine, if you have some problem with my work . . .

—No no, I just, you know, we'll just hope this . . . blows over. Now where are we with this missing property?

Where they were, after an hour, was in a quagmire of missing papers, unfiled requisitions, and slipped cogs of a bureaucracy burdened with irrelevancies to the point of, if not breakdown, at least a deficit of some forty million dollars.

—What does this mean, sensitive property? Classified?

—No no, in this context sensitive means items susceptible to being appropriated for personal use or readily convertible to cash. Cameras, tape recorders, tools, that kind of thing.

—I checked out some classified papers this weekend, if the signout sheets for property are as badly managed it's no wonder, I had to go looking for the guy on duty. Why can't people just, just do what they're supposed to do?

—It's not as bad as it looks.

—What do you mean, we don't have a clue where any of this stuff went, or how it disappeared.

—The way I'd deal with this is to say that you're following DOE procedure

—But we're clearly not.

—as well as you understand it, and point out that other DOE labs have similar problems, or worse. When they broaden the inquiry the pressure will come off you. Now the next thing are these unassigned overhead costs . . . as a folder over an inch thick came to the top of the pile.

—Yes but

—You've looked this over, right? Out of an operating budget of one billion dollars, four hundred million are in unassigned costs

—Four hun, forty percent?

—Yes, and some interesting liberties were taken with what is accounted for, let's see, ten million in defense programs charged to overhead as, ah, Emergency Meal Chits . . .

—But this is, what year was that?

—F Y ninety-one.

—But that's, I wasn't even, I don't see how

—Well we still have to address it.

—Yes okay Jeremy but I'm out of time now, I have to . . . though whatever necessity was pressing him vanished with the closing of the door onto a moment of stillness that brought not peace but a void, as if some paralysis of the spirit commanded in its train a paralysis of the mind. When his attention returned, it was to the items on his desk. I love you, I miss you. Lab Hiring Criticized. How could she? In his mind's eye the line of her mouth, the flare of her lips were set against him, and then they gave way suddenly to another's, Nan's lips, soft and opening to speak, so present that his breath came short, a taste almost was in his mouth, of sandalwood, bittersweet as a pang of long-ing, or of conscience, her absence from his life now as permanent and irrevocable as the closing of those lips. The errancy of his heart stunned him, and he sat in the aftershock of its protest, not under-standing, unable to retreat from its need to pay in full some debt he'd forgotten.

He held his breath through the ring for her voice, its familiar qua-ver, —Nan Adams, and through another tract of silence almost to hang up on the new voice, flat and bored, —is not available. Please leave a message at the tone. Or enter another extension number.

—Nan . . . this is, this is Philip. I, ah, well, would you . . . look some-thing up for me? Employee records for a Devon Null. He was in J Sec-tion a few years ago. Thanks. I'll . . . ah, I'll talk to you later, returning the handset to its base then standing in agitation to pace the room. He raised the blinds to stare down on the flooded construction pit until in the outer office a voice rose, —Hell, Dolores, you know me, moments before the intercom buzzed.

—Who? No Dolores I can't spare a minute not even half a, but already a man filled the doorway, black shirt embroidered red and white in Western fashion held closed by mother of pearl snaps and a string tie in a tooled ivory clasp, over which loomed a ruddy face framed by lank graying hair and a smile that held somewhere in its depths the glint of gold. In one fat hand was a Stetson hat, and the other he held forth like a ham.

—Dan Root. Pleasure to meet you.

—You'll have to make an appointment.

—I just this minute did.

—I'm sorry but

—Not as sorry as you might be. Root dropped his hand and took a step forward, still smiling. —Settle down, you'll make me think you're not sure of yourself. Got an ashtray?

Quine's hand checked itself on its way to the phone as Root took from his shirt pocket a cigar and a clipper. —I'd prefer you didn't smoke, said Quine.

—And I'd prefer the president go back to Arkansas. Root smiled and sat, leaning to drag over a trash can by its rim as he placed the

Stetson on the desk. He trimmed the cigar and dropped the tip in the trash can.

—You kept Highet's people on. Dolores and Conor.

—They're good at their jobs.

—Quite a bloodbath I heard. Was it three associate directors went down with Highet?

—I had nothing to do with that. They weren't fired, just reassigned.

—Siberia. I know. Root struck a match and held it in the air between them. He raised the cigar to its flame and rolled it there until the tip glowed, then leaned back and looked around the room. —You want to get some photos up on the wall. Yourself with the Vice President. That sort of thing. Make the place yours. Or don't you care about things like that, as his eyes ceased their prowl around the room and came to rest on Quine. —No, I guess you don't.

—Please put that out.

—This? Smoke rose in gauzy ropes from the coal of the cigar held at arm's length until Root returned it to his mouth and the smoke flurried in a complexity almost chaos. —Hear you gave Réti what for. Want my advice, course you don't, but here it is. He may be pushing ninety but he's not weak. Give him that asteroid crap. Keep him in the loop on that moon shot. That way you protect yourself, and anyway it's the right thing to do. He did real service for this place.

—Don't you think I know that, he's practically worshiped here.

—So should he be, he's the creator. What you callin that moon shot?

—Persephone.

Root shook his head in silent laughter.

—I didn't name it. Something about going into the darkness forever.

—Education is a damned expensive way to hide from yourself, if you ask me.

—This advice. Why do you care?

—About you? I don't. But I got some projects on and I'd rather have you in that chair than Szabo.

—And you think my position's that weak.

—I surely hope not.

—It's an interim appointment. I'm under no illusions.

233

—Are you not. Root regarded him for a long moment, then mashed the cigar end against the inside of the trash can. —I apologize for the smoke. Filthy habit. See, here's the thing. Mister Orrin Gate is a bud of mine, I introduced him to Leo. Figured to set them both up with a good thing.

—Set them both up?

—Dual use, give Leo's Slingshots some civvy cred, get Orr some tech he could use.

—You're a friend of Highet's?

—A colleague. A sponsor. One of his angels. Root drew out a card and leaned to push it across the desk, DANIEL J ROOT Aerospace Consultant djroot@xfin.com. —Leo got some crazy notion about Gate workin with North Koreans. So he kind of held things up on the CRADA and now it's in your hands, is that right?

—I need to have some aspects of it clarified before I can move forward.

Root spread his hands in the air. —I am here to clarify.

—Are you one of Gate's partners? This, this xfin, is that your company?

—Doctor Quine, Dennis Kihara wants to see you.

—Dolores, just, don't interrupt me here, tell him to see Bran Nolan.

—Good for you, you're delegatin. Highet delegated a hell of a lot to you.

—What's that to you?

—I like to see the cattle bite back.

—Okay now look, Gate's already been in to see me, we've gone over this, and I don't care if his partner's from North Korea or South Korea or, or Canada, he's not getting data from that shot.

—A word from you to DOE would ease our way. But we can go without you.

—How would you do that?

—The head of a NASA lab can approve a CRADA.

—NASA doesn't own this technology.

—Right now we just want the data, son. What can I clarify for you?

—You could tell me what Gate wants with those orbiters.

—See, I don't think he knows himself. A wireless satellite net looks good to shareholders. But reasons are a dime a dozen, and everybody fools themself. Now Gate, he's a Mormon. A Latter Day Saint. Who believes that God was once a man living on another planet. And that men will become gods populating other worlds.

—What does that have to do wi

—See, that's the heart of it. The unreason behind his reasons. You want to know why a man does what he does, look to his unreason, to whatever he follows despite all evidence and discouragement. Gate believes in eternal progression. He wants to go into space because he aspires to the highest places. Look at Highet, you wouldn't take him for a believer, but for all his worldly cynicism, he has no use for the mammon of unrighteousness. He's a child of light. It vexes him that Réti, a Hungarian Jew and a man of science, sups with fundamentalists. His faith in reason is his unreason. Leo thinks religion is ignorance, the enemy of science. But he's wrong. Sir Isaac Newton, Francis Bacon, Kepler, Priestley, Boyle, Faraday, James Clerk Maxwell, these were devout and prayerful men who looked for the apocalyptic coming of Christ. There's no contradiction. They all wanted to bend creation to man's will. To find if the fury in their hearts was God's or some other's. Why, you have quite a few of the saved right here within your walls. And what better place for them? Are they not stewards?

—You're a religious man?

—I am not. That claptrap makes me puke. And you?

—I don't have an opinion.

—Agnostic? Looking for proof? Do you think what Bacon thought, that God left his fingerprints on the creation? Then hid them from us like some cypherpunk? Like Leonardo's mirror writing?

—No opinion.

—I'm not saying He didn't. But if He did hide the sign of His being, would it not be in the atom? The nuclear reaction is the source of light, of energy, of the universe itself. Isn't that why we study it? But Leo never understood that light can't conquer darkness. It only pushes it back for a time. Who wants to live in that light? That's why we build houses. That's why we build churches. That's why we build labs.

—Okay look, I'm

—But what do you believe? What's your purpose here?

—Here? I'm here to serve the national interest.

—The national interest! Why, that's unassailable. Can you tell me what it is?

—According to DOE it's stockpile stewardship and nonproliferation.

—That's quite a job of work. You got the former Soviet republics bein looted, you got Khazakh nuclear scientists gone unpaid for two years, you got four hundred reactors in the world that by the time they shut down they'll have produced a million kilos of plutonium. Somebody kicked over the anthill and you're gonna keep track of every last ant? You can mess with your sensors and analysis techniques and inventories, but that's just playin keep away. Few more years we'll all be nostalgic for two player mutual assured destruction, know what I mean? So there's all the more need now for missile defense, it's a perennial, you'd do well to remember that. Ever since the V2s hit London. Time after time the military studies it and gives it up. But you *can* hit a bullet with a bullet. To hit a hundred bullets, among a thousand decoys, not to miss a one, that's difficult and expensive. But it is possible. The man in the street don't care what it costs, he just wants to feel safe. There's national interest for you. Anyway we have assets in space. Put assets in space you have to protect them now don't you.

—I don't think anyone's really asked the man in the street what he wants.

—You truly want democracy on a thing like this? When everybody's so harassed by daily life they can't think straight even if they'd ever learned how? Mom and dad both working fifty hour weeks to pay down the credit cards while the kids play Nintendo it's no wonder you got all those suburban muscle trucks on the road, corner a wounded animal he'll make a face looks just like that. Democracy? It's a miracle they don't kill each other. Meantime they just want to feel safe, whatever it costs in the long run, fuck the long run, they're livin on usury so why not make them feel safe and help yourself to the float? The beauty part is, you don't have to deliver the safety, so long as they have someone to blame but themselves.

—So money, that's your reason?

—Money interests me as a force. You know, this Fukuyama fellow with his talk about the end of history, the triumph of liberal capitalism, I got news for him, he ain't even seen capitalism yet. Till now we've had the playschool version. Real capitalism is just warmin up. Just you wait. Money? Trillions gone be flyin in the air up for grabs. But I'm only interested as a student of the world. If money was my thing I'd buy real estate. Course I want a decent return on my investment, like everybody else.

—I have to get on with my day.

—Course you do. You're a busy man. Root grimaced as he pushed his bulk up from the chair. —One more thing. Devon Null left some papers here.

—What do you know about Null?

—You shared office space he told me. Thought you might know what become of them papers.

—Do you know, I never once saw Devon Null.

—Did you not?

—Not in all the time we were supposed to share an office.

—See, Dev's a friend. He asked could I get those papers back.

—They're Lab property.

—No they're not. Dev had an arrangement. You can look it up.

—Why doesn't he come himself?

—He's not local.

—I thought he owned a business in Tracy.

Root's eyes glittered. —Did Highet tell you that? He knew Null pretty well. Maybe you should ask him.

—Where's Null now?

—He's a man always had good ideas. Hear you've had a few yourself. Ever want to take them outside the envelope? You know, commercial spinoffs. Lot of good ideas here get put on the shelf. Defense contractors implodin right and left, it might be a good plan to look for the next thing, hedge a little.

—Is that what this, this xfin is, your company . . . ?

—We handle intellectual property, if that's a service you need.

—What is that, exactly, intellectual property?

— Anything you can't fence, eat, or fuck. Root smiled and took his

Stetson from the desk. —Let you get on with your day. Take good care.

Quine rose as Root left. He carried the trash can by its rim to the bathroom, upended it into the toilet, flushed. The cigar bobbed to the surface and he flushed again, then with toilet paper wiped the rim where ash had stuck. He watched the settling water then flushed once more. As its wheeze faded he listened as if for some other voice, but nothing rose over the insentient drone of the building. In the office he scanned his daybook and lifted the phone for a waspish voice already in conversation, —number one the leadership issue, —and how long till he's gone, —classic passive aggress, hello? hel? and dropped the handset, face burning, heat coagulating into rage as he picked up again for —Dolores? Tell Frank Szabo to come by in an hour. I'll be in the laser bay till then.

In the hallway he averted his eyes from passing faces so evidently occupied by matters beyond human frailty that thay seemed at once strained and slack. He'd planned to walk, to shake some of that numbness from his own being, but when he came squinting into the cold wind rippling puddles on concrete all around the dry fountains, he gazed upward as if to confirm the source of this inclemency and in that moment stepped —Damn! into a cold flood up his left foot, his weight on it as if trapped in a mire until a slim figure hurried past him against wind driven drops, —Nan! Nan, wait . . . !

—Hello, Philip.

—Did you get my ah . . .

—Your message, yes. I sent you e-mail. There are no employee records for Devon Null.

—No records? But that's imp, I mean he worked there, he worked in my office, don't you, don't you remem

—There's a file for him, but nothing in it. Just a memorandum of understanding.

—Understanding? Understanding about what?

—Philip, it's raining. If you want the file I'll send it to your office. If you want to talk to me, say so.

—Well, I do, I just thought

—I have an appointment now, but I'll be free in an hour.

—Well okay, good, I could

—In the mall, there's a place that used to be called Café Desapareci-dos.

—Yes I know.

—It's a Starbucks now. I'll see you there at five, all right?

—Yes, I . . . but she had gone. Another gust of wind hurried him on to his car, his foot squelching with each step. He drove to a security kiosk, showed his ID, crossed a barren of shattered rock and motion sensors, turned and slowed, anxiously peering down a nondescript stretch of road, continuing slowly on until the edge of a large building asserted itself above a nearby roof. He circled around, found its lot, and parked.

It rose to five stories in places. In the lobby, a Whig history of lasers led from the first ruby milliwatts down a broadening highway of progress to Avalon, resplendent in artist's cutaway wireframe per-spective, a million times more powerful than its remote ancestor, though, like so much else elaborated into application here, the basic science had started elsewhere. At the door to the bay he put on a dust coat and boots, and went into a cavern of white steelwork supports and the skyblue pipes of beamlines. Bernd Dietz, dwarfed under them, looked up from a clipboard as Quine approached. Bill Snell raised a hand.

—Wanted you to see this, said Snell as Quine reached them. —We're playing around with designs for the new beast. I think it'll go.

—But, said Dietz, turning to draw out a thick glass panel two feet on a side, as somewhere a vacuum pump started up and Quine strained to hear, —for one thing, we need much better glass. These edge claddings absorb spontaneous emissions, and when these heat up about a third of the glass near the edge is unusable. There are also impurities in the glass, mostly platinum from the casting vessel. They absorb energy and lower the damage threshold. Dietz tipped the panel and light glanced from it. —See? For the new laser this glass will be bigger and will have therefore more impurities. We will need three-omega damage thresholds of fourteen joules per square centimenter. That is far more demanding than what we have here. And you see here, yes? where this glass is already failing.

—Shouldn't be a problem, said Snell. —Each beamline has fluence near eight joules per square centimeter at the third harmonic. Plenty of margin for error in the specs.

—And the final focus lenses will be exposed to gamma rays and to neutron energies at fourteen KeV, we have no idea how long they will last. Tests on fused quartz show

—Doctor Quine, we've specified type FS one fused silica, and we're testing the Corning seventy nine eighty

—Yes, at low energies, around one KeV. The scaling factor I would guess at about two hundred times. At three-omega wavelengths you will see fused silica damage at four joules per square centimeter. Then too the Pockels cell and frequency converter require very large KDP crystals, both deuterated and undeuterated. Probably three times the size of our current crystals. These crystals may take two years or more to grow. Any of the typical impurities, arsenic or aluminum or chromium or lead, these will interact with gamma rays even at parts per million . . .

—Well, we've got what, seven years to get online? You worry too much, Bernd. That's why we'll start by building one beamline.

—And when we get that one right, we need to duplicate it one hundred ninety-one times without errors, balance them all to within a few percent, with an aiming accuracy of fifty microns in fifty meters, and I don't know what else.

—As you see, Doctor Quine, Bernd is a pessimist.

—Actually, Bill, I've found Bernd's reality checks to be invaluable.

—Well, of course, but we've barely begun . . .

—Really? I thought Avalon had been on your wish list for several years. What other problems, Bernd?

—There is very much more. But one thing at a time. Because the optics coatings are not perfect we get reflections, and these ghost beams propagate through the system, potentially damaging it. Our next activity will be ghost management solutions.

—Bill, your latest cost estimates are already higher than what we discussed in the meeting.

—Well, that's what things cost. See this? Snell held on his palm a small gold cylinder. —That's a hohlraum. Ten thousand dollars. I could pay off my car with that. But there's a defect in it too small to see, so it's worthless. Here, take it as a souvenir . . . and it went into his pocket to clink against change and keys until his hand found it again to worry as he rounded the doorway into Dolores's outer office where Frank Szabo rose to follow Quine inside.

—Frank, are we still working on missile defense?

—We have support contracts with DoD.

—Is this support coming out of J Section?

—I don't micromanage, I mean, if my people bring in DoD contracts I'm all for

—Just tell me we're not remarketing any Radiance projects.

—What gave you that idea?

—Do you know a Dan Root?

—Root? Years ago we worked together in a group here. Heard he consults for NSA and NRO now.

—He worked in J Section?

—No, that was before J Section existed. He and Leo and I worked on some fusion concepts. Laser-plasma interactions.

—He came by. He suggested that Radiance work was ongoing in J Section.

—Look Philip number one Dan Root isn't reliable. He didn't last a year here. He

—Like what? What are we doing for DoD?

—I don't really, I'd have to, probably some laser work . . .

—X-ray lasers?

—No no, high energy lasers of some other de

—Space based?

—You put assets in space you have to protect them.

—I want to see paperwork on everything we're doing for DoD.

—Everything . . . ?

—Everything J Section is doing.

—Philip I really don't think

—Then I want every active contract transferred to X Section. Suspend all other work pending a review. Then shut down J Section.

—What? Philip that's not fair, a lot of these people are long term

—Fair? Since when are we doing fair, Frank? Look, grabbing papers from the desk, —do you see what I'm dealing with here? Twenty thousand inventory items missing worth forty million dollars. Computers, VCRs, test photos, look at this, four hundred million dollars in unidentified overhead costs on no particular program, that's forty percent of our entire budget, and do you know, I'm out of patience. I'm trying to, to clean this up and every time I turn around another skeleton falls out of some closet, so what happens to a few J Section employees is not a high priority for me. I just want it gone, I want that whole culture of deception and exaggeration dismantled in spirit and in fact.

—They're still good people, I mean, you were one of them.

—And another thing. No more Heinrich Hertz fellowships. I don't want them recruiting for us anymore.

—We can't tell an independent entity not to give grad students money.

—We can stop using them as a recruitment tool. We can make it against policy for any of our people to sit on their board.

—Réti's on their board.

—He should decide whether he's on staff here or with that think tank on the peninsula. If he's here he'll abide by our rules.

—You sure you know what you're

—Just do it Frank!

—Then what's my reassignment? I know we don't do fair here, but I'd rather not be head of advanced nothing in X Section.

—All right. Quine took a conscious breath. —How would you like to be the Avalon project manager? I'll create the post. Associate director level.

—What about Bill Snell?

—He'll still be head of L Section. Avalon needs its own leader.

—And you want me? For a moment Szabo's hunger and mistrust and resentment stood in a visible equilibrium, and a kind of terror rose in Quine at his own daring.

—We've had our differences, Frank, but you're a capable scientist and manager, as he straightened papers on the desk and then looked up suddenly as if to ambush the suspicion and hope at war in Szabo's face.

—I'd want to talk to Bill about it, he said.

—It's not up to Bill. Quine glanced at his watch and picked up the phone. —I'll talk to you tomorrow, Frank.

After the door closed he put down the phone and stood gazing out the window, past the torn and lakeleted pit, past the dry fountains, to where the sun broke for a moment through clouds, its brilliance surprising the white ramparts of Building 101 and illuminating the people before it as though Solomon's House had risen from the New Atlantis and with it these elite and stainless angels of progress, lambent in their moment of instauration, only to be swallowed again in the sullen shadow of a cloud, like a blessing glimpsed then withdrawn, a grace fickle as the air that sustained it and sent the vision's acolytes now scurrying for shelter ahead of its chill, doors slammed and heater punched to HI as he waited through two changes of the light for cars in the turn lane inching forward finally to permit him into the parking lot, where he crept over yellow and black speed bumps past Zany Brainy and REG L C NEM S M X and Linda Evans and New Economy Dry Cleaners and Ψ Psychotherapy Associates, until at Starbucks a heavy truck VANITY driven by a blonde with a phone to one ear backed smartly out of a space, HONOR ROLE PARENT ALISAL ELEMENTARY looming closer and closer between the tires' inch-thick tread until he abruptly geared into reverse and lurched back three feet to the sound of a horn behind him and his engine's sudden stall. The horn blared twice more as he turned the ignition key, and the offended driver shot around him turning sharply into the vacated space. When his engine caught he eased the car another hundred feet to another space and walked back to Starbucks Grand Opening where a line of people stretched out the door.

Up in the gray sky fleeted a ghost of blue. At the door of the café he paused, watching her just inside in a kind of half light before the dimness, the back of her neck aglow where a veil of fine auburn hair traced with gray fell across its paleness. As if sensing his gaze there her hand came up to brush the hair aside, exposing the volutions of her ear before it fell back and she stepped forward into the dimness. When she took her seat he came toward her. There was strain in her face when she looked up.

—Here, sliding across the table a thin manila folder bordered in red and white stripes. —Do you have a need to know this? Or are you just curious?

—I just want to, as he opened the folder and scanned the single page within, Memorandum of Understanding Between Laboratory and Contractor, security clearance, right and title to intellectual property to be negotiated case by case, glancing up to find her eyes steady on him.

—What are you looking for, Philip?

His eyes moved down the single page and back up it in a vain search for he wasn't sure —What? Oh. The university has all employees sign an agreement, a patent agreement, everyone signs it, you have to, but see if Devon Null was only a contractor he could have had a waiver he could just walk out the door with whatever work he's

—I wasn't asking about Null.

—But you see if he never worked here . . .

She sighed and closed her purse. —Philip, I have things to do.

—No wait, I . . .

—This file isn't what you want to talk about. Because you could have called anyone for it, had it sent to your office.

—But yes, it is, I mean

—You won't give me an inch, will you? Philip, it's been over a *year*. I thought you would at least call me. Or even come back, once, to say goodbye. But you didn't. And I gave up waiting. Why are we here now? Because you want employee records?

Her voice had opened further perhaps than she'd intended, and her mouth showed its distress at this betrayal of her defenses by the very tremor of those words trying not to say all of what she meant.

—Yes, but it was, it was also a reason to see you, Nan . . .

—How little you must think of me, Philip.

—To say I'm sorry.

Suddenly his eyes filled. Hers in turn dropped their guard. After a moment she reached for his hand. They sat in silence for a moment as she regarded him, waiting perhaps for the more that, she seemed now to remember, never came. She withdrew her hand and looked down at it, as if surprised and not particularly pleased at its boniness, the lines in the knuckles, the pale skin creased near a ring.

—And now you're acting director. I wouldn't have guessed it. I thought you were ready to have a breakdown or to quit. And it turns out that you were maneuvering.

—That's not what happened.

—You stepped over so many people. What a change in you.

—But I, it wasn't, have I really changed so much?

Again she regarded him with level curiosity.

—No, Philip, you haven't really changed. You never gave anyone an inch. I just never thought . . . but she shook off whatever it was she hadn't wanted to think.

—But, no, I, that was Highet who

—I worked for Leo Highet once. He was a jerk, but you knew where you stood with him. With you I always had to guess. When I guessed wrong, you took it out on me.

—Nan . . .

—You were such a, an artichoke, Philip. I could never find your heart.

He glanced away, as if unwilling to encounter in those gray eyes what he'd failed to see in himself. —Are you well? How are things?

She continued to regard him with that watchful uncertainty. —I'm fine. I'm short on sleep. There's new construction behind my house, it's very annoying, it used to be open space, you remember. Trucks come in at six a m dumping dirt. You know what a poor sleeper I am. Philip, why are we here?

He looked in agony around the café. —I never knew what you wanted of me. What you expected.

Her face softened. —Oh, Philip, I never . . . I just wanted you to be, to be what you sometimes can be, just now for such a brief moment, just to be happy in your skin. To be content with, with things.

—I was, I was content with us. As best I could be. I was content and not content, don't you see . . . As he spoke he leaned slowly forward and opened his hands. But she seemed resolved now to resist contact. Without moving she drew herself back.

—Philip, I'm getting married.

A stone fell in him. —You're, but I, but who . . .

—You remember Ben. You used him as an excuse to break up with me.

—Nan . . .

—The wedding is in July. I'll send you an invitation.

—Nan, I . . . He blinked in fury, then pressed fingers to his eyes.

—Philip. Her hand touched his forearm and he flinched from it.

—I'm sorry, Nan. I have no right. I treated you very badly.

—Yes, you did. But I know that you were in pain. Over your work, and more. I could have tried harder. To allow for that.

—Were you, sorry, when I left?

She seemed to consider. —No, not at first. At first I was relieved. Not to have to deal with it anymore. Whatever was eating you up. Then I was lonely, very lonely. For months. I hated you then. Hated that you didn't call, that you could just walk away like that.

—I was hurting, too.

—Yes, I suppose you were. I told myself that you were. That you'd get through it and then you'd call me.

—I still hurt. The truth of it went through his body like a shock.

—But you're seeing someone.

—Yes.

—That young anti-nuclear activist.

—How did you

She drew back. —Oh, Philip, everyone in the Lab knows. Anyway, you were looking for someone else even when we were together.

—But I, no, I

—Did you think I couldn't tell? That was what hurt most. She's much younger, isn't she.

—Not so much.

Her hand clasped her cup. She said with bitterness, —Does she make you feel younger, is that it?

—Nan, please . . .

—I swore to myself that if you ever talked to me again I wouldn't . . . She looked away and sat stiffly in a kind of abstracted misery until she could face him again. —Did you ever really love me?

—Nan . . .

—Because I did love you. I felt, all that time, despite everything, all our differences, the distance you wanted to keep, that we held each other in trust.

—I, and he swallowed with difficulty, his breath was short, his eyes burned. —I wanted to give you my heart.

She sat looking at his face. —You had a funny way of showing it. No, I'm sorry. I'm sure you did want that. She rose and bent toward him, pressed her soft lips to the hinge of his jaw.

—Goodbye, Philip.

The sun dimmed, bled whitely into opal sky. Everything seemed to lose itself in the middle of time. He'd sat like this, here in this lot, so long ago, when Kate had told him, not unkindly, oh Philip, it's too late for us. The moment's passed. The same sun dimmed in cloud, the same hollowness. He wanted the pain of it again. Anything but this middle.

Seeking an exit his car heaved over one yellowstriped loma after another, past Linens 'N Things, Blenzers, Leather For Le$$, Hacienda House, Mattress Discounters, Dent Removers, heading toward the main road but reaching a curb that cut him off from it, turning parallel to the curb past the back of Circuit City where barriers turned him back from further construction to a blank wall and dumpsters where he turned sharply to brake at DO NOT ENTER SEVERE TIRE DAMAGE forcing him into a smaller lot where Ah-dór-no Hair Salon, En-Dev'R Computers, Try Us Bail Bonds ushered him out upon First American Title and Coldwell Banker to the promise of an EXIT and NO LEFT TURN. As he stared in that foreclosed direction waiting for a break in the traffic, a woe beyond pain rose in him, at what he'd never valued enough to feel the loss of, it came to him now, the pent and denied longings of his baffled heart rising briefly to an apprehension of the true scale of his grief, before submerging again into the remorselessness of the everyday and the freeway to Codornic s XIT NLY, and into his driveway where he stilled the car and sat in gathering darkness listening for he didn't know what. On some road out of sight was some obstruction, a metal plate or a loose manhole cover, and from it came a hollow thump that echoed briefly as vehicles passed over and were gone, echoed through him like a tocsin of loss. As he opened the car door, wind harried the papers on the seat beneath his hand which clamped them and tucked them firmly under one arm before he dashed through a bluster of rain flung from the sky against the door slammed hard on fully gathered night, as he wandered from one room to the next, into the kitchen where it seemed a voice muttered, masked by the refrigerator's motor, rising from time to time almost high enough to make itself understood, until the motor shut off, and in its shadow came the murmurous drip of water in the sink, buried then by the whine of the microwave heating dinner, carried with a glass of golden wine to the sofa where at last he settled papers before him, the mutterings of the house submerged in the unattended flicker of The Truth Is Out There.

Saturday morning came complacently into the house, lingering in the nearly bare rooms, touching blond wood and pale fabric, chrome and glass, browsing at the laminate bookshelf where The One Minute Manager leaned in to touch 7 Habits of Highly Effective People and Principle-Centered Leadership stood up to Managing At the Speed of Change and Stewardship: Choosing Service Over Self Interest had given over its struggle to hold back Thriving On Chaos which sat heavily upon Parsifal's Briefcase upheld by cassette tapes Remember To Breathe, passing all by to follow the path sick sorrow took, finding Quine out in the kitchen for coffee and oranges by a sunny chair, only to lose him again in the one room that showed, in its dim disorder, anything like life, what Lynn called his mess room, a desk with papers strewn like leaves across its surface, a computer monitor topped by a seamsplit cardboard carton sagging like a heavy bough and beside the desk a banker's box DESTROY AFTER and D NULL upended now for a flood of papers folders xeroxes and a curious small white stone figure crudely carved, some kind of dog perhaps, put aside while he sorted printouts, some of them ten years old or more, accordion fold dot matrix, perf edges gone brittle, and some faint pervasive burning smell coming from somewhere, not from the papers, not from the house, not from the air, that edge of burning, the halogen lamp was it? but though he wandered out into the fading sun angling through the outer rooms he kept returning to the dim room like a dog to its vomit, searching compulsively for what he couldn't name, some enemy, whatever but himself that had brought him to this pass, sorting through the box of papers he'd checked out of the vault, Superbright materials, the same he'd been immersed in during the worst year of his life, drawn again into that intensity, into a sense that he was still a part of all that he might have been, while the yellow legal pad Stewardship Notes he'd set out to map the Lab's future and his own was gradually covered over by the past, while outside the drone of rain, the chipping of some bird, the hiss of passing tires went mostly unnoticed until the drone imperceptibly tapered off into a silence more indifferent than accusing yet he looked up in alarm from his preoccupation out to where shafts of setting sun pinned a tanbark oak, green and shot through with redness, against a slategray sky, pinning too his distanced gaze to this offhand splendor in a kind of panic, so he felt like someone moved from his proper time and place, as though this unlooked for appearance and imminent fleeing of sunlight, like that casual flock of pigeons sinking in the isolation of the sky, were a threat as palpable as the wineglass in his hand coming down golden and heavy and refracting cusps of lamplight onto Articles of Incorporation Nullpoint Systems, an S Corporation, shareholders Aron Réti Daniel J Root Leo H Highet.

He woke on the sofa in dimness threaded with rain sound, from a dream of Nan standing in halflight before some darker interior, her hand coming up slowly to brush aside a veil of auburn hair as she turned to face him, a smell of sandalwood from her mouth soft and opening to speak: —I love only you. A sweet bitterness pierced him, as if he'd never before seen this face, this capacity, herself in her fullness: but time and the limpidity of dream made it clearer than the truth he'd never grasped, a truth that slipped from him even as he came into the gravity of wakefulness, to the room where papers still waited for his sorting, as if any truth could be found there, until he looked up in alarm at the darkness which again had gathered unheralded and unheeded around his reach for the lamplight which sent cusps dancing through the golden contents of the wineglass now resting on Stewardship Notes with its scribbled lines, its bullets and question marks not yet evolved into cows nor dogs, some five and a half pages of possibilities and questions that were not yet as clear as the truth he turned from in frustration, retreating to the living room where the sofa grudgingly took his weight as he clicked on the television and thumbed away from the onslaught of cued laughter at —So what was that all about? to a music lugubrious with menace, —she will likely be his next meal, on to a tense, —photon torpedoes on my mark, thumb reflexively pressing as he settled into that stupor of abused attention which promised, without delivering, respite from the next salvo of cued laughter at —thought I'd leave it ou

—you'd expect to pay

—Great American Broadcasting now on television my friends your host Tuck Eubanks doing everything perfec

—ght, now you can use this life-transforming system to be happier, fitter, healthier, to have more money, to

—like the way you look, I guarantee

—ruins are mute testimony to the dauntless vitality of this once prou

—viewers like you

—beautiful knives Jack just look at this twelve inch Bowie

—we have prayer staff that pray for us seven days a

—relentless pursuit of the

—personal power to break through the barriers that hold you back

—from the destruction that overtoo

—seven days a week in Fairf

—double riveted full tang construction titanium blade with serrated edge and blood groove

—can do know how

—when you feel powerful, money is attracted to you

—if it doesn't say Jiffy Lube it can't be Jif

—and by the Venham Foundation, enhancing the wellbeing of the Bay Area by supporting

—material and spiritual abundance

—on easy pay today but it won't be on easy pay past midn

—inspire people to be more than they can be

—three kinds of assets, physical financial and

—the emotional bank account is the essence of win-win

—training you need to land a high paying job in comput

—pledge at the sixty dollar level you'll get

—there we go for ya

—all you have to do is put God where he belongs

—in a Three Tenors at Snowmass tote bag
—another anonymous clump of flotsam in the flood
—DeVry School of
—Academy of Art Coll
—capital flows to the barrier of least resistance
—and the Lord commended the unjust steward, becau
—Maharishi University of Management
—the endtime transfer of wealth
—not available in stores
—within that range of democracy that we can afford
—what we're gonna do right now for ya is we get a lot of questions
—and remember, net worth *is* self worth
—tire collection of thirteen blades yours for the low lo
—plete set of wealth building seminars on videocass
—everything you've ever wanted right here right n
—1-800-ENDTIME or reach us on the Internet endtime at endtime
dot com

—if therefore ye have not been faithful in the unrighteous mammon, who will commit to your trust the true riches? And if ye have not been faithful in that which is another man's, who shall give you that which is your own?

—you'd expect to pay . . . for such surcease of thought, for respite not retreat, harried at every step in pursuit of what can't be bought, to pay and pay again only to be roused from slumber by this voice strident and oracular, —Then he which had received the one talent came and said, Lord, I knew thee that thou art an hard man, reaping where thou hast not sown, and gathering where thou hast not strewn. And I was afraid, and went and hid thy talent in the earth: and lo, here thou hast that which is thine! and if something in Quine were buried in some forgotten place, it would be his heart now groping vainly for what it had missed, but when his eyes filled it was at nothing he could name, it was at the flickering signs that appeared and fled on the screen. —Take therefore the talent from him, and give it unto him which hath ten talents. For unto every one that hath shall be given, and he shall have abundance: but from him that hath not shall be taken away even that which he hath. And cast ye the unprofitable servant into . . . an outer darkness that came promptly upon his press OFF to bring that desired, if temporary, surcease.

—Thought . . . which returned relentlessly as the sun, climbing now over the unfinished facade for a day or at least a morning free of rain, rose struggling above the ceaseless growling and grinding and crashing below with its descant of hammering and beeping as Quine held a tissue to his nose and repeated, —. . . phones getting fixed? —Thought they were, mine's okay, you still having trouble . . . ? as Bran Nolan edged round around some boxes just inside the door and Quine picked up for a waspish voice —ister Dial Tone? seems to have come out of neutral, beating everybody up over this thing, real passive aggr, with his face reddening for —What's all this? as Quine hung up, —Oh, I asked Frank Szabo for some documents, he seems to have dumped a load on me . . . and Nolan dropped a sheet onto the desk, —Sorry, don't mean to dump any more on you, but . . . as Quine loudly blew his nose. —Having trouble since I took over and the noise outside isn't helping it's a wonder I get anything done.

—I won't keep you long, just wondered where Dennis got that tune generator of his, thought it was a little too sophisticated for him, turns out to be some friend of Highet's, "Algorithmic Composition by Rule-Based AI," by Leo Highet Charles Hollis and Jeffrey Thorpe, look at the fine print, "funded in whole or part by Defense Advanced Research Projects Agency order 4796 under Contract F33615-87-C-1499, US patent and corresponding overseas conventions pending." Nice to know DARPA's looking out for the arts, I wonder if they know they're funding a startup.

—Do you think this came out of the Lab? Is there a problem there?

—I don't really care about that, I just think the patent's cute. World's running out of real resources to exploit, so let's commodify the intangible and the unspeakable. Doing a damn fine job of it so far too as far as I can, speak of the devil, hello Dennis.

—Dennis? Are you, are you still here?

—It's my entrepreneurial leave.

—But you haven't left.

—I have, but I signed back on freelance to help the Lab diversify

and manage its post-Cold War R&D portfolio, kind of intrapreneur-
ing. I thought I should talk to you abou

—Not now Dennis, I'm

—because I've identified some scientific project areas I think you
should

—n't you see I'm busy with Bran, just send me e-mail or make an
appointment with Dol

—representing customers at DOJ and they're looking for partne

—. . . Justice?

—to develop law enforcement technologies for drug interdiction,
antiterrorism, crowd control, surveillance, it's quite a menu of programs, I could give you a briefing, I've talked to several group leaders
and there's a high level of interes

—Look Dennis, I wouldn't, I mean, people here are frightened for
their lives right now so of course they'll look interested in anything
that has funding attached, but it's not a good time to be . . . reaching
for another tissue to stanch the tearing of his eye.

—But this is exactly what we need, more military-to-civilian technology transfers, see I have a list here, ah, multiple microphones as
gunshot locators with or without tracking surveillance cameras and
return-fire weapons, there's a chief of police down on the peninsula
ready to buy that as soon as it's available, what else, a way to shut
down auto engines with microwaves, got some real interest from the
CHP there, and a smart gun that can't be fired if it's stolen, crowd-
control devices, strobe light grenades, sticky foam cannons, subsonic
can

—This is what, a DOJ wish list or things we're already working on?

—A little of each, you know just some talking points to help find
common groun

—Dennis I wish you'd, you know I'm trying to keep the science
separate from the fiction here and

—Oh this isn't fiction, just ah science PR, you know, when something has to be clearer than the truth . . .

—Clearer than the

—I'm trying to be proactive you know, put first things first, think
win-win, synergize . . .

—Yes well syner, perhaps you can synergize somewhere else

—Well but this is really what we need

—Dennis, what I really need's an antibiotic for this cold, would you

—Cold's a virus, wouldn't help, said Nolan.

—Oh I see, but an antiviral . . .

—Dennis, please . . .?

—What about Justice?

—Later! as through the swinging office door an orotund voice slipped in, —let's put the dots together, and

—What's the other thing, Bran?

—We need to talk about toxics mitigation.

—At Site Alpha? I thought we'd expanded that area.

—We can't keep buying up buffer zones indefinitely. The plume's about two miles long now, but given the complex hydrogeology of the site it's impossible to predict how far it might go.

—We're modeling nuclear explosions and we can't model this?

—We don't have quite the budget for environmental remediation that we have for blowing things up. But Site Alpha's not the issue. It's the new building, as Quine turned to take in its facade swept by a ray of sun against a slate sky.

—What?

—I brought this up a few months ago, you may recall. Do you still have the files I sent up?

—Yes, I think, just let me, he rummaged through drawers, opening and partly closing them, coming at last upon a folder, Environmental Report New Construction L-301-92. —Chivian-Harris, Soil Analysis, action levels, iodine, mercury, chromium, strontium, lead, nitrates, perchlorethane, trichlorethane, benzene, ethylene dibromide, polychlorinated biphenyls, volatile organic . . .

—Look at the next report.

—The, ah, who is it, Boole and Clay, trace levels of, approved and accepted . . . what happened, did we clean it up?

—No.

—Then this doesn't make sense . . . Quine paged to the next folder. —Soil engineer, I can't make this out, nuclear density tester misaligned, negative readings, visual approval only, signed T Kuhn Engineer, well this doesn't seem very important, but why the two reports?

—It's a discrepancy, isn't it. I thought you should be aware of it.

—Well, but Bran, this stuff is two years old, I mean the building's up, what am I supposed to do about it?

—See, the thing is, a lot of soil was trucked offsite.

—So?

—A good guess would be that it went to other Credne job sites to be used as fill.

—What are you saying? Is that soil contaminated or not?

Nolan shrugged. —Maybe you should take the files home with you, look at them closely.

—I really, you know I've got enough on my pl

—These reports are a matter of public record. Anybody who bothered to look them up would see something's fishy. The CANT suit is tactical, it's about our EIS being defective because we screwed up on some maps. So that's the lever they use to slow us down, but it could also lead to discovery of material we'd rather not let out.

—Like these reports.

—I realize the last thing you want is to, ah, dig this stuff up. Despite what the secretary's saying about openness. But you realize, this contamination could be out in the community.

—We don't know that, or, or how bad it is, and even if we did, we don't know where it is.

—That's true.

—So what are you suggesting.

—Me? I'm not suggesting anything.

—I mean it's Boniface's job to handle this stuff, isn't it?

—Well, Boniface is usually content to let a press release be his umbrella. But if that's what you want . . . as Nolan went out the door past, —lies being perpetated, and Quine followed to pause at Dolores's desk for her quizzical look over God Wants You To Be Rich while she turned down —to error is human . . .

—When's my next appointment, Dolores?

—Jeremy Rector at two.

—Fine, until then see that I'm not disturbed, and that especially includes Dennis Kihara, returning to, as she turned up —his own petty fiefdom . . . or if not that at least a temporary sanctum, where he sat heavily, unfolding Ohlone Valley Herald to his name striking at him like a venomous barb, *Interim director Philip Quine defended the hiring of Jeremy Rector, former auditor with the General Accounting Office. Rector supervised a report that critics say downplayed the Lab's exaggerated claims for the Superbright x-ray laser. Quine said he did not hire Rector but said he was "the most qualified person" for the Lab job and had "no conflict of interest".*

He tapped MEM 2 for, —You've reached the offices of Citizens Against Nuclear Technology. If you know your party's, pressing 303 for —Lynn Hamlin. Is not in her office. Please, hanging up just as the phone buzzed for Dolores's voice, —Senator Chase is here.

—What?

—He says he's sorry to come by without an appointment, but do you have time

—Jesus Chr, yes, all right, give me, just one, one . . . as he held the phone away for the gathering force of a sneeze, —Damn! and smatters of mucus on the mouthpiece, the Herald, his right palm, as he blotted frantically with a tattered tissue the papers he swept into a half opened drawer, dropping the Herald in the trash can as he wiped his palm on its edge, leaving the desk bare except for 1994-1999 Institutional Plan and a small gold cylinder just as the inner door opened to a gray suit, crisply pressed, navy and red striped tie the only color below a patrician face clean as scraped parchment, sharp nose and tapered chin at the point of a wide jaw, gray hair as impeccable as the suit, eyes that same color of a worn coin, taking in Quine's worth as the thin mouth almost smiled. With Chase was a young aide, tall and sallow.

—Doctor Quine, it's a pleasure. Hard to believe you've been here all these months and I haven't visited.

—Senator it's it's quite a, a . . . as he came around the desk half extending a hand then feinting and gesturing with it. —Please sit down.

—Sorry to pop in like this, but I had a gap in my schedule so I thought I'd pay my respects. See how you're getting on.

—Well, it's, as you know, it's a challenging job.

—That's what staff is for, right, Kevin? turning not at all to the blankeyed aide. Chase walked to the window and looked out on the unfinished building, currently in shadow against vivdly green hills swept with dapples of sunlight. —Quite a view. All the way to Mount Ohlone.

—Yes, I, it's quite something.

—I remember when this was all open space. When I was a kid I used to ride out by Camp Jepson. Before the Lab. A long time ago. A different world. Chase continued staring out. —I care about this region. I care about the Lab. I've watched both grow all my life. I think the Lab is good for the region, the region needs . . . although the coincolored eyes narrowed on the scene they'd once embraced with gladness and trust, a scene now hard to make out under the decades of growth and the striving after some good also hard to identify under its accumulated necessities. Chase gave it up and turned back to the room. —But not the Lab as it's been run lately. My top priority now is to restore trust in the Lab's credibility. Kevin?

The aide came to life. —The secretary of energy is going to announce science based stockpile stewardship as part of the F Y ninety-five budget. Next month the Appropriations Committee is going to hear testimony about the program and nonproliferation. The senator would like you to testify about the need for certain program elements, particularly the Avalon laser and its importance in the continued absence of testing.

—I just got back from Washington, Senator. I have a, a lot on my, my . . . Quine reached for a tissue.

—Yes, I know it's a pain in the neck. How's everything going for you here?

—Well, quite well. We're doing quite, quite well with our, our civilian missions, with our CRADAs, we have quite a few success stories . . .

—Dual use.

—We're calling it dual benefit now.

—There's a faction in Congress going after federal programs with a meat axe. They're zealots. They want to abolish whole departments. Health and Human Services, Education, Energy.

—They, they can't be serious, can they? Energy? Who would manage the weapons?

—Department of Defense. We don't want that. We want the university to continue managing the Lab because it attracts top talent and it provides an atmosphere of intellectual honesty. Your predecessor did a lot to damage the Lab's credibility on the Hill. As long as the Lab is perceived as some poorly managed vestige of an earlier time, it's vulnerable to these attacks. If, however, we present a vigorous new Lab with a new post-Cold War mission that requires its scientific expertise, we can resist these attacks. Are we on the same page?

—Well, I think that's, I mean yes, I would support . . .

—So my question is, is Avalon and science-based stewardship the best way to accomplish the goal of safeguarding our nuclear stockpile?

—Well, of course we've discussed other options, sampling, remanufacturing, but in terms of, of attracting talent, expertise, of keeping our scientists interested, I think, in light of what you've said, I think it's clear that the Lab, the Lab's future requires Avalon.

—Good. Then you'll say as much in Washington?

—If that's what, yes, sure, I, and I, I ought to explain the dual benefit element . . .

—The what?

—The dual, you know, inertial confinement fusion . . . ? Quine looked at the gold cylinder on his desk, as if at a talisman or totem. Chase followed his gaze incuriously for a second. —We'll be igniting deuterium and tritium in a fusion reaction. That's essential to stewardship, because only that produces the same high energy physics regime as a thermonuclear blast, and it's really the, the only way to do it without testing.

—Good. That's exactly what I want to

—But it could also lead to commercial fusion power . . .

—Of course I don't want to tell you what to say. Mention that if you like, but we've been funding that since the fifties and I'm not holding my breath waiting for the lights to come on.

—Yes but, but there've been substantial advances, and of course it may reassure those who see only weapons app, oops, excuse me, let me get, as Quine picked up the phone for, —Miss Hamlin is downstairs with a visitor's pass.

To Quine's helpless look, Chase offered, —I won't keep you much longer.

—Ah, all right Dolores, tell them, just, send her up. Sorry, you were . . .

—I assume there are people here upset about the end of testing.

—Well . . .

—Can you manage them?

—What do you mean?

—You're the clean break. Do you have a problem being the bad guy? Because that's not the impression I got from your Taliesin report.

—I can do it if I have to. It's not something I enjoy.

—Good. That was a problem with your predecessor, he enjoyed it.

The office door swung open and Chase's pale eyes went to Lynn for a moment, then back to Quine. Chase turned and extended his hand to

—Lynn, what a surprise. I never thought I'd see you inside the gates.

—You know each other? said Quine.

—Oh, Lynn and I are old campaigners.

—Senator. Her face had reddened. Chase for a moment indulged the ghost of a smile.

—Doctor Quine and I are doing a little horse trading.

She shot Quine a look. —I'll leave you then. Sorry to interrupt.

—No, please, stay, said Chase. —It saves me a trip. I was going straight to your office after this.

—Yes I, I was planning to meet you there.

—Lynn, here's what I have for you. The secretary is almost surely going to approve the Avalon facility. The president thinks it's our best shot at getting the comprehensive test ban treaty ratified.

—But no. Any signal that the US isn't serious about reducing its arsenal will jeopardize both the CTBT and the nonproliferation treaty renewal next year. I've been to Geneva, you should talk to the Indian delegation or the Pakistanis or even the Israelis, because it's crystal clear to them, they see the stewardship program as bad faith, as a way for the declared nuclear states to go right on developing new weapons. They know we're sharing technology with the French and British, technology we won't share with them. They see that stewardship is about continuing US nuclear dominance. The president might as well come out and say we plan to keep our nuclear arsenal forever, treaty or not. I've explained all this to your staff . . .

—Repeatedly.

—Then what don't you understand?

—What don't you understand, Lynn? The Cold War's over. We'll be down to START II levels within ten years. You should be celebrating.

—START II is still thousands of bombs. I want to see zero bombs.

—Lynn, you know why we can't go to zero. The Nuclear Posture Review directs the Department of Energy to maintain the ability to design, fabricate, and certify new nuclear warheads if necessary.

—Can I remind you what Article Six of the NPT says? "Each of the parties to the Treaty undertakes to pursue negotiations in good faith on effective measures relating to cessation of the nuclear arms race at an early date and to nuclear disarmament, and on a Treaty on general and complete disarmament under strict and effective international control."

—You know it by heart.

—"Good faith, effective measures, complete disarmament."

—There's no timetable.

—"At an early date." We signed in nineteen sixty-eight.

—There's no timetable.

—So the US is going to continue to say one thing and do another. That's not just bad tactics, senator, it's immoral.

Chase glanced at his watch. —Lynn, you know what you get when you mix morality and politics? You get Jimmy Carter. Nice man, decent man, very hard worker. He came to Washington committed to eliminating nuclear weapons. He said two hundred warheads was enough for deterrence. He meant it, too. He worked for it. And what did he get? He got the MX missile, the cruise missile, the Trident sub, the B-2 bomber, and Ronald Reagan as a successor. Chase looked again at his watch. —I've got to go.

—Senator, at the very least there should be public hearings about the proliferation issue.

Chase was again looking out the window toward Mount Ohlone. —Talk to my staff, Lynn. Maybe we can arrange something. You realize Lynn's trying to make more work for you, Doctor Quine.

—It's what she does.

—Okay, see you in DC.

—Thank you for stopping by, senator . . .

—Kevin? The aide came to life and opened the door, letting in, —the battlefield of the political arena, if I may be poetic, before it swung to and Lynn turned to Quine.

—What did that mean, see you in DC?

—I have to testify.

—About?

—Aspects of stewardship.

—What's wrong, are you annoyed with me?

—I just . . . Quine held a tissue to his nose and blew. —I just wish you'd told me you were coming.

—You don't want people to see us together.

—It has nothing to do with, Lynn, it's, no, I just think it's not, not wise to give people a chance to, to gossip . . .

—Are you worried the FBI's going to pull your clearance or something?

—It could happen.

—Where are we going, Philip?

—Going?

She picked up Institutional Plan 1994-1999 Draft and dropped it. —Is there a five year plan for us? The time we've been together, I'd expect a little more consideration, not this act that you and I are, are just two opposite ends of a bargaining table. She turned and paced to the window and he followed, looking down at the flooded fountain where Chase and his aide were getting into a black car under a sky dense with the menace of rain. Quine abruptly turned and sneezed and she paced away and picked up the small golden cylinder on his desk. —What is this?

—That? It's called a hohlraum. It's a, a vessel, for indirect drive fusion. It holds the target for the laser.

—It looks like gold.

—It is. Lasers strike it evenly from all sides and it radiates x-rays. They heat and compress the target inside. It has to heat to one hundred million degrees Celsius in order to ignite. The trick is getting the outer layers of the target to, to, do you really want to hear this?

—Yes. What's the target?

—A frozen capsule of deuterium-tritium. Small, about a millimeter. See, you heat it so that the outer layers boil away like rocket fuel and compress the center. You want the increased pressure so you don't have to heat the entire target to ignition temperature. But the heating has to be uniform, if the target doesn't stay spherical, it'll fly apart. The hohlraum helps even out the radiation, but there's always some leakage and nonuniformity, so the lasers have to be aimed precisely. A hot spot forms at the center of the target, the imploding fuel ignites there, and the burn propagates outward. You have to time and shape the laser pulses to pull this off. Nanoseconds. And there are hydrodynamic instabilities that can distort the sphere and break up the hot spot before, before . . . this must be boring.

—No, it's . . . you make it very clear. Her fingers turned the hohlraum.

—The aim is to get more energy out than we put in. That's called breakeven. That tells us it can be done. It's beautiful, isn't it?

She put it down. —This is your work, isn't it. I'm sorry that I forget that.

—Will I see you tonight?

Her eyes lost the edge of calculation they'd had since she walked in on Chase. —Do you want to?

—We haven't spent a night together since you got back.

—I have to work, I'm still catching up.

—I do too. And I have this rotten cold.

—Come to my place. Bring your work.

—No. You come to mine.

The skin of his neck jumped at her touch. Her mouth opened on his. The length of her body pressed against him to turn from his closing arms and quickening pulse with a coy smile and, —Later . . . when the light from outside had ceased to challenge the halogen glow on his desk and his eyes and back turned upward, as if he could see already the dimming of the sky over the line of traffic joining the freeway behind the smoke from a decrepit pickup hauling yard tools, the sound of horns and motors of one car after another passing him trapped by their passing behind it, craning anxiously past the clicking of his left turn signal and the sting of his tearing eye for an opening that didn't come before orange cones forced him onto a banked curve and a vacant road stretching like the last avenue of light toward a wall of cloud dark as slate behind radiant green hills. He slowed before this dire splendor, light tangible as a thick plasma holding its energy for the act of perception that could free it, and he stared dumbly for a minute before turning back into the fierce eye of sunset peering through cloud at a lattice of steel beams now half clad in travertine and bottlegreen glass encroaching on the open land beyond it, past Extended StayAmerica Now Renting and REG L CINEM S IM X, past those expanding edges of a consensual economic reality that had only an estranged and grudging relationship with its natural counterpart, till he rejoined the line of taillights flowing across the overpass, he hadn't thought there could be so many cars, nervously twitching the radio to, —uclear waste repository is a death sentence on Nevada that we cannot live with, silencing it as he pulled into the driveway behind Lynn's Toyota Free Tibet for a second of JAM blinking blue before cutting the ignition with a dead sound. Coming inside, he saw Lynn on the sofa, papers spread on the table before her, a wineglass weighing them down, an empty plate crossed by flatware.

—I ate already, I hope you don't mind, I was ravenous, I still haven't adjusted to the time change.

—No, it's okay . . .

—Takeout lasagna in the fridge, you can heat it in the microwave.

—Yes, okay, later I will.

—In Geneva I met someone who knew you. Andrew Sorokin? He was surprised to learn what you do now. He said you wrote a paper together once, is that right?

—Sorokin . . . ? In Geneva?

—He works at CERN, as Quine came forward to take from her a thick sheaf and to hold the hand. —You should read it, it's about the proliferation risks of stewardship.

He glanced at The Quest for Fourth Generation Nuclear Weapons and the familiar name, the twinge it brought.

—Yes well, I'm kind of under the gun with, paging quickly to Executive Summary, where *The construction of large ICF microexplosion facilities in both nuclear-weapon and non-nuclear-weapon States will give the arms race a fresh boost.* —I'll, you know, look at it when I get a chance but I think he's got the wrong idea here, Avalon isn't to design new weapons.

—No? Look at this . . . at the fall of a printout headed Department of Energy Office of Research and Inertial Fusion, —Lynn please I get this all day at work, can't we . . .

—Just where I highlighted, and he scanned down the page past Core R&AT Program Elements (Detail), flipped to Concept Design and Assessment where, under a yellow highlight, he read *Concepts under consideration in this Program Element range in complexity from relatively minor modifications in the components of existing weapons to major changes in warhead subsystems, or to entirely new physics designs for a proposed or candidate weapon.*

—Look at the next page.

He turned to *new ideas needed to evolve and improve the stockpile,* looked down at her set features, —Keep going, and scanned ahead to Concept Design Studies, *arising out of the experiences during and after the Gulf War that indicated potential military utility for types of nuclear weapons not currently in the stockpile.*

—Lynn, look, I'm not up to speed with ah, as he went paging past Physics, Computation and Modeling, Systems Engineering, High Explosives, Special Nuclear Materials, Tritium, —ah with all the details here but

—Why not? Isn't it your job?

—I'm working twelve hours a day but my God there's hundreds of thousands of pages of this stuff, I read what I have to but my God

—What's so difficult to understand, they're saying one thing in public and here they're saying another, "entirely new physics designs", did you see that?

—Yes but look these are concept designs, it, here, it says right here a concept is supported by the Program Element only through a proof of principle demonstration, and, and at such time that a new concept matures to the point of inclusion in a formal directed study, see, what it means is

—Philip I can read I know what it means, it means they're playing a shell game and not including new weapons under stewardship proper. But they're still doing it and reserving the right to transfer it at any time.

—Well but concept studies are

—It's a program element! It's core research!

—Where did you get this, anyway?

—It's on the DOE's public server.

—So how incriminating is that? Out in the open, why would they put it on the server if . . . as he flipped the pages shut, reading in the upper corner ftp://dp.doe.gov/dp-10/dp-11/detail.d11.

—I'm sure it's there by mistake. They're shoveling documents online to comply with the vice president's National Information Infrastructure program. But we have it now and it shows what DOE really means by stewardship.

—You ah, you didn't use the word stewardship in Geneva, did you? Because it's still, you know, the program hasn't been announced. . .

—Oh Philip, everyone knows, even Chase said it, you've been sharing data with the French Megajoule project, it's practically identical to Avalon.

—Where did you hear that?

—It's common knowledge. Why, what is it, is something wrong? You look upset.

—I'm just, Lynn, I want to be able to tell you things, but not, not if you leak them to the press.

—Leak? What are you, I never

—The Ohlone Valley Herald is running articles about Jeremy Rector. Did you tell them?

—No! But her face turned from him and she frowned at the floor before looking back, her brow darkened by something between anger and chagrin. —I told Tony.

—Lynn, how could you?

For a moment anguish rose in her face, tossed there in a brief tumult of conscience, and subsided in a blush more shamed than chastened over the stubborn downturn of her lips. —I asked you, don't you remember, I asked you if you were telling me. If you want me to keep things to myself you have to tell me, you have to be clear, I can't read your mind.

—Lynn, this kind of thing, it's internal Lab business, I don't want to have to watch everything I say to you, you just, just need to exercise a little judgment when you

—I'm sorry, Philip, but this kind of thing, your hiring records, they're not secret, and Rector, you were disgusted by his Superbright report, weren't you?

—But now I'm taking the heat, and I didn't even hire this guy!

—So fire him.

—No, I can't.

—Why not? Why back some sleazy decision of Highet's?

—Because don't you see it's my decision now! I can't back away from what I said to the Herald. If only you'd let it be I could have

Again the anguish rose in her face, cresting this time into anger. —Don't make it my fault! If firing him's the right thing to do, don't say I've made it politically inexpedient for you.

—Politi, do you have to make everything, it's not, this is, there's nothing wrong here, it's, he just knows the, the ropes, you know, it's like if you, you can hire an ex-IRS agent to take along to an IRS audit it's, it's the same thing, it just helps to clarif

—Make things clearer than the truth?

—That's not what I'm doing! God Lynn do we have to, please, can't we just, please, I missed you . . .

She turned from his outstretched arm, folding hers together, looking away for a moment, as if trying to separate what she felt from what she'd done. —Okay, let's, I'm jet lagged, and I have a lot to process from the conference. I don't want to fight. I shouldn't have told Tony about your auditor. It's not my fault he called the Herald, but I should have guessed he would. You just have to be very clear with me when you tell me something, okay? Okay? Will you? In her urgency she took both his hands in hers, and that pressure seemed to ask more than her words.

—All right, I'll, I'll try, you . . . what is it?

She pivoted away from him wiping an eye with a palm, slumping forward with the collar of her blouse fallen loose and the weight of her breast a pale curve there within. —I can't, I can't do this, keep the parts of things separate.

—Lynn, I'll, I'll try to be clearer, I will . . .

—Could we just go to bed? Please?

—Yes, all right . . . waiting then in the darkness for the gurgle of water in the sink to subside, for her silhouette briefly against the light in the doorway before it went dark and the faint sheen of white briefs and chemise against the dusk of her flesh come against him like a furnace, taking his breath first under seeking lips then under her weight sitting his hips while she gripped the hem of her chemise to pull it off over her head and drop it pooling on the floor as he craned forward, his mouth seeking to consume the pale softness offered there, hands eager as hers slipping close to the rising heat and cloistered moistness opening like petals, and her breath on his neck, chest, belly, —wait, just lie there while I . . . until his gasp as she swung a leg over to settle against the search of tongues coming free in an inarticuate moan sharpened to a cry at the first plunge quickened by her insistence, where the mirror caught the pale blade of her foot clamped around his clenched thighs driving them up the bed to where one hand flung back gripped the bedrail by the air that freshened from the window to a crescendo of rain drumming hard on the roof till its release faded to a murmur to a trickle to a whisper to nothing but the air moving to cool their spent forms in deepening stillness until —What! her leg spasmed against him and he came up on one elbow to still her with a hand on her bare shoulder lurching upward against it.

—Lynn! What is it?

—Huh!

—You were dreaming.

She sat and drew her knees to her chest, looking out into darkness.

—Are you all right?

She shook her head and her voice, when it came, was plaintive as a child's. —I couldn't think the things you need to think to make it go away.

He waited, then said, —Do you want to tell me?

—I was in a city, some strange city at night, and I couldn't remember where my car was, I kept walking around looking for it, and, and I knew someone was watching me. And I knew I was dreaming, but . . .

—Okay, it's okay now, but her face in the streetlight was still and stricken by something distant.

—That's not what scared me. She turned to look at him. —Do you ever dream about nuclear war?

—No . . . But unbidden came the image of slender rods pivoting to point into the black hollow of a crescent earth, where missiles rose in a silver swarm.

—I used to. I'd be at a window looking at the city. At night. The lights and the bridges. Then a flash and I knew it had happened. Sometimes the dream stopped there, sometimes it went on. A roar. A hurricane of fire. I haven't had that dream since I was . . .

Outside, beyond black glass, sudden light froze the yard in an apprehension of windtossed hedge and trees, a moment that for all anyone knew might be their last, until whatever had moved out there stilled and the floodlight snapped off.

—My mother was arrested in nineteen eighty-three, demonstrating. I was sixteen then. Do you remember that?

—I'd just started at the Lab. I remember a lot of people blocking the gates.

—Over a thousand. There wasn't room for them all in jail. The county put up tents at Camp Jepson. It took four days to process everyone. My mother said, even with the overcrowding, the dirty latrines, not enough food, everyone there was positive and caring, she said it felt like a family, like the beginning of a world she wanted to live in.

His hand idled at her hip, gliding across the rise of bone to a softness at the verge of hair where she met and held it with her own, turning her face so that the warmth of her brow lay against his, so that her voice vibrated there.

—I remember the day I met you, I got up very early to drive to the Lab for the demo. It was still dark, the freeway was almost empty. I took the Lab exit and the car in front of me did and the one behind me did too, and on the access road there was a string of lights ahead of me and behind me and I thought, every single person on this road is here for the demo. It felt so right. Then we passed the mustering area for the police. City, county, state, CHP, federal protective, there were so many, I thought how can we win, how can we ever win? Abruptly she released his hand and pulled back her head to look at him. —This is what I can't tell anyone but you. How hopeless it seems. The reach of his hand fell short as the bed jounced to her sitting upright, her expression remote in the dimness. —My father was a lawyer. He did a lot of pro bono work, and he used to say, you never win. I think he got some grim satisfaction from that. From fighting the same battles over and over. He thought demos were futile, he didn't like my mother going. I started going just to bug him. But he'd left us by then, he went off with another woman when I was twelve. I was so angry at him. I saw him only twice after that, once he took me to the zoo, a few years later to dinner, and he looked so, I don't know, so tortured. So embarrassed. I wasn't easy on him. Now I think he was a decent man who knew he'd done a thing he couldn't make up.

She came down on her side, leaning in to him, clutching his probing hand with both of hers, raising it from her warmth into the air. —I think of him when I see you angry, when you don't want to talk to me. I'm afraid of that, Philip, I don't understand it, why people do that, break precious things they've worked so hard to make. She clutched his probing hand with both of hers, raised it from her warmth into air.

—Do you, and he cleared mucus from his throat, —do you ever see him now?

—He died three years ago. Philip? She released his hand. —You never talk about your family.

Her leg came slewing over his and her arm crossed his chest as he rolled from her onto his side, back to her front, eyes seeking in darkness something not visible at the window where circling planes outshone the few stars struggling through the low clouds, listening for something beyond that drone of distant engines but pursued only by the warmth of her voice.

—Philip?

—We're not close. I don't talk to my father.

—What about your mother?

—She died. I was ten.

—I'm sorry. That must have been hard.

—I don't remember much of it. She was in the hospital, then she was sick in bed at home for a long time.

—What was it?

—Leukemia.

The fronts of her thighs pressed hotly against the cold backs of his, and her warm bicep draped over his as out in the darkness 11:38 consumed 11:37.

—How old was she?

—She was thirty eight when she died.

—Oh, my dear. Her embrace tightened around him. They lay in silence for seconds. —What about your father?

—He was, he was ten years older. He didn't. He never. He just, he hired housekeepers. One after another. He went to work, he worked for the state, or he stayed downstairs sitting in his red leather Morris chair.

—You sound so bitter. Is he alive?

—As far as I know.

She came up on one elbow. —You don't know? Where does he live?

—Outside Sacramento. Unless he's moved.

—So near? How long have you been out of touch?

—Since I graduated high school.

She came down off her elbow and embraced him again, pressed to his back. —You make things very hard on yourself, don't you. My artichoke.

His hand came off her. —I'm, what?

—Philip! What's wrong? I mean you're, you're prickly, and you have many layers, but, but your heart is sweet. What is it, have I hurt you?

—No, I . . .

—What's wrong?

—Nothing. Nothing.

—There is. I said something wrong, I'm sorry. Come back! as the mattress rebounded in a sudden flurry of sheets.

—It's nothing. I have to . . .

—Where are you going?

—Just to, to the bathroom.

He stood in the dark voiding. Outside a pale light fled across the sky. Through a break in the clouds, the moon appeared full and racing like a ship through foam. The view from Persephone looking back toward Earth at that moment would have shown, clustered like jewels in a handsbreadth of Aquarian space, the Sun and crescent Earth set against the diadem of Venus, Mars, Mercury, and Saturn, but its cameras pointed the other way, downward, like a man looking for dropped change on the Moon's bright and barren surface.

THREE

Though the equinox bore down, winter hung on, bracketing days of sun with downpours, relenting for a week then returning in force, breaking the banks of rivers, undermining cliffside roads and homes, covering the mountains in forgetful snow. Sun, when it appeared, penetrated his office from unaccustomed angles, striking the corner where twenty-five volumes of Funding Request FY95 were stacked on the floor in piles of varying height as from time to time he carried one to his desk, consulted it, left it open for the drift of papers and folders across it till a chance thaw exposed it to be shut and returned to the pile. Papers accumulated in wire baskets, on the desk, they fell into half opened drawers and onto the carpet, where he bent to recover Core R&AT Program Elements (Detail) as the shadow of a frown passed over his features at Characteristics Of Principle-Centered Leaders, *See yourself each morning yoking up, putting on the harness of service in your various stewardships, see yourself taking the straps and connecting them around your shoulders as you* lift the phone for —Yes? Thank you Dolores, put him through. Hello Reese I, I, wait who is this? Well get off the line! Dolores? Did you say secure line, somebody was just, oh all right, yes I'll. Yes just let me, hello? Oh hello Reese. Yes I, just fine. Oh well, you know, the usual glitches, but overall things are. Yes I do, wait just a . . . scanning the desk and jabbing the hold button to call, —Dolores! Where's that courier package! as she entered with a vinyl pouch and tossed it on his desk for unzipping and the candystriped border on the folder within, —okay I have it, mission need, earth penetrating, reduced yield. Uh huh. I'll pass this on to oh you did, okay then. My approval? Sure, give me a minute to just look over the, uh huh, okay, I see it now, in light of Gulf War lessons, seek new options for hardened nuclear, attack and destroy underground bunkers, earth-coupled shock waves, uh huh, . . . 1987? Reagan admin, yes I see it, capability against deeply buried targets, B fifty three unsuitable for, that's a, the B fifty three is a, a nine megaton device? What they used to call a city buster? What? Crowd pleaser? Oh really? I didn't know that the individual bombs had nicknames. Yes, I can see it's overkill for a bunker. Won't fit in a Stealth B two. Dial-a-yield now that's . . . oh, there's actually a dial? Uh huh. Ten to three hundred kilotons. And that's the existing mark, the, the B sixty one rev seven. Uh huh. I mean we're not, this is a modification right, not a new weap. No change to the physics package? Uh huh. Okay. Yes, I will. Oh, and Reese, one thing, as the restless stir of his fingers found Core R&AT Program Elements (Detail), —We've been saying in our public information that we won't design new weapons. Nuclear, yes, nuclear weapon designs, that's what I mean. But let me read this to you, ah . . . "concepts under consideration range from relatively minor modifications in the components of existing weapons to entirely new physics designs for a proposed or candidate weapon". Yes. That's from a DOE document on a public server. Also this . . . "concept design studies arising out of experiences during and after the Gulf War indicate potential military utility for types of nuclear weapons not currently in the stockpile". Yes well, our public information office asked me to, to clarify it. Because all this might sound like new designs to someone who, who isn't. Concepts, yes of course I understand, I just worry that someone else who, who, might, might. Yes but if, I mean it's on an open server! Anyone could. Yes I do, right here. It's, hold on, FTP colon slash slash DP dot DOE dot GOV slash DP hyphen ten slash DP hyphen eleven slash detail dot D eleven. And just, just one more thing, research on pure fusion weapons is still classified, correct? I thought so, but, as papers flurried off the edge of the desk to settle on the carpet, —here it is, sixteen A, unclassified, fact of research on pure fusion weapons, do you know about that? On the same server. Uhhuh. I see. Fact of research but no details. Well, I ask because of Avalon and the nonproliferation issues, I mean we have a public hearing coming up don't we? Yes, the one Chase asked for. You've scheduled it for, when, May? Yes we'll have the Conceptual Design Report done by then. Yes, just so, so we're on the, the same . . . as the next page was uncovered by the brusque sweep of his hand, pushing aside DOE Performance Agreement, *The Department has changed its priorities, so that we contribute to the restoring of the American Dream, improved communications and trust, a safe and rewarding workplace that is results-oriented and fun,* and DOE Openness Initiative Update: *Appointment of the Advisory Committee on Human Radiation Experiments has enabled the Department to regain control of the controversy and to slow down public,* for UCRL-ID-120738 Avalon System Design Requirements, folding it firmly back to X-Ray Laser Experiments, *needed to preserve our competency in non-LTE design and to develop short-wavelength x-ray lasers for dual-benefit applications.*

The days lengthened, extending the near perpetual twilight of wind and rain that stippled the construction area, the parking lot, the freeway, the driveway of his house, most often empty, with Lynn preparing for the hearing, or away on some retreat. Twice in the month they were together for a night, a bubble of time outside normal succession, a pocket utopia whose boundaries, for that moment, excluded the greater world, but always that world returned, ominous as the dark tower of cloud behind Mount Ohlone as he dropped the blinds and sat frowning at

Attn: Dr. Philip Quine, director
From: Dennis Kihara
Re: DOJ request
UCRL-JC-125797 Abs

To effectualize a Department of Justice request, E Section performed experiments stopping automobile engines with microwave beams. Using Laboratory equipment, we beamed microwaves onto an engine. The engine, which was idling, stopped within a couple of seconds.

Because our equipment could only generate modest amounts of power, the hood was opened to maximize the exposure. Our automo-

bile was a standard government issue sedan. We believe that the microwave confused the computer. A sensor was upset and gave the computer a too lean reading, causing the engine to stall. After the experiment, we drove the automobile back to our office 15 miles away. After hundreds of exposures under various stressing conditions, the sensor did quit.

We will present our data in a classified talk and tell our story about how the media changed our story.

Work performed under Contract W-7405-Eng-48.

—Just the kind of high quality first-principles research we want to effectualize around here . . . he muttered, as it vanished under Ohlone Valley Herald, Critics Charge, and he lifted the phone for —Dolores, tell Dennis Kihara I want to see him in here right aw . . . who? Put him on. Jeremy, how's Washington? Yes fine, the Herald seems to have, at least your hiring's no longer . . . what? No I didn't. Okay, I'll look into it. Listen, those Nullpoint papers I gave you, did you, did you show . . . what do you mean you already, Highet gave them to you? Before he? But, to clarify that he hadn't, but you mean he, no now look you mean, waiving commercial rights, spinning off shell companies you, you mean all that's legal? Yes I know DOE was encouraging technology transfer but that's what CRADAs are for you can't just . . . Yes I do want to bring it up again, there's, there's what do you mean more import, no but look this is important the principle is important! He can't get away with . . . Me? How can it bite me? I had nothing to do with it! Yes I see that but, but and what? Four hundred mill, that has nothing to do with me, how can you even . . . a, a history? Well it's not my history! But, withhold until a full accounting, who . . . Bangerter? Who's he? Armed Serv, and and where did he hear . . . ? Well it's none of his business who I, I, I, what my personal life is or what her politics are, who does he think he . . . well if he thinks he can use any of this to stop Avalon he's wrong because I'm going to do what I think is best for the Lab no matter wh . . . well fine then you just deal with that! He dropped the handset and leaned back in the chair, eyes shut, opening at last to a fly orbiting his head to land on the computer screen, where he came forward for

mQEPAzIqPxOAAAAEIALEPWTHRLZ6xOn75VZkUwjpOFI3coOOVmB35xXcw

Gym+Du8biuNgKrK+KwkHvJxdaywtkixRZkl/IEKEktWviruj520c1tuy5DNV+
MR0pZUDKZbbjlI2PsCuTS9D4qFRXQ/hNKbTtFjQD9RavfBr2kTHEFqzqn-
mJY9KOlm2bK312Wz05
and squandered a minute trying six letter permutations at Password:
••••••, as the fly lighted on Counterproliferation In The New World
Order and he quietly raised Ohlone Val poised to come crashing down
on a white stone dog uncovered by the force of his blow as the fly
entered a new orbit eccentric as any asteroid's. Eyes narrowed on it he
lifted the phone for, —Dolores? Where's Dennis Kihara? He's not?
First day he's been gone since his leave started . . . as the sun broke
briefly upon his desk, finding him unwilling to turn for long from the
ongoing distraction of the present to the eternal reproach of the past
or the future's capricious threats, addressed in gory detail by STRAT-
COM 2010 Potential Uses For Low-Yield Nuclear Weapons In The
New World Order, *We doubt that any president would authorize the
use of nuclear weapons in our present arsenal against Third World
nations. It is precisely this doubt that leads us to argue for the development of subkiloton nuclear weapons, weapons whose power is
effective but not abhorrent . . . An earth penetrator with a yield of just
ten tons could hold buried leadership and C3 at risk while keeping col-
lateral damage very localized . . . The most appealing concepts focus
on nuclear warheads with very small yields and with design and
delivery techniques that minimize fallout, residual radiation, and col-
lateral damage, offering a wider range of targeting options for maintaining a credible nuclear deterrence in the new world order.* His head
lifted for the sharp rattle of rain against the window, only to lower
again to *That the US may become irrational and vindictive if its vital
interests are attacked should be part of the national persona we project
to all adversaries* . . . as he looked up into Nolan's saturnine face, col-
orless and fixed in the rainlight. —Bran?
   —Did you look at those environmental reports yet?
   —The, I'm sorry, the what?
   —Last month I gave you a couple of files concerning toxics?
   —Oh yes, I, I meant to, but you, you can see what I'm up against
here, gesturing vaguely at the clutter around him, surprised as Nolan
seriously followed his gaze across FY95, System Design Require-

ments, FUDGE: A Fusion Diagnostic for Avalon, to the edge of the desk where something hidden behind The 7 Habits of Hi seemed to catch Nolan's eye, —not, not even sure where those files are now . . .

—What's this?

—The, what . . . ? his baffled gaze rising to the white stone dog in Nolan's hand, its snout pointed skyward, its mouth a blue dart back to where haunches were more implied than incised.

—Oh it's, I think Highet left it behind. Do you know what it is?

—Coyote fetish. Navajo, maybe Zuni. He could have got it on a visit to our sister lab in the Southwest. Ten bucks at a roadside stand. So you're not doing anything about those toxics reports?

—I'll look at them, but, what with the Conceptual Design Report and I've really got to finish reviewing the System Design Requirements oh and the budget stuff . . . anyway isn't Boniface in charge of

—Okay, I can see you're busy, I'll handle it some other way.

—Thanks, I . . . as the coyote fetish went back on the desk, to hold down a turned-back page, *The monetary and deferred maintenance costs of more than fifty years of the nuclear arms race rise like a cresting wave to shadow present and future generations. The cost of building our present stockpile was approximately five trillion dollars, and the cost of managing it will be far higher,* glowing more brightly under the halogen lamp as night came on and Quine paused over Ohlone Valley Herald to tear out Respect Fades For Activists, moved some papers aside from System Design Requirements Part V X-Ray Laser Research, eyes falling on The Quest For Fourth Generation Nuclear Weapons, Andrew Sorokin, 1211 Geneva 12 Switzerland. The familiar name lashed out from a past that, like so many of these papers, refused to stay buried.

First generation nuclear weapons (NW) are uranium or plutonium fission bombs, such as the Hiroshima and Nagasaki weapons. They are relatively simple, reliable, rugged and compact.

Second generation NWs are two-stage thermonuclear devices, commonly called hydrogen bombs. A tritium-boosted fission bomb is used to implode and ignite a secondary fusion reaction which produces most of the yield.

Third generation NWs are "tailored" or "enhanced" to increase or

decrease certain effects such as degree of radioactive fallout. A typical example is the so-called neutron bomb.

Fourth generation nuclear weapons are based on atomic or nuclear processes that are not restricted by the CTBT. Their development will be essentially science based. It is likely that the first fourth generation nuclear weapons will be miniaturized explosives with yields in the range of 1 to 100 ton equivalent TNT, i.e., in the gap which today separates conventional weapons from nuclear weapons. These relatively low yield nuclear explosives would not qualify as weapons of mass destruction.

Considerable research is underway in all five nuclear-weapon states into inertial confinement fusion (ICF) and other physical processes necessary to develop fourth-generation NWs. A major arms control problem of fourth generation weapons is that their development is very closely related to pure scientific research. The chief purpose of the CTBT is to freeze the technology of nuclear weapons as a first step toward general and complete nuclear disarmament. In order to achieve that, it is necessary to implement effective measures of preventive arms control, such as internationally binding restrictions in all relevant areas of R&D whether they are claimed to be for military or civilian purposes.

—Easy for you to say . . . as he raised blinds to a night sky the blacker for floodlights glaring below it and the broken grid of lights where some had stayed late working to sketch against that blackness, as it were, some foreseeable future, some extension of these lines of light past the boundaries of the Lab and into a world bodied forth in those pages he returned to, a world in which *High Engergy Laser (HEL) systems offer the potential to maintain an asymmetric edge over adversaries for the foreseeable future. Funding for HEL Science & Technology programs should be increased to support priority acquisition programs and to develop new technologies for future applications. The HEL industrial supplier base is fragile and lacks adequate incentive to make the large investments required to support anticipated DoD needs. The DoD should leverage HEL relevant research being supported by the Department of Energy (DOE),* as he muttered, —Put assets in space you have to protect them, let's sow a few dragon's teeth while we're at it . . . industrial supplier base a little fragile let's pump up the demand . . . what time is it anyway . . . ?

Rain in the early hours abated only for the bluster of wind and a rush of dappled light across the torn and lakeleted pit below, the glistening black piles of gravel and mounds of dun earth cradling skycolored pools like a model sierra, as day made its tentative way into the empty office, asserting itself across *Types of fourth generation weapons* until the blind was dropped to close it out, and the chair creaked under his weight settling back to

1. Subcritical and microfission explosives. With 1 kg of high explosive and under 1 gram of Pu, it is theoretically possible to produce a highly compact weapon with a yield of several tons TNT equivalent.

2. Transplutonic and superheavy elements. These elements are in general fissile, and their critical masses are much smaller than that of Pu, potentially in the range of grams rather than kilograms. The goal is to find a long-lived superheavy element with a critical mass of 1 g or less. $^{267}108$ was synthesized at Dubna last year with a halflife of 19 msec, and $^{265}106$ and $^{265}107$ with halflives of about 10 seconds, confirming Nix's theory regarding stability, suggesting that close to 400 stable superheavy nuclei may be found between elements 106 and 136 and that at least a dozen of them should have halflives longer than 25,000 years.

3. Antimatter. Releases 275 times more energy per unit mass than any other reaction. Antiprotons have been captured and confined in magnetic traps. CERN is building an antiproton decelerator. Could be used to ignite subcritical burn of fissile material.

4. Nuclear isomers. High explosives have energy contents ≈ 5 kJ/g. Nuclear isomers yield ≈ 1 GJ/g. Fission yield ≈ 80 GJ/g. Long-lived isomers in the region of interest have not yet been observed.

5. Superexplosives and metallic hydrogen. Could be used to greatly reduce size of fission trigger.

6. Pure fusion. The challenge is to build a compact single-use device that can replace the huge accelerator, laser, capacitor bank, or magnet that is necessary for laboratory ignition of fission or fusion capsules. Whether or not a fusion driver such as a compact laser can be designed, ICF experiments with laboratory lasers will enable the development of mini-secondaries.

7. Superlasers. There is no fundamental obstacle to reaching the theoretical maximum intensity of 10^{24} W/cm^2. Such devices could be made compact enough to have numerous weapons applications, from fusion drivers to particle beam collimators. Their civilian applications are so numerous that containing such developments will be nearly impossible . . . and the blind lifted onto another twilight overborne by the flicker of the overhead fluorescents, their meandering buzz grating against his rising panic at another day so quickly slipped away, and he rose to snap them off, the evening light at that moment perversely swelling as the sun found space to swim beneath the leaden overcast into delicate bands of salmon and silver cloud figured on the darkness like floating meadows, till it ignited in them like a jewel and sent shafts of fire across the wide air and into the office, washing the wall with rosy light, a quickly gathered promise that as quickly faded as if sorrowed that its luminosity hadn't been seized, but was overlooked for *The Avalon Facility And The Issue Of Nonproliferation DRAFT, This section will explore, within classification guidelines, what weapons science is technically possible at Avalon.*

i. Radiation flow

ii. Properties of matter

iii. Mix and hydrodynamics

iv. Using ignition for weapons science

v. X-ray laser research

For two reasons, Avalon would not be sufficient to develop a pure fusion weapon: (1) its targets are much too small to be a weapon; and (2) the driving mechanisms and conditions that would be required for a weapon are entirely different than those required for ICF.

But that . . . overlooked and forgotten radiance returned soon enough through slats in the blind aligned so that it glazed the white stone coyote, still at attention, holding down Organization For The Creative Person, as his hand reached for it but was checked by, —Hello? Reese? Oh, yes . . . you did? Okay, let me . . . turning to the computer for

> ftp dp.doe.gov

Connected to dp.doe.gov

220 Welcome to the Department of Energy FTP Server.

Name: **anonymous**
331 Guest login ok, send your complete e-mail address as password.
Password: **quine@lucinda.lab.gov**
230 Welcome to the Department of Energy FTP Server.
230 Guest login ok, access restrictions apply.
ftp> **cd /dp-10/dp-11**
250 CWD command successful.
ftp> **get detail.d11**
550 detail.d11: Permission denied.
then lifting the handset, —Yes, I just checked, it's, it's gone. What? Yes it's, I'm just finishing it, the statement of work, I'll e-mail it to you right away . . . bringing up a new window on the screen to type quickly, *The B61 rev 11 will be designed with the help of computer simulations. Hydrotest Shot 3574 will be the basis for certifying the B61 rev 11. Full scale penetration tests will be conducted at Aguas Secas Test Site,* filling in To: reeset@doe.gov and clicking SEND. The stone dog snared his eye again and in annoyance he reached to move it, but once it was in his hand his eyes narrowed and he held it. After a moment he replaced it on the desk, turned to the computer and /highet/pgp/ and typed Password: coyote for a flood of files opening one over another until windows too many to count were overlapped with arched brows and sultry eyes and splayed limbs and grasping hands and pouting lips, where lovely Lyca, tanned in the face by shining suns and blowing winds, lay with Rose and Sharon and Lily and their valleys and the hinds of their fields putting forth what might have been green figs hanging from every man with his sword upon his thigh, while in desert wild the virgin view'd loos'd her slender dress for the threat'ning horn blush'd fiery red, seeking only itself to please, naked in the sunny beam's delight, pressing with slow rude muscle to deposit the fruits of the gushing showers from pent-up aching rivers, his eyes fixed on the lineaments of gratified desire as he muttered, —What, more of these? and the phone blurted. —Yes. Oh! No yes I'm glad you. Yes I miss you too. Yes me too, but I can't, can't come, I mean, no I don't mean it's just I'm kind of chained, to, to my I mean . . . yes but it's hard, no I mean hard to, listen, can you hold it for just a . . . ? as he put down the hand-

set and clicked QUIT to collapse the windows as he muttered —Hundreds more megabytes of smut, what was he thinking? picking up the handset again for —Lynn I'm sorry it's, I just . . . yes I know I said that I'd, that we'd, but I'm just going to have to stay tonight . . . how about Thursday? Oh. Well why didn't you tell me? Good Friday, yes you did say, I did know that but, but is it Easter already . . . ? as the office door swung wide and Dolores deposited two more boxes of papers just inside —What, what about this weekend then? Retreat from what? Oh. I see. Yes okay then I'll, I'll be home Monday by six. I promise. I do? Well yes, things are working out here I think I see some light at the end of . . . Yes, me too . . . hanging up as on the field now cleared of venery new directories appeared, /4thgen/, /icf/, /papers/, and he browsed the scanned images of papers Highet had written or, more often, cowritten, or in which he'd simply gotten a cite or acknowledgment, —Zero Point Quantum Dynamic Energy, Inflatable Kevlar Space Station, Steganography: A Novel Approach To Data Hiding, Perpetual Motion of the Third Kind, typical, not a bit of real science in sight . . . until he opened Laser Compression Of Matter For Thermonuclear Fusion A. Réti F. Szabo L. Highet 1974 and his muttering ceased and after a while he reached for a pencil and paper while his eyes remained fixed on the screen.

Calculations show that one kilojoule of light energy is sufficient to generate an equal quantity of thermonuclear energy. —But, one kilojoule . . . ? . . . staring at his own scribbles that, impossibly, seemed to confirm it, until he went on browsing into 1976, *Calculations show than ten kilojoules of light energy should be sufficient to,* and 1979, *One hundred kilojoules should provide sufficient energy,* and *Funding for the laser upgrade will assure leadership in inertial confinement fusion research,* and *Funding for validation tests of our computer models,* following the trail of increasing energies and enticing predictions and fiscal years to an apparent terminus in LANCET 1979-1991, *Overview: The Lancet series of underground tests has been undertaken to validate and refine x-ray laser codes as well as codes related to the thermodynamic ignition of deuterium-tritium (DT) capsules. The tests in this series are: Alder, Willow, Rowan, Plumtree, Primrose, Raspberry, Honeysuckle, Cherry, Goldenrod, Hawthorn, Appletree, and Taliesin.*

And within this directory was another, /data/, where he found 1013 TALIESIN DOE 911107 ASTS SHAFT P8 80 KT. Columns of numbers. T SYMM PULSE TEMP BURN . . . It was the x-ray laser data he'd spent months trying to square with simulation codes. This was his. What he'd bled over. But there were columns of unfamiliar numbers, measurements he'd never seen. As he'd piggybacked his reflectors, someone had added something else. Every other test in the series the same. Dual use. Attempts to ignite fusion capsules. And these were the roots of Avalon, going back twenty years and more. He stared out the window at floodlights and darkness. A lone figure crossed down there near the dry fountains, his shadow behind him. Quine kicked off his shoes, moved volumes of FY95 from the couch to the floor. He stretched out and shut his eyes for just a moment. Panic flickered there, in the last moment before sleep rose like a cresting wave to shadow present and future concerns.

FOUR

Damp skin against damp sheets. The radio sang softly, —öd und leer das Meer. . . .

He raised himself on an elbow to press the light. He opened Valerian 500 mg and shook out two capsules. Stink of gravesoil.

Ladies and gentlemen, madam secretary, mister President, this solemn responsibility, this prisoner's dilemma, this stinking albatross, I throw it back in your faces.

Sorry I'm sorry

Childhood house. Citrus Way. Predawn window. Cobalt blue sky, high pink horsetail clouds. White dust on the lawn. Snow? Some powder or lime. In the neighbor's yard a young woman sits in the bushes playing a guitar. Mother?

But I

Again the smell of burning, pungent as a halogen lamp.

Her face in the mirror, intent upon itself, as she combed her long auburn hair traced with gray, falling away from the volutions of her ear. Her serious gaze on him.

I

Dawn light gray in the room, creeping with its chill into the bed. He drew in his limbs and lay for a moment gathering himself as on the radio a baritone voice lept and feinted over a mutter of contrabasses and a single horn, stretching the syllables of —Kar, frei, tags, zaub, er . . . and he groped for OFF finding instead —illions of gallons of crude oil have spilled from, stabbing it to silence as he stared dully at the leaves, buds, and blooms so mildly and tenderly scenting the air outside his window, no less than the air outside the gates where, sun risen but absent behind a shroud of gray, protesters in a ragged and dispirited group clustered by the roadway bearing signs AVALON BOONDOGGLE and ZERO NOW as Quine, driving past, glimpsed a young woman in the crowd, elbow raised to rest one hand in the russet gleam of her dark hair while the other hand was up in a gesture perhaps meant to rally the others, though she passed from his sight before she completed it.

—Morning, Philip, said Szabo, suddenly at Quine's side as they entered the conference room. —I see Good Friday is April Fool's Day this year. It's like the anarchists' convention out there. How many have they got, fifteen, twenty? What's that, coffee? Not your usual

—How are you all? I just want to quickly go over our basics, get a kind of progress report from each of you, make sure we're on the, the same page as we go into the home stretch on this Conceptual Design Report. I know that some of you think the, the language we use is unimportant, but I want to, to fine tune this mission statement based on DOE's expectations. First, and I've seen most of your drafts, you all know, you should know that we no longer use the word nuclear in our public information. We say national security, special programs, threat reduction, or NBC.

—What's that, guided peacocks?

—You know what it is, Frank. Nuclear biological chemical.

—Maybe we should get nuclear out of the acronyms too.

—There's an alternative, WMD. Weapons of mass destruction.

—Sure, whatever.

—Frank, please don't take this lightly. Now if you'd all turn to . . . the pages folded back as sighs, short and infrequent, were exhaled, and each man fixed his eyes there, on the exigencies of words trying not to say what they meant.

—"ability to design, test, manufacture, and certify new weapons should the CTBT end."

—Make that "collapse", should the CTBT collapse.

—Don't start out with new weapons, start with "maintaining the arsenal".

—"maintaining the arsenal and the ability"

—make that expertise

—"maintaining the arsenal and the expertise needed to design, test, manufacture, and certify new nuclear weapons should the CTBT collapse"

—We still have new weapons in there.

—How about "maintaining expertise and developing capabilities that would be useful if the CTBT collapsed"?

—Okay, and address, you know, the safety and reliability issues . . .

—David, just, just as a matter of information, would you call a pure fusion weapon a "significant safety improvement"?

—I certainly would. Thermonuclear ignition without a fission primary would be a clear win. Much smaller, more compact bombs, without the plutonium. I hate plutonium. It's dangerous, its halflife is twenty four thousand years, and it has the ugliest phase diagram you've ever seen. I'd love to get rid of it. Of course, since Congress found out about plywood we're not supposed to be working on

—Plywood?

—Precision Low Yield Weapons Development. An Air Force initiative. Too bad, we had to put a lot of neat ideas back on the shelf for now.

—Is there, is there any more coffee? Yes, could you, thank you. Okay, let's go over the Avalon elements from the, from the top. I'm looking for, for show stoppers. Anything that might prevent us from delivering ignition.

—Capsule design and manufacture. If the fuel capsule distorts under pressure, loses its sphericity

—or if it isn't perfectly spherical in fabrication

—. . . what kind of tolerances?

—It's hard to get good data on nonlinearities, but in scaled down tests on existing beamlines, we're saying irregularities should be smaller than a micrometer

—and uniform heating of the target from all directions, within say a few percent. We can overlap beams to smooth the illumination, but

—holhraum coupling at about ten to fifteen percent, think we can get it up to twenty, twenty five

—confident we can get power in the five hundred terawatt range

—not just the power you know, it's the terawatts plus the teraflops.

—Could you say that again in English, Marshall?

—The codes have to validate the experimental data.

—Don't you mean the data have to validate the codes?

—Could we, could we possibly use a different word?

—A different word, what do you mean?

—Teraflops sounds like failure. We're selling this to Congress.

—But, but, that's the word for it. Trillions of floating point operations per second.

—I'm worried about how it sounds. How about teraops?

—Sounds like a dinosaur.

—No, it sounds optimistic. Now, is one point eight megajoules enough? Because without ignition, the case for Avalon as a stewardship element is weak.

—Jesus Phil, the case for Avalon as a stewardship element is almost nonexistent, it's just the hoop we have to jump through.

—I hope you're not sharing those sentiments outside this room, Frank. The fact is, we're selling ignition. Is one point eight megajoules enough?

—Detailed numerical simulations predict

—Any actual data?

A pause, a look, went across the room. —Well, yes, said Mosfet. —We did a test series that put to rest fundamental questions about the basic feasibility of high gain and ah confirms . . .

—Those would be the, the Lancet underground tests?

Again a look. —Yes, that's right. We, while Radiance was ongoing, as part of the underground tests then, we ignited some DT capsules. Using the blast as an energy driver. We got very useful data on

—I've seen some of that data. What I want to know is, did the capsules ignite?

—Well . . . yes.

—And the codes correctly predicted the conditions for ignition?

—Well, these were one and two dimensional codes, that's what we'll refine with the data from Avalon and the new computers. But yes they predicted . . .

—Wait. In the seventies our codes predicted ignition with one thousand joules, isn't that right? And we built a thousand joule laser and it wasn't enough. Then we raised our estimate and it still wasn't enough. Now we're up to one point eight million. Are you sure, Marshall, that our codes capture the physics?

—Not all of the physics, but, you know, those early codes, they underestimated the rate at which instabilities in the capsule could expand, but we're confident now, I mean, our models conform very well to the experiments we've done.

—It sounds like you've been talking to the skeptics, Philip.

—I want to sell this program, David, I don't want to oversell it. Marshall?

—We've been using these codes to postdict behavior from tests, including the ones you've alluded to, and

—Postdict? How about just assuring me that ignition at one point eight megajoules isn't wishful thinking?

—Philip, we've already spent our forty days and nights in the desert on this one. There are never guarantees. But under the circumstances, to protect our scientific interests under the constraints we've been given, we're convinced that we have to have Avalon and that we can do this. You're the team captain. Don't tell us not to fight.

There was a silence while Quine looked at Ware, then at Szabo, who looked blandly back. —Anything else?

—Does anyone know what's going on with the new building? I haven't seen a crew out there for weeks. If Credne wants to bid on Avalon, I mean they're what, a year behind?

—They claim it's because of the toxics mitigation work DOE required.

—I thought is was those Indian remains they found under the retention tanks.

—Never know what you're going to dig u

—tribal council in court with the *state* now, might as well make that pit a permanent feature.

—but the toxics, I mean that was a separate contract, didn't they start up a subsidiary to handle the waste, Glenn?

—It may have happened about the same time. Anyway, it's ongoing.

—Oh one other thing Doctor Quine, we're getting data from the last leg of Persephone's mission as she leaves lunar orbit to rendezvous with a near earth asteroid. That could give us proof of principle on asteroid defense and we should be ready to exploi

—Wait, asteroid def, are you talking about Slingshot . . . ? I thought we were through with all that.

—We have contracts. DoD's a customer, theater defense, and national defense are very active programs at Army, Navy, and Air Force labs.

—I thought Persephone was for lunar mapping.

—Ah, right, the cover story. The mapping was an afterthought, kind of a lollipop for NASA. We've got twelve flavors of infrared sensors onboard, the kind that track missile plumes and so forth. And we're taking a side trip to impact an asteroid at high speed.

—Impact?

—That's the plan.

—So we're still working on this even though J Section is closed.

—These things have a life of their own, Philip.

—Was I unclear, Frank? About shutting these programs down?

—We have contracts. Anway, I don't think this is the

—Fine, I'll talk to you about this later. What else?

—What about this public hearing? Do we have problems there?

—It's just an annoyance. DOE's looking to park the billions from the Texas Supercollider before Congress wakes up and takes back the money. Avalon is made for them, the fusion science makes it palatable and the weapons apps make it bulletproof. If we finish the Conceptual Design Report on schedule it should be a slam dunk.

—Yes but the weapons part, this, ah, this antinuke group CANT, they've done their homework, they're going to raise real issues there.

—Tell you what, Philip. I can get some Avalon supporters to come out for this meeting so it's not, you know, totally onesided. There are concerned parties inside the Lab and out.

—Will you be there, Frank?

—Only if I have to be.

—You do. Anything else that I need to know about? Anyone . . . ? Okay, are we done? Frank, walk with me. Quine stood last and Szabo lagged to follow.

—Are you hiding projects from me, Frank? Why don't I know about these contracts?

—Because you haven't looked? For God's sake Philip, there are thousands of projects and contracts, do you want a daily update on every one of them? I shut down J Section, isn't that enough for you, do you want to get sued by DoD, too? You know Philip, you're breaking everybody's balls in there, and for what? DOE thinks you're Mister Golden. Not long ago they almost had us all up on charges, and now they're waving billions in the scented air. Take the money and screw them.

—Well maybe if I'm, if I'm Mister Golden, maybe I'd like to keep it that way and not become known as Highet the Second. Do you know what I heard in Washington, what somebody said to my face? Some senator said, there's lies, damn lies, and what Lab people tell you. Okay?

—Jesus, Philip, do me a favor, talk to Réti, will you. He knows how this game is played, he invented it. Research is expected to lose money. You just have to go about it the right way.

—Frank, if Avalon is approved, we're only two years from groundbreaking. Not research, not engineering, but actual construction. When construction is complete we have deliverables. I don't want to be sitting here wondering how to deliver.

—Philip, I've run big R&D projects before. If we don't come in on schedule, on budget, if we don't achieve ignition right off, these are manageable problems. You amend, you rebaseline. It's R&D. This isn't the Supercollider, it isn't a snipe hunt for some theoretical particle, it's national defense. Trust me on this.

—And where was Bill Snell?

—Not really his job since you made me head.

—L Section is still involved and I want him at these meetings.

—Okay, frankly he's a little sore but I'm mending fences. Told him to work on that fast ignitor concept, some nice potential spinoffs from that in the area of

—Doctor Quine! Dolores said you

—Oh for

—Catch you later, Philip.

—Doctor Szabo are you, ah, well, I can catch up with him later, but I wonder if you remember the demo I gave back in Janu

—The, which one was that, the screensaver?

—No, the, you know, this Marc Andreesen guy, he started up a company to market that Web browser, I just wondered if you had any interest, he's calling it Netsc

—Dennis, I have more important

—Also there's an M Section initiative I'd like to

—Look Dennis you seem to have all these friends in industry, at Justice, why don't you just take a fly

—and did you get my report on the DOJ pro

—a flyer on whatever looks interesting to you okay, and just leave your reports in my in box okay, and I'll read them when I can.

—Well sure but we should talk about this M Section initia

—Dennis! Either do it or don't do it but stop bugging me about it ... ! as the office at last quieted for his deferred attention to GAO/NSIAD-94-119 Nuclear Nonproliferation: Export Licensing Procedures For Dual Use Items Need To Be Strengthened, —Wait a minute, this isn't ... lifting it to reveal Library Copy GAO/RCED-91-65 Nuclear Security: Accountability For Lab's Secret Classified Documents Is Inadequate, bemused for a moment by —twelve thousand missing documents? Weapons designs, x-ray laser plans, photos of weapons and tests ... what the hell is, nineteen ninety one, that's Highet all right, wonder how much of this stuff Devon Null walked out with ... moving on to —people in southern Utah designated a "low use segment of the population" by the AEC during open air test, what is this, something of Lynn's, Jesus I wish she'd, where's the ... finally finding Laser Performance Requirements, as his highlighter moved through lengthening stripes of sunlight until —What time is it ... ? tossing papers into his case, passing throught the outer office where Dolores had already left for the day, forging around a corner almost headlong into three young men passing him oblivious in jeans and t-shirts NO FEAR, $\aleph_0$, And God Said $e_0 \int E \cdot \delta A = \Sigma q$.

—Dude, did you hear? Persephone found water on the moon.

—Water?

—Water ice, at the south pole. You know what this means?

—Dude! Colonies . . . ! And Quine could see them almost, the domes couched in utter silence at the rim of a crater, near the still point of the turning globe, so that in its fortnightly rotation the sun would hug the horizon, never rising or setting, brushing the jagged mountaintops in that airless clarity, acres of solar panels slowly tracking it, while down below, in the perpetual night of the crater, the billion year old ice is mined for water, oxygen, hydrogen, deuterium, to fuel the reactors that provide heat, power, propulsion. Without the nucleus there is no way out, no way off the planet, no way to leave behind the mistakes, the refuse, the history, no way to transcend the history, what we've done to become what we are, no way to forget the mire held aloft in the jaws of <<ULTRADIG>> where something white and round tumbled free before he turned through the gates toward a last smear of sun dying behind a veil of gray that closed over a violet zenith. He hurried up the walk to where a light already glowed within the house.

—Lynn . . . ? Sorry I'm, losing and regaining his balance as she came hard against him in the hallway.

—Oh, I've missed you.

—Hey, hi, just let me . . .

—I'm coming on too strong, sorry I'll . . . backing away to let him pass into the living room, where he set his briefcase on the coffee table.

—No no, I'm, I'm glad to, that you . . . submitting to an embrace less emphatic but as firm.

—I came straight over, I didn't bring dinner, are you hungry?

—No no, that's okay, I had a late

—I want to turn on the TV to see our coverage.

—Of, of the demo? Yes sure, anyway I, there's something I want to see too, some PBS guy, Armand Steradian, came to the Lab in January, something on post-Cold W

—Steradian? And he didn't call us?

—He talked to me for over an hour, I think he was really interested in . . . trailing off at the sight of a ragged group on the screen, ZERO NOW and a darkhaired woman's arm held out in a gesture perhaps meant to rally the others but cut off for a well groomed woman holding a microphone, —activists continue their lonely vigil. Pete?

—Well there's my two seconds of fame, I hope Steradian did better by you.

—Can I, can I change this now . . . ? and he thumbed to where ordinary citizens were having their heirlooms appraised, all well satisfied that a market existed for the turning of personal history into hard cash; and although some histories were, by the nature of the market, worth more than others, there were no hard losers.

—A lot of people didn't show up. The Herald reporter was snotty about how few we were.

—That reminds me did, did you see this? I saved it in case you . . . rummaging through System Design Requirements, Conceptual Design Report Preface, The 7 Habits Of, coming up at last with Respect Fades For Activists, —"Given the dramatic changes in the world, even some of the activists' sympathizers are questioning recent anti-nuclear tactics and positions."

—I read it. It's all we talked about at the retreat. Tony wants to, what did he say, broaden our focus, find a larger audience. We should add arms sales economic justice and social welfare to our menu if it'll help our funding. Speaks the ad man.

—As Réti says, funding comes from the threat.

—I'll tell Tony. He never met a tactic he didn't like. She crossed and recrossed the room, carrying the clipping, setting it down, glancing at the screen, sitting by him only to get up again.

—Is something wrong?

—Do you have anything to drink?

—I think some, some Chardonnay? But wait, it's almost . . . as he settled onto the sofa for the newly merged Lockheed-Martin creating an instant history for itself as —the proud sponsor for twenty five years of science broadcasting, and Lynn returned to sit cradling the bowl of the wineglass in her thin long fingers.

—And I thought Steradian was on our side. When he was a stringer for CNN he talked to us, but now he's doing this MacNeil-Lehrer routine, that balanced point of view where you get the secretary of defense and a former secretary of defense. I mean, I'm sure Steradian thinks he's doing the right thing and all. But everybody thinks that, don't they. I think I'm doing my job so well and twenty people show up Friday and the Herald disses us and our funding's down and everybody's on my case at the retreat. Tony said I was demoralizing others. Philip, tell me . . . and he looked to her with an apprehension of distress, —Am I fooling myself about you?

—What do you mean?

—About what you want.

—Lynn . . . his eyes came up from an F-22 banking against the dun backdrop of a desert floor. —I want to be with you.

—estimated cost of seventy three bill

—But the rest of it. You told me you wanted to make a difference at the Lab.

His eyes, roving for an answer, came back to the screen where a hawkfaced man, —Colonel "Rip" Whipple, assistant secretary of defense for acquisitions and development, envisions a day when the military subcontracts information and services from the private sec

—Philip, are you listening . . .

—Just a minute . . .

—Cold War over, expect constrained military spending, reap benefits in reduced R&D and maintenance costs by outsourcing to civil and commercial providers and global partners. Military can no longer rely solely on DoD owned and operated assets in order to

—Philip . . .

—He's but wait, he's saying the military will buy services from private companies . . .

—So? They do that now, they subcontract.

—No but not just weapons, he means all kinds of

—launch vehicles, satellites, space assets, we can outsource these functions

—But, but that's just what Gate wants, it would be a perfect setup to get

—funding from both sectors, spin-offs, spin-ons, and future opportunities, let me tell you a success story

—Philip would you please . . .

—Just one

—of our partners, 3Vid, developed a three dimensional battlespace display, spun it off into laptop computers, won the Best of Comdex ninety three award, and I guarantee you we'll all have 3D laptops by the year

—Philip, I'm trying to talk to you!

—What?

—I want to know if you're serious about changing the Lab. Because there's an opportunity. I've lined up people willing to comment at this public hearing, to challenge the way DOE is scoping stockpile stewardship and Avalon.

—And you want me to, to do what?

—To comment. To tell DOE that they need to explore other options besides Avalon.

—Oh but Lynn

—You wouldn't be alone. We have a former head of SAC, a former joint chief, a former bomb designer

—Former, well that's the word isn't it. If I signed on to this I wouldn't last five minutes. What good is a former acting director? Anyway, you talk as if it's up to me. It's not. My job's to implement DOE decisions.

—What good is being current if you don't do anything? Your job's also to advise. If you tell them there's another, better way . . .

—I can't take a political stand on this.

—You already have! The Lab's a political institution! You play a major role in directing weapons policy!

—Lynn, we carry out policy. DoD tells DOE what they need to fulfill their, their goals, and we execute for DOE using best business prac

—Highet and every director before him lobbied. You got the neutron bomb in the seventies, Radiance in the eighties, and now Avalon. You've always opposed arms control treaties, you

—Would you stop, don't compare me to Highet, and anyway treaties, that's exactly what we, why they want Avalon, so that the CTBT will be ratif

—When Chase, did you even hear what I said to him?

—Lynn, please, can't we, I think about this stuff all day long can we just pl

—Listen to your own people, you can remanufacture from blueprints, you can

—but to maintain competence, to keep our scientists interested

—Interested? Do they have a short attention span?

—Lynn it's just not going to, I can't do this, it would be a total failure.

—But isn't that, I mean, that's all we ever get is the chance to, to fail at something worthwhile! I just want you to take the chance.

—national laboratory where cold warriors retool

—oh but, but wait

—Philip don't you see you have this opportunity, this singular moment when nearly everyone agrees that these weapons are useless and obsolete, don't let it

—wait I, I may be on now, as the camera panned past a bank of equipment and followed a figure walking —Who is that, isn't that . . . ? among the skyblue beamlines of the laser bay. —Frank Szabo, but what's he, he wasn't even in that section then, what's he think he . . . as the waspish voice was saying, —building on twenty years' expertise in laser technology, this could be the most important thing the Lab does this decade

—What's he, Steradian's acting like Szabo's the direc, as Quine's own voice came up to cut him off, his face squinting in the lights, querulous, put upon, —You can't wish these weapons away. It's Luddite philosophy to think so, as the camera went quickly back to Szabo, standing inside the laser bay.

—That's it? He talked to me for over an hour and that's, as Szabo went on, —activists may ironically be a greater danger to a test ban than Avalo

—Luddite philosophy? Is that what you think of me?

—What? No I didn't mean

—Wish? Does it look to you like I spend my time wishing? I'm working my tail off! This is so, so disrespectful Philip . . .

—Lynn no no it's not, I wasn't talking about you, I don't even remember saying that, they, they cut me down to nothing, what am I supposed to

—You could say we have a difference of opinion! You could say we're honorable people, not know-nothing crackpots! Do you think I've spent all these hours reading up on the science because I'm a, a Luddite?

—And Szabo, they treated him like he's the direc . . . Lynn . . . ? He followed her into the kitchen, where she was paused with her wineglass over The One Minute and 7 Habits looking at his papers.

—Can I, can I see that before you

—Why, is it classified?

—Well I don't know, that's why I want to

—Our arrangement is that anything you leave out is open.

—Yes but since you haven't been here I, I mean I know it's my fault but could I please . . . taking from her poised hand Avalon System Design Requirements For Nuclear Weapons Physics Experiments, —See, no it's not classified but it's not exactly public . . .

—I guess not, since the title alone seems to contradict DOE's stated policy.

—But no, it doesn't, this isn't about new weapons, it's about understanding the physics of

—Just tell me that Avalon can't be used for new weapons design.

—Well of course it can, but

—But what? Trust you that it won't? Trust you like with the B sixty one rev eleven, isn't that a new weapon?

—It's, that's an upgrade, we're permitted to, but where did you hear about

—Trust you? Like with Radiance, with Rocky Flats, with the human radiation experiments?

—Lynn please stop saying, but where did

—Both Turner and Sorokin say you're trying to make pure fusion bombs.

—Oh, Turner. Turner hasn't worked in a lab for thirty years.

—Oh Philip that's so, don't discredit him, that's what you always do isn't it, how can anyone trust you!

—Will you stop saying you! That you don't trust me!

—I'm sorry, you know I mean the Lab. But

—And, and you've already thrown Sorokin up to me, his fourth gen, you know he's guessing about that, he doesn't have the data he needs to draw those conclusions, and you know something, if it hadn't been for the Lab that experiment of ours would never have come off, did he tell you that? If I hadn't come on that Hertz fellowship . . .

—Hertz? You were a Hertz fellow?

—It was Réti's idea, he was my advisor.

—I never knew that. And I thought you weren't in the inner circle, but you are aren't you, this is how it happens. Denial by degrees so small you don't see it happening . . . She picked up another paper.

—Can I, can I see

—What's this, another of your success stories, hope it's not classified, "In addition to mammography the system can be used for inspection and quality control of materials commonly used in the manufacture of modern conventional and nuclear weapons." There's dual use for you. Is the mammography part supposed to comfort all the women in the breast cancer cluster around the Lab? She threw down the papers. —But it's been dual use since day one, since Hanford, dual use and duplicity, plutonium for the bombs but it's a power plant too, atoms for peace, electricity too cheap to meter, never mind the cancers downwind, never mind the trillions we'll need to clean up the mess, forget all that history because there's something new called fusion . . .

—Lynn will you . . . pausing a moment to shut and lock his case before following her back into the living room, —Why are you so . . . what's wrong with you tonight . . . ? where she dropped onto the sofa. The only light now came from the hallway and from where, in the interval between programs, noncommercial television advertised in plain white type LINCOLN, AMERICAN LUXURY, begging the question of whether that slain President had been a frivolous indulgence of the nation or something it could ill afford now that some toothy woman in a suit grinned and prowled like a panther before a placard that exhorted her unseen but vociferous audience to Dare To Be Rich, before Lynn leveled the remote and with a cocked thumb squashed OFF. In the dark she sat staring at the bleakness of the dead screen. When she turned to him he couldn't see her features. An air of desolation settled like some toxin.

—I'm so tired of fighting.

—Lynn, I don't want to fight.

She looked up at him. —I may not be funded again.

—What do you mean?

—If donations don't go up, CANT's going to cut staff. I'll be back to part time. That's what Tony was telling me. I need this money to go back to school and pass the bar. If they cut me, I'll have to work at some corporate firm in the city. Nobody else will pay me to do this stuff. I already know as much case law as our lead attorneys but I can't practice, I need a place to work . . .

—Okay, . . . He came forward uneasily, further into the darkness where she sat.

—No, it's not okay! She seemed to draw herself together and set down the glass. —It's not okay, but I will be.

—Is this happening because you're seeing me?

—No. Tony wouldn't be so intolerant. Philip . . . could we go to my place?

—But why? We're here.

—We always come here. I know my place is small and the street is noisy but I need, I haven't been home since Friday morning, I need to . . . I just need to be home.

—Lynn, please, I'm tired, it's so far . . .

—Do you smell that?

—What?

—It's, I don't know, like a burning.

—What? No, I don't smell anything . . .

—Oh this is crazy, but do you ever feel like there's something in the air? Something toxic?

A chill went up his neck, as if something had stirred in the dimness behind him. If he stood unmoving it might pass him over.

—I'm cold. Will you turn up the heat? It feels like something died in here.

He turned on a light. The chill of desolation receded but stood by. The thermostat baffled him for a moment, its gray panel blinking 10:22 68F, until he thumbed ^ for a distant rumble lost in a rush of air.

—I'm sorry. I'm in such a mood. Come sit here. Relax with me. You're always on guard.

—Okay, let me . . . She leaned against him.

—It's been a hard month for me.

—I know.

—Do you remember when I first came over here? All those times we'd gone out, and you never . . . and then I came in and asked you to take my clothes off. I was so shameless.

—I couldn't believe that you wanted me. He shifted so that her elbow came away from his ribs. —Listen, Lynn, if you're worried about a job, I could see what's open in N Section, that's the Nonproliferation Directorate . . .

She pulled away. —What? You mean, me, work at the Lab?

—I'm just saying, if you wanted to apply for something I'm sure . . . but whatever certainty he might have had vanished in her laugh.

—I can't believe you said that.

—I mean, you have the expertise . . .

She was on her feet, something between amusement and incredulity claiming her face. —You're not joking, are you.

—Well, but, if you really want to change things . . .

She walked away and turned back to him under the hall light shining russet in her hair, shadowing the hollows of her dark eyes and the deep bones of her cheeks. —I'm going to take a bath. Will you come up in a little while?

—Yes I, in a while . . . turning from the stairs when her feet had vanished to the open briefcase on the coffee table, where Environmental Report New Construction L-301-92, Chivian-Harris Soil Analysis, Boole & Clay Environmental Consultants were pushed aside for a list of Credne Construction Job Sites that failed to claim more of his attention than the television returned to life with —megadittos from a real American woman who, incidentally, isn't a lesbian or a feminist.

—Hey hey hey. Whoa! Whoa! Whoa!

—How anyone can watch this idiot . . . muttering as his thumb held still for the obese figure asserting, —that means you find me attractive then. See, women who don't find me attractive have to be lesbians or femini, as his thumb finally rebelled to move on to —carbon steel blade with Zytel handle, and his attention went back to the list continuing with Credne Waste Management Contract Sites, a few dozen Lab locations, and then, striking at his heart, Estancia Estates.

—Are you coming to bed?

—What? Oh, oh yes, in, in just a minute, I was just . . . looking back in surprise at the papers in his lap, —I just . . .

—Philip. I'm crying.

—What . . . ? The hall light behind her slim figure, slouched there in white briefs and chemise, rushed him with regret, for Nan, for Kate, for Sorokin, for everything in his life that was or would become irretrievable.

—Philip . . . as something new swam into her eyes to regard him from an appraising depth.

—What?

—Are you seeing someone else?

—What? No, that's, no certainly not. Why would you think that?

—I don't know. You're distant. I'm afraid for us.

—It's just work . . . you know I . . .

—We have something, you know. It's real to me. Is it to you?

—Lynn . . . He rose, but she didn't move, stood with her arms pulled close around her and stared as if at some future she could pull into being or banish with her next words. But abruptly she shook her head.

—I'm sorry Philip, I know I come on too strong, it scares people, I don't want to scare you.

He embraced her warmth. Her tongue filled the emptiness of his mouth. What we want from another is so simple. Almost anyone will do. For a time at least the heart bonds as if it's found its other, cloven half. Is this illusion? Something neither commanded nor freely given? If the heart can be so needful and so indiscriminate, how trust it?

—Please come upstairs.

—Yes okay . . . I just want to brush my teeth . . . Water entered a whirlpool, rising and falling around the rim of the drain.

—Will you shave for me?

—Hm . . . ? The chalky water cleared.

—Do you mind?

—No, of course, I'll . . . as he peered closer than he liked at where gray had advanced down his temples to garrison the stubble he now shaved from his face and neck, looking past the reflection to where she gazed back frankly from her seat on the toilet. She smiled as she rose tucking a square of paper between her legs to drop into the bowl. He touched the flesh over his hips, as past their reflection came the lithe muscles of her lean thighs. —I really should, there's a gym at the Lab,

I really should, I just never seem to have time . . .

—I was just thinking how attractive you are. She embraced him from behind, staring in the mirror at the rise he turned to trap between them. —Come to bed . . . where she extended one arm to raise the sheets for the fall of his weight onto bedsprings, their cramp and creak lost in a sudden drumming of rain on the roof.

—Philip, your skin is always so cold.

—You're always like a furnace, a little furnace . . . His hand moved to stoke what grew warmer under it, as if increase of appetite had grown by what it fed on. Her breath harshened. Hot in his ear her gasp at his touch. Her hand turned on the length of him moving against her and he slid one thigh across the tender swell of her pelvis and paused as a despairing sigh left her.

—Yes . . . ?

She loosed her slender dress as though in desert wild, her face tanned by shining suns, half in shadow, tossing and troubled, as, seeking only himself to please, he pressed down with slow rude muscle, seeing her neck naked and pale in the streetlight's beam where it met the volutions of her ear, the strain in her face when she looked up at him before it fell back into dimness. Lightly his hands cradled her head. Deep inside him something drove home and he writhed as pent-up aching rivers, asked for pleasure first, then excused from pain. A dimness like a fog wrapped his consciousness, a languor more suasive than the wetness on his face.

—Philip . . . you're crying. He shook her hand away. Bone by bone he returned to that loathed self, which could not recollect when it began, which had no future but itself, abyss covered with trance.

—Please tell me, what's the matter?

The streetlight was diffused in mist which sent its glow the stronger into the room.

—. . . every day it's like, like waking up from a, a long sleep, to a world where things have, have gone on without me and I don't know how I got here, what day it is, how much time has passed, everything I'll never, never recover, all that loss, every day I wake up that way and every day the hope for, for something else gets smaller, and I have nothing, just nothing . . .

—Philip, look at me. You have me.

He turned to her but didn't look, as if an open eye would drop him.
—I don't know why.

—But it's true. Oh, what is it? You look so wounded . . .

—After I, after I left Nan I'd sometimes walk on the mountain. You know, where you took me that night we walked in the moonlight. One day I heard, I don't know, it sounded like a lost cat crying. Crying with desperate force. It pierced me through. I, I didn't know who I was sorrier for, Nan or myself. We abandoned each other . . .

She cradled him to her breast.

—No but listen. A month later I was walking there again and I heard it again in the same place, and I thought, that can't be a pet, it wouldn't still be there alive. And it wasn't a cat, you know, it wasn't at all. It was a bird calling, some kind of catbird. So you see I'd been living in this, this yes this myth you see, this utopia of loss while things, things had gone on, but in a way it was better to believe in loss than, than in this muddle . . . See, the past, you can carry your past and let it drag you under, or you can let it go but then you're adrift, the present just, just carries you . . . oh my God, what am I going to do?

She didn't answer at once. Finally she said, —You have to quit, Philip. This is destroying you.

—It's all I have!

She held him. When she spoke her voice was dry. —Will you do one thing for me? I'm sorry I asked you to comment at the hearing, that wasn't fair of me. But will you please come? To hear what our people have to say.

—If you want. If I don't have to, to speak.

A murmur of rain had started again. He lay there in the abyss of his thoughts as her breathing beside him steadied and deepened. Almost a voice stirred in him. It starts before Hanford, it almost said. It starts with Röntgen, with the piece of barium glowing in the path of invisible rays, striking out the fire that God had put there. It starts with his wife's hand on the photographic plate, its transparence there, the ashen bones visible within the milky flesh. Who could imagine that this radiance at the heart of matter could be malign? That with its light came fire? (Yet from the first the ashen bones were there to see within the flesh.) It starts with Becquerel carrying the radium in his pocket that burned his skin, and darkened the unexposed film. It starts with Marie Curie poisoning herself in that pale uncanny glow. With Rutherford guessing at this new alchemy, guessing that matter, giving up its glow, transformed itself one element into another. With the miners at Joachimsthal, deep under the Erzgebirge, inhaling the dust of uranium and dying of "mountain sickness". With women who by the thousands in watch factories tipped their brushes with that glow, touched it to their tongues before painting the dial face, women who only much later, when the watches' glow had faded, sickened and died from that radiance taken into their bones. It begins with Ernest Lawrence rushing across the Berkeley campus, the idea of a proton accelerator uncontainable in his mind, calling out, I'm going to be famous! With Oppenheimer at Jornada del Muerte that morning of Trinity. With the scientists who had prised open the gates to that blazing realm past heaven or hell. What were they now at the Lab in all their thousands, but the colonial bureaucrats of that realm, the followers and func-tionaries, the clerks and commissars? Mere gatekeepers of that power. Or in its keeping. It goes of its own momentum beyond Hanford, to Trinity, to Hiroshima, to the prisoners, the cancer patients, the retard-ed children, the pregnant women injected or fed this goblin matter to see would it bring health or sickness, the soldiers huddled in trenches against the flash, bones visible in their arms through closed eyes, star-ing up at the roiling cloudrise, the sheepherders, the farms, the homes, the gardens downwind. And in his sleep the voice long stilled spoke once more. It starts with Sforza; *in case of need I will make bombards, mortars, and firethrowing engines of beautiful and practical design. It starts with Archimedes focusing the sun's rays upon the fleet at Syra-cuse, it starts with the first rock hurled by the first grasping hand. It starts where we start. It is mind, it is hunger, it is greed, it is defense, it is mischief, it is the devil, it is the god; it is life.*

FIVE

Then, all at once it seemed, the sky cleared and the world lay open to the scrutiny of heaven, that skin of blue air beyond which was mere vacuum, below which a scatter of birds turned incomplete spirals, now black, now white, banking into and out of the wind above the pit where CREDNE Waste Management trucks took on their burdens and labored away to parts unknown or at least undisclosed, while from the other direction came a cart trailing two pallets of chrome canisters and turning wide enough to clip the bumper of a parked car, jouncing once as the canisters chimed, and continuing on its way to some project or projects separated from Quine by at least five floors of management passing one at a time until the brushed stainless steel door opened to a vista of identical doors receding in three directions, and he reached the anteroom where an orotund voice proclaimed —it's a straw dog argum

—Dolores, would you pl . . . what's that smell?

—I don't smell anything.

—Like, like a burning . . . ?

—I don't smell anything. Have a donut?

—What?

—A creme donut. Have one. They're lite.

—Light . . . ?

—They're lo fat. She laid down Nanopreneuring and held out a thinwalled box, where a stressed tab and slot threatened to give way until Quine grabbed the sagging edge. —Bernd Dietz wants to see you.

—Tell him I'm busy. Tell him Monday.

The box pushed papers across the desk, exposing, like a thorn he couldn't pluck out, *Nancy Julia Adams* and *Benjamin Daniel Stern* still awaiting the pleasure of his company, or at least the earnest of it, on *16 July 1994 RSVP*. He hid them under System Requirements, but they emerged unabashed minutes later from Laser Compression of Matter, as he held aloft the doughnut to lose them again beneath Steganography: A Novel Method of Data Hiding. On the computer screen was another thorn still awaiting a response he was as unready to give as to forego.

Date: Fri, 6 May 1994 16:20 -0700
To: quine@lucinda.banl.gov
From: sforza@nous.com
Subject: Gate URGENT!
WE HAVE TO TALK.
Highet

He clicked to dismiss the window but as he reached a gobbet of cream fell onto *RSVP* and Earth Protection, and he glared as what was left of the doughnut, grabbed the nearest paper Theodore Turner Comment Preprint to blot the card and wrap the dougnut for the trash, angrily sweeping in after it the stained carboard box, *RSVP*, and Earth, coming up then to what, even in the sun glare on the screen, was clearly not his mailbox, windows overlapped in a profusion of sultry brows, splayed limbs, pouting lips parted to meet the thrust of his legs up from the chair to the window to drop blinds against the brightness out there. As the unfinished mauve and avocado façade opposite vanished behind the clatter he had an apprehension of the hundreds of offices there waiting for their tenants, closeted against the world, of the hundreds upon thousands of offices already occupied, stretching out to Washington, in every one of which decisions were taken in the absolute vacuum of procedure and contingency, and he stood in a kind of paralysis until his phone went off and his door opened.

—Yes? Hel

—problem with these civil liberty types, we have to dither the camera resolution so you can't read the license plates, but

—Damn it! Who's . . . slamming down to click and collapse the windows on that which men in women most desire, as his eyes came up to

Dietz's white beard, his blocky anxious face, the strands of graying hair fallen forward from the thinned ranks of a moist and mostly barren pate. In hands restless and seemingly forgotten by their owner, some papers were clutched.

—I am sorry, but this is urgent.

—What is it, Bernd?

—Avalon. The Conceptual Design Review. The budget and time line. There are grave uncertainties here.

—Yes, I know but

—This will be the world's largest optical instrument. Seven thousand large and twenty thousand small glass components. The entire US optics industry can produce only two hundred meter-class optics in a year. That is ten times too low for our time frame. So, to meet our deadline we must develop entirely new fabrication techniques which will take an unknown amount of time and which are not budgeted. Also, the beamlines must operate near the damage threshold of the glass. Even if the glass can be made pure and in quantity, even if it does not fail under power, we must then integrate and assemble the parts. One hundred ninety two beamlines must focus to the micrometer with a uniformity of one percent. We build these in a room the size of stadium, so how will you keep dust out of the glass? No one has yet answered for me this simple question.

—Bernd . . .

—Then, diagnostics. We need new kinds of sensors and new computer codes to fine tune the array before experiments can even start. Then, targets. Frozen capsules of deuterium-tritium must be made perfectly spherical to tolerance of ten billionths of a meter.

—Bernd, are you saying it can't be done?

—I say only that there are great hurdles and our time frame and budget permit no errors at all.

Quine pressed one hand to a throb in his temple, glancing at Nonprolif. —Bernd, let me be completely frank with you. We're losing funding, jobs, talent. We have to stop the bleeding. If we don't complete Avalon right on schedule, if we don't achieve ignition right off, those are, arc manageable problems that we can address in their time.

—But it is my name, not yours, on the Laser Design Cost Basis document. Thirty thousand pieces of glass, do you understand? I will not put my head on that block.

—Bernd, none of our groups raised red flags. You're the only one.

—Because they remember what happened to Slater and the others. Have you forgotten Radiance? Highet's extravagant claims?

—Of course not. You rescued me. That's why you're on the project.

—But Szabo is head.

—Is that what this is about? Because if you want more responsib

—I do not! But Szabo, he thinks, if this laser does not work out as planned, we go back to underground testing, we continue on with other lasers, it is no problem for him. In fact, one point eight megajoules, assuming we attain that figure, which I do not promise, is probably not even enough. But that is not my concern. I am saying the construction. That is my problem.

—Why do you say it's not enough?

Dietz stared at him with something between dismay and offense. —You know why.

—I don't.

Dietz looked down at the papers in his hand. He stared at them in silence as Quine waited. At last he glanced up and as he placed them on the desk he barely spoke. —Taliesin.

Quine glanced at the papers. Dear Madam Secretary. A finger of unease uncurled in his bowels. —What are you saying?

—I have said too much. I will not sign the Cost Basis Document unless these objections are attached.

—But . . . Bernd, you're putting me in an impossible position. The Conceptual Design Report has been turned in. If you had these concerns

—I told you my concerns! Weeks ago!

—What would you agree to? There's a fifteen percent contingency. I can budget twenty percent more for the optics if you can certi

—Fifteen, twenty, fifty percent is not the point! There are too many uncertainties, we must study more, run more experiments on the lasers we have . . .

—We can do that after Key Decision One.

—Too late. Then the budget is fixed. We are saying one billion?

—One point one.

—Three, four times that, is my estimate. To solve only the problems that I can see from here. I have put my concerns in writing, so there can be no misunderstanding.

The finger inside him pressed harder. —Bernd, you have to sign this.

—Or what? What will you do? Fire me? I will go public!

Quine got up and paced to the window. The pressure in his bowels was desperate. —If I, if I accept your protest, make it an addendum to the report, will that satisfy you?

—It will go to the secretary with the report?

—Yes yes.

—All right. Then I will leave it with you.

—Is that all? Are we done?

—For now.

As the door closed he rushed hobbling to the washroom. He had barely sat when he released a torrent into the bowl. He lowered his head onto folded arms as the spasms subsided and a weakness swept his legs. After a minute he rose to wipe himself and flush away a watery yellow chyle, leaving behind a stink more sulfurous than fecal. The fan labored as he washed his hands, and he glimpsed in the mirror as he went out a face paler than normal turning to Frank Szabo perusing the papers on his desk.

—What that's smell? Like a burning?

—Frank . . . ?

—Sorry to barge in, but I saw Bernd. He leave this for you? indicating Dear Madam Secretary.

—Yes he, he thinks the Avalon optics won't work.

—He's full of crap. You're not sending this, are you?

—I said I'd include it if he signed off on the Cost Basis Document.

—Classify it and bury it. It's an internal memo with sensitive information.

—Can I do that?

—Ask Bran how, he's been studying the new classification guidelines. Listen what about this Earth Protection Seminar, are you on board for that?

—What, I haven't had a chance to

—Space thing we're hosting in July, international community, blah blah. Can you give the keynote?

—Talk to Dolores . . . who looked up from How To Profit From the Coming Chaos.

—Dolores, those doughnuts . . . did you eat . . . I mean, are they okay?

—Do you like them? My cousin works for a food company. They're testing a fat substitute.

—Substitute?

—It doesn't get digested or something. But it tastes like the real thing.

—Do you know where Bran Nolan is?

—Some seminar I think.

—Right, okay, I'll . . . hurrying down the hall to pass a couple of men, —going to launch these things on their Long Dong missile or whatever the hell it's . . . trying E-233 which opened onto a small group watching a coatless man with tie askew and sleeves rolled up prowling back and forth before a placard Motivating Faster Failure With Peter Paul Thomas, —the great Swedish playwright Hendrick Isben and his great play Enema of the People, where Dean Stockwell goes up against the grain of his community to save them from themselves and the toxic plume of distrust corroding the fabric of their society where his news is unwelcome at first until the townsfolk see that it's in their own interest to be self-interested, the point being is that they

—Excuse me, Bran . . . ? who rose from a seat in the back and followed Quine out the door muttering, —Must be the hundred drachma course, all this time I thought Isben was the guy who invented book numbering, won a Barnes and Noble prize for it didn't he?

—How do I classify an internal report?

—What section?

—L Section.

—Those used to be born classified, but under the new openness regime I'll have to look it up.

—Something Bernd Dietz wrote. I want it put through an internal review.

—Fax it to me. Do I have your comments?

—My what?

—The document for the public hearing tonight? I know how you like to work over the language, but it goes out at four.

—Oh, the nonprof, I mean the nonproliferation thing. That's right, just thought I'd get a, a, a little breather after the Design Report. Okay I'll

—Just send it to my office.

—Yes okay . . . as a hand went deep into the trash pressing aside a stained cardboard box ALESTRO Test Product S to come up holding between two fingers *RSVP* and Earth Protection. A gobbet of cream still clung to the hand traveling to intercept the phone's bleat, pausing only to ward off, ineffectually, the opening door.

—Yes? Hold, hold on Conor I'll be right with, no hello go ahead . . . out of, of gas? Course correc, isn't that NASA's . . . But I mean after the lunar, why are we calculating the course correc. Uh huh . . . as Conor waved for his attention and wrote something on a scrap of paper. —Okay. I'm still not clear why we were doing those calculations at all but maybe you can explain that to me when we meet. Quine put down the phone and pushed aside *RSVP*, Earth Protection, seeking the more absorbent Ohlone Valley Herald Critics Charge, with which he wiped the heel of his hand and the telephone.

—That was about Persephone, right? On the scrap in Conor's hand was written aXon.

—That was Tom Young. He said that NASA failed to convert our units from miles to kilometers.

—Miles? Who uses miles anymore?

—Legacy codes, apparently.

—Legacy codes? Running on aXons? I don't think so. I know what happened there. Those guys didn't fix their math chips. So their results put Persephone's thrusters on full burn and depleted the fuel.

—Yes well, I'll have to, to deal with it later. Come here a second, as Conor leaned into the screen while Quine clicked LANCET 1979-1991 to open TALIESIN. —I know you have some expertise with Rayleigh-Taylor instabilities . . .

—Wow, ignition, burn rate, this is DT fusion, right?

—These codes model radiation transfer, hydrodynamic evolution of the plasma . . .

—This is great, whose work is this?

—Some of this I worked on but not, not this side of it . . . see, x-ray energy is pumped into the capsule here . . .

—I didn't know you did fusion.

—I, I didn't. This is . . . just started to look at this really, see, these are the data sets for the DT burn . . . here, look at the rho-r values, for the first twenty nanoseconds they're going up and with these energies you'd expect burn to take off, but

—Yeah I see. Instabilities cooling off the hot spot?

—That should be accounted for in the underlying code libraries . . . as he pushed Steganography aside for Laser Compression of Matter.

—The classic paper.

—Yeah well, they predicted ignition with one kilojoule and underestimating the Rayleigh-Taylor instabilities put them so far off. But the current codes should have fixed that. So I want to know what's going on.

—Shouldn't you, I mean Szabo actually worked on this all along, he'd be the guy to ah

—Frank's got a lot on his plate right now. Anyway this is a long term kind of project, and I've heard great things about your expertise in this field, just thought it's something you could sink your teeth into . . .

—Well definitely, I'd love to, I just, you know, don't want to step on anybody's

—Let me worry about that.

—Well that's, that's . . . wow. So that's like a whole lot of energy going into that capsule. Our lasers can't do that. Is this from a bomb test?

—It's better that you don't know the source of the data.

—Listen I know it's late but, have you had lunch? Maybe we could grab something, if you're not too busy, I can show you the Rayleigh-Taylor work I did last year . . .

—Feeling a little queasy actually but maybe tomorrow I mean Monday we could, I mean after you've had a chance to look at

—This is really great of you, I really appreciate . . . lingering to pick up Steganography A Novel Method of Data Hiding. —Hey cool. You know I did some stuff for Highet on this, did you ever see

—Philip where the hell is your summary?

—My, my what?

—Hey Bran, how's it

—Messenger's waiting in my office.

—Oh yes that page I, I, I'm sorry I'll, tell him I'll, ten minutes, I'll fax it down to you in, in five . . . sorry Conor, I have to . . . pushing a stained and shopworn Earth Protection and RSVP under the fall of Steganography to retrieve Avalon And The Issue Of Nonproliferation, where Part V X-ray Laser Research reminded him that *Experiments on nuclear directed energy weapon concepts, while technically possible, are not planned.* He read on to *X-ray lasers have military applications as well as peaceful ones. The results of Avalon experiments could provide data for comparison with codes and could be used to further interpret the results of past underground experiments on nuclear-pumped x-ray lasers.*

For a moment he was back in the office he'd shared with Null in those despised years of Superbright. The loss and the waste of it were a hook through his heart. He lifted the phone to press MEM 1 but hung up before it rang. After a moment he pressed another number.

—Reese? Sorry to bother you. Just want to check something. The x-ray laser or, or similar Radiance components, are those considered proliferation risks? I mean for purposes of. No this is for, for a possible Avalon application. No, Title One phase, the Conceptual Design Report is already, it's at the printer, yes you should have it any day now. Really? She has? A, a done deal, well that's good news. So, on the x-ray laser, we can pretty much do whatever . . . okay then.

He walked to the window and stood in what might have been motionlessness except that it brought no stillness, no elsewhere, no immensity, it brought only a stifling anxiety at the stubborn progression of all he was enmeshed in, so he turned from it as something in him hardened and at the same time gave way, as it might have been the unprovoked slide of dirt down one wall of the pit there below him. He strode to the desk and wrote:

Research on x-ray lasers has multiple applications. Therefore, it would be unwise to restrict peaceful research in this area in the interest of preventing weapon development.

—Dolores, fax this down to Bran Nolan . . . oh, is that the time? I have to go.

—Will you be back today?

—I don't know. Is our voicemail back up yet?

—No, they're still working on that virus.

—Virus, how can voicemail have a virus? Never mind, I'll call in later . . . racing down the hallway for the brushed steel of the elevator door shutting against —Wait . . . ! an entreaty that was ignored then and there but perversely answered at the exit gate, where two gondolas of CREDNE Waste Management backed beeping across both lanes of the road, and at Mariposa, where under the blunt barrel of the traffic camera the light flicked from yellow to red at his approach, and again at the plinth welcoming car after waiting car to Circuit City Toys "Я" Us Barnes & Noble Starbucks, and by car after creeping car searching and pausing for the hope, seldom met though often indulged, of a parking space about to be vacated, a hope at last interrupted by the blare of a horn which, Quine realized in angry surprise, was his own.

—Sorry I'm late, I

—I'm used to it. Can you believe this line? stretching from the sidewalk through the doorway into halflight where, a few people ahead, at the threshold of dimness, a woman brushed a veil of auburn hair from the pale skin of her neck, revealing the volutions of her ear. Quine felt sweat spring from him. —Listen, maybe this isn't the

—Relax, we're moving, and the line surged forward, while a woman in red pushed to join the auburnhaired woman with just a glance at the people in line behind her.

—Some crowd, said Lynn as they entered the dimness. The boy behind the counter turned to the woman in red with an expression not quite a query, —Me? Oh no I'm not in line, I'm just talking to my friend, but as long as I'm here, what kind of herbal teas do you have? and as the boy indicated the menu board and the woman slowly took it in, —Is the hibiscus tea sweet? I mean, is it sweet hibiscus tea? and the boy didn't know and as the auburn head turned Quine turned to Lynn.

—Maybe we should . . .

—Are you in a hurry?

—No but I, and the woman in red carried on, —well then, how about a decaf mocha latté, is that with foamed milk? Can I get lowfat? And lowfat, is that one or two percent, and the boy didn't know and turned to another boy while the woman in red resumed talking to her auburnhaired friend.

—Lynn, really I don't want anything, why don't we

—Neither do I, but as long as we're here.

—Yes but, and the boy answered one percent and the woman pulled from her conversation looked vaguely annoyed until, —oh, all right then, and can I get just a dollop of whipped cream? while the steaming nozzle hissed and spat and the woman interrupted, —oh, and can I get that in a mug? not a paper cup? and the boy dumped the contents of the cup and started over while the auburn head moved again.

—Lynn . . .

—Come on, we're up. Espresso please.

—Ah, capp, no, make that just some steamed milk please, nonfat milk . . . as the auburn head began to turn and Quine turned away to study two chromed machines Gaggia and Rancilio in full steam drowning out further talk.

—Grab that table if you can. I'll bring the drinks.

Across the room the woman with auburn hair and the woman in red joined a wiry man, white teeth in a tanned face, his blackhaired forearms resting on the table. He glanced over as Lynn set a cup before Quine and Quine looked down.

—I wanted to see up close who put my friends at Café Desaparecidos out of business. This espresso is terrible. Have you seen this? She opened a folder and spread out papers Chivian-Harris, Boole & Clay, Soil Engineer.

—Where, where did you get . . . ?

—From UC through the California Public Records Act.

—But how did you, Lynn tell me, did you see these in my briefcase?

—In your briefcase! Do you think I'd . . .

—Okay I'm sorry I just, I don't know what to think . . .

—You don't think you can trust me that far?

—No I'm sorry, Lynn, I do trust you.

—But, in your briefcase, so you do know about them.

—Bran Nolan wanted me to look, I didn't even have a chance . . .

—So you know what they mean.

—No, I just said I haven't had a

—Then I'll tell you. This first report showed EPA action levels of metals and volatile organic compounds. The second report is a whitewash, which incidentally gave permission to start construction. Now this, this is a soil report, but the results are nonsense, the soil density meter was marked defective. But when the instrument was tested later, it worked fine. Do you know how those meters work?

—No, how, how would I?

—They measure how much radioactivity passes through a sample of the soil.

—With what, a neutron source?

—I don't know, I can find out. But if the meter was working, this means the soil was radioactive. And that soil went offsite.

—Where?

—Well, we don't know. That's the problem. The nearest Credne job site is a residential community called Estancia Estates.

Quine turned to the table where the auburnhaired woman and the red dress and the dark forearms had left. Four teenagers sat there now. Lynn followed his stare.

—What is it? What are you looking at?

—Estancia Estates? You're sure?

—No, of course not, that's just a guess based on it being nearby. The point is it could b

—Have you tested the soil there?

—We tried to interest the Department of Health Services, but they won't do it.

—Well no wonder, you have no evidence . . .

—Philip, that soil is somewhere. Maybe in people's yards.

—Why don't you go to the developer? Make them test it.

—Catullus Development owns four thousand acres in this area. If we say a word about this they'll sue us.

—Sue you? What for?

—Oh, tortious intereference with economic advantage, for instance. There's a dozen ways to craft a SLAPP suit. A whisper of this could cost them millions in lost property value, they won't sit still for that. The mayor and the council won't sit still for it.

—Slap . . . ?

—Strategic lawsuit against public participation. For them it's a cost of doing business, for us it's disabling, the point is we don't have a way to get this information out.

—Information? It's not even a rumor . . .

—But you could, Philip. You could pressure Credne. All that work at the Lab is worth a lot to them.

—Oh Lynn . . .

—Philip, dual toxics reports, that's not good. You're covering someth

—Are you threat

—A threat? Is that what you think this is?

—Well, what am I suppo

—It's a chance to do the right thing! Tell Credne to test the soil! At Estancia, or wherever else it could have gone.

—And you think they'll just, for God's sake Lynn, they won't like it any better coming from us!

—Tony said you wouldn't do it.

—Tony? Since when have you and Tony have been strategizing about me?

—Look, would it hurt to ask them?

—Yes, it would, it would damage a relationship that's already strained.

—Strained how?

—You don't need to know that.

She sat back. —All right.

—Look . . . will I, will I see you later?

—Of course. At the hearing. She was putting the papers away.

—Yes but I mean . . . it's, where is it again?

—First Unitarian Church of Kentwood. Eight. I have to get going, because I need to talk to people before it starts. You know how to get there?

—Yes, I . . . Kentwood . . . ?

When she'd gone he looked up from the flyer she'd left to the table opposite, now empty. The sun, so bright and warm an hour before, was now a mere glow within sullen bands of cloud climbing the western sky, winter's last obduracy. The paling blue overhead was specked with gray puffs sailing steadily east. A bright contrail arched above the sullen glow, scoring a straight line that wavered only at its end. In the vastness of the parking lot the sky's radiance diminished and a wind came up. The clutter of Ψ Psychotherapy Associates, Zany Brainy, Taco Bell, Bed Bath & Beyond, nearly blocked out the green of the distant ridge where, halfway down and hardly visible in the frame of Blenzers and Leather For Le$$, grass and earth had been torn by the orange dots of trucks now idle there. A blare of horn and a flicker of headlamps just behind him brought his eyes up to the glare and moving mouth of a driver jabbing a finger at his space. His radio came to life with, —injury accident at Christopher, as he rounded the cloverleaf <- Oakland Sacramento -> where a travertine and glass building, touched by the sun's last rays, ignited in a red glow as he came down the onramp joining a myriad of red and white lights in a stream heading west and east past Codorn c s XIT NLY to Kentwood RIGHT LANE as he searched the dashboard and the seat beside him for the flyer left behind in the café, unreadable in the last glimmer of the darkling sky over a cul-de-sac among lighted homes. He turned his watch into the pool of a streetlight, 8:20, then circled back to the small sign he'd missed, First Unitarian, and lurched onto a rutted dirt road.

So many cars were parked in the lot that for a moment he lost his faith that this meeting was an irrelevancy, an ironic genuflection to a democracy that even the governed no longer took seriously. He scanned warily and in vain for a red Miata SFORZA, past pickups SUVs Volvos Hondas Acuras with their various blazons ⸷ IXΘΥΣ, CARPENTERS UNION LOCAL 713, PLUMBERS STEAMFITTERS 342, SHEET METAL WORKERS 104, WWJD What Would Jesus Do,

ETERNITY Smoking Or Non-Smoking, JESUS DIED 4U, 98.9 SOL, Got Crypto?, POWERED BY FREEBSD, ✝ DARWIN, 94.1 KPFA, Nobody For President, Free Tibet, U.S. Out Of North America, If You Think Education Is Expensive Try Ignorance, parking at last by a truck where sun had bleached the red from MY   BELONGS TO DADDY. He walked back into the light from the entranceway and the spill of people there, voices laboring under the obligations of a world grown too complex to compass except by traversing from one likely story to the next, resting the weight of preconceptions upon them for only so long as each held. The crowd wedged him against a folding table bearing any number of available fictions in pamphlet form, The Challenge Of Stockpile Stewardship, What Would Ghandi Think?, Countering the Lies of the Lab, The Avalon Facility And The Issue Of Nonproliferation Preliminary Draft Study, which he opened to *On February 7 1994, Senator Samuel Chase requested that the Secretary of Energy resolve the question of whether the Avalon facility will aid or hinder US nonproliferation efforts.*

He pressed through the crowd, unable for the most part to tell Lab personnel from civilians in their common motley of nylon windbreakers, jeans, polyester pants, herringbone jackets, to the refuge of the far wall covered with laserprinted signs <- OHLONE VALLEY QUILT GUILD, DOE PUBLIC HEARING ->, CLOUDSTONE STORYTELLER ->

—scheduled everything on the same damn night
—standing room only in there must be two hund
—sending their scientists out to the local schools in radiation suits, hey kids even bananas are radioactive so don't worry about plutonium
—can't get arrested tomorrow I have to pick the kids up from sch
—sixties scumbag jerk
—my wife said people in Washington don't wear beards
—says here they're going to host the
—Dali Llama?
—him and Ghandi here could have a spelling bee
—people so stupid it's a waste of time trying to reason with them
—see people have always been stupid, problem today is technology's a kind of amplifier

—don't worry, they'll end up eating their young as usual.

Through an open door BREAKOUT ROOM a dozen or so people sat wincing under the grate of an amplified voice.

—opportunity to, to give you sort of a overview to stockpile stewardship and a bit of an overview to the Avalon mission requirements. As my viewgraph indicates, I'm deputy assistant secretary for research, development, and simula

From the next doorway came a woman's keen, a woman in a long white dress clasped at the waist, raven hair over her shoulders, a woman pacing, halting, declaiming, —When everything needed was brought into being, when everything needed was properly nourished, when heaven had moved away from earth and the name of man was fixed, Enki gave his daughter Inanna blessings, and she took them. He gave her truth, descent into the underworld, ascent from the underworld, the art of lovemaking, the art of forthright speech, the art of slanderous speech, the art of treachery, the plundering of cities, deceit, kindness, the kindling of strife, the making of decisions . . . Quine pressed on toward PUBLIC HEARING -> stopped by the crowd in the doorway, as within the room an electronic whine rose and died at a raised podium visible through a sea of heads.

—I want to start out with making, making sure that everyone understands. The stockpile stewardship program is the policy of the nation. Its, its, its roots derive from the presidential directive.

—From the great above she opened her ear to the great below. When she entered the first gate her crown was removed. Inanna asked, what is this? Quiet, Inanna. The ways of the underworld are perfect. They may not be questioned, as from near the podium he saw Lynn pushing her way to him with fury in her eyes.

—The secretary of energy reaffirmed the, the following reaffirmation by the President that it's the policy of the nation to maintain its no-test policy. And the secretary is, has been very forefront in, in maintaining for that. It's one of her most respon, most important responsibilities to ensure that the US nuclear stockpile remains safe, secure, and reliable without nuclear testing. The US nuclear deterrent remains a supreme national interest, and those are very special words in treaties, the supreme national interest clause. What we have to do is while we're going along, maintain the institutional viability to respond to all parts of the, of the stockpile mission, including reconstitution if we, if we are asked by the President.

—When she entered the seventh gate from her body the royal robe was removed. She was naked. Inanna asked, What is this? Quiet, Inanna. No one ascends from the underworld unmarked, said Ereshkigal. If Inanna wishes to ascend she must send someone in her place. Take him! cried Inanna, and the galla seized her husband Dumuzi, as she grasped Quine's arm and drew him inside the doorway. She led him to the far wall and edged them along it to the front of the room.

—This is a very comprehensive facility. It serves a very wide spectrum of, of user communities, all the way from very specific bomb designers, to some of the, look, looking at some of the things you can read about in the newspaper about our, our astronomy discoveries. This is a needed flagship high-energy density facility for stockpile stewardship. We, we need ignition and nuclear burn. We need implosion and radiation physics from this facility. It's a magnet for world class talent. It provides key validations of computer simulation. Ignition in particular is one that I am particularly focused on because it is a clear dividing line. This is going to be a very, very large validation element for validation. Sine qua non. I mean, this is essential, basic and applied science exploration. And we have to have that. This is where we are, we are seeking to reach the temperatures of the stars, and, and, and also the same similar to the temperature at the inside of a nuclear device as, as it goes off.

Now he could see the podium upon which stood a shield vert, thunderbolt in bend sinister Or, on middle chief an atom, dexter chief a sun radiant of fifteen points, in fess a derrick and a windmill, on base a turbine, all of the second, the shield ensigned by a wreath of colors out of which an eagle's head couped proper, the whole within a roundel azure with bordure of the field bearing the motto, DEPARTMENT OF ENERGY UNITED STATES OF AMERICA, of the second.

Lynn's whisper was fierce. —There's about a hundred people here from the construction trades. They're all signed up to speak, it's going to take all night. Did you call the unions, put them up to this?

—No of course not I, glancing over to where Szabo stood like a post.

—continue now, our next commentor

—I'm tempted to blow your cover, make you get up there and explain a few things.

—hundreds of jobs

—Please Lynn, I'm, I came, didn't I.

—God they're eating into our time and they're saying the same thing over and

—jobs over the next five years adding a hundred million dollars to the local econ

—That is so untrue, she muttered and as yet another man stood to take the wireless microphone passed to him, she waved her hand and called out —Excuse me! Excuse me, I don't want to cut anyone off, but are we going to hear the exact same thing from another fifty electricians?

From next to them a voice growled, —Hey girly, wait your turn and don't disrespect the trades.

—I have the greatest respect for the construction trades, but a lot of other people are waiting to speak. Could we summarize please? and a stir behind the podium as —I think in light of the advancing hour . . .

—Got em, she muttered and without a look back at Quine began to make her way across the room.

—Doctor Quine, hello, I saw you in the audience, wasn't sure if I should introduce you or not.

—No no, I'm just, just stopped in to see how, how things were going, I'm about ready to

—I saw you talking to that rather well informed young lady.

—Under the pretense of maintaining the safety and reliability of the stockpile, stewardship is intended to preserve the capacity to maintain, test, modify, design and produce nuclear weapons, with or without underground testing.

—That is not the department's stated position. We are committed

—Ah yes she's, that is, we're acquainted of course, her group is a, a kind of, kind of a watchdog group, we hear, hear from them a lot, kind of a, our, ah, keep us honest . . . you're, ah, I don't believe we've . . .

—Carl Schlecht. We met in DC, just after the New Year. But I'm sure you met dozens of people on that trip.

—Sure, yes, of course, I ah, good to

—I work with Reese in DP. We're on tour here, kind of a sideshow really, but the chairman of Appropriations put pressure on the secretary. We've got ten of these things scheduled this month, from here we go to Amarillo, Sante Fe, South Carol

—documents posted on DOE's own Defense Programs server state that the US will continue to introduce new weapons, as per the B sixty one rev eleven

—Just a, just a moment, what documents?

—Core R and AT Program Elements from the DOE Office of Research and Inertial Fusion, in the section headed Concept Design and

—Just a . . . The two DOE representatives huddled out of microphone range.

—So you're not going to be speaking tonight, Doctor Quine?

—Yes, no, I mean I

—documents have since been removed from the site, an action that we regard as highly suspicio

—I must say, Doctor Quine, this young lady has excellent sources.

—Yes, we're aware of those, of those, those documents, and, and they were removed from the site because they shouldn't have been there to start with. The

—Once you make something public you can't just withdraw it because it's embarrassing.

—Those documents were outdated and had been superseded.

—There's no date on the document.

—Doctor Quine . . . ?

—The online version may not, not be dated, that's an oversight, but the document itself is from nineteen ninety two.

—What? No, no I won't be speaking.

—But the language and the programs listed are virtually identical to your F Y ninety five. These are clearly statements of intent to design new weapons.

—The US policy is to develop no new nuclear weapons.

—Are you willing to stand here and say that there is no consideration in the labs, that no scientists are thinking about pure fusion weapons?

—There is no pure fusion weapons program at any Department facility.

—That wasn't my question.

—We never tell scientists to stop thinking, but there is no program.

—Then what are your scientists thinking about? Can you be more specific?

—As to specifics, we're not at liberty to discuss them.

—What about the B sixty one rev eleven? Isn't that a new weapon?

—The physics package of the B sixty one has not been changed, therefore it is not a new weapon.

—The modification gives the weapon entirely new strategic uses. Is it US policy to upgrade existing weapons into what are, essentially, new applications?

—We will replace or rebuild existing designs as needed but we won't be adding new marks.

—Just about any nation looking at this is going to consider it a new weapon. It doesn't matter what your stated policy is if your actions contradict it.

—Thank you. I think five minutes is, is our limit, if we can move to the next commentor, ah

—Anyway Doctor Quine I just wanted to tell you how grateful we were for the, the heads, oh hello Miss, Miss Hamlin is it? I was just saying how impressed I was with your presentation.

—I didn't feel I made much of an impression.

—Oh, I think you may underestimate, ah, just how seriously the department takes ah your group. Anyway, what was I

—last ten years the number of chronically hungry children grew from

—and Doctor Quine, wanted to thank you for the heads up, I know that Reese was, ah

—US should invest in peace, trust, and equality

—Reese Turbot?

—Oh you know Reese, Miss ah Hamlin?

—We've had dealings.

—money could be better spent on schools, hospitals, housing

—think the, the commentor might be confusing the Department of Energy with the Department of Health and Human Services

—I really should get back up there, nice seeing you again, Doctor

Quine. You too Miss ah . . . as Schlecht's extended hand fell back unmet by the hard resolve in Lynn's eyes that turned to Quine.

—Yes, give my, my best to, to, to Reese . . .

—Reese Turbot. At DP.

—Yes . . .

—Did you happen to mention this ORIF document to him? Because boy did it disappear fast, like the day after I showed it to you.

—US is legally committed to disarmament as a signer of the non-proliferation trea

—Lynn, how can you, when you've been going through my papers for stuff like that B sixty one

—Going through your, I did not!

—weapons program necessary to ensure national sec

—Keep your voice, well where did you get it then!

—justified by potential for fusion energy

—Do you think, listen, we have plenty of sources, do you think for one minute that I

—Lynn please keep your v

—treaties depend upon Avalon

—If you can't trust me that far, then keep your briefcase locked.

—kay I think if we can move along

—Do you mean that I need to?

She didn't answer, but stared grimly as a slender bearded man in caftan and sandals stood to declaim pacifist couplets punctuated by arabesques on a flute while murmurs and snickers ran through the audience. When he'd finished she muttered, —Friends like these. As Quine turned to her he confronted a tanned face with a well managed smile, and a wiry tanned hand resting on her shoulder.

—Tony.

—Nice job, Lynn, you had them sweating. You must be Philip. Thanks for coming out.

—Honestly Tony, couldn't you have restrained Bernie?

—Oh, his heart's in the right place.

—I wish it'd check in with his brain once in a while.

—Look Lynn, I'm up next, are you in the office tomorrow?

—Till noon. I'm at day care in the afternoon.

—Lynn . . .

—I don't get in till three. You see this on the handout table? He held up Avalon And The Issue of Nonproliferation.

—I haven't looked at it yet.

—take a recess

—Lynn is this about

—Excuse us a minute Tony . . . ?

—Sure. Nice seeing you Philip.

—What is it?

—My head, I just need to

—Did you see Turner? He's here. Did you read the preprint I gave you?

—What? Look Lynn, I've got a terrible headache. Can we go now?

—Go? You mean leave? Philip, I have to stay to the end.

—But you've had your say, you

—There's a member of the Indian CTBT negotiating team here, I met him at Geneva, we're all going out afterwards so we can talk

—But I thought afterwards you and I would . . . as the crowd took them into the hallway, where —thanks to Ms ah Cloudstone's ah compelling performance, you can see that elements of the Inanna myth persist in that of Persephone, just as ah Grail romances can be traced back to Celtic

—I want you to hear Turner give his comment, he's very compelling, did you read the preprint?

—or even Russian

—Ah no, I . . .

—how dangerous it is to allow, as he was pushed against the wall by another surge exiting BREAKOUT ROOM.

—surrounded by a fence made of human bones

—oikonomia, literally "house management", a very powerful word, Jesus speaks of his father's

—Lynn I just . . .

—house on chicken's legs, Baba Yaga, the Bone Mother, breaks down the boundaries of personal

—you all right?

—forcing us to examine ourselves in the dark mirror of

—really can't take any more of this, can you please, can we go now?

—Go? I thought you understood that I was here for the evening.

—I didn't know it was going to be the whole time.

—I, Gopal! Hello yes, you've seen Tony . . . ?

The lot was half empty. Under the full moon his car glowed white. He lurched onto the rutted road and drove past the freeway and up Crow Canyon Road. As he ascended a mist gathered in the headlights. A fear in his heart, that he'd be judged. That he wouldn't be. Soon he was at a closed gate. PARK HOURS 6AM-8PM. A building was set back among the trees. In the second story window a dim line flickered, a fluorescent tube neither on nor off, stuttering between states. A broad path rose winding under black oak and bay. A deer came into the beam, the moist dark of its eyes on him, ears athwart, antlers forked like lightning. It raised one hoof as if inviting chase, then with no sense of hurry bounded into a thicket. Nothing more stirred but the mist, droplets brightening and thickening there, then vanishing into the dark.

The morning was clear. Eucalyptus blossomed and a new warmth urged out its pungency. In among the sickles of leathery green leaves were white blooms, each made up of thousands of twined filaments. In a breeze they drifted down like a sunshower. Just outside the kitchen window a live oak leaf spun like a coin, suspended in air by spidersilk that vanished and reappeared as it spun.

—Will you drive?

—Sure, I . . .

—Your CD player's jammed. She reached for, —No don't touch, the sudden growl of —who are you this time? under his —Damn it! I had that all . . . as he fidgeted the buttons for silence returning with the blue blink of JAM.

—You like Tom Waits?

—No, it's, the stereo is broken, the eject button doesn't work and the last owner just left this disk stuck in here so I had to, to figure out how to, to, what's so funny?

—Here I thought I was seeing a new side of you, and it's just some technical problem you haven't fixed yet.

—Yes well the dealer, it's not a factory install so, so . . . well I'm glad you think it's funny, his hand pulling back from the buttons when she stopped it with hers and held it.

—No you're not, you're annoyed.

—Well . . .

—Philip, believe it or not, I like you as you are. When you let yourself be.

—Well, but it is annoying, I actually can't turn it off, just to play the radio I have to, to, and as he held ^ to demonstrate the blue segments of the display flashed JAM before the radio boomed, —a fewer percentage of

—Please turn it off.

—Can't even do that, have to, what's so, so damn funny? as he pressed SRC to silence the voice and JAM flashed again.

—I'm in a good mood. It's a beautiful day, Mandela is president of South Africa, and I'm still working for CANT.

—Tony's keeping you on? You should get it in writing.

—Gopal convinced him that I know what I'm doing. Slow down, this is it.

Off the road a gate EBMUD No Trespassing Day Use Permits opened on an unpaved circle. He parked in dust and gravel.

—Shouldn't we, it says permit needed?

—Oh pooh. I'm not driving to Lafayette for a damn day use permit.

An edge of the coming summer heat lay half hidden in the sun-roasted smell of sage. Hills still green were specked with the yellow blossoms of Scotch broom and mustard and the pale blue spires of lupines. Sky spilled over water held back by an earthen berm. On the dirt road over the berm was a vacant aluminum trailer Mills College Crew. Redwinged blackbirds darted in metallic song. The trail climbed through oak and bay. Even in the treesoftened sunlight he sweated. She waited on a clear rise above the reservoir. The sky was so empty there he dizzied almost. On a day this warm and clear last summer he'd touched her for the first time. They'd watched a redtailed hawk bank and soar. Her dark eyes squinted, her lips parted in what was less a smile than delight arrested and contained at the moment it was born. Her head was tilted and sunlight moved glittering through her cropped black hair to the base of her neck. A muscle stood out where her jaw met her ear. His hand went out to touch the down of her neck and her head tipped back into it. The warmth of her hair and the weight of her head filled his hand.

Now a bird flock was scattered on the sky, white flashes that vanished into blue, reappeared black, vanished again wheeling, flickering it seemed in and out of existence. The glitter of light on water also moved in and out of being. He was on the verge of something, as if God, as extravagant with bounty as he was stingy with meaning, might have hidden the clues to being somewhere in being's very abundance and superfluity.

Lynn's warm hand slipped into his. Startled, his thoughts fled.

—I'm sorry about last night. It was crunch time for me.

—It's all right. I was, just wasn't feeling all that . . .

—Turner was good. I wish you'd stayed.

—How about here? Quine moved into the shadow of a bay tree.

—Look out! Poison oak. Rhus diversiloba.

—Sacred to . . . ?

She smiled. —It's a New World plant, Western states only. Coyote, I guess. It's probably sacred to Coyote.

—Coyote . . . ?

—Trickster. It's a tricky plant. Even the genus name was changed, from Rhus to Toxicodendron. Its leaves can be dark green or bright red. Even the bare branches and the roots are toxic. Tricky plant.

She unpacked small plastic tubs of lentil and chevre, fennel and red onion, olives, pears, a baguette. Acorns and leaf trash littered the hard dry ground. They sat in silence as he stared across the glittering water.

—What is it?

—I was, I don't know, I was thinking about light. About energy. I just, I had an idea about something. There's this effect that happens in, in plasmas . . . do, do you know about Rayleigh scattering?

—No, tell me.

—The sky's blue because of it. Sunlight is scattered by air molecules, and the short wavelengths like blue scatter most so that's what we see the blue. Lord Rayleigh discovered the effect, actually he discovered much more, an amazing scientist, all the work he did in the nineteenth century on fluid dynamics, wave equations, we're still, I mean well, anyway . . . and, and you see near the horizon, how the blue shades into white? That's Mie scattering, light bouncing off larger particles, larger than a wavelength, so the light remains white but most of it comes forward, but see, these are both forms of elastic scattering, they don't actually change the wavelength of the light. But in plasmas, Raman scattering and Brillouin scattering are inelastic, the photons gain or lose energy, they actually shift their frequency, so it becomes an issue in, especially in laser-plasma interactions. Anyway I was just thinking that at certain energies you might get another kind of, of sort of a resonance effect that might . . .

—Quine scattering.

—Don't joke, I'm just

—But no, why not? Why couldn't you discover an effect?

—But that's, no I mean, it's only an engineering problem. It's still physics I guess, but not, not . . . A sudden desolation welled up in him, from that nowhere he couldn't name or manage, the warmth and the scent of the day receding even as they came forward to overwhlem him, turned against themselves in mockery of his anxiety, some unnameable burden that had just caught up with him sitting there in his vortex of vanished peace.

—Not what?

—Not . . . not what I ever meant to do.

—You sound so resigned.

An annoyance came over him, but passed off into the depth of that nowhere. —If I'd had it in me to do, don't you think I would have? That paper with Sorokin, maybe that was all I had.

—Oh Philip. If you feel this way why did you take the director's job?

—It was a last chance for me. I just couldn't believe it when I was offered this . . . but I was a terrible choice, don't you think I, everyone in the Lab knows it, I know Szabo wants to get rid of me, but maybe Réti's right, this is what science is now. Maybe my role is to enable others.

—But enable them to what? Walk your path, from science to weapons? She took his hand. —You remember last summer? Right here. We kissed for the first time. Nothing seemed impossible then.

—No.

—And now we're so much closer!

—Closer . . . ?

—To each other. To what we want. You don't have to go on with the bad choices of the past . . .

—But that's just it, I'm surrounded by all these bad choices, bad ideas, relics of some past, there are whole groups, departments, sections devoted to them, we have contracts and deliverables, it's like a maze you have to run, there's no time to, to reflect on what direction you should take just get to the next corner and go on from there.

—Yes, I know. Sometimes I think it's impossible. That you can't convert these entrenched ideas. That nothing good can ever come of them. That we'd have to close down all the weapons labs. And even then it wouldn't end. It does seems impossible sometimes. But

—But I mean, how do you keep on with it when you see how impossible it is?

—I can't live with myself if I don't try.

—I just, sometimes I just want to give up. But if you think it's all so compromised, what about me? Why are you with me?

—Because I trust you, Philip. That you want to do the right thing. And it's so hard for you. Do you trust me?

—Trust? as something fled across his face looking for a place to hide, and was trapped there. —Yes I, of course I, I mean . . .

—Because that's all there is finally, that fragile skein of trust. Without it everything falls apart.

—Yes, I . . .

Her dark eyes engaged his. —And with it, you know, it's not hopeless. We do have a chance. With Turner's comment, the other comments from the hearing, we can convince DOE, to halt Avalon or scale it back. The Lab could

—To halt . . . ? Oh but . . . something like alarm rose in him. —But you know it already went in. The Conceptual Design Report. The secretary okayed it. The baseline budget was accepted, I mean it won't be formally approved for a few months, but, but even Chase signed off. It looks like a sure thing, even the x-ray laser, we . . . Lynn? She was on her feet, standing against that flawless sky, fighting it seemed for breath.

—What? When did this. Did you.

—Lynn

—How long have you known?

—It just I just

—Even, going into that meeting last night, you knew? And all my. You. You'd think. By now you'd think that I.

—Lynn . . . he scrambled up to follow her pacing.

—You mean that everything we've talked about, Chase, Turner, Sorokin, the public hearing, you're saying it's all wasted because this decision was, was made. Like Tony said, it was a done deal. And I believed that you really wanted to to to

—Lynn, I did want, I do . . .

—All my experience with politicians and I wasn't ready for this. Damn!

—But . . . he reached for her.

—Don't! Don't you understand, my own foolishness that's bad enough but how I've behaved, used up favors, credibility, thrown CANT's resources into this, because damn it I trusted you, thought you were being honest that there was a, a chance to turn it around . . . and now this, this makes me feel so stupid!

—Lynn, please, isn't there more between us than . . . stepping up to where she whirled in dappled sun to push him away, —Don't! as his heel turned on a loose stone, gave under him, and toppled him into the brush. Under his hand and against his face were the waxy green leaves and white berries of Rhus or Toxicodendron.

—Oh God. Wait, let me, she bent to unscrew the cap from a water bottle as he thrashed upward. —Don't touch me! I mean, wait, just lie there while I . . . as she wet a kerchief he gazed at the burning sky. She dabbed at his face.

—Shut your eyes. This is to get the plant oil off, the urushiol. Your skin oil will protect you for an hour or two. When you get home, take a cool shower. Don't use soap or hot water, they'll break down your skin oil before the urushiol.

—Aren't you coming home with me?

She dabbed in silence at his hands and forearms. She folded the kerchief and poured water from the bottle over her hands one at a time, then threw kerchief and bottle into her pack.

—Lynn . . .

—I'll see you at the car.

She turned from him and went steadily into the sun, where, ruffled by a wind, her hair spread out in fiery points. The sunlight was so bright now it was hollow, the reality leached from everything. It was a few minutes before he followed. She was waiting near the gate, across the circle from the car, and came toward it only when he unlocked the doors.

They drove in silence down the winding white road to the freeway.

—You weren't such a bad choice. The x-ray laser, that's the real kicker, that you hated so much, now you're protecting it.

—Lynn it's not the, the Superbright it's

—Maybe if you solve your Quine scattering problem all those undead Reagan assholes can bring their missile defense back to life.

—That's not what

—God I'm so mad at you! We're keeping our bombs no matter what so fuck you.

—Lynn, I said, you know, if you wanted to have an impact you should, you could have come on board with us, you say you're trying to go to law school but

—Philip, don't say anything more.

At a red light he looked away from the barrel of the traffic camera to FAST DIVORCE BANKRUPTCY on a bus stop bench.

—Lynn please, I didn't mean . . . will you let me . . .

—CANT's sending me back to Geneva. For the second CTBT session. It starts May sixteenth. I'll be gone six weeks.

—You didn't tell me.

—I was waiting for you to ask.

—But I didn't know, how could I . . .

—To ask about, I don't know, about anything that's important to me.

He reached for her and she backed away. —I really don't want poison oak.

After she'd gone inside he watched a cloud of insects move in and out of sun. At home in the shower he turned the water as hot as possible. He stood laving and scrubbing until his skin was red.

S I X

—ten minutes we'll bring you the world, which suddenly loomed closer in the form of HOW AM I DRIVING? CALL 1-800-328-7448 as he braked and —North Korea said it's started withdrawing spent fuel from a nucular reactor without international inspectors present, an action that senior US officials warned, pressing ^ for the blue blink of JAM where a red Miata SFORZA was parked between a Mercedes and a dumpster CREDNE Waste Management. As he released the seat belt he caught a glimpse of himself in the rearview mirror, the left half of a face distended in forsakenness and misery, and swollen with welts now crusting and beginning to weep clear fluid. He dabbed with a handkerchief already stiff and yellowed, holding it there through Soon Yet OPEN Visa Mastercard PUSH, from blinding heat into bone chill, a crowded foyer, and up to an impassive Chinese, —Excuse me, is Leo Highet, who pointed to a table behind a potted ficus.

—Sorry I'm late, the traff

—What happened to your face?

—Poison oak.

—You get a cortisone shot? Benadryl's good. Hot water releases the histamines, gives you some temporary relief. You know, this is what M Section should be working on, allergies and autoimmune reactions, not that genome stuff. Try the jellied duck feet.

—I'm not hungry.

—Suit yourself. Highet speared a dumpling and brought it to his mouth. —How's your girlfriend? Still speaking truth to power? Is power listening yet?

—Look, I didn't come for

—He'll have two of these and two of these. Keep your strength up, it's a stressful job.

—What is it you want?

—Right to business, wow. Somehow I thought we'd start out comparing notes. How to get the washroom sink to drain. Keeping Dolores's radio down. Figured everything out yet? Seems to me I had file an environmental impact statement just to eat lunch.

—The new secretary of energy's changing that.

—Oh right, Little Miss Openness. How's that working out for you? You find that the Lab's becoming a "safe and rewarding workplace that's results-oriented and fun"?

—Look, I don't have time, what about Gate?

Highet pried opened a dumpling with his chopsticks and examined its interior. —He's working with North Koreans.

—I've been all through this with your friend Dan Root.

Highet looked up. —Dan's not a friend. We worked together once.

—Well I need to know just what

—I won't forget your needs, but there's something more pressing. Eight thousand fuel rods sitting in a cooling pond near Yongbyon. That's five bombs' worth of plutonium without even violating the NPT. If they've been pulling spent fuel since the reactor started up in eighty six they could have built five or six bombs in the fifty kiloton range. They're on their way to a nice little arsenal. All they need is a delivery system. The CIA thinks they're fifteen years from an ICBM, but the CIA can't find its ass with both hands. Anyway they don't want an ICBM. They want satellites. With another stage, their No Dong could put things into orbit.

—Why are you so concerned about this?

—It's what I do now. I'm a nonproliferation researcher at NOUS.

—You mean, what, you . . .

—We advise NRO, CIA, DoD, that kind of thing.

—Good God.

—It's not as glamorous as it sounds.

—Glamorous, it doesn't sound, just, if you're bringing the same,

336

the same level of truth you did to Radiance to this job, it sounds dangerous is what it sounds.

—World's a dangerous place. But I'm wasting your valuable time with all this history. All I want to know's if the Supreme Leader's getting flight data from Persephone.

—I held up the CRADA. Root said he'd go to NASA to get the data.

—Okay, I know who to call there. My guess is they're getting the data.

—This is absurd, Gate told me his Korean partner is Hyundai, but even if, so what, what if they are getting some data?

—Hyundai, that's cute. Suppose it's true. How will Pyongyang react when they hear that their neighbor to the south is checking out a missile defense component? Look, this data is the camel's nose. If Gate's CRADA goes through, the whole package is out there, thrusters, sensors, everything. The North Koreans are very resourceful. Our intel keeps saying they're on the verge of economic collapse, yet somehow they hang on. Somehow they've built nuclear reactors, missiles, sure they had Russian and Chinese help but not lately, and they were always smart enough to play the two off against each other. You've got to admire the feisty little fucks.

—And you're worried that they may launch a few satellites?

—Right, who cares about some piece of junk playing The Immortal Hymn Of Bum Suk Kim on the ten meter band until its batteries run down. But have you looked closely at the Slingshot technology?

—We're no longer doing missile defense.

—I see why Chase likes you so much. Do you know what Persephone is carrying?

—Sensors, we designed the sensors . . .

—Right, you're an executive summary kind of guy. The Slingshot is a kinetic kill vehicle that

—I know all

—that can carry a payload of up to a hundred kilos. That's either a dieting engineer or a small nuke. You want five, ten, fifty of those things in low earth orbit?

—What makes you think

—"States parties to the treaty undertake not to place in orbit around the Earth any objects carrying nuclear weapons." Outer Space Treaty, nineteen sixty seven. North Korea never signed.

—Well, so what, they're a, a rogue state, you were always so contemptuous of treaties . . .

—Did you notice that they announced their intent to withdraw from the NPT? They take those commitments seriously. They have a sense of honor. The US has fucked them and helped Japan fuck them for fifty years. Now President Bubba is yelling about sanctions over these fuel rods. How do you think they'll take that?

—Look, even if they get the Slingshot, even if they can launch these things, even if they do have bombs

—Sure, Space Command can track an object the size of a softball, but how do you prove there are nukes on board? Are we going to start shooting down satellites on suspicion? And with what?

—So this is your way to, to hit a bullet with a bullet, a Slingshot with another Slingshot, to keep that whole program alive? You're going to claim we need to deploy these things before anybody else does.

—Me? I just provide information. For example, a nuke dropped from an orbiting platform takes under five minutes to hit the ground. Or, you can set it off in low orbit and the EM pulse will take out military C3, computers, telephones, broadcasting, banking, toasters, gameboys, you name it.

—So you sell this fear, this, this farfetched story, beginning middle end, you're still doing that, telling a story instead of, of the truth.

—Well, Philip, truth is a story. Or do you know better than that? Help me out here. What's the truth of your situation?

—You've got some some some . . . after you . . .

—After I what? Tried to keep my Lab going in the face of impossible demands, incoherent policy, and ignorant policy makers? You getting a taste of that now? Ever had to explain anything to a congressman?

—Chase . . .

—Think Chase is your friend, the very first time you forget to say mother may I he'll be on you like a wolverine. No, believe it or not I'm here to help you Philip. So don't insult me. Don't make yourself out to be the victim, sitting in that chair you pulled out from under me. Pissing me off will only make me irrational and vindictive. Didn't you have something to ask me?

—Who's Devon Null?

—Talented physicist. I think he's on Wall Street now. Using chaos theory to model financial trends.

—Records show he was never an employee.

—You don't say.

—So giving him an office was a little unusual, wasn't it?

—Everybody has to be somewhere.

—It was my office. He was never there. Nullpoint, what is that?

—I have no idea.

—Conor recovered the deleted partition on your computer.

Highet set down his chopsticks and touched a napkin to his mouth. He chewed in silence for a moment, then looked around the room, as if someone out there might be easier to talk to. —What a great kid. Isn't he a great kid? Okay, about Nullpoint. You've probably never read your contract, but as an employee of the University of California, you agreed to certain things. "In the event that any such invention shall be deemed by University to be patentable, I shall do all things necessary to assign to University all rights, title and interest therein." See, people at the Lab commit to an unusual scientific career. They do classified research that can't be published. They invent things they can't patent or sell. Occasionally the Lab waives commercial rights, but it's always a pain in the ass, especially now that the university's gotten so greedy about patents. So we set up a shell company. To shelter intellectual property.

—It's, it's all about the money for you, isn't it?

—What's it all about for you, Philip? Being right? I could care less about the money. I did this for my people. If they feel they're getting ripped off they'll rip you off.

—That would explain the forty million in missing inventory. How many people have profited from this setup?

—Profited. Maybe once in a great while somebody got enough to pay off a loan. Profit? That's change that fell out on the car seat. Christ Philip you bought a house with the rise in your salary, you know what's being tossed around. You want to talk real money, ask Dan Root. He's the one with irons in the fire. I'm just a semi-retired consultant with condo payments to make and white papers to write. Or ask Rector, he's already looked into this.

—So everybody thinks they're entitled, is that right? Employees running insider land deals, walking out the door with equipment, taking kickbacks from patent agreements, you think that's, that's, there's a GAO report on my desk about twelve thousand missing documents, nuclear weapons designs, x-ray laser plans, photos of tests, did any of those documents pass through Nullpoint?

Highet shook his head again and lowered it, as if tired of contending with missed points, to push the remains of a dumpling through a dark sauce on his plate. Quine put the coyote fetish on the table.

Sun slanted across the chopsticks idle in his blunt fingers, flesh pale as the wood they held, skin creased around the burls of the knuckles. On his face the light was even and unforgiving, etching a map of time on his features like a wrinkled shroud, spotted here and there with a brown fleck or a broken capillary. His voice, when it came again, was tired.

—The thing about passwords, you should use a random string, never a real word. Seven characters minimum. Put some numbers and punctuation marks in it. And never write it down. But does anyone follow these simple rules? Highet put aside his chopsticks, then picked up the fetish and put it in his jacket pocket. —You have any other questions for me?

—You worked on fusion for quite a while.

—And many before me. Szabo . . . Réti . . .

—You wrote that a thousand joules was sufficient for ignition.

—Long ago.

—Your computer model was optimistic.

—It looked good at the time. Why are we talking about twenty year old computer codes?

—Our codes still use many of the same assumptions.

—When you simulate a complex process on a computer, you always make assumptions.

—You piggybacked fusion capsules onto Superbright tests, didn't you.

—We did that all through the eighties. More buck for the bang, you know?

—The Lancet series. Alder, Willow, Rowan . . .

—Keep it down, even those names are classified.

—Taliesin.

—Right, your shot. You're upset we didn't tell you.

—Those shots were to verify your codes?

—Those shots were a proof of principle. The basis for Avalon. You want Avalon, I wouldn't look too closely at that test data.

—Why not?

—I know how demanding you are. It might not meet your high standards. Personally, I wouldn't have promised ignition. I would have emphasized the weapons aspects. But I know you're down on bombs.

—Well, we've got Avalon. That's for sure.

—Who's heading it?

—Szabo.

—Ah. Get your goats lined up. Let me give you a little advice. Watch your back with him. If he gives you any trouble, check his school records.

—Why do you care what

—What happens to you? I don't. I care about the Lab.

—Sure, you care so much you rigged those codes back in the seventies to show just what you wanted, to get the funding, so now the entire laser program is based on a deception, that's how much you care.

—You really despise me, don't you, Philip. You think I stole secrets, you think I faked data, why don't you call the fucking FBI if you're so sure. If you've read my laser fusion papers you know the science is good. Despite how you feel about me.

—You were always after the money.

—You amaze me. Only someone who doesn't know what the fuck he's talking about could be so sure. You know Bill Venham? No? Close friend of Dan Root. Ran direct mail for Goldwater. Claims he got Reagan elected governor in sixty six. Now he runs the Arete Foundation, heard of them? No? They own NOUS. They own broadcasters. They fund right wing causes. That loudmouth Eubanks on the radio? Ven-

341

ham started him out eight years ago on a Sacramento station. They want to shut down DOE, give all the nuclear weapons work to the Pentagon, you think DOE's fucked up talk to some ambitious Air Force colonel's read too much Tom Clancy. Bill wants creationism taught in the schools, he's got Senator Bangerter on board for that one. Oh, and Bill sponsors the Hertz fellowships. You've heard of those. At least I know where my money comes from.

Highet pushed back his chair. —If you've had the time to crack my PGP, you must have found those GIF files on my disk. Not my thing, but I wondered why the hell they were on an open server, so I saved copies. Ask Conor about steganography. You're so clever, you'll work it out.

—That's all?

—Yeah, I think so. Tell me Philip, you ever get any joy out of life?

—Joy . . . ?

Highet regarded him with the dour look of a man who's missed a long-awaited chance. He dropped a few bills on the table. —This is my treat.

The red Miata was gone when Quine emerged under a sky full of Mie scattering, a haze that magnified the sunlight by diffusing it into almost an opacity settled over the bridge as an unyielding glare while the battering of crosswinds tore free the fluttering Profit From Your Knowledge from under his wiper blade, and an orotund voice proposed that someone or something —wouldn't stand a prayer, before being silenced by a quick thumb jabbing 5 for the temporary solitude of brushed steel doors and —The hell . . . ? a breastwork of boxes stacked in the front office.

—The Conceptual Design Report is back from the printers. They sent ten copies.

—Good God I can't get by them, how did

—It's twenty seven volumes.

—Well can't we . . . ow! What's

—That's the new GAO report. Twenty copies I think? Jeremy Rector called, he'll be by to discuss it.

—Dolores, I can't work with this stuff here, can't we move it to the library or something?

—They have copies already. Oh you have a call from Armand Steradian he wants to ask about Bernd Dietz.

—. . . yes I'll, listen Dolores can you get me Frank Szabo's academic transcript from, from Yale I think . . . jamming the inner door against a stack of boxes that tottered but stabilized as Conor, face crimsoned, came up from his chair, —Jefe! You're back early, I mean, wow, like what happened to your face?

—Poison oak, as he pushed around to where splayed limbs and pouting lips held out a promise of, if not fulfillment, at least distraction.

—. . . oh uh listen I was, I had a thought about these files, you probably already thought of this, I saw that paper on your desk but

—Could we please get rid of . . . he leaned in to close the windows open on that plain of venery.

—actually Highet thought of it back when they found this stuff, you know, that it might be steganography?

—What?

—Data hiding? Goes back like centuries. There's a fifteenth century manuscript, the Steganographia by Johannes Trithemius, about the science of knowledge, the art of memory, angelic magic, it contains passages on cryptography. Then there's Gaspari Schotti's book from sixteen sixty five

—Listen Conor, I've got

—and a fourteen ninety nine anonymous work, the Hypnerotomachia Poliphili, published by Aldus Manutius, where the first letter of each chapter spells out in Latin "Brother Francesco Colonna passionately loves Polia", which is something you definitely don't want your abbot to read.

—How do you know all this anyway?

—I read the cypherpunks mailing list.

—So this, this is just some archaic method of

—Oh, not archaic. Large computer files like graphics have slack space in them, redundancy. You can embed other information in that space and the file doesn't even look encrypted. Highet asked me about it when they first found these files. I wrote a decrypting program for him, it might still be on his, I mean your disk, it's called stego.

—Yes thanks I'll, be with you in a second Jeremy, oh look out for . . .
as the calfskin case came up over the corner of some boxes and banged
against the doorframe. —Conor let's do this another time, I have to

—And my Rayleigh-Taylor work, can we talk about . . . ?

—Yes, later Conor, I'll see you . . .

—in an hour or so . . . ?

—see you haven't opened, my goodness, what happened to your
face?

—Just an, an allergy, it's nothing. Opened what?

—The report, but there's not much to worry about. We have to put
a new property management system in place, that's about the worst of
it. But I ah, may I, may I . . . ? Yes if you'd just move that, thank you.
I'm concerned about this Dietz fellow. Did you get some kind of a letter from him?

—I shut him down. That letter's been classified.

—That's probably why he's upset. He's been telling everyone that
his letter should go to the secretary. Not my business at this stage, but
it might be best to let him make his point.

—No, I'm, I've really had it with people taking advantage of my,
my good nature, Bernd is just going to have to, to, to come to terms.

—Yes I'm sure he will. There's one other thing I'm concerned
about . . . pushing aside Time Tactics Of Very Successful People to
make space for Chivian-Harris, Boole & Clay, Credne Waste Management. —Have you seen these?

— . . . no.

—No?

—Well I've glanced, but not, not in the context of any actionable, I
mean any ah proactive kind of ah action . . .

—Well, it could turn nasty. This CANT group, I have to say, they're
very adroit. You ah know someone with them, don't you . . . ?

—Not really.

—They settled their Site Alpha suit, but there's a number of other
toxic plumes. The effluvients are covered in our Superfund documents . . .
as three more thick folders came out of the calfskin case and Rector
freed a sheet. —Volatile organic compounds, polychlorinated biphenyls,
ethylene dibromide, benzene, trichlorethane, perchlorethane, lead,

strontium, iodine, merc

—Look Jeremy is this, I mean you're basically saying that there's no immediate, I mean nothing's wrong, right?

—Nothing's wrong? But, we're a Superfund site. We're getting federal money to clean up th

—Yes but that's, I mean that's baseline right that's not news, we're dealing with . . .

Rector squared documents against the calfskin case. —It could be made into news if it seems we're not doing our part. The EPA took a baseline reading in a schoolyard a half mile away and found plutonium concentrations of one point th

—Plutonium? A half mile away? How did that happen?

—No one's sure. It could have come from a smokestack with a bad scrubber, but the concentration is localized. There was one incident in sixty seven, some plutonium released into the offsite sewers. One EPA official guessed that contaminated sludge might have been collected and sold as fertilizer.

—But how could that happen, aren't there safeguards?

—There are radiation gauges at our outflow points, but they were often turned off because of too many false positives. The waste could have entered the city sewers.

—Okay, so people make mistakes, but, but, nineteen sixty seven? How is that news?

—It may have been there that long, it's just the readings that are recent. Also there's the two mile long tritium plume, well at least tritium has a fairly short halflife, unlikely to surprise you thirty years later, but

—But this is, I mean . . .

—I'm just sayng, with the new construction and suspicions that might arise around these dual toxics reports, these older incidents could be used as a lever, you see?

—But no, I don't see.

—Case by case these aren't really my concern, but a pattern and practice of abuses is something I need to be aware of, especially if Superfund monies have been misused.

—But, pattern and prac . . . ? Rector stood, snapping shut the calfskin case. —But what should I do?

—Senator Chase is still in your corner, isn't he?

—As far as I, I, I mean I haven't talked to him lately but

—Well, you might want to touch base there . . . as the door shut on the binders and spiralback volumes of Conceptual Design Report now laid out like a patient on the table, diagrams and wireframe perspectives littering the floor where —Conor! came sliding —Look out! across the carpet on the skid of 1.1.2 SYSTEM MANAGER APPROVAL Optics Bernd Dietz, crumpling it against the leg of Quine's desk. —Yo dude! This place is like . . .

—What is it?

—Sorry, jefe, but do you want to talk about my Rayleigh-Tay

—Just, is that? just leave it here, I'll take it with me and read it tonight and maybe tomorrow or I mean Friday we can

—Okay but this is like, something I think you really want to

—Hello . . . ? Senator! Yes, thank you for. Well I'm very glad to hear th . . . Dietz? He's the manager of, of the . . . he did? Well yes, that's why he's manager of the optics and . . . well no but and you know the value I place on, on intellectual freedom but I do think his criticisms are yes as you say untimely. That, that's why I've spoken to the project manager and told him to, to review . . . yes an internal review there's no reason this should be on, on anyone's radar, and anyway Dietz did sign the, the . . . going down on hands and knees for the crumpled page under Conor's Air Jordan, —the System Manager Approval for Optics and the, the Cost Basis Document so . . . yes I do know his concerns, they're well within the parameters of ah . . . well, he's been under some, some stress with our deadlines and I think he just, just, yes exactly. Yes I'll make sure he . . . and what? Hearing ? Environmental manage, what's that got to do with . . . oh. Yes I. Well of course we are. Planning for, for waste disposal sites, well but do you think that's really our, our . . . yes we do generate . . . yes we do have toxics mitigation progr . . . our expertise, yes I see I'll, okay I'll call Glenn Boniface and . . . but, but me? But why? Uh huh. Yes, well I'll have to, to get up to, to speed on . . . when is this . . . ? reaching for a pen and turning over 1.1.2 SYSTEM MANAGER for a blank surface. —Okay. Yes. Yes I will . . . tapping the phone for, —Glenn Boniface please.

—Jefe . . . ?

—Not, not now, Conor, I've got to . . .

—Okay, I'll leave this on top of uh, is, is this your in basket . . . ? the door closing on —Glenn, this is Philip. Can you get me some documents . . . ? and a minute later he was stepping over Conceptual Design Report and FUDGE and Ohlone Val Anti-Nuke Group Brings Superfund Suit to reach the sink, where he stared into the mirror at a face almost healed of poison oak but looking no healthier for it, rummaging through Naproxen Valerian St Johns Wort Gingko Biloba for an unmarked amber bottle, some blue pills incised with triangle sitting in a residue of blue dust like a diorama of some distant and peaceful planet that offered a languor of the life more imminent than LANCET 1979-1991, or Growth Rate of the Rayleigh-Taylor Instability in an Ablating Plasma, or DOE/RW-0184-R1 Characteristics of Potential Repository Wastes Volume 4, a drowsiness diffusing a dimness like the ground fog thickening to obliterate the distant ridges where <ULTRADIG> had slit the hills and was scooping a new interchange past Codorn c s XIT NLY, solid with unmoving cars as somewhere up ahead blue and red flashes stained the fog and ƎƆͶA⅃UꓭMA came up the shoulder in a blast of klaxon, but whatever misfortune or mortality had manifested there was gone with the fog next morning, leaving behind only a litter of bright glass pebbles, an oil stain, a crumpled strap of metal. The snout of a camera presided over eight lanes of cars waiting then rushing at the patterned alternation of lights. Quine in his turn edged past FAST DIVORCE BANKRUPTCY with a pang more conspicuous for the singing of some bird, for the minute effulgency of bus exhaust blowing through the window rolled quickly shut against the bluebird's tune which proved to be only the mechanical chirp of the traffic signal offering to assist any blind passerby foolish enough to brave those eight grumbling and irate lanes, chirp changing to a cuckoo as he turned to brake for EBMUD rolling away a stone, or was it only a manhole cover.

Back in the office he sat in what might have been silence but for the tinnitus in his ears, the construction coming to life out by the dry fountains, the inexorable press of the daily round, the sound of people trying not to say what they meant, yet he went on listening for that unheard stillness within, as if some clue to his heart or to its safe passage through the world could be found in the world's very exigency, if only he could wait long enough.

But each passing moment brought its new exigencies, like crows coming to land among the sheafs and binders and Growth Rate of the Rayleigh-Taylor Instability. He gazed out from his desk at Mount Ohlone, its slopes covered with the long grasses now dried to dun and pale gold and amber and mauve and gray and violet. *Capsules below a certain energy failed to ignite because the hot spot will not achieve sufficient rho-r and temperature.* Scotch broom and lupines, their flowers fallen, stretched out hard and hairy seed pods for the heat, orange poppies and purple thistles bloomed. *Typically, the computational mesh is too coarse to resolve steep, inhomogeneous plasma-density structures that might arise from uneven illumination or hydrodynamic instabilities.* High above arroyos Cathartes aura soared. *Because we lacked adequate models for certain pieces of the physics,* the leathery leaves of Rhus diversiloba were dark green and shiny with resin, innocently holding forth their pale berries.

—See, Bill Snell's group measured the inflight aspect ratio of the capsule and here see these radial lineouts are Abel inverted, providing density profiles as a function of t

—yes I see that's great Conor

—doped and undoped ablators

—really great but could y

—basically I think Bill's group majorly underestimates instability growth. They're getting their confirming data from flat foils. They assume axial symmetries, they assume linear or weakly nonlinear regimes, but our capsules are spherical and this stuff is three-D and nonlinear out the yin yang. The codes don't capture that.

—Does the Lancet test data square with the codes?

—Eight out of ten Lancet test capsules fizzled. According to our codes they all should have ignited. Of course the conditions were different, I mean those were bomb tests that's obvious but still, something like twenty megajoules went into some capsules and that's like over ten times what the codes predic . . . hey, you okay?

—Just a, a little headache.

—kind of to be expected really, I mean you put a little droplet like that under that much pressure, the instabilities are going to spin right out of control. What do you want to do with my paper?

—Yes well I'm sure Bill Snell will want to, to review it, we'll have a meeting soon, okay and Conor . . . ?

—Yes?

—For now this is between you and me.

—Yeah, okay. You should take an aspirin or something . . .

—Yes I . . . In the bathroom he pushed aside Naproxen Valerian St. John's Wort for the amber bottle and shook out the last of the blue tablets. Outside the clamor of construction was continuous. When Szabo entered he barely looked up.

—What's with Dietz, Frank?

—What, his protest? We classified it.

—He called Senator Chase, then he called a reporter.

—Well, shit.

—Reassign him. Revealing anything in that letter is a classification breach.

—Philip, look, let me talk to him, I can manage him.

—Do what I say!

—I'll take care of it, okay? What's the trouble?

—Trouble? Tell you what the trouble is . . . as he rummaged through Waste Repository Preliminary to come up with Growth of the Rayleigh-Taylor Instability, —trouble is some tests done in the eighties the Lancet series you've heard of it?

—Yes . . . as a kind of wariness came into Szabo's voice. —I worked on those, they gave us our first proof of principle, kind of the basis for Ava

—Proof? You call two out of ten capsules proof? You call that a basis?

—I call two out of ten pretty damn good considering.

—Considering our codes predicted ten out of ten?

—Philip you've seen the codes you've even worked with them you know we're not capturing all the physics but

—Listen to me Frank construction starts in two years Bernd is screaming that Avalon might not come up to spec and now I find out that even if it does we might not get ignition, I don't need this. Why did I never see this data?

—Lancet? It's been out there. It was gone over by review panels. I assumed you were up to speed.

—Okay. I see a problem here that threatens our deliverables. And that is not going to happen. I want you to write a full report on all the Lancet data, emphasizing any uncertainty in Avalon's ignition threshold. I want this laid out for Reese in black and white.

—Philip, there's no need. Reese knows. Talk to him. You submit a report like that now it's just a red flag, he'll have to respond. He might even have to postpone Key Decision One, nobody wants that. That happens, then the elections, who knows, we could lose this, to another lab, or altogether. What do you want Philip, to blow the whistle on yourself? Reese knows there are no guarantees, he's fine with our unknowns.

—You seem awfully damn sure of what Reese is fine with.

—We've worked together. We understand each other. I'll talk to him if you want, get some assurances in terms you're comfortable with if that

—I'll talk to Reese. Meantime, write the report, Frank. I want to see it when I get back from this damned waste meeting in DC.

—What, next week? I don't have time to

—None of us has time . . . and the door had barely shut when his face hardened and the phone was in his hand for —Dolores, did you get Frank Szabo's academic transcript yet . . . ? and lingered there for MEM 5 as, waiting, he opened GAO/RCED-91-65 to *an organization saturated with cynicism, an arrogant disregard for authority, and a staggering pattern of denial,* dropping it for —Reese . . . ? I just wondered if you'd talked to Frank Szabo recently. He seems unhappy about something . . . not sure what the problem is, maybe he feels slighted because he was passed over for director, but I can't help that, I mean I promoted him to Avalon, doing everything I can think of . . . not really, just hard to work with, this Dietz thing, you know? Thought he had that covered and now Dietz is calling everyone he can think of . . . And this report he's writing, about some test data from the eighties? Lancet? You've heard of it? No, I don't know what he means to prove by it . . . just wondered if he'd shared anything with you . . . don't mean to trouble you with it, anyway I'll see you next week, we can talk then. Yes I'm, I have it here, Characteristics of Potential Repository Wastes, is that, no wait, Radioactive Waste Inventories Revision Nine, is that . . . ? Yes I'll get up to, up to speed here . . .

Night had fallen again out there beyond his notice, beyond his open blinds, where *375,000 cubic meters high level waste* awaited disposal, and the moonlit slopes of Mount Ohlone seemed as though his window gave upon the sylvan scene, *100,000 cubic meters transuranic waste,* where an owl left the harbor of a eucalyptus, *2.5 million cubic meters low level waste,* where two raccoons growled circling a squirrel carcass, *iodine neptunium cesium uranium zirconium half-lives of a million years,* where a rat crept softly through the vegetation.

He pulled the blinds closed. *To ensure isolation from the biosphere materials are placed in a geologic repository, buried underground in shallow pits, dumped at sea, or discarded by hydrofracture injection.* Some planet set in the west. *The latter two techniques were past practices and are no longer performed.* Saturn by its color. *This report does not report civilian nuclear waste.* A grove of live oak blocked all light except for shards of the moon fallen like leaves among them. *This report also does not report inventories of radioactive materials not classified as waste.* Crickets chirred. *Steel drums are certified for 300 years.* Moonlight rinsed the open range land, and further off the valley was filled with glittering points. *Pretreatment and immobilization processes have not yet been finalized.* On a breath of warm air Umbellularia broadcast its waft of mint and resin. *Estimates for certain other waste categories are not fully reported because of the current unavailability of data.* —Artemisia tridentata, Lynn said, breaking from a sagebrush a twig of gray leaves, pungent in her cupped palm. The warmth of her came with it. And at the far verge of the sylvan scene was always the floodlit terrain of the Lab.

—Stop, he whispered. A nausea came over him and he pushed aside the papers. A desolation gaped, engulfed him. He started

To: lhamlin@igc.apc.org
Subject: Avalon uncertain igniti

then collapsed it in fury. He delved into /highet/ seeking some reminder or revelation to feed that which grew by it, halting at /xxx/ where he brought up that anonymous wilderness of flesh where heat went unsuccored by warmth, where the most sinuous invention devolved to the same predictable end, rousing within him something that sought a release not offered by this image or the next, until he was staring at russet highlights in cropped black hair fading to a fringe of down where it met the neck bent to sup at what in the next image sought lithe thighs to nest between until he pulled his attention from the figure to the ground, to the empty wineglass on the bedside table, the fallen shoe, the philodendron wilting in its tub there against the bare wall whose pixels, when examined closely, were suggestive as the brush-strokes of some secret writing. Over these he opened a new window for >stego a0001.gif At once a flaunt of tongue vanished behind columns of numbers sleeting down the screen to stop with ZULU_DATE 560527 ZULU_TIME 1756.00000 LAT 11.360000 LONG 165.230000 HOB 3M YLD 3530KT OPERATION REDWING EVENT ZUNI DEVICE BAS-SOON. His face wore a kind of stubborn denial belied by his fingers clicking back up through measurements of radiation, neutron flux, x-rays. As if refusing to learn what he didn't want to know, he command-ed his fingers to close the window, but they betrayed him with >stego *.gif, and one after another the enticements of parted lips and unclad limbs were lost in a blizzard of numbers that no rhythm of his frantic clicking could halt.

The names crowded there like demons invoked and impossible to put down, each with its date, time, latitude, longitude, height of blast, yield, weight, diameter, slant range, ground pressure, temperature, neu-tron flux, fifty years of it, every bit of data gathered at every test in the desert or on Pacific atolls, in shafts or tunnels under collapse craters, the wealth of an empire transformed into blasts that returned in their radi-ance the promise of some greater empire, the names of Trinity, Cross-roads Able, Crossroads Baker, Sandstone X-ray, Sandstone Yoke, Sand-stone Zebra, Ranger Able, Ranger Baker-1, Ranger Easy, Ranger Baker-2, Ranger Fox, Greenhouse Dog, Greenhouse Easy, Greenhouse George, Greenhouse Item, Buster Able, Buster Baker, Buster Charlie, Buster Dog, Buster Easy, Jangle Sugar, Jangle Uncle, Tumbler-Snapper Able, Tumbler-Snapper Baker, Tumbler-Snapper Charlie, Tumbler-Snapper Dog, Tumbler-Snapper Easy, Tumbler-Snapper Fox, Tumbler-Snapper George, Tumbler-Snapper How, Ivy Mike, Ivy King, Upshot-Knothole

Annie, Nancy, Ruth, Dixie, Ray, Badger, Simon, Encore, Harry, Grable, Climax, Castle Bravo, Romeo, Koon, Union, Yankee, Nectar, Teapot Wasp, Moth, Tesla, Turk, Hornet, Bee, Ess, Apple-1, Wasp Prime, HA, Post, MET, Apple-2, Zucchini, Wigwam, Project 56-1, Project 56-2, Project 56-3, Project 56-4, Lacrosse, Cherokee, Zuni, Yuma, Erie, Seminole, Flathead, Blackfoot, Kickapoo, Osage, Inca, Dakota, Mohawk, Apache, Navajo, Tewa, Huron, Project 57-1, Boltzmann, Franklin, Lassen, Wilson, Priscilla, Coulomb-A, Hood, Diablo, John, Kepler, Owens, Pascal-A, Stokes, Saturn, Shasta, Doppler, Pascal-B, Franklin Prime, Smoky, Galileo, Wheeler, Coulomb-B, Laplace, Fizeau, Newton, Rainier, Whitney, Charleston, Morgan, Pascal-C, Coulomb-C, Venus, Uranus, Yucca, Cactus, Fir, Butternut, Koa, Wahoo, Holly, Nutmeg, Yellowwood, Magnolia, Tobacco, Sycamore, Rose, Umbrella, Maple, Aspen, Walnut, Linden, Redwood, Elder, Oak, Hickory, Sequoia, Cedar, Dogwood, Poplar, Scaveola, Pisonia, Juniper, Oliver, Pine, Teak, Quince, Orange, Fig, Argus I, Argus II, Argus III, Otero, Bernalillo, Eddy, Luna, Mercury, Valencia, Mars, Mora, Colfax, Hidalgo, Tamalpais, Quay, Lea, Neptune, Hamilton, Logan, Dona Ana, Vesta, Rio Arriba, San Juan, Socorro, Wrangell, Rushmore, Oberon, Catron, Juno, Ceres, Sanford, De Baca, Chavez, Evans, Humboldt, Mazama, Santa Fe, Blanca, Ganymede, Titania, Antler, Shrew, Boomer, Chena, Mink, Fisher, Gnome, Mad, Ringtail, Feather, Stoat, Agouti, Dormouse, Stillwater, Armadillo, Hard Hat, Chinchilla I, Codsaw, Cimarron, Platypus, Pampas, Danny Boy, Ermine, Brazos, Hognose, Hoosic, Chinchilla II, Dormouse Prime, Passaic, Hudson, Platte, Dead, Adobe, Aztec, Black, Arkansas, Questa, Frigate Bird, Paca, Yukon, Mesilla, Arikaree, Muskegon, Swordfish, Encino, Aardvark, Swanee, Eel, Chetco, White, Tanana, Nambe, Raccoon, Packrat, Alma, Truckee, Yeso, Harlem, Des Moines, Rinconada, Dulce, Petit, Daman I, Otowi, Bighorn, Haymaker, Marshmallow, Bluestone, Sacramento, Sedan, Little Feller II, Starfish Prime, Sunset, Pamlico, Johnnie Boy, Merrimac, Small Boy, Little Feller I, Wichita, York, Bobac, Raritan, Hyrax, Peba, Allegheny, Androscoggin, Mississippi, Bumping, Roanoke, Wolverine, Chama, Tioga, Bandicoot, Checkmate, Bluegill 3 Prime, Santee, Calamity, Housatonic, Kingfish, Tightrope, St. Lawrence, Gundi, Anacostia, Taunton, Tendrac, Madison, Numbat, Manatee, Casselman, Hatchie, Ferret, Acushi, Chipmunk, Kaweah, Carmel, Jerboa, Toyah, Gerbil, Ferret Prime, Coypu, Cumberland, Kootenai, Paisano, Gundi Prime, Tejon, Harkee, Stones, Pleasant, Yuba, Hutia, Apshapa, Mataco, Kennebec, Pekan, Satsop, Kohocton, Ahtanum, Bilby, Carp, Narragaugus, Grunion, Tornillo, Clearwater, Mullet, Anchovy, Mustang, Greys, Sardine, Eagle, Tuna, Fore, Oconto, Club, Solendon, Bunker, Bonefish, Mackerel, Klickitat, Handicap, Pike, Hook, Sturgeon, Bogey, Turf, Pipefish, Driver, Backswing, Minnow, Ace, Bitterling, Duffer, Fade, Dub, Bye, Cormorant, Links, Trogon, Alva, Canvasback, Player, Haddock, Guanay, Spoon, Courser, Auk, Par, Barbel, Garden, Forest, Handcar, Crepe, Drill, Cassowary, Parrot, Mudpack, Sulky, Wool, Tern, Cashmere, Alpaca, Merlin, Wishbone, Seersucker, Wagtail, Suede, Cup, Kestrel, Palanquin, Gum Drop, Chenille, Muscovy, Tee, Buteo, Cambric, Scaup, Tweed, Petrel, Organdy, Diluted Waters, Tiny Tot, Izzer, Pongee, Bronze, Mauve, Ticking, Centaur, Screamer, Charcoal, Elkhart, Sepia, Kermet, Corduroy, Emerson, Buff, Maxwell, Sienna, Lampblack, Dovekie, Reo, Plaid 2, Rex, Red Hot, Finfoot, Clymer, Purple, Templar, Lime, Stutz, Tomato, Duryea, Fenton, Pin Stripe, Ochre, Traveler, Cyclamen, Chartreuse, Tapestry, Piranha, Dumont, Discus Thrower, Pile Driver, Tan, Puce, Double Play, Kankakee, Vulcan, Halfbeak, Saxon, Rovena, Tangerine, Derringer, Daiquiri, Newark, Khaki, Simms, Ajax, Cerise, Vigil, Sidecar, New Point, Greeley, Rivet I, Nash, Bourbon, Rivet II, Ward, Persimmon, Agile, Rivet III, Mushroom, Fizz, Oakland, Heilman, Fawn, Chocolate, Effendi, Mickey, Commodore, Scotch, Absinthe, Knickerbocker, Switch, Midi Mist, Umber, Vito, Stanley, Gibson, Washer, Bordeaux, Lexington, Door Mist, Yard, Gilroy, Marvel, Zaza, Lanpher, Cognac, Sazerac, Worth, Cobbler, Polka, Stilt, Hupmobile, Staccato, Brush, Cabriolet, Mallet, Torch, Knox, Dorsal Fin, Russet, Buggy, Pommard, Stinger, Milk Shake, Bevel, Noor, Shuffle, Scroll, Boxcar, Hatchet, Crock, Clarksmobile, Adze, Wembley, Tub, Rickey, Funnel, Sevilla, Chateaugay, Spud, Tanya, Imp, Rack, Diana Moon, Sled, Noggin, Knife A, Stoddard, Hudson Seal, Welder, Knife C, Vat, Hula, Bit, File, Crew, Auger, Knife B, Ming Vase, Tinderbox, Schooner, Bayleaf, Tyg, Scissors, Benham, Packard, Wineskin, Shave, Vise, Biggin, Winch, Nipper, Cypress, Valise, Chatty, Barsac, Coffer, Gourd, Blenton, Thistle, Purse, Aliment, Ipecac, Torrido, Tapper, Bowl, Ildrim, Hutch, Spider, Horehound, Pliers, Minute Steak, Jorum, Kyack, Seaweed, Pipkin, Seaweed B, Cruet, Pod, Calabash, Scuttle, Planer, Piccalilli, Diesel Train, Culantro, Tun, Grape A, Lovage, Terrine, Fob, Ajo, Belen, Grape B, Labis, Diana Mist, Cumarin, Yannigan, Cyathus, Arabis, Jal, Shaper, Handley, Snubber, Can, Beebalm, Hod, Mint Leaf, Diamond Dust, Cornice, Manzanas, Morrones, Hudson Moon, Flask, Piton, Piton A, Arnica, Scree, Tijeras, Truchas, Abeytas, Penasco, Corazon, Canjilon, Artesia, Cream, Carpetbag, Baneberry, Embudo, Dexter, Laguna, Harebell, Camphor, Diamond Mine, Miniata, Bracken, Apodaca, Barranca, Nama, Baltic, Algodones, Frijoles, Pedernal, Chantilly, Cathay, Lagoon, Diagonal Line, Parnassia, Chaenactis, Yerba, Hospah, Mescalero, Cowles, Dianthus, Sappho, Onaja, Longchamps, Jicarilla, Misty North, Kara, Zinnia, Monero, Merida, Capitan, Tajique, Haplopappus, Diamond Sculls, Atarque, Cuchillo, Oscuro, Delphinium, Akbar, Arsenate, Canna, Tuloso, Solanum, Flax, Alumroot, Miera, Gazook, Natoma, Angus, Colmor, Starwort, Mesita, Cabresto, Kashan, Dido Queen, Almendro, Potrillo, Portulaca, Silene, Polygonum, Waller, Husky Ace, Bernal, Pajara, Seafoam, Spar, Elida, Pinedrops, Latir, Hulsea, Sapello, Portrero, Plomo, Jib, Grove, Fallon, Jara, Ming Blade, Escabosa, Crestlake, Puye, Portmanteau, Pratt, Trumbull, Stanyan, Estaca, Hybla Fair, Temescal, Puddle, Keel, Portola, Teleme, Bilge, Topgallant, Cabrillo, Dining Car, Edam, Obar, Tybo, Stilton, Mizzen, Alviso, Futtock, Mast, Camembert, Marsh, Husky Pup, Kasseri, Deck, Inlet, Leyden, Chiberta, Muenster, Keelson, Esrom, Fontina, Cheshire, Shallows, Estuary, Colby, Pool, Strait, Mighty Epic, Rivoli, Billet, Banon, Gouda, Sprit, Chevre, Redmud, Asiago, Sutter, Rudder, Oarlock, Dofino, Marsilly, Bulkhead, Crewline, Forefoot, Carnelian, Strake, Gruyere, Flotost, Scupper, Scantling, Ebbtide, Coulommiers, Bobstay, Hybla Gold, Sandreef, Seamount, Rib, Farallones, Campos, Reblochon, Karab, Topmast, Iceberg, Fondutta, Backbeach, Asco, Transom, Jackpots, Satz, Lowball, Panir, Diablo Hawk, Cremino, Cremino-Caerphilly, Draughts, Rummy, Emmenthal, Quargel, Concentration, Farm, Baccarat, Quinella, Kloster, Memory, Freezeout, Pepato, Chess, Fajy, Burzet, Offshore, Nessel, Hearts, Pera, Sheepshead, Backgammon, Azul, Tarko, Norbo, Liptauer, Pyramid, Colwick, Canfield, Flora, Kash, Huron King, Tafi, Verdello, Bonarda, Riola, Dutchess, Miners Iron, Dauphin, Serpa, Baseball, Clairette, Seco, Vide, Aligote, Harzer, Niza, Pineau, Havarti, Islay, Trebbiano, Cernada, Paliza, Tilci, Rousanne, Akavi, Caboc, Jornada, Molbo, Hosta, Tenaja, Gibne, Kryddost, Bouschet, Kesti, Nebbiolo, Monterey, Atrisco, Queso, Cerro, Diamond Ace, Huron Landing, Frisco, Borrego, Seyval, Manteca, Coalora, Cheedam, Cabra, Turquoise, Armada, Crowdie, Mini Jade, Fahada, Danablu, Laban, Sabado, Jarlsberg, Chancellor, Tomme, Midnight Zephyr, Branco, Branco-Herkimer, Techado, Navata, Muggins, Romano, Gorbea, Midas Myth, Milagro, Tortugas, Agrini, Mundo, Orkney, Bellow, Caprock, Duoro, Normanna, Kappeli, Correo, Wexford, Dolcetto, Breton, Vermejo, Villita, Egmont, Tierra, Minero, Vaughn, Cottage, Hermosa, Misty Rain, Towanda, Salut, Ville, Maribo, Serena, Cebrero, Chamita, Ponil, Mill Yard, Diamond Beech, Roquefort, Abo, Kinibito, Goldstone, Glencoe, Mighty Oak, Mogollon, Jefferson, Panamint, Tajo, Darwin, Cybar, Cornucopia, Galveston, Aleman, Labquark, Belmont, Gascon, Bodie, Hazebrook-Emerald, Hazebrook-Checkerberry, Hazebrook-Apricot, Tornero, Middle Note, Delamar, Presidio, Hardin, Brie, Mission Ghost, Panchuela, Midland, Tahoka, Lockney, Borate, Waco, Mission Cyber, Kernville, Abilene, Schellbourne, Laredo, Comstock, Rhyolite, Nightingale, Alamo, Kearsarge, Harlingen-A, Harlingen-B, Bullfrog, Dalhart, Monahans-A, Monahans-B, Kawich A-White, Kawich A-Blue, Misty Echo, Texarkana, Kawich, Ingot, Palisade-1, Palisade-2, Palisade-3, Tulia, Contact, Amarillo, Disko Elm, Hornitos, Muleshoe, Barnwell, Whiteface-A, Whiteface-B, Metropolis, Bowie, Bullion, Austin, Mineral Quarry, Randsburg, Sundown-A, Sundown-B, Ledoux, Tenabo, Houston, Coso-Bronze, Coso-Gray, Coso-Silver, Bexar, Montello, Floydada, Hoya, Distant Zenith, Lubbock, Bristol, Junction, Diamond Fortune, Victoria, Galena-Yellow, Galena-Orange, Galena-Green, Hunters Trophy, Divider.

He stared into the heart of that comfortless light he could not remove from. Everything had been revealed, all secrets exposed, and yet nothing had changed; somewhere his heart was crying like an abandoned pet, all was given up and given away, and the burden was still on him. In the darkness he pressed his fingers to his eyes, imagining what was out in the world now for the taking by any who guessed the key, and sparks bloomed on his lids, like the wheeling of birds, now black, now white, against a blank sky.

SEVEN

Morning sun, insulting his sleepless eyes, glared from three folded newspapers each a day more distressed than the last: ivory, wheat, urine. On the hand extended to pick up Record Heat Wave More On Way, a mole he didn't recall drew a blunt shadow over the ham of his thumb. In the house he paused long enough to drop his suitcase and pass the phone blinking 4, a clutter of styrofoam cartons in the kitchen, an empty box PapaGeno Pizza and a trail of ants moving across it, and then he was back out under the heat of the sky, that molten blue shell beyond which was mere vacuum littered with the stony threats of a hammering that echoed off the walls of Building 101 where he turned the wheel to skirt Putzmeister P30 growling at the dry fountains where RIDGID shot a halo of sawdust into the air and turned again around a motorized cart loaded with canisters Dichlorodifluoromethane CFC-12 Freon while the radio informed him that —the nuclear weapon is obsolete. I want to get rid of them all unquote yet while applauding General Horner's sentiment the secretary of defense was skep, stilling it as he set the brake under RESERVED DIRECTOR.

On media vans KGO CNN KNBR ABC microwave dishes angled skyward. Cables thick as firehose snaked through open doors and an exhalation of cool air met him two steps before the entrance. Just inside stood placards CAUTION UNCLEARED VISITORS UNDER ESCORT IN THIS AREA. A large man in a blue serge suit passed muttering, —Doverai no proverai. At the elevator a federal protective officer glanced sullenly at Quine's badge.

His outer office was vacant and silent. He went through and sat heavily, pushing aside with his case Earth Protection, FUDGE: A Fusion Diagnostic and *RSVP*. As he let drop Ohlone Valley Herald Secretary Steals Secrets, a binder slid off the desk and hit the floor in a spray of papers. He bent to retrieve them but was unable to fix his attention for long on *Idaho Rocky Flats Hanford Savannah River 109 of the 144 sites under DOE's care will require long-term protective stewardship after remediation end states of the sites are not reliably known and the activities that constitute stewardship are not yet defined long-term centuries millennia myriadennia 36 million cubic meters legacy waste 1 billion curies 86% high level will take decades and substantial resources comparable to the level of effort expended for the 50 years of nuclear weapons production and research activities thus far. RSVP Nancy Julia Adams 16 July* had come to rest against his daily calendar, and he reached forward to tear off pages to Monday 18.

—Jefe, you missed it . . . as *RSVP* went into the trash and he came up glaring, —Missed what?

—The Trinity Day picnic? Saturday? Come for the burgers stay for the comet. Réti was playing Mussorgsky on a rented Bösendor

—Comet what comet.

—Shoemaker-Levy? as he followed Conor's gaze down to Ohlone Valley Herald Black Eye Smears Jupiter.

—We had a live feed from the Hubble. The seminar

—Seminar what seminar.

—The, didn't you see this? I thought you

—Philip are you Jesus all these boxes, you ready?

—Ready for what?

—The seminar, Philip? Earth Protection, don't tell me, you're supposed to introduce this session.

—Session what

—been in your box for weeks now, if you can find it in all this, as Nolan pushed aside Organization For The Creative Person, —When's Dolores getting back and why don't you get a temp in, here . . . thrusting Earth Protection Seminar into Quine's hands, —have you even looked at this?

—I approved the damned thing didn't I to placate Réti but I didn't give permission for this film crews newsmen this this circus

—Kind of to be expected with the comet. Highet held a press conference Saturday when the first fragment

—Highet? Here?

—Informal kickoff after the Trinity party lots of people glad to see him actually, listen Philip we have to get down there it's

—So wait, they, they timed this whole show for the, for the comet?

—Thought you knew that. Kihara's suggestion, pretty good one actually, gets himself a nice twofer.

—Participants StarQuest Productions Burbank California who the hell is that?

—Kihara's client that's what I mean by twofer, he gets to plug his asteroid movie along with the Radiance technology.

—Movie?

—Schwarzenegger, Bruce Willis, somebody like that, ought to give Friends of Missile Defense a nice bounce in the polls. Look can we

—All these Russian names what are they doing here?

—International problem getting hit by an asteroid needs an international response wouldn't you say?

—Russian Federal Nuclear Center, and this Vassili Maksimov from what the hell is the Tsiolkovsky Association?

—Aerospace consortium. Surplus hardware and skill sets looking for a mission. Blow up an asteroid you need launch guidance warhead got em all right here. Have to say I underestimated Kihara when he used to stumble around here with his shoes untied. Can we get going?

—What's this, I'm down as a speaker?

—What I'm trying to tell you Philip in about five minutes. It's just an introduction. Réti will do the keynote. You just say welcome, and you're out of there.

—Is this Highet's idea of how to get back in here? Is this some kind of coup?

—Philip . . . relax, you can't keep him out of a thing like this just go along with it he'll be gone in a few days.

—These preprints what is this thing it looks like a cheese slicer, and is this what is, is that Slingshot? I mean we can't sell missile defense this year so let's do asteroids instead, a little life support until, just listen, Ballistic system of antiasteroid protection, Nuclear weapons impact on hazardous space objects, Nuclear explosion effect on dangerous cosmic objects, The numerical simulation of the planet's explosion with massive icy envelope, and what is this There is high extent of global and regional dangerous? Heavy cosmogenic bombardment of the earth has been going? It's not even English.

—I've read it all Philip, including the bad translation.

—Earth Protection is it, quite the racket. Nice little planet you've got here, pity if anything were to happen to it . . .

—Not disagreeing with you Philip, just trying to make things run smoothly it's in my job description somebody's got to be standing on that podium in five, in three minutes I'll do it if you won't but that might be kind of a bad move especially after missing the picnic, people were wondering

—Let them wonder, I was in Washington, anyway what's to, to celebrate about incinerating a hundred thousand civilians?

—Didn't realize you felt that way about it. So you're not coming?

—I have nothing to say to these, these hucksters.

—I've got to go then. Why don't you take it easy up here Philip you seem a little excited.

—Where's Szabo?

—Downstairs, I imagine.

—Tell him I want to talk to him.

—I'll tell him if I see him.

Conor had edged toward the door and now he followed Nolan out. Quine dropped the blinds muttering —thinks he can hijack this program use it for his personal career advancement I'll . . . closing out the mauve and avocado facade and the media vans, then picked up the phone for —Reese please. Philip Quine. Hello Reese I'm glad I caught you, listen . . . oh he did? Yes I spoke to him about how he handled this Dietz business. That call to Steradian. I think it's contained but. I agree Reese, Frank is a capable scientist but here's my thought, if he can't exercise openness with something like this . . . Well yes but this has been a recurring problem, his what can I say pushiness his confrontational style insistence on having things his own way, playing fast and loose with . . . Yes but my point is isn't it better to send that signal now? I mean if we get some, some show stopper coming up later will he be honest with us? I mean we agree don't we that Bernd's problem with the optics is, is fixable, right? But I worry about this Lancet . . . Review panels, I know, but do they know all the details because I've been looking at. And are you sure you've seen everything, because I thought I had in fact Frank pretty much said I'd seen everything and then I found out . . . well that's what his report is supposed to address . . . yes I do think it speaks to his, his reliability. And something else just came up, hate to, but look can I fax you something? Hold on for one . . . minute to avoid boxes binders papers on his way to the outer office where he stared at IntelliFAX Hook Hold Redial Function Mem and began touching buttons at random until DOE DP appeared in black on the gray panel and he pressed Start for COMPLETE LIST? Y/N, —Oh god damn it just . . . jabbing Start again and as Yale University began its crawl into the machine he returned to, —Reese? Did you get it? Uh huh. You see what I mean? I think we need to take this seriously. Yes okay I will, I'll handle it. Just thought you, thought we should be on the, the same page . . . fallen to the floor beneath the fax machine which went on humming as Quine rushed into the small theater where Réti was addressing perhaps a hundred people. Behind him was a whiteboard and flanking him were two large video monitors, the crystal image of a full moon on one, on the other a blurred amber limb of Jupiter marred by black dots. In the vacant back row Quine sat behind a couple of men who broke off their whispering to glance at him.

—Tunguska in nineteen hundred and eight. It was an explosion of ten million tons equivalent. Had it happened near a populated region

—. . . OJ's internet address?

—Colon slash slash escape.

—Oh you heard it. What's the only thing worse than being married to Lorena Bobbitt . . . ?

—This I think is a very interesting threat.

—his lawyers want a change of venue to West Virginia? Because everybody there has the same DNA.

—still larger objects may require more destructive force

—'s the last thing Nicole saw?

—and so we see there is a use for nuclear explosions in space after all. We see there is reason to reevaluate certain treaties we have signed, even as a new administration tries to enter into an even more terrible treaty, with the connivance and cooperation of some who should know better. But I will say this to you. No administration lasts forever. And I say that if this administration follows its present course, by ignoring this great threat and even more obvious terrestrial threats, it will have blood on its hands.

—bad news your blood's all over the crime scene, good news your cholesterol's one thirty, lost under a scatter of uncertain applause that swelled without conviction as Réti limped from the podium.

—kay we have film now from last night's I should say yesterday morning's impact quite spectacular maybe the biggest yet circa zero thirty three hours little behind the predicted ah okay Kev? Do we have that? Can we punch that up on a monitor?

Réti reached a seat in the front row. Next to him someone rose to help him sit, a bald spot turned and a broad nose appeared. Highet. On Réti's other side was Szabo.

—punching holes in the Jovian atmosphere each the size of the United States give you some idea what one might do to us

Szabo and Highet both seemed to be conferring with Réti. The second video monitor showed —lunar images sent back by Persephone themselves a compelling argument for asteroid defense. You can see how many hits our neighbor in space has taken over a few billion years.

Szabo rose and walked toward the back of the theater. Quine made his way to the aisle a few steps behind. —Frank . . .

—give us some perspective on this threat welcome back our former director, Leo Highet.

Something like rain began. It took Quine by surprise, in the enclosed space, this growing rustle soon a freshet then a torrent. Highet came to the podium and waited for the applause to fade.

—The nuclear weapon is *not* obsolete. There *is* a use for nuclear weapons in space. We've just seen one.

The applause started again. Szabo was standing at Quine's side. —It wouldn't be a bad idea to have him back. Make him a director at large or something.

—At large? You mean like an escaped felon?

—We can't get rid of these devices. That's Luddite thinking. So why not use them to protect ourselves?

One monitor showed over and over in timelapse closeup the entry of fragment G into the Jovian atmosphere while piano chords crashed into Baba Yaga's Hut trembling under the impact but springing back undaunted for the next pass.

—very high likelihood that our recent brush with comet Swift-Tuttle will be a collision when it returns in twenty one twen

—I've had enough of this. I want to see you upstairs.

—Upstairs? What's the

—first priority's to get some telescopes up there, constellation of a few hundred small cheap CCDs in low earth orbit

—Doctor Quine!

—Oh Jesus Ch

—continuously monitor near Earth space cost about ten million dirt cheap

—Hey Dennis how's it

—dual use of course, some other agencies interested in what you can see with these sensors when you look down

—looking forward to your paper, StarQuest is very excited about your giant tungsten knives it's a great visual

—Tungsten knives . . . ?

—See you chop chunks off the asteroid and

—Frank, let's go.

—But Doctor Quine I really need to . . . as the importuning vanished behind the brushed steel doors closing for his stab at 5.

—Why is Highet here and why are you presenting a paper with him?

—Didn't know I had to clear it with you Philip, next time I'll . . . as doors slid open on an empty hallway. —What's the trouble anyway? I should be down there . . .

—Where's your report on Lancet?

—I'm working on it.

—I said I wanted it when I got back.

—I know, but this asteroid con

—I consider that extracurricular.

—Philip, you know we really have to talk about this report, I thought I'd wait until

—Sit down. Show you what I've got here Frank . . . rummaging for Growth Rate of the Rayleigh-Taylor Instability, —Listen to this . . . After some growth, instabilities enter the nonlinear phase with mode coupling and saturation and convergence effects . . . Mixing of the ice and gas layers instigated by the growth of irregularities will have a detrimental effect on fuel compression . . . The nonlinear growth and turbulence properties are almost entirely a mystery . . . The modeling of convergence and saturation effects have not been confirmed experimentally . . . No general analytic solution for instability growth has been found, indeed there is no reason to think one exists . . . Experiments on inner surface instability will commence soon . . . soon, Frank? In other words we haven't done anything yet . . . ? The linear growth of instability is well understood in planar geometries . . . Planar, Frank? Aren't we compressing spheres . . . ? However, a simple argument based on numerical work makes it reasonable to assume . . . is nature *reasonable*, Frank? Do the planets move in circles? Took over a thousand years to correct that *reasonable* assumption, and look at this from nineteen seventy four here's the same damn equation we're using now, tweaked the coefficients, fitted the curve, added a, a, a few epicycles, this isn't physics it's numerical analysis it's, this is what I did on Radiance, we don't have a clue what's going on but let's pull the curves into shape and claim quantitative agreement! Look at this, Frank, would you look at these curves, there could be an energy cliff here between ten and twenty megajoules, you see it? same damn equations from the seventies, Highet's in fact, the ones he used to sell the first kilojoule laser, only now the curves have been goosed, some coefficients changed to make one point eight megajoules looks like the threshold because, because that's what we want now? This whole damn project I'm on the line for it's just more tweak and squeak isn't it!

—Philip will you calm down I've worked on this for twenty years, we don't have to capture the physics in every det

—Frank it's all like this!

—With the new computing tools we'll have improved models better visualization graphical interf

—So, what, we put a really nice graphical front end on twenty year old codes get animated full color videos, tart it up with a John Williams score if you want but do we understand it?

—Philip believe me everything's fine, the CDR is accepted, we're a slam dunk for Key Decision One, we're right on track.

—On track for what, another billion dollar scandal?

—Philip there are unknowns, everybody knows that, I mean Reese is fine with our unknowns they're known unknowns we all know that

—And what about the, the unknown unknowns? Everything that comes up in the next year two years four years six years that we can't see yet?

—I'm telling you, talk to Reese.

—I did. He's upset with how you handled Dietz.

—Upset . . . ? The annoyance Szabo'd been holding in check flickered into caution. —I thought I had your support there.

—And he's upset that your Lancet report isn't on his desk. Frank, I supported you on Dietz but this Lancet stuff is over the top for me. I specifically asked you about it weeks before the CDR went in. I got vague assurances from you and I trusted them. Then I find out all this, and now you're stonewalling on your report.

—Stonew, I haven't had time! And I'm trying to, to . . . The caution was losing coherence, trembling into something like fear. —What is this Philip? What are you really after?

—Frank, I did some checking. You don't have a PhD.

—Jesus . . . Szabo's face was red, his voice shaking. —That's . . . for God's sake. What is this? Everyone knows that.

—It surprised Reese.

—I . . . I did the damned work! But I was hired straight on here, I was a Hertz fellow. So I didn't finish my dissertation. They gave me seven years to finish it, but Christ Philip I was here, I had other priorities, you know?

—You should have told me.

—Christ Philip. Réti knew, Highet knew . . . What are you doing to me?

—Protecting the Lab.

—No, this is bullshit. I've worked here for twenty years. No one ever cared about my damn degree. What difference does it make?

—Our integrity has to be above reproach. Because finally Frank trust is all we

—Is it Bill Snell? No, it's you, isn't it. You set me up. Promoted me to make me vulnerable. This is what you did with Superbright. I watched that kid Thorpe crash and burn while you came up roses as the whistleblower. I don't know what you said to Reese but it won't work this time because you don't know what you're doing. This isn't some cowboy scheme of Highet's you're messing with, this is the future of the entire nuclear weapons program.

—I don't want you hiding potential problems on this laser.

—A complex project like this, you give me a year to prove myself, but you can't afford that can you because you're a screwup and everyone here knows it and your interim appointment will be up before then and I'll have your chair. That's what worries you isn't it.

—We'll find you another position, Frank.

—In Siberia? In X Section with Dietz? Don't bother. I'll take a personal leave.

—Doctor Qui

—Oh Christ . . . as Szabo pushed out past —Dennis this isn't a good ti

—But I just, gee is he okay? You just need to see this before

—God damn it Dennis can't you understand English I said

—faxed this up last week but I guess you here that's it there here let me oops, as he slipped and lurched forward jabbing Quine with Executive Summary M Section Participation And Potential Liability In Anodyne Placebomycin Trial.

Placebomycin was developed by M Section under a Cooperative Research And Development Agreement (CRADA) with Anodyne Medical Response, Inc. Doctors and HMOs have been seeking a pharmaceutical that could be prescribed for patients with self-limiting viral infections, such as flu or cold, in place of costly and inappropriate antibiotics that patients often insist upon.

Placebomycin has no active ingredients. The pill is an inert mixture of calcium carbonate, glucose, and magnesium stearate.

Clinical trials proved effective in 35% to 65% of cases, with patients receiving placebomycin recovering more quickly from self-limiting viruses than patients who were told outright that they were receiving a placebo.

After development, Anodyne entered into agreements with various HMOs to provide placebomycin in quantity for specific use against self-limiting viruses. However, after distribution, production, and marketing costs were factored in, placebomycin proved to be as costly as conventional antibiotics, and the HMOs backed out of the agreement. In an attempt to recoup costs, Anodyne sold stocks of the drug to hospitals and clinics in various Third World countries, where unfortunately it has been used outside its intended application, as a broad-spectrum antibiotic against pneumonia, staph, typhoid fever, meningitis, and other life-threatening bacterial infections. Since these diseases are not self-limiting viruses, placebomycin has proven less effective than in its clinical trials, with 5%-10% of patients recovering, a percentage which is slightly worse than those patients receiving no treatment.

Anodyne faces legal actions from several customers and has brought suit against the Laboratory for alleged violations of the CRADA. Our position is that the suit is frivolous and without merit and that no settlement should be offered.

—See we wanted to jumpstart the enterprise, get an object oriented production model in full fluence but you know how long traditional model pharmaceutical R&D takes so we

—So you sold useless drugs to Third World hospitals.

—Well no, that was our customer Anodyne and anyw

—Did you consider, even for a second, what your customer might do with this stuff?

—Not really our concern as long as we execute in accordance with best business prac

—Dennis they were placebos!

—Well they were supposed to be used as antivirals not antibiotics that was part of the guidelines and anyway you see what counsel said we don't have to worry because we

—Do you realize what you've done? People have died!

—Well, they were sick anyway. I mean, it's not like they had much of a chance. And some of them did get better.

—I, I don't even know what to say to you. This is, talk about the Auschwitz touch, this is not even, you can't even pretend it's science it's only money is that all you understand?

—Well you don't have to get all huffy. I thought I was doing you a favor. It's not like anyone around here knows how to run a business.

—This is a laboratory!

—Oh and that reminds me this is from another client of mine for your immediate attention, if you could . . .

—invoice, System Concepts and Methods, use of proprietary algorithm for multiplication, running on an estimated two thousand Lab computers and an average of ten million operations per second, an estimated two percent of which are multiplications, royalties to be assessed at point oh oh one cents per operation, for a year-to-date total in the amount of fifty bil, is this some kind of a

—What should I tell him?

—fifty bil, you can tell him to f, in fact, you know what Dennis? All of this, that StarQuest asteroid film you're pushing, the screensavers, the microwaved cars, this bogus invoice, the placebo drugs, you know what? You're finished. Whatever agreement we've got with you it's terminated. You're out of here.

—No offense but you've got kind of a negative attitude. I was hoping we could work out a win-win synergy, look at our alternatives

—Alternatives? What alternatives do these people have? They're dead! Get out!

Outside the din of construction had resumed. Behind him his phone went off.

—Christ can't I get one single moment . . . he dropped Executive Summary on the desk and charged into the hall, the phone fading to a suspicion of voices somewhere just around a corner as he turned for brushed steel doors that opened on Highet, insolent and at ease. —Just coming up to pay my resp, as Quine seized his arm and steered them both around a corner into the mauve and avocado of MEN swinging shut behind them to muffle the threat of voices approaching and passing.

—Nice office, you ought to put some pictures on the wall, make the place yours.

—What are you doing here?

—You seem stressed, Philip. Are you taking your meds?

—You think you can still get those things up there one way or another.

—You mean Slingshot? Oh, they will be up there one way or another. I like my way better than letting North Korea do it.

—That and your setup with those rigged fusion codes. Those Lancet tests.

—Rigged? What are you talking about? You ought to thank me for that. You're getting Avalon.

—You know Avalon won't be enough for ignition, no more than the first laser was enough twenty years ago, all along it's been just tweak and squeak, keep raising the threshold for the next round of funding, and now I, I, I'm stuck with this this . . .

—If you'd worked half as hard on Superbright we might have something to show for it.

—Superbright never had a chance of working.

—You know that Stones song? You can't always get what you want to? But sometimes you can get what you need.

—Where do you get off telling me how to run things?

—Sorry, I forgot what a great job you're doing.

—What about those pictures.

—You mean my smut collection?

—Did you do that? Hide that data there?

—Even you don't believe that.

—Then who?

—Who? Probably some disgruntled employee who felt ripped off. Probably could have avoided it if Nullpoint had worked out.

—Conor says these files were downloaded hundreds of times. Copies are in the open. And you didn't tell DOE?

—Did you?

In Quine's silence, Highet passed his hand under the sink's photocell. The faucet came to life for an unstable flow of water that died to a drip speaking measuredly of an accommodation between surface tension and gravity.

—How bad is it . . . ?

—Having that data out there? Without the design codes the test data is fairly useless. But it's not that hard to write the codes. A few sharp grad students or for-hire Russian physicists could do it. A small dedicated group could build working fission weapons without testing them. Maybe now you see why I want those Slingshots up there.

MEN swung wide for two figures, one in black mohair and one in blue serge, —We-hell, Leo, can't seem to get away from you can I.

—Hello Bill. You've met Philip Quine? Philip, Bill Venham.

—You remember Vassili don't you Leo, as blue serge turned to spraddle a urinal and Venham raised his voice above the chiming porcelain. —So you're the fellow kneecapped Radiance are you. Venham turned to the wall and raised his voice further. —I was set to make a few hundred million when production geared up. But I don't hold a grudge. Maybe this asteroid thing will work out for us. Venham bounced on his toes as the Russian's stream tapered off, and reached into a pocket as he turned from the wall. —You ever need a job, you call me. Quine by reflex took a debossed business card νουσ from the hand that Venham then wiped on his pantleg as the Russian stepped back from the urinal, adjusted and zipped himself with a heartfelt sigh. —Bozhe moi.

—Wait how did you . . . the seminar is restricted to the first floor . . .

Venham smiled as he held MEN wide for blue serge. —I'd say you have bigger troubles than us taking a leak in an SRD pissoir.

—I'm still Q cleared, Philip. I'll see that these two aces get downstairs . . . as MEN swung to and Quine, turning past the mirrors, caught sight of a face so gone in forsakenness and misery it could scarcely be accounted human, although those eyes still exposed a trapped and implacable sapience, caught without its diadem of reason.

Back in the office all was still but the mutter of his voice sorting through a lack of possibilities —talk to to to someone, she should be back by now . . . as hands moved papers pausing at the torn edge of Test Ban Talks Break Off. He lifted the phone and tapped MEM 1 for —This is Lynn Hamlin. I'm not at home right now, but . . . He tapped MEM 2 and waited. —You've reached the offices of Cit, punching 303 for —Lynn Hamlin. Is not in her, and dropped the handset on its hook.

—Maybe she, those messages at home, how the hell do I . . . from a

drawer he pulled out cards papers Coldwell Banker Daniel J Root
Washington Mutual Gate Cellular AT&T Cordless Answering System,
—retrieving your messages . . . dial your personal code what the hell
was it . . . he dialed, waited, punched, waited, slammed it down. —God
damn it can't anything just work! He punched again with a different
code and waited for, —Christ is that how I sound . . . his expression of distaste going dumbstruck yet rapt in the dry whisper of a distant voice settling as it might have been some weighty judgment. His eyes took in the
tumulus of papers on and around the desk but the sapience behind
those eyes regarded it all as some landscape seen from far off and
already passing into irrelevance and forgetfulness. He was writing
something down as Conor came into the office and began to speak but
stopped as Quine reached for the phone again and jabbed at numbers.

—I need to speak to someone about a Robert Quine. I'm the son.
Yes I'll hold, for the unguent of strings sliding through some Beatles
tune as Conor stood at respectful attention. —Yes this is Philip Quine.
I was out of town. That's all right. So what do I. Yes I can do that.
What's your address. Yes and the, the remains? I'm sorry, can you say
that ag. With a c? Cremains? Are, are you serious? That's what you
call it? For Christ's sake they're ashes! Why the hell can't anybody say
what they mean! Why can't you say ashes!

He stood there trembling with one hand braced on the desk, the
other holding the handset.

—Jefe . . . ?

—I have to go to Sacramento.

—Why? What's wrong?

—My father died.

—Oh my God. I'm, I'm really sorry . . . Can I do anything?

—No. Wait yes. Erase those sparta files from my drive.

—Sparta . . . ? Oh yeah, those GIFs, I meant to tell you, the sparta
node is online again.

—It is? Well shut it down and erase all the files. Do it right away.

—Thing is, I can't. It's not on any of the local networks. The logfile
shows it someplace called ARIES . . . ? Jefe? You look pretty bad. Why
don't you lie down for a little while?

—Too much to do.

—. . . think you should take it easy. Let me get you . . . He returned with a glass of water in one hand and two blue tablets in the other.

—Yes I, I, thanks. I have to go.

—well but I mean maybe you shouldn't drive . . .

Bran Nolan stood in the doorway. —Conor, give us a minute here will you.

—Sure . . . call me if you need anything, jefe . . .

—What now?

—Herald reporter called me. He wants to confirm an anonymous fax he got that Frank Szabo never finished his doctorate.

—What? How did he find out . . . ?

—You send any faxes today?

—Earlier, I sent one to Reese Turbot.

—See what the last number dialed was . . . as Nolan went out to the machine and returned holding a sheet. —Think I see what happened here. Dolores has macros to manage fax lists. Reese's number is at the top but there's about fifty numbers on the list, looks like you sent copies to various offices in Washington, some local numbers, yes, here's the Herald, number forty . . .

—Not, not really sure how that happened, I didn't mean to . . .

Nolan looked pained. —Kind of a shame. Frank didn't deserve that. You okay . . . ? Where are you . . . ?

The lobby was quiet but for two men passing —know what PhD means? possibly has doctorate . . . as he went out into heat hammered into splinters against the white pavement and fumbled out his keys under RESERVED DIRECTOR and settled into the sear of the seat and the stale blast of A/C HI slowly drying his sweat as he turned onto the access road, loosened his tie and collar, horns blazoning his career to ◊ LEFT LANE BUSES AND CARPOOL ONLY 6AM-9AM 3PM-6PM MON.-FRI., with REGAL CINEMAS IMAX NOW OPEN surtout, Sacramento RIGHT LANE, needle touching 90 at the apparition of a city wavered in the broiling air and brown smutch, BANK of the WEST 4:05P 102F, and on through unlovely outskirts, Exposition Blvd Arden Way El Camino Ave Elkhorn Blvd, turning and slowing for Citrus Way more distressing than familiar, in the manner of a dull dream turned ominous without warning.

In the late afternoon heat the street was a desert of frame houses poorly shaded by stunted sycamores and a few columnar cypresses. A heavy breeze rose and died moving nothing but hot air. Quine was sweating by the time he separated the worn key from the others on his ring. The door lock was bright and the key didn't fit it.

—Damn . . . !

Sweat ran down his ribs. He twisted the iron thumbscrew of the mailbox and the flap fell open. Under three letters was a key.

The door swung partway then stopped. He forced it further and edged into the dim foyer. A smell was there, stale smoke and old sweat. Heavy blinds were drawn tight to the sills. Stacked boxes made a path to a bench near stairs piled high with magazines, more boxes, piles of paper ascending out of sight. From beneath the door he dislodged the torn Reader's Digest January 1971, wedged there with LIFE March 5 1965 A MONUMENT TO NEGRO UPHEAVAL. More boxes were stacked three and four deep against the rooms' walls, piled on chairs, under tables, on all but one cushion of a sofa. He edged down a narrow aisle between the dining table and a small desk, where he dropped the mail and went on back into the kitchen, one end of which was given over to black plastic trash bags. The nearest had sagged open in a spill of envelopes.

—Geico . . . UC Alum . . . you may already be a . . . tossing envelope after envelope onto a counter lined by cans of creamed corn, kidney beans, Le Seuer peas, Bartlett PEARS in Heavy Syrup. A scrap of paper was taped above the stove.

*How to light oven pilot
(if pilot goes
out.:
Press in on little button at
lower left. Hold match
for at least one minute, it
takes time.*

He retreated to the dining room where in the silence and dim warmth nothing stirred but his heart, tapping out its irregular distress. A lamp teetered at his touch and he steadied its light on Pacific Bell SMART Yellow Pages, opened to Estates Appraisal & Liquidation, full clearance a specialty, prompt service, shortest time, we do all the work, estates cleanout and hauling, discounts for salvage and old stuff, one finger at last falling on one of the numbers there while the other dialed. —Hello . . . ? as he edged out a chair between Beringer Gray Riesling and CÔTÉ A OUVRIR where a faded green card offered him Congratulations on the purchase of your new SEARS HOME APPLIANCE! FOR SERVICE PLEASE CALL ENterprise 13971, — Yes hello I, I need to, to have an estate appraised. In Roseville. Yes well but I mean, is there any way you could come today? I mean as soon as poss. I know it's late but I haven't got I mean I'm here only for the day and I. Well it's a whole house full. I mean I don't know a piano some furniture some books a lot of old magazines . . . He freed a pen from a checkbook. —Yes I could stay until then. Yes okay. The address . . . ? as his eye was drawn to A Visit To The New York World's Fair With Peter And Wendy. —Okay, thank you, yes, I'll, I'll see you here then . . . He sifted through the box muttering —Captain Hook in here too? Whole box full of . . . Official Views Official Souvenir Map Official Souvenir Book when did all this . . . Peter and Wendy accompanied him into the living room where he moved boxes from the sofa to the floor, blocking the fireplace. Back in the dimness of the mirror there he saw an alarmed and disheveled figure working at some Sisyphean torment watched in sober sympathy from the mantel by a photo of his younger self.

—God damn it, I'm surrounded by, by things! Always hated that photo, can't I just . . . as he came round a cordon of XtraTime Firelog duraflame contents 6 and CASCADE X-9000 BLANCO/BLANC WHITE 20 lb 10M 8 1/2 X 11/GL to discover the piano. John Thompson Teaching Little Fingers To Play. Diller-Quaile Book One. He raised the lid. JANSSEN Elkhart Indiana. Photos sat on the cigarette scarred blond wood. Aunt Lil, his father's sister, a big unsmiling woman. Next to her another woman, slender, young, a smile brave and fragile, the sunlight caught in fine auburn hair pushed back from the volutions of one ear. — It was . . . he returned to the sofa and opened OFFICIAL GUIDE NEW YORK WORLD'S FAIR 1964/1965. Just after she died. Visiting Aunt Lil in New York. They'd stayed a week. In a blankness he'd wandered the well lighted pavilions of the Fair, those gardens of promise, that heaven of (as William James had said in another connection) atrocious harmlessness, where everyone and all things were to be well. Toward those ideal worlds and painless utopias one was led, like a flatworm into light, by unreasoning hope, but those tomorrows never arrived, nor had they ever been meant to, but were purposed to distract from the present just long enough to move the unwary on to the next station of whatever might befall. See The Future First General Motors Futurama New York World's Fair. DU PONT PRESENTS Wonderful WORLD OF CHeMIStRY. The Westinghouse Time Capsules. No matter to what great heights we ascend or to what great depths we descend, we of the Twentieth Century bequeath to the Seventieth Century proof that man not only endures, but he also prevails. GENERAL ELECTRIC PROGRESSLAND On the Avenue of Commerce beside the Pool of Industry, the epic struggle of man to control Nature's energy, Awe-inspiring Atomic Fusion, a man-made sun, demonstrated to the general public in the U.S.A. for the first time.

—Awe inspiring demonstration wish I could remember it, could have picked up a few pointers for the next design review. Remember the picturephones the flying cars the undersea farms but that's where it really begins isn't it, this crossroads of ignorance and credulity, all this hope on one side fear on the other side between the two you can sell just about anything . . . during the last two decades the pace of science has quickened so that now the man in the street is reluctant to question any prediction, no matter how bizarre. Cars riding on cushions of air, bubble-top cities with conveyor-belt sidewalks, orbital post offices for the almost instantaneous transmission of picture-mail around the globe, large scale mining of the oceans, and perhaps even of the moon and the asteroids. Weightless orbiting for sport, synthetic foods, transplanted organs to replace worn-out parts of the body, interplanetary travel, that recent discovery in optics called the laser . . . well at least one of these panned out, not too bad one out of ten . . . as a beam widened to pin him there squinting at the silhouette in the doorway.

—Mis, mister Quine? Is that . . . ? Oh there you are. My there's a, a lot of

—Careful!

—I have it, steadying a stack of National Geographics, from which several slid and slapped the floor in a riot of technicolor birds, pale maps, and ebon limbs. —Are you quite all right? Sitting there in the dark, you looked a little . . .

—I'm fine.

—Here perhaps if we move

—Don't! Move anything you'll never get out.

—Is, is there someone else here?

—Why would there be someone else?

—I just thought, thought I heard you talking to, to . . .

—Just reviewing a little lecture I have to give on this recent discovery in optics called the laser happy to explain it to you useful for anything from playing music to shooting down missiles . . .

—Yes well perhaps another time . . . for now, ah, why don't you walk through the house with me and . . . ?

—I've already walked through. You go right ahead. I'll be sitting here brushing up my physics. Leave a trail of breadcrumbs if you like . . . as the light penetrating around the blinds slowly relinquished its fierce white edge and a spider ventured out from behind the roll.

—Yes well I, I think I've got an idea now, it's quite a, a . . .

—Quite the treasure trove for some cultural anthropologist don't you think? Life magazine from nineteen sixty eight, Co-ed Dorms An Intimate Revolution On Campus, The Grandeur Of DeGaulle, Sunset Western Living, form five forty tax return total wages twelve thousand eight hundred not bad for the sixties, how about this Kenmore laundry guide for your new automatic dryer, not to mention all the junk mail, know who's on the five cent stamp?

—Yes well of course I can only give you a rough appraisal now, and you probably want to go through things carefully, to see if there's anything of sentimental value or

—I don't need to do that.

—or, or even material value, I've seen people hide cash in books, sometimes quite a lot, one gentlemen had over five thousand dollars stuck between pages of the Encyclopedia Britann

—I don't care, I just want it all hauled off.

—All? Well, but, if you give me a few weeks I'm sure I can get a decent price for

—Look what's so hard to understand just haul it will you, haul everything off to a landfill think you can do that?

—Well, yes of course, I can hire some haulers.

—Fine. Send me the bill.

—But I, let me make you an offer on, on the furniture and the piano at least, and and that could help offset the hauling cost . . .

—Fine.

—Well . . . let me see . . . the piano . . .

—Just, look, you have my address and phone, I'll leave you the key, just let me know okay?

—All right, if that's wh, oop

—Careful!

—Yes I see, that's a dead end isn't it, this must be the, the path to the door . . . ? You'll be all right . . . ? I'm sorry for your, your loss . . . ?

Light lengthened there outside the upstairs window in a room with no furniture or familiarity but the nodding weight of a sycamore limb sharing what remained of the day with this vacancy of bare floor and walls. Down the hall the other bedroom was tidy. A single bed, a small night table, a lamp, the —same damn chair with the cracked red leather same cigarette burn on the arm he moved it upstairs brass tacks coming out at the base friction tape on the cushion same damn chair . . . as he put Peter and Wendy on the arm to cover the burn, —sat here every night just just just sitting there, staring at nothing, just . . . just . . . mourning. His throat constricted as he caught his breath in the heat, the dust, the filtered slanting sunlight hidden by hands covering the moistness on his cheeks, lost in the spasm of his diaphragm and the occasional apneic gasp that subsided at last into the dusk. —Christ . . . I need to, to, to rest for just a . . . as he settled onto the cushion, staring at nothing, until he picked up Peter and Wendy making their way around the Unisphere, past dinosaurs, underwater, to the Moon, and back again to some improved and lucent Earth where the Electric Power and Light Pavilion seemed like a huge Church. Philip thought it was more like a palace, all made of light. And Mother was there! Mother was sure the whole thing was a piece of magic. She was rather annoyed when Father pointed out that the effect was created by megajoule searchlights. Philip said to his father, I hate you! I hate you! It is magic, Mommy's right! But the light faded and she was gone. What did you do to her!

His father sat in the red leather chair, head down. Réti's head came up in a cold glare. Never forgive, never forget.

—Huh!

He stood unsteadily in the dark and switched on the lamp. Somewhere outside, some great thing lumbered over, shaking the windows, coming in for a landing at McClellan. Water trembled in a glass on the bedside table. Dust was held to the water by van de Waals forces and kept from sinking by surface tension. A dial telephone rested on a book and after a moment he lifted the handset. He held the book and opened it as he waited through six rings.

—Huh. Since when did he get rel . . .

—This is Lynn Hamlin. I'm not at home right now but if you'll

He dialed again and waited, paging past First Edition Fascimile as the regular chirrup sounded over and over, BY JOSEPH SMITH, JUNIOR, AUTHOR AND PROPRIETOR. PALMYRA; PRINTED BY E. B. GRANDIN FOR THE AUTHOR. 1830. Northern District of New-York, to wit: BE IT REMEMBERED, That on the eleventh day of June, in the fifty-third year of the Independence of the United States of America, A.D. 1829, JOSEPH SMITH, JUN. of the said District, hath deposited in this office the title of a Book, the right whereof he claims as author, in the words flowing, to wit: "The Book of Mormon: an account written by the hand of Mormon, upon the plates taken from the plates of Nephi." In conformity to the act of the Congress of the United States, entitled, "An act for the encouragement of learning, by securing the copies of Maps, Charts, and Books, to the authors and proprietors of such copies." R. R. LANSING, Clerk of the Northern District of New-York.

—This is Lynn Hamlin. I'm not . . . he dropped the phone.

—Look for some spiritual consolation get a copyright notice, just a little more intellectual property aspiring to the highest places . . . as a strip of paper fluttered from the book to the floor.

while I thought that I had been learning how to live I have been learning how to die

A moon not yet full had climbed into the sky, high as a winter sun slipping over the empty street, the ribbon of freeway, sparkling on the delta waters around the dark ranks of spavined battleships, ghosts of earlier wars, rays scattered but not blocked by thin cloud near Mount Ohlone, where it was joined briefly by an orange globe 76 as Quine punched 87 REG and left the light emitting diodes to their fervid counting for REST ROOM and the sound of a flush and the metal door slamming shut just ahead of a flood of water and —Shit! Can't anybody just, just clean up after themselves . . . ! pulling away from RECEIPT Y/N? with a squeal of tires repeated at Cod rn ces XIT NLY.

He left the front door open as he went past a blinking 4 to press MEM 2 and wait through four rings that seemed to space themselves further and further.

—This is Lynn Hamlin. I'm not . . . The door slammed on his broken mutter that barely rose above the engine, —All right, needed to tell her, tell somebody . . . one crisis to the next . . . no solution . . . those things will be up there one way or another . . . this, this history we carry around, the waste we leave behind . . . God damn him anyway! God damn the whole goddamned . . . couldn't we just, just stop . . . ? and died away at Estancia Estates An Adult Community New Units Opening Soon as he peered down a prospect of identical bungalows for the one he sought.

A light was on. He went up the steps, rang the bell once, then again. Through a gap in the curtains he saw a lamp. Its light fell on a pile of mail and three folded newspapers. Again he rang the bell. As he stood there the lamp shut off of its own accord. He walked around to a chainlink fence that cut off the yard from a terrain of broken ground and hillside where in the moonlight a backhoe sat parked CREDNE CONSTRUCTION. On one knee he reached a handful of dirt from the sift through the fence and let it fall through his fingers. Under or within the mutter of freeway, voices were there in that moonlight. If you could hear them.

I had cancer in the other breast too.

We watched those clouds going over.

They discovered he had it in the liver too.

They kept saying it won't hurt you.

We just had one case after another, and we began to wonder.

We would see the flash out west and then later the sound would come.

The whole sky is alight as you've never seen.

I was by the window, looking to the southwest, and it went up like a fan of colors.

Every color in the rainbow.

The ground shook and the wind came up, and it was full of little gritty things.

The dust would settle over our farm area, land on everything.

We trusted the government.

I thought probably she had a sunburn.

It was early summer because we were out in the garden picking peas.

They were purplish sores, they weren't like anything I've seen before or since.

All I done is take the readings and send it in.

We would play in it like that was our snow.

They claim they have lost the data.

Sometimes it would be big pieces, like burnt pieces of paper, like if you burn a bonfire.

There is a philosophy that the Latter-Day Saints have, that all will be well, no matter what.

They had less respect for us than for the money it took to train us.

Joseph Smith said in the Doctrine and Covenants that as soon as a person gets a little authority, they rule unrighteous dominion on their fellow man.

If there isn't any truth we can't be free, can we?

And there's not a damn thing you can do.

Nobody gives a damn, why should I?

I love only you.

He realized he was speaking. —Nan . . . ? What could I do. How could I stop it.

From the freeway the distant floodlit perimeter of the Lab receded behind him. Jupiter, the concussions there ongoing but unseen, led the declining moon across a sky otherwise blanched by OHLONE LIN-

COLN MERCURY and DA-NITE SELF-STOR 24 HRS and BAIT BEER GUNS until the stars came back point by point above dark orchards and wheeled over foothills of pale grass pocked with dark stones that seemed to have fallen from the crowded sky whose lucidity revealed them clear as day. He passed a lighted but unmanned kiosk at the start of the road's climb up through pines. For an hour he wound through this darkness and came out of it among great domes of granite phosphorescent in the moonlight. At a lakeside he stopped while the moon, wearing an aureole, vanished in the teeth of the southern peaks as he stood near a whitebark pine, voiding. A bolide slanted down the sky in silence leaving a bright lingering trail.

Beyond the crest the road tipped down in switchbacks tracing the edge of some chasm just emerging in the predawn. He stopped where the road leveled in the valley and stood there drinking a can of iced tea and fueling the car under BP REGULAR 1.29^9 as the sun came up over waste and infecund desert. He turned south and the sun rose higher and its light fell like copper on the buttresses of granite to the west. The highway curved in toward that glowing splendor. Through the window came a rush of morning air, already warm. Ahead the white road wound into mountains. On either side sang cicadas and dry grass.

He parked by an empty cistern and an exhausted well. His car was limed with dust. From somewhere sounded dry sterile thunder. Two military jets were gone far ahead of it, already vanished behind the scarp where snow still clung in rags. He climbed the dirt path, passing a rib of granite so cleanly broken that its pieces seemed cut and placed side by side, but for the sand and gravel in the crevices. The thin air scoured his lungs while the intensity of the sun for a moment seemed to suck the color from things.

On a peg inside the open door hung a nylon windbreaker and a billed cap $e=hf$. Past the dimness of the entranceway in a large room stood cardboard boxes half packed with books, binders, tapes, diskettes. Against one wall blue and white and black and gunmetal equipment was racked or piled, Verity Systems V91M Bulk Tape Degausser, SparcStation 10, Cisco 7505, KSV Instruments CAM200S, Tritium Alarm Monitor TAM-100, GC-8A Gas Chromatograph ☢, SALD-201V Particle Size Analyzer, ThermoFinnigan Delta E, Seistronix

RAS-24, Vax 8500, each tagged with the silver foil of a Lab property sticker, some plugged into the wall with their pilot lights on, with their faint smell of burning, of ozone, or of heated ceramic, or of stale wood ash from the fireplace, or perhaps of the neglected cigar dead in an ashtray on the low table between two couches. A murmur of woodwinds rose from speakers on the mantel, and below its mirror was an open CD case, HISTORIC BAYREUTH 1951 HANS KNAPPERTSBUSCH. At a noise behind him he looked up and in the mirror saw a black shirt in the doorway, red string tie and tooled ivory clasp, fat ruddy face around ice blue eyes framed by lank gray hair and beard. Two great hands hung as if they'd forsaken their grip on something. Quine turned.

—What the holy hell are you doing here?

—I might ask you the same.

—Don't tell me you got a key.

—It was open.

—How'd you find this place?

—I've been here before.

Root came forward then, smiling to expose a mouth of carious teeth filaded with gold. —That's right. You were a Hertz once.

—And you, you're not even a Lab employee, what business do you have here?

—This here's a private ranch. Lab uses it grace of Bill Venham. He's sellin, so I'm closin up shop.

—Most of this equipment has Lab property stickers.

—Decommissioned. Why, you want a PDP-10? Run a few legacy codes on it? I got some used Cray parts I'll let go cheap.

—I'm looking for a Vax 8500.

—Got one right here.

—Did you ever hear of steganography?

The murmurous woodwinds had lost an unequal battle with swelling strings and a baritone, all cut off by Root's easy gesture. He went deftly among the boxes on the stone floor, examining items and placing them here or there.

—Don't mind me, got to keep workin, get this stuff out. Bill's sellin to some Silicon Valley cashout. I'm peeved with you there. If you hadn't shut Radiance down you'd still be on his A list and I'd still be in business here.

—Shut down? I thought it just moved offshore.

Root paused at the round table to pick up the dead cigar from the ashtray. He studied it and lay it down again on a sheaf of papers. —You're learnin, but not fast enough.

The cigar rested on Department of Defense Laser Master Plan. From where he stood he could read, *DOE is funding laser technologies with potentially large payoffs if leveraged properly to DoD weapons applications. New programs have opened the door to new lethality mechanisms with lower power thresholds than previously thought.* He looked from it to Root.

—These things have a life of their own. Used to upset me to miss out on action. Once I worked at Hughes and lost a whole radar detection system to a manager claimed it as his own. But eventually I come to realize that's just ego. That's just the way things get done. Managers change, credit and money falls like rain on the just and the unjust, but the work endures and the people who know, know.

—There are files on that Vax. Did you put them there?

—Someone did. Does it matter who?

—I think it would matter to the DOE and the FBI.

—I don't believe I know what we're talkin about. But that steg, whatever you said. I do recall somethin about that. Trimethius was it? A book of occult knowledge. Doctor John Dee translated parts of it into English. Here was a man who claimed to speak with angels.

—I thought you disliked education.

—I say that? It's a handy thing in others. An educated man always thinks he knows where he stands, even when you've turned him around. I study up subjects when I can get some use of them but I'm not educated. You ever read up alchemy? Ought to be part of the science curriculum. Terrible frauds and mountebanks they were, taking kings and princes for fortunes. But I see that tricksters don't interest you, and you're right. As the flower maidens say, wir spielen nicht ums Gold. The ones who thought themselves learned, those were the real specimens. With their angels and demons and archons. Those strange and terrible powers that seek to possess and lay waste to the

Earth. Course you don't need the Gnostic gospels for that today, just read your Investors Business Daily.

—What about those files.

—There's more, it might be, than what you've found. Hidden in the plain sight of some eye or other.

—Have you put up something new? Design codes?

—Think I did it? I wouldn't take such a chance.

—Then who?

—Some bored bomb geek, may be. One of the old guys, ten or twelve tests under his belt, now he's doin library work, one day he says, is this it? All I did to be locked away and forgotten? To hell with it. Let everybody know. What we did, what we learned. Or maybe someone just wants a better retirement package. Maybe it's some peacenik who wants a, what do they call it, transparent regime of nonproliferation. A level playing field. And you, do you think there are things that shouldn't be known? And you a scientist?

—What I think isn't important, these are national secrets.

—And will you say that the crown jewels of America's nuclear program went missing on your watch?

—I'm not taking the blame for treason.

—Treason? Let me tell you of a greater treason. Did you ever meet Turner? Turner could have been a world class drunk or gambler but he went into physics. A great man, mind you, a visionary. He worked on Aeneas, you know what that was? A spacecraft propelled by atom bombs, one after another spit out the back like watermelon seeds. I worked on that with him when I was barely out of grad school. A great man. He also did the first work on pure fusion bombs, he wanted them for Aeneas cause they were clean, cut down on its radiation shielding. Then he turned round and he did the neutron bomb, dirtiest weapon ever made. He taught me we could do anything at all, anything we wanted to, if we could get someone to pay for it. But more than just pay. To believe in it as well. To share in its unreason more than in its reasons. How he believed, how he could share that belief. Then one day he looked deep into the fire and he flinched from it. Went to the other side and tried to undo all he had done. But you can't put that fire out. It's what we're made of. That stardust. That nuclear waste.

—What do you know about waste.

—I know a thing or two. Turner is a waste. Much of my life is a waste. But it's no treason. And what are you? A creature that won't ensign or renounce the thing that's in you. A man engaged in treason against his very being.

—You don't know anything about me.

—Do I not? I know that every quantum of light in this world is a mark of our compact with that fire. We're signed to it! Its name is written in our every atom. It's not devil's work. It's the work of men like you and like me, and that's why those outside the fence can't countenance it, because it shatters their idea of humanity. Every man is called to it but few overcome the corruption of their hearts. And welcome it into their lives. You did for a time. Why betray it now? Don't you know that every life lived is over in an instant? You don't pick and choose your moment. When it comes, nothing is left of you in this world but your baseness and corruption, the corruption of matter. Unless you've heeded that energy in you longing to be freed. Listen man. You pledged yourself to a fellowship but you broke from it. You scrupled and stepped back and judged your work and the work of your fellows before it was done. You lacked faith and you lacked trust not only in yourself but in the very work that was meant to redeem you and your fellows from all your baseness. For their sakes at least you should have set aside your selfish scruples. Have you never poured your soul into anything without asking: what is this? Never known the awful daring of a moment's surrender? I see in your face that you have. But you wouldn't keep on at this work. Why is that?

—What do you know about it? There's no truth in you.

—In me? I should hope not! Is that where you look for truth? In the self? What is that? Is it this? Root gripped Quine's shoulders and turned him so that the two faced the mirror. Root's head loomed over Quine's and almost affectionately he cradled Quine's head between his great hands. —Do we explain the unknown by the unknowable? The truth if it's anything is made by cunning and persuasion. By what we say. Didn't Bohr believe that physics concerns only what we can say about nature? Even Jesus preached. Was he the Son of Man because he made miracles? Or because he said he was? What if he'd kept silent?

What if he'd doubted, but lied? Truth, is it? I say, *who says?*

—Let go of me.

Root lowered his arms and stepped back, holding them out as if pleading some doctrine.

—What is it you want? To shut down that Vax? Go on, I don't care. I'll do it myself. He strode to the far wall and reached behind a console. Panel lights went dark and a fan fell silent.

—You want the disk? Like some conjuring act an electric screwdriver was in Root's hand. He put it whining to screws in the console's rack and one after another they fell on the flagstones. He grabbed and pulled free by its handles a unit the size of a dictionary. He offered it to Quine and spoke in a tone almost cajoling.

—Take it with you. As evidence for some trial if that's what you want. No? What are you really after? Happiness? Is it that? Peace? But there is no peace. A reckoning is coming, don't you feel it? Too many people, too many wants. There's not world enough. Do you think the so-called truth will protect you when that time comes? When the grids go dark and there's no food or warmth and every man's sapience is set against every other for survival's sake. You'll want every weapon possible then. You'll want every spark of your fire. That's the world you're aiming to enter armed only with your scruples and your faltering. But you could survive. I could teach you how. You could be a power, not one of the wrecked and the wretched for whom the only peace is defeat and death.

—I don't want anything from you. Just that disk.

Root held the heavy thing out in both hands like a salver. —Step closer then. Take it from me. Come and see what a reckoning is like.

—You're crazy.

Root turned and placed the disk on Verity Systems V91M Bulk Tape Degausser. A red light on the machine blinked for part of a minute as Quine and Root stood watching each other.

—Is that it? Is that what you want? That knowledge gone? It's gone from the disk now. Let's see you take it from the world.

Root smiled and swung the disk in one hand. He stepped forward and Quine moved to keep the table between them.

—Hasn't it come to you yet that there are matters weightier than this mote you call a soul?

Root dropped the disk. It rebounded on the flagstones. —Go you forward. I haven't given up on you yet.

On the crest of the range he stopped in the afternoon light, stepping out into a roadside lot where thick cumulus hung overhead trailing a chill when they moved before the sun and cast their shadows over that long emptied riverbed of ice hewn when the first men ran chattering in packs on the savannah of another continent. He drove down the western slope into pines and a haze of smoke, slowing for Visitor Center where in a flash of lightning the cock on the rooftree flailed between compass points in a damp gust bringing a promise of rain unfulfilled as he came out from under the mutter of dry thunder and the towers of clouds rising behind him to darken the pines with shadows only and into the blaze and heat waver of the dry sea bottom, burning in the lens of the late afternoon, past BAIT BEER GUNS and DA-NITE SELF-STOR 24 HOURS, eyes burning, throat burning, all his senses burning in a worry of incitements as they sought some story, some rasping voice to explain this —hostile world, the demise of the Soviet Union dunt mean we're home scot free, we have Korea out there we have Iran out there we have Iraq out there we better be prepared to take these turkeys out, now here's what Merica should do, we should tar and feather every congressman who votes against defense spending who votes against building a missile defense . . . while the traffic thickened as countless cars flowed from its tributaries into the widening freeway while the rasping voice went on, —I'm a tell ya, most Mericans don't know we can't stop a missile attack. Most Mericans don't know we're defenseless. Most Mer, and he stabbed it to silence as the dash blinked JAM and he accelerated into the next lane with the needle climbing past 80 past 90 when the CD player blinked PLAY and a falsetto whined, —gonna be just dirt in the ground

—Damn it! Shut up . . . ! banging the dash as his wheels trilled on the raised lane dividers and a horn snapped his head around to the panicked face of another driver too close as he yanked the wheel and the road slid on despite his foot wedged on the brake and the yank of the wheel back against a fishtailing swerve into a chorus of horns and gaping faces traveling sideways past him until the car came up hard against a curb and stopped. He was on the shoulder turned sideways. Through the passenger window he saw traffic rush toward him and pass behind him. Ahead of him, smoke rose from fields of stubble, and a flight of birds, scattered by some disturbance, wheeled, now black, now white, against the empty burning sky.

In the heart of that light, lucid and inevitable, all that was scattered cohered. Superbright and all its progeny stood plain before him in conception and in detail and in its component parts and its deepest strategies and in its awful and enticing radiance. He saw the design and the making of that device complete, and of further devices without end, and he stood apart from them as if it mattered not at all whether the deviser was himself or some other or whether they came into being sooner or later. Trembling he stared across the burning fields and whispered, —Stop. Stop. But the traffic rushed on.